Windthorn Rose

Book One

M.J. Burr

For Doah.
Because you believed,
endlessly.

Prium

The Sareth Isles

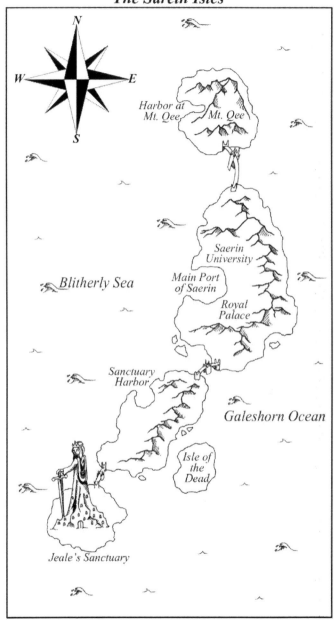

Prologue

The worst part about these darn crutches, Sylvia Eldritch thought, *is the complete inability to carry anything!* She juggled her crutches about, making room to sling her backpack over one shoulder to rest at the small of her back. *The second worst thing has got to be doors.* She grimaced as her crutches and one movable leg beat a staccato rhythm on the alternating blue and gray tiled floor of her high school. Sylvia paused in front of the closed double doors leading out of the dreary public school, sighed, and roughly heaved one of them open, working fast to get a crutch against it before it could swing shut on her.

Even as a senior, she was one of the shortest girls in her class. Contrary to her stature, however, Syl had been a force to reckon with on the rugby field. Her small body had been agile enough to keep out of the tackling arms of the more traditionally large and stout players of the other teams, making her a veritable scoring machine for her state bound squad, along with gleaning the interest of college scouts all along the west coast. At least they *had* been interested. Now she doubted their interest would continue in a rugby player with a shattered knee. Just yesterday, Coach had regretfully asked her mom to make a round of calls to the various college scouts who had been planning trips to see her play in upcoming games.

The moment still repeated itself in her nightmares, the moment that had changed everything. It had been September eleventh, obviously a day for disasters, when her team played their top rivals, Western Valley. Number fourteen topped her by a good foot, and at least fifty pounds, and when they collided perpendicularly, all the weight and momentum of her opponent had slammed into the outside of her planted leg. She would never be able to forget the sickening noise emanating from her own body. A sound so foreign and detrimental; the crumbling of rock when you are miles into a cave, the flat lining of a heart monitor, the crushing of bones and snapping of tendons.

At least they managed to win the game, she thought, her chest feeling tight as she envisioned her team making their way upstate today to play in the first round of playoffs. They would still be on the bus this early in the day, laughing and talking, pump-up music blasting despite Coach's attempts to make the girls turn it down. Syl gave a small smile at her imagining of the scenario, Coach hated their music. She, on the other hand, waved to her parents as they pulled her mom's clunky 'soccer mom van' into the bus loop and hopped out to help Syl maneuver herself onto the bench seat.

"Surgery bound!" Her mom smiled falsely, "lets' go get this taken care of and over with honey." Syl attempted a smile in return, and knew she had failed as her mom's eyes welled with tears and her dad gripped her shoulder tightly before tucking her crutches into the car behind her.

The waiting room at the Surgery Center was crushingly silent, the small clusters of people waiting eyed each other stealthily, wondering who the patient was, looking for signs of illness and injury in the bodies jittering impatiently in the uncomfortable chairs. Syl's leg brace spared her from the searching eyes, but afforded her lots of sympathetic looks she would have rather not have had to endure. A young man a few years older than her caught her eye, a wide smile breaking out over his chubby face when he realized he had her attention. Sylvia averted her eyes as quickly as possible when she saw his cast laden arm begin to raise in a wave. Hoping he hadn't taken their brief contact as an invitation to come talk to her as they waited.

"Eldritch, Sylvia Eldritch" a nurse suddenly called. Syl and her parents twitched as one at the breaking of the silence, and then rose to follow the smiling nurse into the sterile white hall behind the ominous double doors reading 'Employees only beyond this point'.

"Ready to get that leg all fixed up, sweetie?" The smiling nurse's name tag ready Susie, *a suitably chipper name for this perky, rotund woman*, thought Syl.

She managed to part her lips in a smile with great effort and reply, "I guess so, it has to be better than being like this, right?" she gestured loosely to her crutches and leg brace that covered her from ankle to upper thigh. She hadn't realized how much of her identity was wrapped up in her physical body until she was stuck sitting on the bench during their games. Suddenly everything was harder, and not just the menial everyday tasks like showering, or sitting on a darn toilet when one of your legs didn't bend; but fitting in with her teammates now that she couldn't play. And relating to her friends and their endless boyfriend drama when she was facing something so life changing.

Susie beamed and placed her warm and slightly sweaty hand on Syl's shoulder, "That's right, kiddo! Dr. Attebury and the gang will get you right back on your feet!" Susie giggled huskily at her own witticism.

Surgery prep passed in a blur of horror. She got into the open backed hospital gown with much awkward, hands-on help from her parents, while she silently wished she had worn any pair of underwear but her Sponge-Bob ones. Then she had to look away as she saw the size of the needle Susie unwrapped for the IV placement, watching her mother's face instead as she winced in commiseration when the needle entered the crook of her arm. All the while the nattering of the anesthesiologist answering her father's questions pattered on somewhere to the right and behind of the rolling bed she had been ensconced in.

"And you'll know right away if she has a bad reaction to the anesthesia? I was reading online that it's fairly common for people to have trouble..." Her dad's voice was intense and serious. Even without being able to see him she knew that the deep crease between his eyes would be showing, it always appeared when his voice hit this level of agitation. Although it was usually when he was mad at her, rather than concerned for her.

She dimly followed the questions and concerns of her mother and father, now talking to the surgeon, as she stared at the lumpy and discolored knee that Susie was unwrapping. And then an apple cheeked resident was telling her to count backwards from ten as the drugs were administered. "Ten" Syl said steadily as her mother tearfully kissed her hand. "Nine" she noticed a cold creeping feeling emanating from the needle prick in her forearm even as her dad smiled at her before kissing her forehead fondly. "Eight", the prep room spun a little as they wheeled her towards the surgery room and the voices around her began to sound like they traveled to her from underwater. "Sev…" and she was gone.

The surgeon palpated the girl's knee aggressively, searching for the shape of the bones beneath the swelling. He oriented himself, considered briefly, and then smoothly opened a gash in the leg to reveal the destroyed joint. Humming tunelessly, his gloved fingers expertly probed the pulpy, abused tissues. Next came the arthroscopic cameras and a suction tube that began the long process of cleaning up debris that had broken loose at the incredible impact of injury. Floating scraps of cartilage and the now loose ends of the girl's snapped tendons darted into the tube on the screen as the doctor cleared the area.

Dr. Attebury remained so intent on his work that at first he didn't hear the desperate alarm of the heart monitor join in his thoughtless music making. It took longer than usual for the anesthesiologist to rouse the surgeon from what his staff fondly called his "zone". But the insistent lessening of the young lady's vitals pushed him into action without the direction of the surgeon. By the time the doctor had everything safely removed from the incision, the crash cart was already barreling into the room, guided by the competent hands of Susie, her ever present smile temporarily replaced by intense concentration.

Chapter 1

Sylvia

The first sense to return to her was smell; the sweet scent of crushed grasses and mulchy wet soil. Then the actual wetness of the ground beneath her wormed its way to the front of her mind, bringing attention to her pruned skin and the deep cold which seemed to have settled into her very bones. The chaotic impressions that filtered in reminded her that she should be able to see where she was, as she should still possess eyes. So she pried her gummy lids apart to a slate gray sky and weak moonlight filtering through tall objects located somewhere behind her. The moon looked to be floundering in the sky, its girth was so great. Its pale, pocked face swam giddily before her eyes as she struggled to move into a sitting position. Groaning, she levered herself up on her elbows and the distant horizon swung into view, craggy with blue mountains that looked to be supporting the almost lavender colored crescent of the moon upon their jagged tips.

She sucked in a sudden ragged breath of horror, "A crescent moon!" As she tipped her gaze skyward her breath shuddered out of her again. "And a full moon" she breathed. Two moons. TWO moons, when it should have been the numerous harsh fluorescent lights of the Surgery Center's recovery room.

"Where the hell am I?" Her cry echoed eerily, and a smattering of cold rain brought to her attention the fact that she was completely naked.

"This has got to be a nightmare," she muttered, pinching herself vigorously. The cold had marbled her skin with a spread of veins. The snaky blue lines showing clearly through chilled skin where she wasn't splotched red and white from the elements. Her grasping fingers suddenly paused as she reached her knee; her intact and un-bruised knee. She bent it experimentally, without a twinge of pain, and then sprang to her feet, arms pin wheeling for balance as her bare feet slipped in the dewy grass.

"Okay," she said out loud, "Okay." She turned in a circle, feeling at a loss. "Crap! I don't even know what to think." She spun again, taking in the dark forest around her and the meadow-like clearing she had woken to. "I was going to have surgery, and now...And now this." Her wide eyes fixed once more on the two moons above her, one a normal looking silver but the one on the horizon looking decidedly purple. Her gaze moved to the foreign looking plants at her feet, much like grass, but softer, and a little fuzzy, with a blue coloring clearly illuminated by the excess of light from the two orbs above.

"So I'm obviously not on earth, right? And that means, well that means I am completely crazy...but let's just run with that theory for now. Not on earth, not injured, no clothes and no sign of civilization. Logical next step? Shelter, food and water, I can do that." She spoke into the bleak landscape, but the silence was broken only by the plops of raindrops falling.

"Oh god, I'm crazy aren't I?" Her body was beginning to shake in earnest now, a reaction to the cold that had been delayed by shock. The shivering made the words come out in a high chatter that would have been quite funny in different circumstances, but the alien cast to her own voice simply edged her closer to the hysteria she could feel building slowly inside. Wrapping her arms tighter about herself she tipped her face back to survey the unfamiliar sky again. "Even crazy people get clothes," she said sullenly to the pocked face of the larger moon above her.

Pushing the sick feeling in her stomach to the back of her mind, she spun in another shaky circle, zeroing in on the smaller details this time. The slant of the light and the length of the reaching shadows in comparison to the position of a purplish lichen coating the trunks of the huge trees behind her, told her that the moons were very close to slipping behind the horizon. At least that would be true if the sun rose in the east and set in the west here. Wherever here was. She congratulated herself on her choice to take "Wilderness Survival" rather than one of the more hip fitness classes offered at school. *Score one for the nerds,* she thought as she turned yet again, looking farther out this time, searching for something, anything, to give her direction.

There, was that a flash of light in the distance? She had hoped for the reflection of light glinting off a body of water, or maybe the glow of light pollution from a distant city, but the flicker was too far in the distance for it to be a reflection, and too small to be the lights of a house, let alone an entire city. *Alright, that way then,* she thought, pushing down that sick feeling in her gut, stirring again as reality tried to assert itself once more. The untouchable knowledge that this was *not right,* made her close her eyes, tempted to go back to sleep so she could wake up in the recovery room like she was supposed to.

A particularly hard shiver forced her eyes open, the cold quickly becoming more important to her than the question of reality. She needed to get moving or the risk of hypothermia would be a certainty. "I have a plan," she chattered to herself, "find out whose fire that is, hope to God they have some extra clothes and can tell me what the hell is going on here." And with that cheering thought she trudged to the edge of her clearing, hands rubbing up and down her arms vigorously to stimulate blood-flow, and began to make her slow way towards the distant light.

Ryland

Ryland squinted his eyes against the fire's glare as he struggled to maintain Control over the squirming blaze. He plucked at the unwieldy stream of magic he was pulling from the damp ground beneath him with his mind, trying to meld it to the ever changing flames so that he could harness their power, bringing forth a greater amount of heat to ward off the evening chill, regardless of the wet wood sullenly acting as fuel for the magical flames. With an angry hiss the campfire went out altogether, and his elder brother gave a great guffaw of laughter, making the blood beat hot and angry in his cheeks.

"Don't you dare laugh! I'm using Earth magic to control Fire!" He stood abruptly, glaring at his sibling across the empty fire pit, "I watched you do far worse when you came of age, and you were handling an element you actually have an affinity to!"

Torman stood up, his tall frame bulky in the firelight, and, still chuckling, ruffled Ryland's hair. "Yes, and someone was there to laugh at my best efforts also, little one, as it should be. You fear your magic too much, Ryland. Don't be afraid to call more, the power will help you keep Control. You've barely tapped into your potential, and already your magic surpasses mine," the big man said humbly. He moved towards the towering Steelskins surrounding their camp, tossing his final words over his shoulder, "I'll try to find some drier wood so we can laugh some more." Mirth was evident in his deep voice.

Ryland growled softly in annoyance and then allowed himself a small smile at his brother's retreating shadow. Five rebirths his senior, his brother was his only real friend within the walls of Jorgenholm. Well, he supposed he could count Torman's longtime lover, Metra, as a friend also, but truly his sibling was the only reason that quiet, sweet woman spoke to him at all. In truth, a better friend than Torman could not be found. Regardless of their age difference, Torman was patient and kind to a fault to his bumbling younger sibling. Ryland sighed heavily, looking down at his lanky frame, thinking of the well-muscled warrior currently fetching firewood, and wondered how that man, with lush dark hair and laughing green eyes, could possibly be his brother. *He was right to laugh,* he thought, *it was a pretty pathetic show of Control when all is said and done.*

He heard the snap of a branch behind him and whirled towards the sound, wondering if Torman was playing some sort of game at his expense, but seeing only smooth Steelskin and sappy Listenbark trunks dappled by weak moonlight. He listened hard, ears twitching, holding his breath and reaching for his magic to sharpen his senses. But there was not a sound in the Reedwood forest. No sap beetles singing. No stalkwings beating the air in hunt. His eyes focused on a pale strip at the edge of a massive Steelskin trunk, but when he blinked, the tree looked as dark and solid as the rest of its brethren. Ryland slowly rose from his crouch, and hearing the return of his brother at his back, turned his head, without relinquishing his view of the tree, calling to Torman, "Brother! I think we are not alone."

Torman picked up his pace, dropping the logs he had scavenged to the ground and moving lithely into a fighter's stance. He was soon at Ryland's side in a defensive crouch, sword naked in his hand. "Hinterlanders?" he queried. "We are not too far from the Skypeaks to encounter one of the tribes."

"No," Ryland shook his head, eyes still probing the darkness between the trunks. A strange sense of foreboding shook him, like an icy finger running down the length of his spine. He suddenly wished he was anywhere but here, camped in the middle of the Reedwood forest, with a thick fog drifting between trees that he could barely make out in the moonlight. He shook off the feeling irritably, "I think we should go see." And with his words he began to pick his way noiselessly toward where he had seen the pale shade, his brother at his side.

Sylvia

Sylvia could hear them coming. She knew she should have stayed farther away and continued her surveillance for a while longer, but the glow of the fire had called to her chilled bones and the heartfelt laughter she had heard drew her ever closer to the camp. And now they were coming. *Friend or foe?* she wondered, her breathing rapid and shallow. Her heart was pounding too loud to gauge their distance from her hiding place behind a tree. "I should say something," she hissed to herself, feeling as if she was failing to get air with each breath she took, paralyzed with fear. But by the time she had pulled in enough breath to speak, they had already reached her. She gasped the precious oxygen out in astonishment as they whirled into her sight, a light suddenly bursting into life, blinding her until she shrank down at the base of the tree, arms wrapped tight around her nakedness, shaking with fear and cold.

The light dimmed until it was at a bearable brightness as she studied her dirty toes, with a quick glance up before she tucked her head back down, she saw what looked like a miniature sun floating between the two figures before her. Sylvia stayed huddled between the solid roots at her back, but curiosity eventually got the better of her as long moments passed with no movement or words from her pursuers. She lifted her head from the cradle of her arms to survey the, beings, before her and gave a small exhale of surprise. "What are you?" she asked, forgetting to be afraid in the wonderment of long equine legs standing atop cloven feet. Narrow hips flowed gracefully to wide shoulders draped with the elegant folds of deep red cloaks. Long aquiline features set in disgruntled confusion stared at her from an unusual height, and from her low vantage point she could just barely make out a crown of antlers set upon each figure's head. They were speaking to her, but she could not put a name to the language, nor understand what they were asking. The words lilted enchantingly, as fluid and graceful as the creatures in front of her.

She tried speaking again, trying to make her voice firmer than the squeak the question had sounded like before. "What are you?" They stopped speaking, and glanced at each other, eyes wide in surprise. Then the larger one knelt, his massive frame folding over gracefully, even as her eyes bulged at the startling revelation that his knees bent backwards. He sheathed his sword in a practiced movement as he lowered himself to her level. His skin was a soft fawn color, complemented by the darker chocolate of his hair and brows. Peeking through the thick curls on his head, she could just make out the elongated tips of strangely shaped ears. His face was graced with high cheekbones that carried a flush of red, but it was his eyes she focused on, forgetting the rest of his face and foreign attributes. His eyes were kind in the flickering light of the tiny sun, and she suddenly felt like she might be able to breathe again.

Her eyes fell to his lips as the creature haltingly spoke in heavily accented English. "Greetings small one. You need no fear of us." He gestured to himself and his companion; and the lips she stared at peeled back to reveal startlingly white teeth in what Sylvia fervently hoped was a smile.

Ryland

As Torman spoke to the creature in the antiquated scholar's tongue, Ryland stared in fascination. He had never seen something like this before, and he was as well-educated as anyone in the Holm but his noble father and their Maegi, Camus, who had also studied at the King's Academy. She, for her small stature and high timbered voice must mean she was female, was curled protectively about herself, hiding what he assumed would be the most interesting parts of her body from view with her milk white limbs. Long, silky dark hair framed her face, cascading messily over fragile shoulders to pool like inky water in the valley of her crossed arms. The hair fell thick and unbroken from the top of her head, no antlers of any sort parting the tresses. Only the secretive traders from beyond the Galeshorn ocean boasted no horns on their heads that he knew of. Even serfs and the peculiar Hinterland tribe that ritually filed down their natural horns had small bumps visible upon their skulls.

Her legs were bent in a strange manner, folded in front of her and tucked tightly to her chest at an angle he didn't think even the most accomplished tumbler could replicate. And at the ends of those bizarrely shaped legs, her anatomy became even stranger. Little lumps of flesh ballooned out from her ankles where hooves should have been. He looked away quickly, afraid that she would catch him staring at her deformities, but her face was turned up to Torman in rapt attention. He let his gaze drift back down, wondering if this defect rendered the girl incapable of walking.

He had seen depictions of various strange birth defects in his studies. One book in particular come to his mind, a rambling account of a traveling troupe of performers who catered to the strange and unbelievable. The actors of the troupe were the true attraction, sporting extra limbs, freakishly malformed antlers, hair on their bodies where no hair should grow, and one man had even claimed to have a tail. *Could she be a descendant of one of these actors?* he wondered, knowing that the troupe had ceased to exist many years before, when the novelty of their existence had faded.

With a start he realized his brother had been speaking to him. "Ryland! By Garrin's bones boy! Are you back with us now?"

Torman grinned, switching back to Layette, "A pretty little thing if I ever saw one, I know Ry, but she would really appreciate some clothes I think. If you could grab some of your spares, she would be fair swimming in mine."

Face flushing hotly at getting so lost in his thoughts, Ryland met the eyes of the girl, and swallowed hard. Lush black lashes surrounded the startling blue orbs. "Blue! Torman, her eyes are blue."

"I know Ry," Torman sighed heavily, "go get the clothes and we will take our time to think on this mystery."

Sylvia

Sylvia dressed hastily in the clothes the younger man brought to her, fingers stumbling over the unfamiliar garments in her haste to cover herself. With a great breath of relief, she surveyed her borrowed outfit of loose pants in a soft material and an engulfing shirt of sorts with baggy sleeves. She hiked at the sagging waist of the pants and turned ruefully to the chuckles of the larger male, who handed her the leather belt from his own waist so she could girdle both the pants and tunic to her hips to keep them from falling off.

Finally, as at home in the unfamiliar clothes as she could be, she took a deep, steadying breath, and addressed the elder of her two rescuers, determined to find out the nature of their claim on her. "If I wanted to," she said, "could I leave now?"

"Yes." The antlered man said calmly. "But it is… unsafe." He paused, obviously searching for words. "Better at our fire, this night."

She nodded and followed their gracefully rolling gaits back to the camp she had been stalking. Once they had all settled around the empty fire pit, a smattering of flames sprung to life at a gesture from the large man. She stared, too numb to new experiences to even jump at the startling revelation. *It's a dream, magic can be real in dreams right?* she asked herself silently.

The larger man pointed to himself, "Torman" he said, and then, "Mine brother, Ryland" pointing to the younger man, who had still not said a word she could understand.

Sylvia pointed to Ryland and asked, "Can he speak this language too?"

Torman laughed and looked to his brother, speaking in their own tongue briefly before Ryland turned to her and spoke himself, "Yes, I speak the scholar's tongue better than that uneducated lump over there, but I have never, ever, seen something like you."

His tan face colored at his frankness. Ryland's cheeks were rounder than his brother's, still bearing the baby fat of his youth, but in the bones underneath you could see the shadow of the man he would grow into. The antlers sprouting from above his hairline, smaller than his brother's, looked much like those on the deer that populated the woods and towns of Oregon. Her eyes darted between the brothers, weighing their similarities. Ryland's eyes were a lighter, golden brown, to his brother's startling green, his lips fuller as he grimaced at himself for his bald statement. But the ease of the familiar words coming from his mouth was a balm to Syl's raw nerves and she laughed at the absurdity of the situation, until suddenly it was not laughter but tears. They ran down her face in streams, rivers of salty water that she could taste. The men shifted uncomfortably across the fire but she had no control over her sobbing, crying until the terrible tension of the last few hours of uncertainty finally ebbed from her body.

Torman touched her gently, grave concern in his eyes as he touched each of her arms and legs with exceeding gentleness. "Hurt?" he asked, his eyes lingering on her bare feet and their coating of grime.

Sylvia shook her head. "No. Confused, scared." Torman shook his shaggy head, not understanding, until Ryland moved out of the shadows and translated for him. The giant man then nodded in understanding and pointed to a stack of blankets warming by their fire. Torman took her gently by the arm and set the blankets over her one by one, like her father used to do when she still required 'tucking in' at night. She snuggled down into the warmth, happy for the moment to forget her other problems in the comfort of being clothed and warm once more. At least for now.

Ryland

Ryland and his brother stared in fascination at the sleeping girl. A delicate frown creased her fine features, easing ever so slowly as she fell deeper into sleep. Her hair reflected the light of the fire, the flickering flames revealing intriguing glints of lightness in the strands that gave way to shadows so dark they appeared almost blue. The hair fell straight and heavy from her head, shorter wisps curling slightly around her face, framing it in shadowy tones of midnight.

"She speaks a most ancient tongue" Torman said softly, "where did she come from?"

"I have no idea," Ryland replied, "at first I thought her deformed, like something went wrong before she was born. Then she got up and in moving all of her strangeness seemed to fit with the rest of her, rather than encumber her." He paused for a beat before continuing, "In all my studies I have never seen someone shaped like her. Did you see her legs? And feet. Those are feet! Like a banded monkey from the Isles! Not hooves."

"So slight, so tiny," his brother breathed, "it makes me want to take care of her, she looks to be so easily harmed. Maybe she is still just a child?"

Ry nodded his head in agreement and then shook it at his next thought, "Torman, they are going to want her."

"I know," his voice was sad, his face grave, "The question is, are we going to let them have her? And if we aren't, how do we keep her a secret?"

Ryland slid his hands over his face, pushing at his tired eyes with the palms of his hands. Lamenting that their few day's trip out into the Reedwood forest to escape the Holm had veered so far from the much needed break from stress it had been intended as. "We have to find a way to sneak her into the Holm," he said, "Camus will know what to do with her, won't he?"

Torman nodded in agreement with his younger brother's plan, "Yes he will, but father cannot know, or her life and our own are forfeit." He grinned fiercely and began rolling himself into his cloak, "And with that happy thought I am going to try to sleep, I suggest you do the same."

Ryland settled himself into his own cloak, throwing an envious look at the girl, snuggled warmly in both his and Torman's blankets, as the garment gaped open to let the cold air in. He tried to pull his chaotic thoughts into some semblance of order. How could they possibly make it into the Holm tomorrow without being seen? The border patrols were no problem as Torman's position as the Jorgen's Captain at Arms meant he was aware of all the patrol patterns and they could easily slip through and around the scouts, at least until they got to the Wall.

The Jorgen family had helped in the ascension of the current ruling King, and in reward His Majesty had sent them a resident Maegi to aid in the defense of their homeland. Camus had come from the capital city where the King resided, full of arcane knowledge and modern theories. His very appearance spoke volumes on the differences between Seaprium and Ryland's own isolated country home. Camus's features were more refined, his face thinner than the broader cheekbones and coarser attributes of the Trewal who had been living in the rugged mountains around Jorgenholm for centuries. His antlers rose from the crown of his head like two slightly curved blades, and bore thick ridges along their entire dark length. Slowly, over Camus's years living in the Holm, the strangely styled clothes he wore gave way to more traditional garb. The long pointed hoods and gaily colored ribbons that edged his robes disappeared, and the tightly cinched sleeves of the Maegi of the King's Academy loosened into wide, bell shaped cuffs that were rife with pockets, always hiding some sweet or treat for his pupils. His face still set him apart, and the most obvious difference of his Galmorish antlers, but his long time appointment to Jorgenholm overcame any ill will that those differences might have originally brought.

Camus's magic was earthbound, meaning the defensive Wall Camus had spent years constructing around the Holm was made up of all things earthly and deadly. Hundreds of varieties of thorn bushes tangled themselves into an impenetrable mesh, the sweet, blood-red blooms of wild and Windthorn roses perfuming the whole Holm in the heat of the mountain summers, such a sweet scent to come from such a deadly tangle. Bougainvillea and the small, electric green fronds of poisonleaf intermingled into an impervious screen of living organisms guarding his ancestral home. The defense was fed with magic, and the blood of the Hinterland raiders the Wall had claimed.

The tangled barrier encircling Jorgenholm usually evoked a feeling of safety for Ryland. But then again he had never had to contemplate breaking through his home's defenses until now. There was only one entrance that was not blocked off by Camus's Wall, the heavily guarded main gates. But there would be no bringing the strange girl through that very public entrance without the Jorgen hearing of it. His own budding magic was also earthly, giving him a better shot than most against the hyper-natural defenses, but it did not make it a guarantee. If only he could talk to his teacher, then Camus could open a path to them in secret, allowing them to slip through one of the tunnels running beneath the battlements that supported the growth of the Wall. But the magical barrier was exactly that, a barrier to magic, even farscrying. They would have no way to contact the Maegi.

Which left him, his brother, and this exotic creature they had stumbled upon almost solely dependent on his fumbling attempts at magical Control. A shudder shook him. The consequences were dire, for everyone involved. He thought longingly of the King's Academy, his home until his late blooming powers had enticed his father to bring him home. Books did not expect you to perform daring deeds to save damsels in distress, and his studies had had consequences no more dire than extra work. *The good old days*, he sighed heavily and began the five step Opening he had been taught to access his power. *That's usually enough to send me right to sleep*, he thought ruefully.

Sylvia

Sylvia was awake, and she desperately didn't want to open her eyes, but from the bird song she could distantly hear, she knew exactly what she would see when she did crack open her eyelids. She just didn't want to admit it yet. With a groan she squinted her eyes. A fuzzy picture of two very interested faces, heavily back lit with the rising sun, and gloriously antlered, swam into view. She clamped her eyes shut again, wiggled down into the blankets and curled her arms around her head. *Definitely NOT the two faces she wanted to see!*

"I was hoping you weren't real," she said aloud to her arms. "Because really you should be my mom and dad, watching me wake up from surgery, with a nice new knee and a head full of painkillers. Oh! Maybe you ARE my mom and dad, they just gave me too many drugs!" She struggled out of her woolly cocoon, hope blooming in her chest. But the deer-men were still there, startled eyes wide at her sudden movements. She giggled, *deer-men in the headlights.* And just as suddenly her mirth was gone. There were definitely no such things as headlights here, or cars, or painkillers from the look of things. The scene before her was positively medieval, complete with abnormally large pack horses and swords.

The larger man, she dredged up his name from the blur of last night, Torman, grinned easily in response to her hysterical mirth. "Good morning! Will you please share your naming with us?"

"Sylvia," she said, her eyes glued to the crumbly bread each man had in his hand. She was ravenous, the hunger an intense gnawing in her belly she hadn't noticed until her eyes lit upon the crumbs at the corners of Ryland's mouth. The mouth stretched into a smile as she stared at it and the young man stretched out the hand holding his portion of bread to her. "Hungry?"

She reached out slowly, grappling with her impulse to grab the food and stuff it into her mouth as quickly as possible. Torman produced a wicked looking knife from a sheath on his thigh, and sliced off a slab of creamy white cheese that he plopped on top of her bread.

"Fanks," she said, spraying crumbs and nibbling happily on the cheese. It was soft and mild tasting, a little bit like goat cheese, but lacking the overpowering 'goat' taste. She sidled closer to the fire, feeling the morning chill now that she wasn't draped in blankets. The scene around the campsite was eerie, a low mist wafting dampen through the underbrush, making the towering trees look like they were wearing silvery skirts. *It almost looks like home,* she thought idly, inspecting the thick vegetation around them. Then her eyes came back to the deer-men with their avid stares. *Almost,* she clarified to herself.

Torman handed her a mug of hot liquid, spicy smelling and wonderfully restorative as she sipped at it. It reminded her of the Chai tea she favored at home, Tazo for her while her mom adamantly stuck to the sweeter Oregon Chai. With a sigh she brought herself back to the present, "So," she said, considering the two pairs of eyes glued to her face, "where are we?"

Ryland and Torman exchanged looks. One answered "Reedwood forest" while the other said "Between Jorgenholm and Seaprium." They chuckled and reaffirmed the others statements.

She shook her head, "Neither of those means anything to me. And I don't know of anywhere on Earth where people look like you do, rather than like I do." She felt her face flush, a hot sweeping of embarrassment making her eyes water. "Not that that is bad," she added hurriedly, her eyes sweeping once more over the two brothers, catching briefly on the bulging shoulders straining the seams of Torman's shirt, and the proud arch in each of their strong necks. *Surely all those muscles didn't only come from having to hold up the weight of antlers on their heads?*

Ryland's smile seemed unworried as he replied, "And we do not know of anywhere where your kind reside." A puzzled look replaced his smile, "Earth?"

Sylvia felt the fluttering wings of panic begin again in her stomach. "Yes! Earth, the United States of America, the West Coast, Oregon! That's where I belong. SO WHERE THE HELL AM I?"

The men looked taken aback at her vehemence, and stumped by the string of locations she had given, but Torman tried his best to give a similar accounting of her actual location, rather than the one she wished she was at. "Reedwood forest, near the eastern coast of Prium, next to the Blitherly Sea." he continued, "We are Trewal, and everyone in this area are subjects of the Kingdom of Prium. What are you called, Selva?"

He had stumbled on her name a bit, "Syl is fine," she said, her eyes catching again on his antlers "and I'm human. Do you have those here?"

Torman shook his head regretfully, neck muscles bulging as they compensated for the extra weight on his head. He tried out the new words on his tongue like he wanted to actually taste them, "Syyyyl," he said experimentally, and "hooman."

Ryland, however, began nodding his head, a faraway look in his eyes. "I've read that name somewhere; I know I have. Some old dusty book in the library, but I've read so many old dusty books," he mused.

He turned to his brother, "If I have heard of her people then we might be able to find out where she belongs." He faced Syl again, intensity etched in every line of his boyish face.

Torman rolled his eyes at his brother's antics and told Syl, "He will interrogate you now, please do not run away."

Ryland, his eyes fixed on her, made vague shooing motions towards the horses, "Go pack us up you great lummox, I'm going to get some answers!" Torman stood with a good natured grin and sauntered off to their cluster of huge horses, whistling as he went.

"How did you get here? Do you remember anything? Was it on a ship?" Ryland's questions piled up on each other rapidly.

Sylvia shook her head, "I woke up in the forest, a small clearing quite a walk that way." She pointed back towards the painful, barefoot path she had followed the previous evening. "Before that, I was at home, where I belong."

"Some sort of magical transport then," Ryland mused, "that takes some serious power. More than anyone around here has got on hand in any case. But it does let us know that you are deep in someone's game. No one would put that much effort into bringing you here without a good reason. But it has to be someone powerful. I'd say no one weaker than the King and his Demandron, or the Gods themselves!" He laughed a little nervously and said to Syl, "But the Gods haven't messed with mortal doings in a long time, so that isn't very likely…" He frowned worriedly and Syl felt her stomach tighten with nerves, making her wish she had skipped the breakfast the brothers had so kindly offered. "I hope." Ryland finished with an apologetic shrug before he too got up to join his brother to ready their mounts.

Ryland

The girl has obviously ridden a horse before, Ryland thought with appreciation, *that's a good sign, she might even be able to walk after the grueling ride back to Jorgenholm.* It would be a full day's ride through rough terrain until they reached the Wall in the murky light of dusk, in the sun's fading glow and before the true luminescence of the moons. At least they hoped to have all of the latter concealing elements in play. They needed every advantage they could get.

Syl's movements atop their placid packhorse were captivating, her dark hair capturing glints of light and her fine features showing her every emotion in minute changes of facial expressions. The Demandron would snap her up in a moment, even if she had been Trewal and not the strange race of Humans. He shivered with the thought of her in the hated harems. The stockpile of beautiful and exotic women and young children that the Demandron had at their beck and call.

He, like nearly everyone in Prium, had had someone beloved taken by them. His elder sister, Fria, had been seized when he was just ten rebirths old. He could just barely recall her face; the benevolent smile and merry eyes that could be both sharp with mischief and so calm and loving. He could, however, clearly remember the face of the woman the Demandron had returned to his family; those hollow, haunted eyes held absolutely no part of the sister he had known and loved.

Shaking himself free from his memories, he saw Torman and Syl giggling snidely from the corner of his eye. Turning to face the pair, he realized that his clothes were wreathed in flames, and it took all of his will power not to jump from his horse and start rolling on the ground to put them out. Instead he held very still and tried to sound nonchalant, "Very funny Torman, now if you are done showing off, we have actual magic to discuss, rather than your petty tricks".

Torman simply grinned and the magical flames grew larger, beginning to sting the flesh beneath his tunic. Ry gritted his teeth and glared at his brother. "Which one of us is the elder again?" he asked through his teeth.

With a final laugh and a flare of flame, Torman extinguished his sibling and nudged his horse to walk beside Ryland. "You always spoil my fun brother, but fine, let's strategize".

"Alright, so we get through the patrols to the Wall. And we make our way to the 'back door'."

"Yes," Torman replied confidently, "And then you call on your Earth magic to convince that tangled mess of plants to let us through. I'm guessing Camus will be alerted right away, but the fact that we are at the back door near the escape route may make him investigate before he sends the whole garrison down on us."

"May."

"May," agreed Torman.

Ryland was glad their planning had been done in a language Syl did not understand; he would have started riding hard in the other direction if he had heard their conversation and was in her precarious position. He glanced back at her, riding solidly on the dun pack horse he and Torman had brought with them on their little escape. She was so small that she looked like a child on the big boned gelding. Syl was wincing slightly at the rough portions in the trail, but examined the scenery around her with interest, making him wonder if anything looked familiar to her. He dropped back to ride alongside and began to point to plants and trees, telling her their names in Layette, the most common tongue of Prium. She repeated the words back to him, her pronunciation flawed at first, but quickly improving. The glowing light of curiosity never left her extraordinary eyes. Teaching her quickly chased his nerves away, her easy laughter and tendency to poke fun at herself so far removed from the peril of the situation. Ryland found himself laughing back at her, the dangers which lay ahead all but forgotten.

Chapter 2

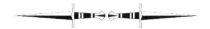

Camus

Camus felt old. His bones seemed to ache more now when he did magic, like the power was resonating in his tissues, vibrating his fragile frame and trying to shake him to pieces. He gently stretched out his arms one at a time and took a sip of the herbal concoction he made especially for his more arthritic patients, like himself. The tang of licorice saved the caustic brew from being completely undrinkable, but he made a note to tone down his use of the bitter nettles in the next batch.

He had felt some sort of disturbance during the previous night, which had woken him from a fitful sleep like a bolt of lightning. He had tasted the magic on the air, thick enough as to seem like he was suffocating on the metallic taste, so similar to blood. Ever since then he had had this niggling feeling at the back of his mind, this feeling of something important coming.

There! It was back, like an itch that has no physical place to scratch, so there is never any relief. *No, wait, this crawling feeling was different from the sense of impending doom, this was the feeling of someone interfering with his magic, but not anything current. The Wall!* He thought suddenly in abrupt understanding.

Camus rushed to the side of his tower room where a large table held a perfect scale model of Jorgenholm, the barrier surrounding it glowing softly, alight with the copper of his Earth magic. At the rear of the model sparks flew from the Wall, exactly where he had spelled in a backdoor for emergencies. There the growth had only put down cursory roots, easily nudged to the side so that a small passage would open up in the mesh of the Wall. What was the probability of that? That someone would be attacking exactly where the Wall was weakest? *Oh no*, he thought, *Torman! Ryland!* They had been out of the Holm, escaping their tyrannical father for a brief time, it had to be them! No one else knew about the escape route but the Jorgen himself.

Camus hurled himself out of the door of his tower room, hooves clattering on the stone steps spiraling away from his cozy abode. He began moving more sedately once he spotted serfs cleaning in the halls; if the boys were coming in the back they did not want to be seen, and nearly every serf working in Jorgenholm was in the Jorgen's pocket. He made haste to the Wall, urging speed from his tired body which even he was surprised it was willing to give, wondering what new complication the two young lords were bringing to him this time.

Ryland

The Wall stopped fighting him after a quarter of an hour. He slumped gratefully to the loamy ground, breathing hard, his head feeling like an overstretched water bladder. The tangle of growth parted before him and a tall skeletal figure appeared through the opening. "Camus!" Torman breathed, "So glad you heard us knocking".

The knobby old man reached down toward Ryland, stiffly holding his lower back as he knelt. "That was some mighty magic to Control son. Are you well?"

Ryland nodded, fighting his way back to his feet. "We need to get in and hide her Camus. Were we detected?"

"Just by me" the old Maegi replied, eyes locked on Sylvia. "By the Gods themselves", he breathed, "We DO need to hide her. Quickly, inside child. You boys need to return by more standard means, we can't have you appearing inside the Holm without having come inside!"

Ryland nodded wearily and allowed Torman to tow him back to his ill-tempered gelding. The big boned bay gave a halfhearted attempt to close his teeth over Ryland's forearm as he swayed too close, but Torman rebuked the attack easily with his free hand. "We should have thought of that Torman; we would have just gone in with her."

Torman heaved his brother up into the saddle, lifting him as easily as a sack of grain, and he landed in the saddle with the same amount of grace as the sack would have had. "Thank Garrin for Camus little brother. Again. We would both have been killed long ago if that man had not cared for us."

"She'll be safe now right?" Ryland mumbled. *By the antlers of Garrin himself he was tired.* He should never had tried calling so much magic. He'd been horrified by the amount of power that had answered, but it hadn't blown the circuits of his mind, which meant he could call even more than he had today. The Windthorn blooms blurred into a smear of red on his left and the mottled shades of green in the Wall began to run blearily together. He vaguely felt a large hand clamp down on his shoulder, securing him in the saddle as his horse shied sideways, unsettled by the limp rider upon his back.

He shuddered, grateful for his older brother's support. The stronger a Maegi he was, the more he had to fear from his father. Just the thought of the Jorgen knowing what he had done today sent icy shivers racing down his back and he could feel the apprehension tangle his already wobbly stomach into tight knots. *I'll hide my magic,* Ryland thought, *I'll just have to hide it.*

Sylvia

The old man reminded Syl of a sandpiper; one of the stick-legged wading birds that bobbed up and down the Oregon coast. But this old sandpiper had twisting horns like a gazelle, and his feet made ringing sounds as they hustled down a stone corridor. She was bundled in a thick, robe-like garment made for a far larger person, hood down to hide her face, greatly obscuring her view of their surroundings. The trailing hem threatened to trip her at every step. She got the vague impression of dark stone walls and towering castle-esque architecture, but mainly she saw her own feet, just barely peeking out from the hem as she kicked it out of her way with each step. The man's grip on her arm was surprisingly strong, even when the occasional tremor shook through his body. The eyes that peered around corners and flickered constantly back to her were bright with intelligence, not at all dimmed with the man's obvious age.

"Hush now child," he said absently. Sylvia crooked an eyebrow in confusion as she hadn't spoken a word since leaving the brothers at the staggering wall of vegetation they had led her to, but the old sandpiper spoke on, "Not far to go".

They rounded a corner and began to climb a spiral stair so tight and steep she began to feel dizzy as they toiled upwards. She eyed her guide with appreciation as her breathing became labored, and noticed with chagrin the elderly man was not winded at all. *He must be stronger than he looks!*

They rounded one last corner to find a small landing dominated by an intimidating wood door. The dark wood looked ancient and impenetrable, fitted with elaborate metal embellishments draping seamlessly down the cracks between planks in gorgeous whorls and inlaid designs. The old man, seemingly immune to the beauty of the entryway, pushed the door open with a little effort. They strode into a cluttered room that looked half laboratory and half library, along with having a cozy living space tucked into the farthest reaches of what was obviously a circular tower.

He secured the door behind them and heaved a sigh of relief, tension she hadn't even noticed in the old man shed like a cloak. His warm chocolaty eyes fixed themselves on her as he strode towards her, tutting softly under his breath. "Ah child," he breathed, running his hands down her arms to grasp her hands in his bony grip, seeming to examine the air around her rather than her body itself. She shifted under the borrowed robe, uncomfortable with his astute perusal.

"The Gods have their hands on you for sure, I can barely see your pretty face for the glare of their light." He blinked owlishly, then squinted his eyes shut tightly before opening them once more, "There you are! Be glad the Sight is not a talent shared by many, else you would have no chance to hide, shining like that."

Sylvia changed weight from one foot to the other uneasily, unsure if a response was expected to his rambling. After a short pause, he turned to the door and cracked it open to talk to someone on the other side. She surveyed the room covertly, turning a small circle to take it all in. Rich colors and textures softened the harshness of the dark stone walls, and warm yellow light spilled from the fireplace to illuminate what the weaker light from the slim window slits didn't reach. She liked the herby smell of the room, and the kind eyes once more regarding her put her nerves at ease more than anything in the last harrowing day had managed to.

"I have a bath and a meal coming up for you," he said to her in his shaky voice, "The serfs come in after one knock, so make sure to get hidden quickly." He gestured to the screen sectioning off a portion of the room near the bed, obviously a changing area. She nodded in agreement to his words before sliding off the robe he had wrapped her in to enter the building. She hung it on the pegs holding other such garments near the door and then walked over toward her hiding place, ready to sneak behind the solid screen at a moment's notice. *At some point I hope they tell me exactly what I keep having to hide from,* she thought irritably. But she would feel more comfortable posing such a question to genial Torman than this stranger, no matter how grandfatherly he appeared.

Said stranger smiled encouragingly at her, saying, "We will talk about what is next when the boys arrive, after you are settled and fed." At that moment a knock sounded at the door and Syl plunged behind the screen, listening to the slosh of water and the rustling of many bodies moving into the room, as she crouched down next to a large hamper filled to the brim with neatly folded clothing.

Torman

Torman scooped Camus into a bear hug the second he entered his tower, gentling his exuberance for the old man's sake, and setting him down carefully once he had greeted his oldest friend. "Thank you Camus, I don't know how much longer Ry would have lasted if you hadn't shown up when you did."

He frowned, remembering the electric crackle of his brother's Earth magic. He had never felt so much magic from a partially trained youth, even one who had come into his power as late as Ryland had. In this household, more magic meant more attention for his younger sibling. He rubbed a hand tiredly through his hair, his fingers tugging through snarls in the curly brown mane. His eyes meeting Camus's, he saw the same worries reflected there. His mentor sighed, smiling slightly as he lightly berated Torman, "Do you have any idea what you have brought into this ice lion's lair, Torman? I think I prefer the injured animals you used to sneak into the Holm for treatments. They caused much less ruckus than this girl has the potential of creating."

Torman nodded in agreement. Sylvia was a few hundred steps closer to fatal trouble than his various secret pets had been. As if thinking her name had called her to him the girl herself stepped out from behind Camus's elegantly painted changing screen, raising a hand in greeting before continuing to comb her fingers through her damp hair. The detailed hunting scene depicted behind her on the screen was heavy with brilliant oranges and deep reds, highlighting the flush of her freshly washed skin and accenting those brilliant eyes with contrasting colors.

He sighed heavily again and moved towards the fireside, dragging various stools and chairs with him as he encountered them in the cluttered space. "I'll go get Ryland, he's probably fallen asleep in his bath, the boy's that wiped out." He fixed his eyes on Camus and Sylvia, "And then I am calling a secret meeting," his voice was teasing as he voiced the cliché, but darkened again as his eyes lingered on the blue eyed girl, "We need to talk".

After dragging his dozing sibling from his tepid bath, and prodding him repeatedly to get him up the stairs to Camus's workshop, Torman settled his baby brother in front of the fire. He immediately launched into the heart of matters, knowing Ryland would likely not last long before sleep claimed him again.

"Syl, you are in great danger here." Camus obligingly began translating, knowing Torman was too worked up to spend the time he would need to find all of these words in her language. Her vibrant eyes widened, flickering between Camus and Torman as he continued on.

"The King of this land holds his power only through the use of dark and filthy magic. He keeps the realm's most vibrant youths cloistered in dark harems, stockpiling their life forces and the potent emotions bred from fear and violence for the use of the Demandron, who are the base of the Royal family's true power. The leaders of the Demandron, the so called Circle, drain our best and brightest, returning only husks to their families. It's this threat to our loved ones, along with the terrible power the Demandron create with them, that keeps the court's noble families in check and beneath the King's thumb."

He took a deep breath and continued, staring into the fire to avoid the sapphire eyes latched onto his face. "Blue eyes indicate great magic in our land. It means you are a Mage, capable of wielding all the elements once you come into your power. Children born with such eyes are carefully tracked and contained so they may become a part of the Demandron's Circle when their special brand of magic awakens. There has never been more than twenty Trewal with eyes such as yours at a time, the ten in the Circle, and the ten being groomed to join it." He tracked Syl's hand as it arced gracefully to her face, lingering on her cheek next to her eye. Her features looked perplexed and her mouth popped open to voice the protest written there, so he barreled onward before she could get the words out. "Being a, human is it? Yes, a human, puts you at risk, but it's those eyes of yours that write your death sentence. The King is very powerful, and his subjects fear him. Anyone who sees you will turn you in to our Lord father," Torman's face flushed with anger, "who is the King's foremost supporter, and also his cousin." He looked to Camus, "She is not from here Camus, and I believe that all she wants is to go home; everyone would be safer if that were to happen. What can we do?"

The old man shook his head sadly, eyes lingering on the girl. "It is not that simple son," he said gently, "She is lit up like the sun with the touch of the Gods. Even if we could find the otherworld pathway that would get her home, it would mean much research in the King's Academy itself. But the Gods brought her here, so maybe, she is meant to stay."

"No." Syl abruptly stood, gathering the too-long folds of Camus's robe in her hands to free her delicate feet so she could step nearer to Camus. "I AM meant to go home, because that is where I am MEANT to be. If you don't want to risk helping me because of the danger, or even because of your Gods, fine, I understand. But please tell me the way to the Academy so I can find this path my-, myself." Sylvia's voice rose in pitch with her intensity, cracking at the last word.

Her face was fierce in the flickering light from the hearth, her body taut with the tension of the moment. Camus ran a hand through the air near her, touching the aura no one else could see. "Child, sometimes the Gods use us lesser beings harshly in the pursuit of the greater good, no matter what our own desires may be."

Sylvia

Sylvia held the smooth recurve bow with shaking hands. The string felt like it would cut through her raw fingers at any second but she forced herself to draw it, once again, back towards her cheek. Her shoulder muscles trembled at the strain, protesting the rough treatment of the last two hours.

Torman tapped the hand bracing the bow, "Higher!" he called to her, "Keep it steady and align the top of your bow hand with what you are aiming at."

She wished she hadn't agreed to this training. At first it had seemed like a great idea, and a welcome distraction for her constant worrying about what was actually happening to her. Plus, the thought of learning archery had intrigued her. She had not pictured the grueling lesson she was to receive. Torman hadn't even let her *see* an arrow yet. She had spent the last two hours perfecting her grip to his satisfaction, and then drawing and holding that position for as long as her arms could take it. *I am an athlete dammit!* She yelled at herself in her head. *How could standing in one spot possibly be this hard?*

"And release." Torman stalked towards her from the window he had been peering out of in Camus's tower. "That's a good introduction to the bow. But with those eyes, and no antlers to speak of, the only disguise for you is going to be as a serf, where you can keep your eyes lowered at all times, and head coverings are the norm. And serfs don't carry weapons unless they are hunting for their lords." He began methodically pulling weapons from his person and depositing them on the worktable.

Syl watched incredulously at the ever growing mountain of daggers and throwing knives Torman had had secreted about his body. He pulled them from his sleeves, the tops of his boots and from beneath the folds of his tunic. It was a marvel he didn't cut himself with every breath he took. He selected a few of the smaller knives, which he called Fen, and began instructing her on how to hold them for close combat. It was at this point Torman realized she had no fighting training whatsoever. His mouth opened and closed multiple times before he asked in an unbelieving voice, "Do people not make war in your world?"

"Some do, but it's a choice; and children," she motioned to herself, "are not allowed to be in the military until they are at least eighteen."

Torman was silent for a long while before answering. "No wonder you wish to return to your home, where only those who wish to make war need kill others." He looked at his hands as if inspecting for blood. When he raised his eyes to hers there was pain lurking in their speckled green depths, "You are in my world now Sylvia, and if you do not learn to kill, then you will die yourself. Only there are things worse than death waiting for you and your blue eyes here."

Syl shuddered at the sudden chill she felt race through her body. Everything she had experienced in Prium had seemed so fantastical, like she was stuck in a fairy-tale with brave knights and their towering castle. But Torman's expression was real. So very real, and so tortured. She had done a report the year before for a psychology class about lucid dreaming, and had been vaguely thinking that was what she was experiencing here with the handsome deer men. She had been going along with the story line like one of the heroines in the fantasy novels she read back home, all the while keeping the picture of herself in a drug induced delirium sleeping in her bed at home, in her mind's eye.

But where would her mind have picked up the knowledge of a tormented soldier so obviously needed to create this character in her hallucination? Her life back home was simple, it was beautiful, and full of light, and the love of her family and friends. Torman's anguish was so outside of her realm of experience... she didn't even want to contemplate how her mind had dreamed this larger-than-life creature up, or to acknowledge the terrifying fact that it was beginning to feel like this couldn't be the work of her mind at all.

Ryland

It took him two full days to feel himself again. Two days of headaches and a ceaseless urge to sleep left him cranky and irritable. *Cranky and irritable and completely unable to keep my mouth shut,* he chided himself. It was his own fault he was stuck respelling his Lord Father's entire armory for the majority of the third day after their return with Sylvia. During his weekly audience with his father, the Jorgen, concerning his magical progress, which always felt like he was the goose being checked to see if it was fat enough for the cook pot, Ryland had foolishly let his snide thoughts slip from his mouth rather than keeping them inside where they belonged. Hence the respelling.

At least the hours of quiet work in the armory gave him a chance to think the events of the last few days through. Respelling armor was child's play at this point in his life. He had been punished with it numerous times since his magic had begun to mature and his father had snatched him back to the Holm. He placed his palms flat on the cool metal of a polished half-helm, next came the steps, the five steps of Opening, now as familiar to him as the back of his own hand. Breathe In. Look Inward. Wake the magic coiled latently inside. Breathe Out. Push the coppery magic out to the very edges of his skin, ready for whatever he next asked of it. He pushed it further, past the boundaries of his flesh and into the helm until the entirety of it glowed, the metal stronger now, lighter. *Now the harder part.* He punched his awareness through the stone under his feet, his mind trickling through the tiniest cracks, down and down until he felt soil.

True Earth. He pulled the power of it to him, using his own magic to entice it upwards from its slumber, and then he bound both magics into the half-helm with a quick word of binding.

"Starsh." He set the helm aside and moved on.

He had plenty to think about. Even omitting the dark haired girl who had recently turned his precarious position in his father's Holm into a balancing act involving knives, he also had his magic to worry about. He sighed loudly over his great, great grandfather's dented breastplate, and watched as his reflection slowly reemerged out of the fog of his breath on the marred surface. He started heavily at the sight of a serf waiting patiently behind him and then dropped the breastplate with a clatter as the serf's head lifted and bright blue eyes met his from under the cowl of the robe.

"Syl!" he hissed. "You shouldn't be out of Camus's tower! What in Garrin's name do you think you are doing?"

She smiled impishly back at him and he felt, momentarily, that his chest was too tight to allow breath to be drawn into his lungs. How could she risk all of them like this? Didn't they explain the consequences? Her beauty would be snuffed out by the debasement of the harems in days. Her lovely smile could be snatched away from the world so easily, and here she is taunting the Gods to make it happen.

Syl's face blanched at his obvious ire and she took an involuntary step back, her head lowering so the cowl darkened her features. Her voice filtered breathily through the thick cloth and barely reached his ears, as she rather sullenly told the floor, "Camus and Torman thought I should test out the disguise we've been perfecting for the last few days."

Ryland breathed out a breath he hadn't realized he was holding. "I'm sorry Syl, I didn't mean to yell at you, I just can't, we can't let- we have to make sure no one finds out."

The lowered head nodded in assent, and then her eyes were back on his face, "Torman says to stop taking your time down here and finish; you need to be training with us if we are going to be able to start out for Seaprium anytime soon."

Ryland cocked his head to the side, "Training with *us*? Is Torman training you in magic?" He wondered idly if his new found strength in magic was the reason his brother hadn't approached him to train since Sylvia's arrival in the Holm. The amount of magic he had Called to the Wall far surpassed even the greatest amounts his brother could summon with magical aids.

Syl shook her head, "I don't have any magic, silly," she said with a roll of her eyes, "We're training with weapons. Torman is teaching me the bow and hand to hand with *fen,* but he said he wants you to be there when we try the quarterstaff."

Ryland groaned inwardly, he had taken to the sword easily enough, having had one in his hand since he was a child, but the quarter staff's extra length and blunt tip confounded him. "Great, he wants to beat me with a stick again," he grinned at her ruefully and shook his head, "or maybe he wants to make *you* hit me with a stick. I'm sure he'd find that amusing."

Syl smiled back and nodded in agreement, "I think the idea is to have us hit each other, and maybe learn how not to be hit." Her face fell and she rubbed her arms tenderly before she grudgingly said, "Although if his staff training is anything like the archery, then we will just be standing facing each other holding the damn sticks for hours."

They stood in contemplative silence for a minute, each considering the impending punishment their bodies were in for. Ryland shrugged, "You head up, I'm on the last set of armor so I should be done soon. Plus, serfs don't accompany the lord's family unless they are too drunk to walk on their own, so we should go separately anyway."

She nodded her head, keeping her eyes down and bowed carefully in a very good imitation of a serf's humble obeisance. He watched her walk away, troubled by something until he realized her feet made no sound on the stone floors of the armory. She would need some sort of shoe that sounds like hooves if this disguise is to work, he decided. He bent to retrieve the ancient breast plate, rubbing a scuff off the emblem of the Jorgen Ice Lion, and began the Opening again, his mind busy devising a shoe made of horn for their dangerous guest as his body preformed the task by rote.

Camus

Training was much more fun to watch than to participate in, Camus thought with an inward grin. *One of the perks of old age I guess, getting pleasure from the young ones struggle and strife.* He gave a little chuckle at the fierce look on Syl's face as she attacked Ryland with the quarterstaff. His chuckle turned to outright laughter as Ryland stumbled back, eyes wide and hands frantically spinning his staff to block.

Torman's deep laugh joined his own from where the big man leaned against the wall near an arrow slit. Their eyes met, both crinkled with laughter. Torman grinned at his mentor, "Ry has never worked this hard before, and I do believe he fears being beaten by a girl. I finally have the key to make my baby brother train hard."

They turned as one as a particularly loud thwack, followed by a yelp of pain broke apart the fighters in the center of the tower room. Syl was nursing her hand to her chest and leveling a heated glare at her sparring partner, who had a very smug grin on his face. Torman strode into their midst, "Ah, bother mine, if I had known that all it took was a pretty woman with a stick to make you into a warrior, I would have been holding your training sessions in brothels from the beginning!" Ryland's face flamed as his brother turned to Syl and repositioned her hands on the staff, wider this time so that blocking would not put her fingers in as much danger of being smashed. "Go again," he commanded.

The trainees faced off once more, when an abrupt knock at the door sent Sylvia scurrying for shelter behind the changing screen. Torman was left staring bemusedly at the quarterstaff that had suddenly appeared in his hands. As the Jorgen strode arrogantly into the room, Camus was intensely grateful for her quick reaction; there

31

was absolutely no explanation they could offer the boy's father as to why a serf, and a woman at that, was involved in weapons training.

The Lord stared haughtily at his sons with eyes as dark as onyx, and then locked eyes with Camus. "Get out," he spat at his offspring without a further look. The boys tumbled towards the door in their haste, each studiously avoiding looking at the changing screen in the farthest reaches of the room. Camus bowed to his master, trying to gauge by his demeanor how dangerous a mood he was in today. Jorgen moved unhurriedly to the table holding the miniature version of his stronghold and sat stiffly in Camus's favorite chair, leaving the old man to trail after him and perch precariously on the stool across from him.

"We have news from the capital." The Jorgen's face was all hard planes and ice cold eyes. His rack of antlers was magnificent, large tines all filed into wicked points and banded with hammered gold that was beautifully complemented by the deep, blood red brocade of his robe, and mirrored the rich gold embroidery that edged the garment. "We war with Saerin." His voice was cold and clipped.

Camus's head snapped up in surprise. Last he had heard the King had successfully concluded the betrothal of his son Fragon to the Saerin princess, who was only a few years younger that the realm's only prince. *Why would we go to war with our allies after months of negotiations to cement them as friends*, he wondered?

"The King calls me to him, along with my forces, to make a full scale attack on Saerin. He wishes to conquer the Sareth Isles as soon as the troops can be assembled." His thin lips twisted into a sneer, "His plan is utter stupidity, and I will turn his mind to other methods as soon as I reach the capital. But until I can show him how foolish he is, our forces must march to Seaprium."

"Yes my Lord." Camus kept his eyes down, it was not required of him, but he had found in his years at Jorgenholm that the volatile Lord was less likely to take out his temper on someone who showed him the deference of hiding their eyes. This turn of events had obviously angered him beyond words. With the Hinterlanders from the North pressing their borders as they did every winter when heavy snows forced them down from the Skypeaks, marching

Jorgenholm's main fighting force to Seaprium, and then sailing across the Blitherly Sea, would leave the Holm dangerously unprotected. A fact the King either did not care about, or had failed to take into consideration.

"You will hold the Holm until my return. Torman will remain to advise you on military tactics, and military matters *only,* it is obvious that is all he will ever be capable of. If he tries to marry that commoner girl of his while I am away, put a stop to it, that is a command Camus." The old Maegi could feel the Jorgen's eyes boring into his lowered head, as if he could make Camus obey with his will alone.

"Ryland comes with me. The boy grows soft under your tutelage. His magical capacity will increase starting now, and if it does not, then I have no use for him anyway."

Camus kept his face blank as he replied, while inside he recoiled from the harsh tone the man took towards his own blood, "Of course my Lord." He tucked his horror into the recesses of his mind. Their plans had just been accelerated beyond anything he had imagined, and poor Ryland was being placed at the epicenter of the storm that is his father, a very dangerous place to be. And Garrin help him, he was going to send that sweet girl child right along with him.

Sylvia

She slowly peeled her hands from her mouth as she heard the door shut resoundingly, and took a deep breath. That man was scary. Scarier than almost anything she had experienced before. But she couldn't put her finger on *why.* While he was a large man with a thunderhead for a face and venom dripping from every word he uttered, he was smaller by far than his gentle eldest son, and not nearly as physically formidable. It was the energy he moved with that she feared. It followed him around like a personal rain cloud, dispensing dread instead of rain and bolts of fear rather than lightning.

This man was Torman and Ryland's father. *Unbelievable.* The two brothers had been nothing but sweet and caring with her. Intense sometimes yes, but only intent she remain safe. And then there was Camus, it broke her heart to hear kind, competent Camus, bowing and scraping to someone so cold and uncaring. Her entire life she had been taught to respect her elders, and even when her grandpa had been tied to his wheelchair in the last few months of his life, his war stories holding not even the smallest grain of truth, she had listened with deference to his occasional words of wisdom. But this monster treated Camus like he was dirt beneath his feet, or hooves, or whatever these deer men have at the end of their long legs.

In this moment, crouched uncomfortably behind a large wicker basket in the changing area of Camus's tower, all she wanted was home. She wanted her mom and dad, her good friends Arianna and Sarah, she even missed her snarky co-captain of the rugby team, Rachel. How did she end up here, so far from everything she understood? It was unreal, and impossible, and why the hell was she just going along for the ride? This had to be a dream, and she was done dreaming. It was far past time she woke up and started rebuilding her life, and her knee.

She pinched her upper arm viciously, wincing at the pain of her sore muscles beneath the skin. Then she took her hand violently to her cheeks, "Wake up! Wake UP! WAKE UP!" Anxiety began to rise in her chest, a tightening and constricting of her lungs, blurring the comfy confines of Camus's tower room. Bony fingers with swollen, angry looking knuckles snaked around her wrist, and pulled her hand away from her face with surprising strength.

"Hush child, that is not going to help." Camus's voice was calm and soothing. His kindness was suddenly too much too handle, the last emotional straw that completely broke her, because she knew, she *knew* somehow, that all of this was real, no matter how much she clung to her idea of hallucinations and drug induced dreams.

"I am sorry child, but you have to believe. You have to believe so we can keep you safe. This is a very dangerous place." He stroked her hair gently, his eyes going distant, "And I have to believe too Sylvia, I have to believe someone brought you here to make this place better, to help fix all of the things that are going so wrong here. The Gods cannot stand by and watch their children hurt one another for so long. You *must* be here to help. You have to be."

Camus's lined face blurred as tears made her vision swim and then she was crying so hard in the old man's arms, that she didn't even notice Ryland and Torman creeping back into the tower room, only to be banished with a dismissive wave of the elderly Maegi's hand. She didn't want to be his hope, it sounded far too hard and dangerous. Her parents didn't think she was responsible enough to get a puppy! How could she suddenly be responsible for a whole world's wellbeing? What God would be so cruel as to think *she* was a heroine?

The tears streamed messily down her cheeks, and she knew from experience that her face was turning blotchy and her nose was running, but it was hard to care. All she could see in her mind was her mom and dad in her house back home, laughing over a game of Uno in their cozy kitchen. All she could think about was her bed that was almost never without one of her two large, fat, cats and how she never made it the day she was going to have surgery, even though her mom hated it when she didn't.

All she wanted was *home*.

Chapter 3

Ryland

Ryland couldn't help himself from turning for one last look at Jorgenholm and the tiny figures of Camus and Torman looking over the battlements as the party rode away. His father, riding beside him, barked out mercilessly, "Stop squirming boy!" And he reluctantly turned away from the familiar figures, facing south again, looking down the long road to Seaprium.

His father continued talking, his regular speaking voice not far off in strength and venom from his harshly voiced command. "Fill yourself with magic, as much as you can, and kill that sapling." He gestured ahead of them some ways at a small Listenbark tree with feathery silver-green needles starkly contrasting the Autumn browned brush surrounding it. "The tree and *only* the tree," his father clarified.

This was a show of Control far beyond what someone with his training should ever be attempting, especially filled to the brim with volatile Earth magic. Luckily Camus and Torman had been falsifying their reports on his progress since his return from the King's Academy. He had much better Control than his father thought, but it was imperative to keep his prowess from the Jorgen, or he would never be free of him.

Ryland sucked in a deep breath and widened his eyes, hoping he looked afraid. It wasn't that far from the truth, so it should look convincing even if he was more afraid of revealing too much than of losing Control. Closing his eyes briefly, he breathed in. At his center he could feeling the wellspring of bright power, and he reached carefully inwards, nudging it to life. His breath left his body, pulling the magic up and out. He began pulling magic from the steady earth beneath his gelding's feet, adding its golden glow to the power inside himself. He pulled it from the bedraggled greenery along the edges of the Reedwood road and fought to suppress the joy holding the magic brought him. He ignored the sharpening of his senses, the beauty that become apparent to his eyes as magic filled him. Ry took another deep breath and focused intently on keeping his face in a mask of fear and concentration, easing a tendril of magic from the larger ribbon filling his chest to slowly bring sweat to his brow. He allowed his arms to shake to complete the illusion of being at the brink of how much power he could hold, and then arrowed his concentration towards the sapling as they neared it. He strangled the pulsing life within it, wrangling the wily Earth magic with intense concentration lest it slip free and stamp out the life of the surrounding flora. He started at the top. Near the bottom he allowed his Control to slip slightly and the bushes around the Listenbark browned slightly. Not a huge amount, but enough to let his father know the exercise was very difficult for him. At least that was what he hoped his father drew from his performance.

Jorgen sneered and then cracked his hand across his youngest son's face. The backhand knocked Ryland from his horse, and the soldiers of his father's guard riding close behind them sniggered at the spectacle. Ryland scrambled back up, drops of blood from his nose spattering the oiled leather of his padded saddle. He wiped at the red splotches, grimacing as they smeared, marring his tack further. Once he was seated again he forced himself to look to his father, pushing down his anger and shoving aside his various throbbing pains to deal with later. The older man did not gaze back at him, simply stared straight ahead and said, "Again".

Ryland's hands were shaking as he wiped more blood from his nose, his breath came hard as he roughly tore magic from his surroundings once again. A large Steelskin tree ahead of the riders crumpled alarmingly, drooping and blackening as Ryland smiled grimly, pulling the life from the tall tree with violence fed by his rage. Branches and leaves littered the road as they approached, the mounts of the soldiers ahead of them shied at the unnatural rain of debris the tree loosed as it withered.

Jorgen smiled his cold smile and smugly watched the Steelskin die. "Better," he said, "much better".

Sylvia

Her feet hurt. The odd shoes Ryland had contrived for her made convincing ringing sounds on the occasional rock she hit on the dirt road, but they were also much heavier than anything she had even worn before. They rubbed in the wrong spots and made her ankles work harder than she was used to. She had been too wary of prying eyes to check, but she was fairly certain a large crop of blisters had sprouted around the crude straps. The Trewal had little reason to hone their shoe-making skills.

She had always taken her athleticism for granted, what everyone else could do at home, she could likely do just as easily, whether it was hiking or paddling a canoe. At least it had been like that until her injury. This world, however, was *not* her home, and every physical task here seemed harsher and longer than anything back home would have been. She had a sneaking suspicion gravity was heavier here, weighing her down slowly but surely. They had been walking for hours, and after a very brief stop where all the serfs waited in line to get some stringy dried jerky and stale flatbread, they kept right on walking.

So it was with swollen feet and wobbly ankles that she made her way to Ryland's pack horse when a halt was called for the night. She and two other serfs were in charge of setting up the younger son's tent for the night, along with bringing him washing water and food. Ryland was nowhere to be seen as she helped with his tent. She had caught brief glimpses of him all day and with each sighting had grown more worried. The last time she'd seen him, his face had been so pale she was concerned he would fall out of the saddle.

By the time she and Ryland's head chambermaid, Lana, had heated water for his bath, and begun the long trial of hauling the buckets of water to his tub, she was silently frantic. Trying to remain outwardly calm was difficult. *What if he had died? Then she would be all alone in this camp, pretending to be something she was not. Could she sneak out? Even if she could get out of the camp, where would she go?* She passed Lana on her way back to the fire for more hot water and was silently grateful for the older woman's grim demeanor. At least without small talk she was free to worry in peace.

The scalding water in the buckets she carried slopped wetly onto her robes as she ducked to enter Ryland's tent with the last of his bath water. A small gasp of relief left her lips as she saw the young man slumped on the sleeping roll she had helped lay out for him earlier. She hurriedly dumped the last two buckets into the tub and then tied the tent flap closed. The other serfs wouldn't miss her at this point, she hoped; it was finally time for them to find some shelter and rest themselves, after making sure the camp was set and fed. She turned and surveyed Ryland grimly. His face was ashen beneath the bruising on his left cheek and blood spattered the light green shirt he had worn today. His ear on the same side sported clotted scabs at the pointed tip, and she could see the dried tracks of blood running down the curved inside. Two of the buttons that ran up the left side of his chest to secure his tunic were missing. His riding gloves had even more dried blood staining them than the shirt. She approached him and began tugging his gloves off. "You look like hell, Ry," she muttered as she tugged at the snug leather gloves on his hands.

"What's hell?"

She glanced up quickly, glad to see some spark of interest in his gold flecked eyes. "I thought he was going to kill you. Is he, is he always like this?"

Ryland sat up with a groan and pulled his other glove off, taking the one she had in her hands from her. "He isn't always this bad. He's angry with the King right now, that's why he was so, harsh, today. I'm also working twice as hard as he thinks I am to keep him from knowing how much magic I have Control over."

He struggled out of the stiffly starched shirt and tossed the bloody garment into the corner of the tent with his saddle bags. Syl bit her lip, wincing at the myriad of bruises on his arms and torso. She had hoped she had been translating wrong when she overheard some of the Jorgen's soldiers talking about the young lordling not being able to sit his horse, but the telltale bruises covering Ryland were a sad testament that her language lessons were coming along quite well.

He stood and moved towards the large metal tub, his hands beginning to work on the complex ties at his groin that held his pants on his gangly frame. She stood abruptly and started for the tent entrance, knowing her cheeks were flaming. "I'll just be, um... I'll wait outside until..."

She struggled with the ties of the flap and glanced back at Ryland who was standing with his head cocked to the side in confusion, his pants held loosely around his hips by his hands. He looked down and seemed to realize he was nearly naked for the first time. "Oh! Syl I'm sorry, the chambermaids they usually help with... they stay and," he yawned hugely and blushed as he looked down again, "your disguise is really quite good if I'm forgetting you aren't a serf," he finished sheepishly.

She nodded with a smile and slipped out of his tent, calling over her shoulder, "I'll be back in a little bit with your food, my Lord."

Ugh! Syl shook her head at herself, here she is, in terrible danger and she's getting all embarrassed at the first boy with no shirt she sees! They aren't even the same species! Her cheeks flamed hotly once more as she considered the implications of that. It was easy to forget the Trewal were not human, their only visible differences being their antlers, backwards legs, hooves, and overlarge and pointy ears. They looked mostly the same as her, and were obviously intelligent beings just like humans. But maybe other parts of their anatomy were different. She wrenched her thoughts away from the muscled abdomen that had been on display in the golden candlelight of the tent. "Stupid hormones," she muttered to herself. Teenage hormones were constantly wreaking havoc in the lives of her friends back in Oregon. After a particularly potent episode of Arianna's relationship drama, Syl had decided it wasn't for her. But that decision certainly didn't make her blind. Or take away hormonal urges for that matter.

She ran into something solid and warm and barely caught herself from looking up into the face of the soldier she had collided with. The drunken man stumbled and made a grab for her with a slurred, "Ah, you swanna splay wench?"

Desperately keeping her face averted so he didn't see her eyes, she struggled away from his grasping hands, earning herself a pinch on the bottom and some muttered curses. Sylvia spun away and ran as fast as her tired feet could carry her, adding some curses of her own at the stupidity of letting herself get distracted. Torman had warned her about the promiscuity of soldiers, high ranking and low. She wasn't to sleep in the serf's tents, as the men could come choose any girl they wanted from the base-born indentured servants, regardless of whether they wanted to be chosen or not. She was to sleep in Ryland's tent if she could slip in undetected, or find a spot in a supply wagon hidden from view if she couldn't attain the safety of Ryland's tent without raising suspicions.

Swallowing her fear and taking a deep breath in the hopes it would calm her pounding heart, she started making her way to the cooking line for the young lord's evening meal, trying to ignore the trembling in her legs, the rush of blood beating in her ears at her near escape. Her blue eyes round and wary, she pulled the cowl of her robe as low as it would go over her face.

Ryland

Ryland smothered yet another yawn in his hand as he sunk his aching body into the steaming water. Muscles long tensed from riding, concentration, and anticipation of a blow, began the process of relaxation in the soothing water. With a sigh he folded his long body into the tub to maximize the use of the water while it stayed hot. *Garrin's bones he was tired!* The day had been long and brutal with his father raining down blows whenever he was particularly displeased by Ryland's performance, which Ry had to make sure was almost every time. His father's mood was black and foul, darkening further with every mile that brought them closer to Seaprium, and farther from Jorgenholm.

Stepping from the tub with a covert glance at the tent's entrance, he gingerly toweled off his bruised body and smiled ruefully, remembering Syl's face as her eyes traveled down his chest to his hands on the ties of his braises. *She looks adorable when she blushes.* Laughing at himself he realized he urgently needed sleep, or at least he needed to get a grip on his wandering thoughts, or he would be the one with the red face when she returned.

At that moment a group of serfs made their way into the tent with his supper. He scanned the hooded figures for a clue as to which was Sylvia and when he spied a tendril of dark hair escaping from the cowl of a particularly small and slender serf, he motioned in her direction, "Stay to serve me, everyone else is dismissed."

After the tent emptied Syl flung off her cowl and eyed his dinner. "Are you going to eat all of that? They haven't let us eat yet".

There was an edge to her voice he didn't hear very often. "You okay Syl?"

She looked up from the roll he tossed her, eyes surprised. "Yeah, well no, really, but I'll be fine." She sauntered over to the bathing tub and looked into the murky water, giving a heavy sigh, "Serfs don't get baths do they?"

He grimaced, "I should have let you go first, you are a lot cleaner than I was." The bath water was tinted a light pink from the blood he had washed off. "I'll make sure you get a bath tomorrow," he apologized.

Syl shook herself from her deep contemplation of the water and smiled at him, "If you give me half that fish," she gestured at the steaming plate of food she had helped to bring in, "all is forgiven."

They settled at the folding camp table with companionable ease and fell silent quickly, intent on feeding their exhausted bodies. The Spineback was succulent, stuffed with herbs and breadcrumbs and the cooked Cheerum and vegetables heaped around the edges of his plate were plentiful enough for the both of them. Syl put some more of the flaky white fish in her mouth and began chuckling to herself; when she swallowed she asked him abruptly in the scholar's tongue, "Do you know what a vegetarian is?"

Shaking his head, he regarded her thoughtfully, "The word indicates..." he found himself chuckling also, "someone who believes in vegetables?"

She laughed outright at his dissection of the archaic word. "It means someone who doesn't eat any meat, only plants." She peered up at him, blue eyes astonishingly bright in the candlelight.

"No meat? But surely they would eat fish then? Many commoners who live on the coast eat fish and only rarely have cattle or chickens they can afford to slaughter." He gestured with one hand, balancing a bite of fish on his knife.

"Fish is meat too! Back home I was a vegetarian, but I don't think I have ever tasted anything as good as this fish. It seems a little silly now..." Her face grew sad and far away, as it always did when the subject of her home came up. Ryland watched the sunny atmosphere in the tent darken as Syl's expression fell. He pulled a grin onto his own face, swollen tissues complaining of even that much movement, determined to cheer her up. It was going to be a long journey to the capital and with the training his father had planned for him, the evenings would be the only good portion of his days. He was determined it would be fun, not melancholy.

He knifed the large bite into his mouth. "I could never give up meat," he decided cheerfully, "it's far too tasty!" He made a clumsy lunge for her portion with his knife, which she laughingly fended off.

"Hands off my fish, buddy!" She playfully shoved him back, eyes widening when his body continued toppling backwards far past the point the stool should have arrested his fall as the leg of his camp chair folded and tossed him unto his rump.

"Oof" the air abruptly left his lungs upon impact with the tent floor, but the hilarity in Sylvia's eyes was enough consolation for his embarrassment. She started giggling as a blush suffused Ryland's cheeks and by the time he had managed to get back onto his feet she was bent over in her camp chair, clutching her stomach as she attempted to laugh quietly.

He settled back into the chair carefully, checking the position of each leg before easing his weight down onto it. Once he was sure the traitorous chair wouldn't send him back to the dusty floor, he watched Syl try vainly for seriousness. And couldn't help but chuckle. She wiped her watering eyes, breathing heavily. Every time she seemed to have stopped her laughing she would try to meet his eyes, only to break eye contact as giggles took over once again.

"Glad to entertain," he said wryly. He could still feel the embarrassment heating his face.

"Sorry!" She managed, biting her rosy lips to try to keep a smile at bay. With a large inhale she got control over herself and managed her next sentence with a mostly straight face. "I haven't laughed like that since I came here. Are you okay?"

They both laughed this time and his smile was genuine as he told her, "I'm fine; well, my pride is a little damaged but that seems to happen with you around."

"Someone has to keep you in line when Torman isn't here," she deadpanned. They both grinned again, the silence of the tent somehow more intense when their gazes were connected. She looked away first, fidgeting with her robe. "So, can I sleep in here? I managed to bring a lot of extra blankets without anyone noticing."

"Sure," he replied easily, moving over to the pallet. He sorted the various furs and blankets his status as the Lord's son awarded him, setting aside one of the Fabriel feather pillows for Sylvia. The danger was minimal. Even if she was discovered in his tent it would be assumed he had simply wanted a woman and chosen one, like most of the soldiers in the camp had likely done.

He knew what men and women did behind closed doors, his education was the best a nobleman could find in Prium after all. But cloistered in the Academy he had had little to no interactions with the fairer sex. His peers, however, had sought out female companionship when their studies had allowed, ribbing him with their ribald jokes afterward, knowing he had never lain with a woman. There was a sudden tension in the tent, like the air had thickened and grown hotter. He made up a bed across the small space from the pallet and laid down without looking at Sylvia, afraid his wandering thoughts might be written on his face. After an eternity of awkward silence as Syl watched him, and he avoided her eyes, she spoke softly, "You should use the pallet Ryland, I can't be in nearly as much pain as you are. You fell off your horse at least five times today."

He flinched at her careful wording. Yeah, he had 'fallen' all right, with some very physical help from his father dearest. He rose from the makeshift bed, "How about we switch every night? Then at least one of us will be well rested."

Ry collapsed onto the pallet, sinking into the cushioning of the woven ropes gratefully. He unlaced his boots and removed his tunic, opting to keep his braises on even though he usually slept unclothed. Reclining now, he watched Syl through half closed lids. Her hair was so dark and glossy it seemed to attract all the light from the lantern, gleaming with the captured luminescence. She shrugged out of her over robe and shoes and made her way to the lamp. As she bent over to extinguish it he could see her form outlined through the thin shift she wore. Darkness settled over him softly and he heard her settling in amongst her blankets. He tossed and turned a little, restless despite his exhaustion.

"Goodnight Ryland." Her voice was soft and sleepy, bringing a smile to his lips.

"Goodnight Syl."

Sylvia

The rising tide of noise in the camp woke her before the sun was fully up. She sat up shivering, as the ground had sucked away most of her body heat throughout the night, regardless of the blankets underneath. Ryland was still asleep. She could just make out his tousled hair upon the pillow through the gloom in the tent. She held the blankets close for another minute, hoping to warm up before she had to go out and begin striking camp with the rest of the serfs. Giving up warming herself as a lost cause, she clambered out of her makeshift bed and donned her robe hurriedly. She stole silently out of the tent flaps, pausing in the doorway with a wry smile on her lips. Ryland looked so young in sleep, his usually serious expression softened, deep brown hair a mess around his face, his antlers pressing solidly into the pillow. She had seen many of the soldiers in the camp sharpened their antlers and similarly shaped horns, the higher ranking officers of the army even adorning the forks with bands of metal. She wondered how many of the men woke up with pillows skewered on their heads each morning.

Today would be another long day of packing everything up, walking and then unpacking everything again. To make things more miserable, the good weather of the day before seemed to have left them. Tendrils of fog snaked along the rows between the tents and dew was heavy on the grassy plants that Ryland called Roan, beneath her feet, wetting the leather of her 'shoes' so they chafed painfully at her blisters. The sky above was slate gray, fading into a darker, angrier looking charcoal to the southeast, forecasting rain as they moved towards Seaprium.

Prium reminded her of the Pacific Northwest. At least here in the Reedwood forest it did, with dense forests sprinkled with a variety of different trees and lots of mountains spiking towards the sky in the distance. The foliage was different, admittedly, Steelskins, the trees most resembling oaks, had spiky leaves, smooth, pale bark, and grew to astonishing heights. The spread of their limbs shading the forest floor beneath them for so many yards that sunlight often never touched the ground at all before the next shadow loomed. In fact, almost all of the flora here seemed gargantuan in comparison with her home. Everything was on scale with the redwoods she liked to visit in northern California and the southern coastal towns of Oregon. The colors were a little off also, vegetation tending towards the blue and purple spectrum of green rather than the deep emeralds and grass green she was used to.

But this place smells like home, she thought, taking in a deep gulp of cold air. Even the piney scent of evergreens was present in the fresh odor of the outdoors, along with the mulchy earthiness of an old growth forest. It's beautiful here, and if she wasn't so set on finding her way home she would probably love to explore this magical place; with the exciting and comforting company of Ryland and Torman, she could happily wander this forest for days. She had loved camping every summer at home. But this wasn't a vacation. She had no way to know what state things were in back home. Was her body still there? She tended to think it must be, theoretical magical travel didn't miraculously heal devastating injuries did it? And if her body was still there, how freaked out were her parents?

Maybe no time has passed, she mused. *And one day I will wake up in the surgery recovery room like nothing has happened.* She hoped to the God she had never quite understood her friend's fascination with, that was the case. All of the other scenarios she had come up with would leave her parents devastated. She hated to think of her mom and dad standing above her hospital bed while she rotted away in a coma, or crying uncontrollably at her funeral. As an only child she was acutely aware of her parent's need to keep her safe. The knee injury had shown that clearly, both her parents had been frantic.

Shaking herself out of her contemplation Syl headed for the ever growing crowd of serfs gathering near the cook tents, receiving a slab of bread and cheese to break their fast, and also their assignments for breaking camp. She was once again assigned to the loading faction, so she spent her morning hauling items from tents to wagons until the army was ready to move again. The good thing about loading duty was that her work was done when the force began marching, and she could concentrate on placing her sore feet carefully on the rough road.

Once again she only caught glimpses of Ryland throughout the day, a feat made harder by her ever compelling need to keep her head down and her eyes out of sight. He seemed to be faring better today as his father's attention was often occupied by messengers riding in and out. Usually from the direction of Seaprium. The messengers were much more colorfully attired than the contingent from Jorgenholm, favoring rusty reds, and startling yellows that contrasted wildly with the small flags of deep purple bearing the royal insignia, which graced each messenger horse's withers, making them highly visible from miles off. The army itself, not including a few nobles who were obviously not fighters, wore muted tones of gray and some greens and blues with accents of the same blood red that flew on the flags above Jorgenholm. The soldier's uniforms buttoned up tightly on the left side of the chest, holding small, stiff collars snugly closed about the neck. Riding into the subdued mass of the army, the messengers looked like parrots mistakenly flown into a dove cote.

By the time a halt was called for the night she was exhausted, her feet so swollen that she was surprised the special shoes Ryland had made her hadn't ripped at the seams. She had the good fortune to be assigned water duty and while dipping her bucket into the nearby stream she waded right in, shoes and all, desperate for some relief. The icy water sent needles of pain into her abused feet, causing her to bite her lips to stifle a gasp. The Trewal could travel amazing distances on foot, but their feet were also more bone than flesh. Since she was supposed to have hooves also, she needed to act like nothing was wrong. Gritting her teeth, she tried her best not to limp on her way back with the heavy buckets of water.

By the time she slipped into Ryland's tent, darkness had fallen over the camp and the air of the little valley they were nestled in was smoky from the camp fires spangling the indentation from crest to crest. The inside of the tent was cozy and warm with a brazier of coals keeping the chill from the air. The mouthwatering aroma of meat wafted in her direction from where Ryland sat at the little camp table, grinning at her. Syl discarded her shoes as soon as her bottom hit the chair, and soon thereafter had tucked into the delicious remains of Ryland's meal of succulent venison and seasoned vegetable broth.

Finishing her meal in record time she realized Ryland was staring at her bare feet with wide eyes. "Are they supposed to be that big?" he asked. She groaned as she saw the tightness of the skin of her feet and ankles. The swelling made the smattering of blisters from her shoes an angry white, although a few of them had popped and were glaringly red. She had been so sure she was a strong and resilient athlete before coming to Prium. She had felt lean and mean with four years of daily doubles under her belt and playing rugby year round. But the harsh conditions and lack of proper footwear was wearing her body down. She had never worked so hard in her life.

"No," she said wearily, "they are definitely not supposed to be that big, they're swollen." He examined her feet again with sympathy in his eyes. Their attention on her feet, neither noticed a shadowy form approach the tent, and they both started in surprise as a voice sounded from outside.

"Lord, may I take away your dishes?" The shadow cast on the canvas bowed grotesquely, appearing to fold into a small writhing ball as the campfires outside made the serf's form jump and dance upon the walls of the tent.

Neither she nor Ryland spoke, their eyes wide. Syl looked around the room desperately for somewhere to hide. She was *not* supposed to be in here with him. The silence was dragging on too long as they frantically looked around the cramped space. She threw herself into motion, elbowing Ryland hard in the ribs as she flew past him towards the bed. He grunted at the impact and seemed to realize he needed to speak to the waiting serf, "One moment!" he called hoarsely.

He turned to Syl and she had just enough time to see the question in his eyes, before she ripped her robe off over her head. By the time her eyes were free from the clinging fabric his expression had turned from curiosity to burning red embarrassment. She hopped in the bed, dragging her shift off her arms and pulling the coarse blanket up over her breasts so that it appeared she was bare beneath the coverings. Glaring at the staring boy she hissed at him, "Ry!" propelling him to the door to let the serf in. She hoped his red face didn't completely spoil the ruse.

Eyes glued to her hands on the blanket, she kept her head bowed as she listened to Ryland open the ties and let the serf into the tent. Camus had warned her that many of the serfs in the Jorgen household were essentially spies, making up a network of eyes and ears throughout the Holm so the Jorgen knew all that was going on with his people. It was impossible to tell which of the serfs reported to him. So the old Maegi had bade them be cautious in front of every single one.

She raised her eyes only when the tent flap had been tied closed once again, and met the shaky gaze of the young lord. They both let out a long breath, which she hadn't even realized she had been holding in, and his eyes slid from her face to her partially exposed cleavage and then darted away like a frightened animal. His face colored again. She burst out laughing, the tension of the moment passed. Flopping back on the bed she guffawed helplessly. Fighting her giggles, she pointed at him accusingly, "You've never seen a girl naked before!" Finally getting a hold on her mirth she faced him again, surprised by his surly expression.

"I had better things to do, like study," he spat at her. Taken aback by the uncharacteristically sullen remark she studied him for a moment.

"It's not a bad thing Ryland..." she let her words trail off until he met her gaze again. "I think it's incredibly sweet. It also makes sense you haven't, it's not like you guys have porn websites here."

"Porn websites?" He stumbled on the foreign words and she grimaced, loathe to describe the crudeness of pornography to her friend.

"Never mind. Do you think he bought it?"

Ryland considered as he began making up the pallet on the floor, "It's unusual enough for me to have a female in my chambers that if he is a contact of my father's, he'll tell him. But if we're lucky, he's not one of my father's contacts and nothing will come of it. I guess we will just have to see what the morning brings us."

She nodded, feeding her arms back into the gaping neck of her shift. "So I get the bed tonight right?" She snuggled down into the blankets, suddenly somber and worried about the morning. "I'm exhausted."

"It's all yours. Sleep well Syl, and don't worry about tomorrow, I'll be the one dealing with my father. They have no way to tell which of the serfs you are." Removing his shirt, he blew out the lantern and lay down. Smiling, he realized from the continued silence that she had already fallen asleep.

The Jorgen

Shadows waxed and waned across the worn paper in front of him, making his tired eyes work for every word he read. He reached for the sand, ready to be done with this latest missive and send the messenger on his way, but the fall of his cuff carelessly draped across the freshly penned words on the parchment, and ink spidered out from the neat letters to mar the exactness of his penmanship. With a growl he crumpled the ruined note and threw it forcefully across the room in a rare show of temper he would never had allowed himself in the presence of another person.

He hated incompetence. Loathed it actually. And yet he was constantly surrounded by it. Was it any wonder that he was always angry then? And now his only ally, his own cousin, who had, up until this point, showed no signs of inability, was spiraling downward in a blaze of bad choices fueled by greed. And Gartlan was pulling him down with him.

He had helped to put the King upon his throne dammit! And this is how he was re-paid? With curt orders and impossible tasks, all to the detriment of his own responsibilities on his land and to his people. Before the King became His Majesty, he had been a lowly lord, a distant cousin of the second son of the ruling Jorgen. Together they had plotted, and just as Gartlan had helped him kill his brother so that he could be Named to the title of Jorgen, he had helped Gartlan from that lofty position, gaining him a place and prestige at court from which he executed a masterful game of intrigue and many instances of backstabbing to eventually gain the throne.

Now he wanted more, always more. He wanted Saerin with its lush tropics, and rocky mountains, rich in minerals. And he was counting on his old partner in crime to go and fetch it for him. The only problem this time was that Gartlan far surpassed his cousin in power, and there was no way for the Jorgen to say no. He had to talk to him in person, without the poisonous presence of the Demandron pushing the King to further folly.

He swept dark hair from his brow and studied the papers in front of him again. It was late, the candles had burned far down and his lantern needed more oil soon or it would gutter out. With an exasperated sigh he began tidying the travel desk, burning the missives the King had sent him today, to keep them from any prying eyes. As the flame bit into the delicate parchment he noticed the gentle noises of the camp growing into a chaotic roar of activity. At the first clash of metal on metal he threw himself into motion, his hand finding the familiar, leather wrapped pommel of *Warbringer* from the camp bed just before he ducked through the flaps of his tent.

He glanced at the serf stationed outside his door. The skinny young man tugged fretfully on his scraggly beard, his gaze wavering between his Lord and the sounds of fighting beginning on the edges of their encampment. The Jorgen snapped his fingers in front of the man's face, resisting the urge to smack some sense into the nervous boy. "Fetch my son" he said forcefully, snapping his fingers a few more times beneath his nose for good measure. Scared brown eyes finally focused on him and the serf scurried off for his son without a word. Jorgen breathed in, and then out, his magic flooding into him with his exhalation. He began pulling magic from the moist night, filling himself with the dangerous burn of Air, he augmented his own magic with the seductive swirl of power he pulled from the heavy jet stone around his neck, his connection to the Demandron, still far away in Seaprium. He pressed the bland stone in its overly ornate setting hard into his chest, feeling the gold filigree bite into his flesh as the cold rush of Demandron magic rushed into him like an icy tide.

His sight sharpened, a glow suffusing the landscape so he could see almost as well as if it was full daylight. He pinpointed the various fronts of attack, his hearing heightened by the magic sizzling through his veins, and noted five separate attacking forces. The enemy had successfully surrounded their camp without alerting the main force of the army. The woodland skill needed to achieve such a feat could be accomplished by only one force he knew of, other than his own disciplined troops.

With a roar he freed his ancestral sword from its sheath, leaving the tooled scabbard of the Relic behind in his tent before making his way towards the loudest of the battle fronts. From his mouth the harsh incantation of his forefathers fell in a guttural rhythm, the cadence so familiar to him, and yet spoken in a language no one living could understand. *Warbringer* grew fiery and bright in his hand, the blood of all the victims of the Jorgens of Jorgenholm feeding his blade until it grew too bright to look at, heating its ancient metal so it would slide through flesh and bone as if it were butter. The flat of the blade crowded with symbols as foreign as the words he still spoke, only seen when the incantation was voiced. His own men shied from him as he passed, flinching away from the unnatural light the Relic gave off.

Ryland

Both Sylvia and Ryland were up before his father's summons came to the tent. The noise rebounding in the small space was terrible, the screaming of injured horses and men mingled in a terrifying way with the war cries of what Ryland knew to be one of the Hinterland tribes from the Skypeaks north of Jorgenholm. They were attacking the camped army, which made no sense whatsoever. The Hinterland tribes had a long standing war with the Jorgens of Jorgenholm, one which had lasted longer than anyone could remember. But by all of Jeale's logic they should have been attacking the Holm, not the well-equipped army marching days to the South.

His gaze strayed to Syl as they both slipped from the tent. Her eyes were huge in her pale face. He pulled the hood of her robe up over her dark hair and rested a comforting hand on her shoulder before pulling her close and asking quietly in her ear, "do you have the Fen Torman gave you?"

She patted four or five spots on her body absently, "Of course" she said, her eyes still scanning the surrounding tents and the soldiers rushing past with swords, spears, and bows drawn.

"Good, then stay in the tent" he said just as a serf broke away from the milling people around them and began tugging Ryland towards the sounds of fighting.

"Your lord father sir, he needs you now sir!"

He instinctively began following the thin serf who had spoken, dread slowly making its cold way from the pit of his stomach into his limbs, causing him to tremble. His father could only want him for one reason, and it wasn't to make sure he was safe. He wanted his magic, either for siphoning purposes, to bolster the

Jorgen's own talents, or to direct at the enemy through Ryland. He was going to ask him to kill with his magic. A cold sweat broke out all over his body at the thought, and he felt a little bit nauseous. He flapped his arms a bit to relive the sudden dampness at his armpits. He had never killed a man before, period, but killing with magic was a much more personal and intimate experience than killing with a weapon. It was not something he had ever thought to have to do.

Syl's voice barely registered in his tumultuous thoughts, but he turned all the same to see her duck back out of their tent and bound towards him with his metal tipped quarterstaff in hand. She shoved it into his limp hands breathlessly, her face fierce as her blue eyes blazed at him, "Don't you dare die and leave me here alone, Ryland. Don't you dare." and with that she turned and hightailed it back to the sanctuary of the tent.

He turned back to the anxious serf, hoping the solitude of his tent at the middle of the encampment would be enough to keep her safe, and with a fortifying breath told him, "lead on" hoping he sounded braver than he felt. The poor wretch shivered and cast his nervous glance around constantly as they started off towards the fighting. He looked like he could use reassurance almost as much as Ryland could.

Sylvia

She thought she would go mad from the noise alone. Battle raged around the camp like a living, breathing, and *roaring* beast. The cacophony of men's' screams and grunts warped sickly with the twang of bows and the squealing of dying horses. In the flickering light from a dozen campfires, men fought grotesque battles across the walls of the tent, bending and dancing from step to step, accompanied by the beat of metal on metal. The canvas walls of her sanctuary were considerably less comforting than they had seemed previously, when all they were trying to keep out were prying eyes. Eyes could not shear through cloth as sharp metal weapons could, and the flimsy walls wouldn't stand up to a stampeding warhorse, driven mad by pain or fire.

One shadow on the wall grew darker, more substantial, and she knew, as the form solidified, her sanctuary would soon be breached. She could only watch, paralyzed, as the figure grew ever larger upon the wall beside the camp bed. He held a sword that looked as large as a spear in one hand and the antlers upon his head rose to wicked points, lending his shadow a demonic edge. Her subconscious suddenly registered squeaky English pleas reverberating in the tent and she realized with horror they were coming from her own mouth, but she couldn't seem to stop their flow. "Oh god, oh my god, go away, please go away...Oh please, please."

The noise of the canvas ripping seemed like it should have been lost in the clamor of the fighting outside, but it was deafening, reminding her of that moment on the rugby field when her leg was torn apart in a sickening collision of bodies. What happened next was relatively silent, as the monstrous barbarian plowed through the tent wall, face a snarling mask of fury, and his battered broadsword seeking her unerringly. She scrambled backwards, hastily slipping Fen from her hidden sheaths, hearing Torman's calm voice in her head, *"Relax, hold the hilt gently, breath in, throw with the release of your breath"*.

Glittering Fen after Fen glanced off of the overlapping discs of burnished metal sewn into the big man's vest as he continued his advance. Left with only one, she felt the wall hit her back, and frenziedly turned to swipe at the coarse material, opening a gash that she threw herself at, scrambling to exit the deathtrap their cozy tent had become. Syl screamed in terror as her hips caught in the fabric, even her petite frame too wide for the cut she had made. A hand so large that it engulfed her whole calf grabbed at her; flailing in panic, she kicked out hard with her unrestrained leg, wincing as it connected solidly with some part of the man's anatomy. A heavy grunt, followed by the release of her leg, allowed her to scramble frantically away from the tent. Gaining her feet, she began a headlong dash away from the giant groaning amidst the collapsing canvas.

Absorbed with her flight, Syl didn't notice the fur clad figure on horseback approaching at a tangent to her escape path, and when the hammer of his ax found her skull with a resounding crack, she fell, loose limbed into the bloody mud and trampled Roan. Darkness rushing up, enfolding her. The Hinterlander on the chestnut mare dismounted with a fierce grin, his soot streaked face triumphant. Ribbing his comrade still struggling to extricate himself from the ruins of the tent, he hauled the unconscious girl into his arms and tossed her easily across his horse, laughing again that such a tiny thing could so confound his friend. Mounting, he rode away from the softening sounds of the battle, his spoils draped gracelessly across his horse's withers in front of him.

Ryland

The Jorgen's hand on his shoulder felt like heavy stone, and emanated the icy cold tingling of Demandron magic down through his body, gripping his chest like a vise, making it hard to breathe through the vicious cold. Only the twisted Demandron magic could siphon another's power like this. Only the Demandron would *want* the ability to so violate another. He could feel the essence of his father scrounging around like a fist inside his chest, grasping for the column of swirling magic at the center of his being. He had read descriptions of how it felt to use another person's magic like this, how from his father's point of view the sensations would be fiery and hot, how wrestling Control from him would burn. More frighteningly he knew his father would be made completely aware of how much magic Ryland could call, because he would be the one doing the calling through his son's body.

With a gasp he felt his sire finally catch hold of the ribbon of light in his chest, and he began to draw it slowly out through his hold on Ryland's shoulder. A fraction of Ryland's awareness went with that small stream of magic, flowing into the Jorgen's body and then flying outwards at a dizzying speed. He knew this attack. It was brutal in its simplicity, small jagged stones from the ground around them sprung to attention, and with a flick of his wrist the Jorgen sent them flying outwards, punching devastating holes in any object or soldier in their way.

The stones, heavy with his magic, tore through a Hinterlander's shoulder and Ryland took in a sharp breath. He had read about this too, how when your magic touches another, enters their body in any way, you are made aware of them. He had felt it before, as Torman instructed him in Healing. The steady beat of his brother's heart, the constant flow and ebb of his blood as loud as a river in his ears. Now he could feel the searing pain of the wound in the Hinterlander's shoulder like he himself had sustained the injury. Ryland could hear the man's screams resounding in his head, and feel the overwhelming panic the man felt as his ax dropped from his weakened arm just as a Jorgenholm soldier swept his sword in an arc towards the wounded man. His death brought a chilling silence to the bundle of sensation Ryland had been feeling, but it was all too quickly replaced by awareness of another Hinterlander downed by his magic.

The battle ground onwards. The grunts of men and screams of sword on sword filling the air around him paled in comparison to the more personal pain he was linked to inside his head. He couldn't tell how long the torment had been going on. His chest felt like it was encased in ice, and his limbs shook from the struggle to contain the torrent of magic being pulled from the land through his body. He felt the life leave each of the men his magic had injured or straight out killed, like a candle being snuffed. His father was ruthless, wielding Ryland's magic masterfully to cause the most destruction amidst the enemy. It was as if the land itself had turned against their enemies. Tears tracked slowly down Ryland's face, their salt stinging in a small gash that had appeared on his cheekbone. *Oh Garrin, huntsman of the Gods, this has to stop soon! Please make it stop!*

The withdrawal of his father's hand was abrupt and left Ryland stumbling without the support of his crushing grip. His lungs tried futilely to pull in enough air, leaving his body so weak he fell to his knees, gasping. Vaguely he realized that the skirmish was nearly over, and in his relief that the torture had finally ended, he released his struggle for consciousness and flung himself gratefully into oblivion.

Chapter 4

Camus

The Holm was a lighter place since the Jorgen left. Torman's boundless good cheer and humor bolstered up those around him and for the first time in Camus's memories of this stone Keep, laughter rang unfettered through the Greathall each evening, and smiles graced the faces of everyone he met as he made his slow way to the Southern Battlements. Camus made the agonizingly long pilgrimage here once a day, usually around now, sunset; when the sun blazed to his right with its golden, dying light. The Holm, with its rough stone towers and steady, chipped walls, looked eternal; it seemed it always had been, and always would be, perched upon the side of this mountain, overlooking the vastness of the Reedwood forest. Sometimes Camus felt eternal too, leaning here, wedged between two crenels, the parapet holding his weight like an old friend and the entirety of Prium stretched out before him. He felt like a sentinel upon the wall, part of the rough-hewn rocks that comprised this place where he would spend the rest of his days.

His Sight was acting up. Most rebirths of the seasons he saw only one or two glimmers of the gold and green light he associated with the unusual magical Sight he had been born with. But since seeing the blindingly bright aura of tumultuous colors surrounding Sylvia Eldritch, there had been flickers of that godly light around many of the Trewal in the Holm. Serfs, common folk, soldiers, even a few of the noblewomen who stayed behind as their husbands journeyed to Seaprium with the Jorgen. It made no difference who, the light seemed wholly random. It seemed to linger at his periphery, just out of sight but still there, still distracting him, but never directly visible. It was maddening. Sunset quickly became his favorite time, when the whole world seemed bathed in a similar light, and the flickering at the corners of his eyes ceased as the light encompassed everything. Camus was startled out of his reverie as a thick cloak dropped into place around his shoulders. Strong young hands tucked the soft, silky collar of ice lion fur down under his chin so it overlapped, engulfing his aging bones in the lingering heat of Torman's body.

"Every night, my sentries tell me. Every night the old Maegi comes to the Southern Battlements as the sun falls. And every night he forgets to bring a cloak."

Camus smiled out at the panorama. *His sweet boy.* Torman's heart was too warm to be contained within these frigid rocks.

"I didn't believe them, you know," Torman continued, "I thought to myself, not Camus, he was the one who taught me to never repeat a mistake, to learn from my missteps. But here you are trying to freeze yourself to these damn battlements. Have you finally gone senile on me old man? Or is there a reason you keep coming up here trying to catch your death?"

Torman leaned out between the neighboring crenels in order to meet his gaze, and Camus saw worry in those soft green eyes, no matter the lightness of his tone. "Did you know, Torman, that I was born down there, in a hut outside these walls? My father was a simple trader, peddling his wares from Jorgenholm to Seaprium to Galmorah and back, buying this, selling that. He was loathe to miss the birth of his first child, and so he took his young wife with him as he traveled, rather than leaving her with her family to come to term."

Camus snuggled down a little more into the warmth of the borrowed garment. He could not get warm lately, which was why he didn't bother with a cloak when he ventured out here. Ever since waking up to the tingle of magic suffusing the air the night Sylvia arrived, he couldn't shake this chill. No amount of fire or layers of cloth and fur could melt the cold that filled him.

"She died in that hut, and her family never forgave my father for taking her from them, for letting her die in a strange hut on the side of a mountain none of them had ever seen. And so in repayment for taking their daughter, my father gave them a grandson. I grew up in their Galmorish house, with its open doorways and arched windows. I barely remember it, but the arched windows in Galmorah always evoke a feeling of home," he reminisced wistfully. "When I had seen four rebirths the newly crowned King of Prium, the good fellow our current King replaced, paraded through the streets leading to the Sacred Square. I sat on the cool stone seat of one of those windows to watch him pass. That's when my Sight first made itself known. The King was glowing, he was shining with this golden light, like a hero in a story, and the Demandron at his side, he exuded a darkness that ate away at the godly light of our sovereign."

Camus looked over at the man who had become like a son to him. Finding Torman's eyes raptly on his own, he rambled on about the past. "My mother's family gave me to the King's company without a backward glance once I told them what I saw. The Galmorish people may worship the Gods, all of them, but they worship because they fear them. They worship to fend off their attentions, good or bad. My grandparents wanted nothing to do with the Gods or the ones they touched. *Weiring*, that's what they called someone like me. Someone with God Eyes.

"So that's how you came to train at the King's Academy," Torman said, his eyes faraway. "And now you are back here, where you were born. You have lived in each of Prium's great cities, but come back to your birthplace in the end."

"I have. I have lived long. I have lived in many places, and learned many things. But I think what I learned that day, so long ago, under a Galmorish arch, I think that is the only thing which had really mattered in this long life of mine."

"What did you learn old man? That the Demandron suck the life out of people like the darkness sucks in the light? That, I think, we have all been witness to."

Torman's voice holds great bitterness for such a young man, Camus thought, *but his bitterness could not hold a candle to that of a man three times his age, a man with three times the losses as he had felt. Three times the pain.* Camus's own bitterness burned like the cold trapped inside him.

"I learned the Trewal are the playthings of the God's. And that I can tell which God is pulling the strings, because I am a *Weiring.* Our great Garrin's touch is gold. His brother Freyton's a chilly green. Once I met a scholar from the Sareth isles, and he glowed blue as the Blitherly Sea with Jeale's light. And then that darkness. That utter blackness which encompasses every Demandron. Well, that is the very hand of death itself. The touch of the God most of us fear too much to even voice his name. But what has never been made clear to me, in all my years, is how this knowledge helps anyone."

Torman

Preparations for the winter gripped Jorgenholm, whipping its population into a frenzy of harvest and store, can and cure. Torman was touring the granary with Perlt, Jorgenholm's head steward, when a tired and shaky messenger found him. The bleary gaze of the exhausted soldier was worrying enough to put the accounting of supplies for the Holm on hold, so he hurried the fatigued man to his father's study and positioned him in front of the fire with a steaming cup of bone broth, which he saw drained, before he let the man speak a word more than, "Urgent news from the Jorgen".

The young man set the cup down, a promising flush of color back in his tan face, and promptly launched into his message, "Hinterlanders sir. Attacked our forces night afore' last, a day's ride south of the Crossroads." He wiped a dirty hand across his brow and then fished an equally dirty messenger's bag from beneath his tunic, pulling out a small curl of paper packed tightly with the Jorgen's severe handwriting. "O'er two hundred dead, lots o' supplies taken, it's all there sir. Your lord father sent me back to warn the Holm." He pulled yet another scrap of parchment out of the dubious looking pouch, "An ere, orders for you too," he shook his shaggy head, "the Jorgen din't look happy to be marching away from Jorgenholm with those mountain barbarians on the loose."

"My brother? He lives?" Torman pressed.

"Oh aye sir! Sorry, shoulda said that first off. The young lord is fine except for a mighty headache from all that magicking he an the Jorgen did, we would'a been lost without them for sure." The young man scratched at his beard tiredly.

Torman let out his breath slowly. Ryland was still alive, thank Garrin. But if his father and brother had been 'magicking' together, things were likely going to get complicated for his younger sibling. Torman threw himself up from his position leaning against his father's massive claw footed desk, gathering the missives absently. He clapped the youthful soldier on the shoulder, "Thank you for getting this to me right away. What was your name?"

"Chir, sir." The man replied with a tired smile.

"Well Chir, why don't you head on down to the kitchens, tell the cooks to roast you up a Fabriel chick from the cotes. Eat, bathe, rest. I might need you to ride back to my father soon, so enjoy your time out of the saddle while you can." Torman was already halfway out the door as he finished the last sentence, his restless hooves carrying him towards Camus's tower with hectic energy.

When he burst into the tower room Camus was at his worktable, mixing a concoction of herbs over an open flame, releasing an acrid smell that filled the tower and made Torman's eyes tear up immediately. "Camus! Put that damn flame out," he sniffled, waving the parchment in his hand about his face in an attempt to clear up the air. "We have word from the Jorgen." He cleared a pile of dog eared books off a seat across from Camus's desk and began writing out the missives from his father, transferring the notes from the special shorthand code his father had taught him, into actual sentences.

"The Hinterlanders attacked them!" he told his mentor as the man picked his way across his room to take the seat across from him. "Ryland is fine, though it seems that my father used his magic during the fight, which does not bode well." He scratched out the next line impatiently, "Two hundred and seventeen soldiers fell, fifty-eight serfs killed, and an estimated twelve taken or run off..." He paused in his translations, defeated. "There's no way to know if Sylvia is alive."

Camus shook his head, saying calmly, "She's alive Torman, someone like her doesn't die by happenstance. She's too important."

Torman looked up at the elderly Maegi. His mentor sounded so sure, but he needed confirmation. He wanted to talk to his brother, and hear from *him* what had happened, mostly the reaction of their father when he called upon Ryland's magic and felt the colossal tide of Earth magic which answered. He had a sudden and piercing need to see both Sylvia and Ryland, to make sure they were okay, to verify the most important thing in his entire world, his baby brother, was still breathing in the air of Prium.

"Breathe Torman," Camus said quietly. "Ryland is resourceful, we know he lives, he can figure out the rest on his own, your father included."

Torman sucked in a breath at Camus's command, stilling his frantic thoughts by reaching within himself for the still center of Control, the slight burn of his Fire magic as he embraced it steadied him, and he released the breath. "You're right. Ryland can take care of himself, and the Jorgen now has a very good reason to keep him safe while they are in the capital. I just wish we knew Sylvia was alright." The only way he would be able to get that information, he knew, was from Ryland. Except days of travel and an army of informants lay between him and the truth. They needed to get a message to Ryland, securely.

There was Chir, Torman pondered. But no sure way to know the soldier would not put a message for Ryland into the Jorgen's hands first. "I'll send a letter of thanks that my brother still lives, a personal note between brothers is not so strange. But maybe we can word it so he knows to get word back to us about the fate of our little human...And the response of our lord father to his use of Ryland's magic," he added darkly.

"A good plan." Camus stood wearily and swung his cast iron tea kettle out of the flames in the hearth. "Now let's have a look at the orders from the Jorgen. I have a feeling this unusual Hinterland activity means some changes are to be made here in the Holm."

Shuffling papers, Torman found another blank sheet and began deciphering the second slip of paper the messenger had brought. His father's orders did indeed involve some changes within the Holm. The most severe directive concerned the village straggling out from the barrier of Camus's living wall. "All citizens living outside the Holm are to be sheltered within the Wall," he read out woodenly.

Camus started in surprise, sloshing tea water over the edge of the heavy ceramic mug he had been pouring into. The steam came wafting towards Torman as he hastily rescued his notes, and the acrid steam set his eyes to watering once again. Blinking back tears he glared at Camus, "Trollit! That concoction is vile Camus, what are you poisoning yourself with now?" Waving a hand under his nose to clear away the offending substance, Torman began mopping up the spilled liquid with the edge of his tunic.

Ignoring the younger man Camus spoke out, "If every inhabitant of Jorgenholm is brought inside the Wall it will be utter chaos. There isn't *room* for everyone, especially not for the winter! New housing will have to be built so the people don't freeze and if the commoners abandon their personal gardens outside the Wall the communal harvest will have to feed many mouths that used to feed themselves!"

Torman read out the next line of instruction in response, "All workers harvesting outside the Wall to have an armed escort. Rationing to begin immediately." Their gazes met over the scarred wood of the desk, "He suspects the Hinterlanders will burn the fields doesn't he?" Torman queried. Camus nodded in grim ascent, "Your father may be many things, but a fool is not one of them. The easiest way to capture Jorgenholm will be to starve us out. Our position is too strong otherwise. And if this raid is a precursor to an all-out war, that will be the next logical step."

Silence fell in the tower, the fire crackling away merrily, seemingly unaware of the gruesome picture being painted in the minds of the two men left to rule the massive Keep. *I was already so busy*, thought Torman. The harvest and preparation for the harsh winter to come had been keeping him hopping from one problem to the next, but this would add hundreds of tasks to his already overflowing to-do list.

"Why were they so far south?" He wondered aloud.

"I don't know," Camus looked apprehensive, "but it obviously has the Jorgen worried. He had never felt too threatened by the northern tribes, but traveling so many miles to attack the Holm's forces on a march...This is a new tactic, one with more cunning than we have ever seen in the leaders of those bloodthirsty men. I think your father's cautionary actions are the right ones. This Autumn is already falling into freezes, and much of the fruit is still upon the vines. Winter will be hard enough without a siege, and it may be the Hinterlander's are finally ruled by one with vision unclouded enough by blood that he can see our weakness."

Torman pulled another blank sheet of parchment from his untidy stack, "Well," he said resolutely, "we have a lot to do, let's get to it. The most important is to get the harvest in and stored, safe from the cold and wet. Then builders, and we will send chambermaids to clean out all unused rooms in the Keep; the more people that can stay within Jorgenholm itself, the less work we will need to do in the courtyards and gardens." He gave a grim smile. "We can send out the children to search for empty rooms, along with someone who knows their letters, to map out the sections which can be used." Meeting Camus's eyes he said, "It's time to explore the warrens beneath the Holm and put them to good use." He clapped his hands together as he stood, and held out an arm for his old friend. "Ready to get busy, Maegi? We have endless meetings with countless people ahead of us. Let us summon the Acting Captain of the Guard first, we have some changes to make."

Kaur

The flame of the torch danced whenever he passed this section of the corridor. At all other times, in the dead air of the passages beneath Jorgenholm, the flame rose steady and brilliant from the torch. But here, every time he passed back through at the end of another day spent exploring, his shadow jumped and danced as if trying to get his attention.

It was pretty regular as far as corridors went. This far down below the Keep the rooms and halls were carved out of solid rock, the dark speckled granite which lay underneath the fertile soil of the entire Skypeaks range. The strange spot was about fifteen paces from a doorway on both sides. The walls were unbroken stone, the ceiling more of the same. He brought his torch down low, towards the floor, as it flickered and waved, only to find more stone, smoother here, from ages of feet wearing away the rough edges.

He had tried to tell Lear about the strange spot. But the man only wanted to hear the number of rooms he had found, if they were empty, and on which side of the hallway they lay on. He *was* rather busy, Kaur knew; mapping out the warrens had taken five days already, and whole sections had yet to be opened for the children aiding the mapmaker to start exploring.

He had been assigned the northernmost section, the one that started two levels down from the Greathall and stretched out underneath the tall cliff backing Jorgenholm. He had been chosen to take the section because of the fur coat his mother had sewn him last spring, when his father, a hunter, had brought down an aging ice lion, and the Jorgen's son had awarded his Da the pelt for his bravery. His mother had spent months on the stitching, painstakingly piecing together the fine fur as lining so her only son would stay warm in the coming winter. His assigned tunnels under the great cliff were much colder than the catacombs under the Keep proper, and damp with ground water that collected in the silent halls. Lourn and Retcha had gleefully told the soldier about Kaur's new coat when they were being assigned to their areas, and how since Kaur had such warmth that *he* should be the one exploring the bleak northern warrens.

He had gotten them back for their treachery the next day, as they slipped into their blankets in the kitchens, after a long day of walking the tunnels and reporting back what they discovered, they had found their tired feet encompassed by sticky sourdough starter rather than fire warmed blankets. Cook had been furious, setting them to washing and cleaning the mess from their bedrolls, and then assigning them to feed the sourdough starter for a month with no reprieve, and with no lessening of their other tasks. Kaur laughed to himself gleefully. While they had been losing sleep due to extra work, he lay snug in his parents bed in their small house in the shadow of the Wall. He missed their little house. The day after his revenge on his friends the entire village had been moved inside the Wall, and now his parents and he bedded down in the stables until the many rooms he spent his days discovering could be cleaned out and made habitable for the common folk.

He had been scared that first day, making his way into the stale hall hidden behind the heavy door that had previously barred off this section of the Holm. The door hadn't been opened in so long that they had to take an ax to it, as the hinges had rusted over. Knowing the door couldn't be closed again had been the only way he had convinced himself to walk into the maze of passages the Jorgen's themselves had forgotten about. But in the last five days, his section had lost its mysterious horror, and the cold dark passages became his kingdom. Each new door he came upon was his next great adventure, and he would sidle into each new room with his torch held before him like a sword, pretending he was Vorrion the Brave entering Firetongue's lair with the great-sword *Fortune*, his ever-present companion.

But there was this strange corridor. This one section within his realm he could not help but rush through each day, trying not to think of why the flame danced here, but nowhere else. He tried to will away the chills that crawled up his back, despite the warmth of an ice lion pelt. Today, as he made his way back through, he made himself stop. Despite his goose pimples, and the faint scent of blood in the air, he stopped to examine the spot thoroughly. He would go to the Lord Torman if this corridor still rang strange with a closer inspection. If Lear wouldn't listen, just because he thought that Kaur was a little boy scared of an empty hallway, then he would take it to the Big Lord, the one who smiled so kindly at him every time they passed in the Greathall.

Holding the torch before him he watched the flame raptly. A quarter turn to the right and the flame leaped like it was trying to escape its tether to the wood below. Turn back to front and the flame calmed. He turned to the left this time, and the torch remained steady. Turning fully to face the right-hand wall, the flame grew agitated again, and he raised it to gaze at the blank stone before him. He had a terrible feeling, a cold certainty he did not want to touch that wall. But that terror, that fear was just kid stuff, he told himself. He could be brave. If he was brave and figured out what was different about this wall then the Big Lord would like him, and think he was courageous like his Da.

Reaching out a trembling hand, Kaur traced his fingers gently down the wall. And nothing happened. With a boyish grin he began running his hands around the rough surface, tracing a chisel mark here and there, but finding nothing different about the stone. Perplexed, he moved the flame in again, gauging how close he was to the strangeness by the flame once again. He moved the torch over the wall slowly, revealing in stark light the pitted surface. Standing on tip toe he reached the brand up above his head to look at the junction of wall and ceiling when a glow caught his eye. Struggling to remain close to the wall so he could reach as high as he needed, he arched his neck back to get a clear look. And sure enough, when he passed the flame over the highest portion of the wall in the corridor, an angry red symbol lit up to match his torch.

Excited now the young boy gave a whoop of triumph. "Wait'll the Big Lord sees this!" he cried, turning to run full tilt down the corridor and up a set of stairs to the central larder, where Lear had set up his supplies and the children made their reports each day. He pelted past the grumpy warrior and up another set of stairs to the kitchens, passing his friends as they fed the sourdough levain, twin looks of disgust on their faces as the sticky and sour material clung to their hands. He called gleefully over his shoulder, "You'll never believe what I found!"

Kaur traveled the Keep at the same frantic pace, asking serfs and soldiers for the Lord Torman until he finally found him, helping to raise one wall of a new section of the stables, where the village animals would be kept separate from the Jorgen's stock. The Lord looked like a giant as Kaur approached him; he had stripped down to his undershirt and breeches in the crisp Fall sunlight, and his thick arms glistened with sweat from the hard labor. Tentative now, Kaur approached, only to be swatted away from his goal as the stable master passed.

"Away with you, lout! Leave the men to their work and get out from under our feet, boy!" The man smelled of wine and stale sweat as he smacked the back of Kaur's head. Forging ahead despite the blow, Kaur dodged the man's second attempt to dissuade him and nimbly danced ahead of the cursing drunk, until the commotion they were causing attracted the attention of the Big Lord himself.

"Lord sir! Lord!" He called frantically, dashing about to evade the stable master's grasping and punching hands. "I found something sir!" A strong blow caught him in the side of the face and he staggered right up to his target, cringing in anticipation of another hit as he came to a stop. "Found-ah-magic-wall-neath-tha-Keep!" he blurted out before raising his arms protectively above his ringing head. But the blow never fell. He carefully raised his head to find the Big Lord holding the arm of the stable master in a crushing grip, his eyes cold on the man's sweating face.

"Get out of my sight before I decide to ask you how much wine you've consumed before it's even noon," the Big Lord spat. The chastised man slunk away with a brief glare for Kaur, promising retribution for later.

"Big Lord Sir!" Kaur breathed, a huge, gap toothed smile breaking out over his small face. "There's a glowing wall! A magic corridor! A strange spot! My flame danced!" The words tumbled from his mouth incoherently in his excitement. With an easy smile Torman knelt down so that he was on the same level as the small child and ruffled his dark hair.

"Let's try that again boy, slower this time. You're helping Lear explore under the Holm, yes?"

"Yes!" Kaur agreed, taking a breath to try to calm his excited babbling, "The northern tunnels, there is a wall with a symbol. But you can only see it when the flame is close, and it looks like embers burning in the wall! The air is strange there, it's always strange, but today I found the glowing!"

Torman turned to his comrades with a smile, heaving his big frame up from the ground. With a wink to the head builder he said, "Best go see the magic wall then." Turning to Kaur again he asked politely, "And what is your name, little explorer?"

"Kaur, sir," Kaur replied shyly, before leaping into motion again as the Big Lord motioned for him to lead the way to his discovery.

Torman

Torman had followed the little boy, Kaur, down beneath the Holm indulgently. But now he stood before the blank wall, and the air did indeed feel strange in his lungs. He could taste a hint of magic in the air, but it was different than the tang his little bit of magic left after he used it. This was... stale. Stale and old. He glanced down at the small child beside him as Kaur bounced excitedly on the balls of his feet. If the boy could tell that the air was "strange" here, he would very likely be developing magic in the next few rebirths.

Torman was rarely able to deny young children anything, whether it be sweets, attention, or protection that they craved. But since this morning he felt like all he could see were children. The little ones of Jorgenholm running about with such sweet innocence and happiness on their faces. Boys and girls nearly indistinguishable under seven rebirths, but all active, helping in the daily tasks of the Holm, helping with the extraordinary effort his people were putting forth to survive this winter.

Metra had stopped him as he left their bed this morning, a brilliant patch of morning sun highlighting the exquisite smoothness of her skin where the tousled bedclothes failed to cover her. She had stopped him and told him something, but he had been too mesmerized by the sight of that golden light upon her equally golden skin. She had to repeat her words, and even then, the temptation of her body was great, and it took him a moment to realize what she had said... She was pregnant, she was going to be having his child.

A child! A sweet babe that was a part of him, and a part of the woman he had loved for the last five rebirths. Would it have her eyes? Those deep pools of hazel that he loved so much? Or would the child take more after him, with the high cheekbones and broad planes of the ancient line of the Jorgens? He truly couldn't care less, whatever his babe looked like he already loved it, and couldn't wait for the small being to join him and his lover in their lives. He would be having a conversation with his father upon his return, and they would revisit the same argument they had been having for the last five rebirths. But this time, this time he would *make* him say yes. He had to, for the sake of the life growing within his lover.

The small hand in his had wiggled free as Kaur danced around in excitement, Torman's slow pace too much of a tether for his exuberance. He rushed past a bemused Lear without a passing word and plunged into a chilly hallway that quickly dried the sweat on Torman's body, sending a chill down his spine. Kaur had stopped his frantic dash in a corridor that looked much like all the others this deep in the warrens. Approaching one wall Kaur leaned into the vertical stone, running his torch close along the face, as far above his head as he could reach.

"Can you see it?" he asked, craning his head back and nearly toppling over backwards in his effort to both see and reach. "Lord? Like embers in the wall, see it? There!" The child squealed excitedly, and sure enough the faint outline of an arcane symbol looked to be smoldering in the rock itself.

"I see it, lend me your torch, son." Kaur turned over the light gratefully, hurrying back to the other side of the corridor in order to get a better view. The warrens beneath Jorgenholm were short enough that Torman's antlers nearly scraped the carved roof at its lowest, so he examined the magical symbol with ease. Holding the flame close to the emblem caused it to glow brighter, but when he retracted the torch the glow faded. "You did good work here, Kaur," he complimented the child leaning against the wall behind him. "Let's see if we can figure out what it is you found." Bringing the flame close again he held it steady on the design, carefully monitoring it as the unknown symbol grew brighter and brighter.

Just before it grew so bright he was forced to look away, the light emanating from the stone was abruptly extinguished. A soft "oof" sounded off behind him and he turned to check on his young companion, only to find the corridor empty. He rubbed his eyes trying to encourage the afterimage of the emblem to fade, calling, "Kaur lad?" His voice sounded different than it had before, the echoes less intense, like the air had snatched his words from the hall and taken them somewhere else.

"Kaur?" He called again, his eyes finally clear enough he could distinguish that a segment of the wall Kaur had been standing against was now black as pitch. His torch flickered incessantly as he took a step towards that black maw, its erratic light finally revealing to Torman's dazed eyes the small, cloth wrapped feet of the little explorer. "Kaur!" He rushed over to the fallen boy, finding him curled in upon himself, gasping desperately for the wind that had been knocked from his chest. He lay head downward, his back resting on the tread of a large stone step, his feet resting on the stair above.

Pulling him up out of the newly revealed stairwell, Torman patted his back gently as Kaur's eyes bulged and he tried vainly to pull air into his shocked lungs. Torman smoothed circles into the child's back as he struggled, and sat with him for a few minutes afterwards as the relief of being able to breath once more, and the horrifying feeling of suffocation led the young boy to dissolve into tears.

"S-so-sorry sir" Kaur stammered, embarrassment asserting itself now he was regaining his composure. "It just sc-scared me s-sir. The wa-wall was there, then it wa-was-wasn't!"

"So it was," Torman said bemusedly looking at the new doorway in the underground corridor, "And now we have a new passage to explore. I wonder what secrets you have uncovered?"

"Should we go down?" Kaur asked tentatively, peering down the staircase from the safety of Torman's arms. The stairs descended farther than the reach of the torch, and with the slimy wet growth permeating the warrens anywhere water seeped into the Holm, they looked treacherous and slippery.

"Yeah, I think we should," said Torman, giving the boy a grin, "It's like when Vorrion the Brave found the secret lair of the Bejeweled Witch, and descended into its depths to slay her and put an end to her black magic ways!" Torman saw the fear recede from Kaur's eyes with satisfaction, and the glow of anticipation return.

Hand in hand they began the descent, steadying one another if the footing became treacherous. The stairs took a sharp left turn some ways down, and forked into two level passages after fifty more steps. They paused there, chilled in the subterranean tunnel, faced with two identical hallways and unsure which to take. Torman began to get the feeling he should have told someone where he was going, in case the ancient structure decided to collapse now that it had been disturbed, or something more sinister happened. He shivered a little, wishing he had thought to grab his tunic from the fence he had draped it over before following the boy into the Keep. "We'll take the right hand passage, just a bit further, and if we don't find anything then we'll go and get some others to help us explore. How does that sound Kaur?" The boy nodded his head, dark eyes huge in the light of the torch.

"Adventures are scarier than I thought they would be," he said solemnly.

Torman clapped him on the back with a smile he tried his best to keep hidden, saying agreeably, "That they are lad, that they are," as he led them both into the hallway on the right. The stones were different on this lower level, he noticed. The rough granite that comprised the majority of the Keep slowly gave way to a lighter and smoother stone that was polished to a mirror-like sheen under their feet. Dark whorls of texture marbled the walls, and he kept seeing strange images and faces in the designs from the corners of his eyes that faded when he gazed at them head on.

The hall opened up after a time, into a room larger than Torman would have thought possible this far underground. The walls were lined with shelves. Shelf after shelf soaring high up towards a ceiling the light from his torch didn't reach, He and Kaur wandered in among numerous pillars dripping down from the ceiling, also encircled with shelves, all packed full of books. Books, large and small, hide and fur bound or with supple leather covers, some titled in languages he recognized, and many more that he did not.

"It's a library," Kaur said wonderingly, breaking the awestruck silence that had reigned since they entered the room.

"Careful now," Torman said, taking his hand from the young boy's so he could take a closer look at the shelves. "Don't touch anything, it smells of magic down here. Old magic." He touched the frame of one of the ledges, marveling at the masonry work. Each shelf was stone, the same light stone as the walls, shot through with darker streaks that glimmered darkly in his torchlight. It looked as if every flat surface of this cavern had been carved into shelves, including some truly magnificent stalactites that reached the floor from the unknown height of the ceiling.

"Is that what that smell is?" Kaur asked, his nose wrinkled up as he sniffed deeply. "That's magic? I thought it was mildew, or blood, it kinda smells like blood..." he trailed off as he and Torman wandered farther apart, examining details here and there, but in general, simply marveling at the enormity of their discovery.

Torman knew he should go get Camus. The elderly Maegi would be able to make much more sense of this strange library in the bowels of the Jorgen's Keep than he could. *Whose library was it?* Torman wondered. *Was it one of his ancestors? Or did the books in this cave-like room predate his family altogether?* Reaching out tentatively he reached for the spine of one large tome, feeling a slight resistance as his fingers neared. He snatched his hand back as the resistance became the sharp tingle of magic. He called over his shoulder to his young friend, "Don't touch the books, Kaur!"

He backed away from the shelf, feeling more apprehensive by the moment. He was in over his head here, and the child with him even more so; who knows what safeguards this ancient library held? He, for one, had no interest in finding out without the guidance of a formally trained Maegi. Whirling briskly, he turned to find Kaur at the edge of the torchlight, hand outstretched towards a strange looking object on a shelf at his eye level.

In the split second Torman had, between his first glimpse of Kaur, and the words erupting from his mouth, he identified the object as a skull. The twisted cranium Kaur faced was staring back at the boy, empty eye sockets leering, much larger than any Trewal Torman had ever seen. The bone was yellowed with age, its teeth many, and sharp, crowding the jawbone crookedly. Cheekbones were nearly invisible as the front of the face elongated into a snout-like projection that terminated abruptly in a gaping hole. The forehead bulged above the eye sockets, sloping upwards to a strange hole in the bone, rounded like the sockets below. But what creature had a third eye at the top-center of their head?

Torman took a hurried step towards the boy, calling out, "Don't' touc-" but it was too late, and the wondering curiosity in Kaur's eyes quickly turned to alarm as his small palm flattened on the skull's wide forehead. A brilliant flare of shockingly green light erupted before their eyes, Kaur's hand turning almost translucent, the fragile bones briefly visible, with the vivid glare. He screamed, the sound seeming to come from every direction at once as the strangely angled shelves bounced the sound back at them. Then the limp body of the small child collapsed to lay unmoving on the white floor.

Camus

A frantic and contrite Torman brought Camus's latest patient to the tower room himself. The young boy looked like an over-sized rag doll in the man's arms as he burst through the door, interrupting Camus's quiet contemplation of the scale model of Jorgenholm and the surrounding countryside. Torman was breathless after ascending the steep spiral stairs that led to Camus's tower, and his words made little sense as he brusquely cleared off a table to lay the child on.

"Magic library, there was a skull. I *told* him not to touch anything! Old, old magic-"

"Calm down boy!" Camus barked out, stilling the tumbling words with a bit of pleasure that the burly man before him could still be called to task by his former teacher. Old habits die hard. He knew that from experience. "Put the tea water on Torman, there's a good lad."

As Torman automatically moved across the room to the kettle, Camus finally had the space to move in on the small form laying on his breakfasting table. The child was pale as milk, and cold to the touch, but his heart beat steady beneath his breast and the breath escaping from his lightly freckled nose was warm and moist as it should be. Reaching within to his center, Camus embraced his magic with familiar Control, encompassing the wily Earth power within the confines of his mind and bending it to his will.

He let the magic flow, glowing coppery gold to his eyes, into the boy before him, directing it into each crevice and cell within the still body until the child emitted light like a small sun. He could find no reason for the loss of consciousness, and no harm in the body itself. The only anomaly was a small hint of magic in his hand, radiating from the palm. It was an unfamiliar magic and its essence tinged his own golden power a sickly green in his Sight, a shade of green he usually saw from Hinterland Maegi, the color he had always associated with their God, Freyton.

"Torman, where were you? Was it outside the Wall?" The questions fired off rapidly into the still tower, just as the kettle began to whistle shrilly.

Swinging the kettle from the fire absently Torman launched into his story, and Camus's confusion grew with each word. What was the taint of the Hinterland God doing in the bowels of Jorgenholm? And what had the hapless explorers unleashed when he and Torman opened the door to the library? Stilling the endless stream of questions running through his mind, Camus directed Torman to lay the sleeping child on his bed, snugging a warm blanket up around his ears to combat the chill in his body.

"We need to block off the passage until I can get down there and see what you've found. But before we go exploring I want to make sure my new patient here wakes up. He could have triggered some sort of defense in the library, and there is no telling what its effects will be." Camus locked eyes with Torman, speaking sternly as he remembered what a precocious youth he had been, "No one, and I mean *no one*, is to go down there until we know that Kaur here has suffered no ill effects."

"No need for the scolding tone old man," Torman said, shaking his head, "that place scared me silly, and I have no desire to return unless you and all of your magic is with me." Torman moved to Kaur's bedside, tightly gripping his small hand in his much larger one before striding out of the tower and downward, to make sure no one entered the newly discovered rooms of the Holm.

Camus puttered about his tower idly for the next few hours, keeping a close eye on the boy snoring contentedly in his bed, his head a chaotic swirl of thoughts and questions. If this was an attack by the tribes, it was cleverer than even the Jorgen had anticipated. And if it was not, then what was magic touched by the hand of a foreign God doing in Garrin's stronghold? The Jorgens were believed to be descendants of the God of the Hunt himself, and he had only ever Seen the gold light of Garrin around the people of the Holm. So what was the putrid light of Garrin's tempestuous brother doing within Jorgenholm?

A stirring from the bed drew his attention outwards once more. With a creak and a wince, he made his way to the bed to find two eyes peering out from beneath the ice lion pelt that kept his old bones warm at night.

"Sir?" the confused boy squeaked timidly, wide eyes taking in the tower room full of books, arcane instruments and herbs. "What happened sir!?"

"You collapsed when you were down beneath the Holm with Lord Torman" Camus said as the little boy struggled out from beneath the fur and blankets, a ruddy flush upon his cheeks. "What's the last thing you remember?"

"We found a library," Kaur said haltingly, stilling warily as Camus neared to lay a hand upon his brow, afraid the pink tinging the child's cheeks might indicate a fever. "And there were strange things on the shelves. Kinda like these things!" The boy said triumphantly, ducking out from underneath the Maegi's hand and approaching his worktable to point to the mortar and pestle and other instruments of potion making.

Camus followed, reassured that the flush on Kaur's cheeks was from being wrapped up in so many blankets during his unscheduled 'nap'. "What is the very last thing you were doing child?"

Kaur bit his lip thoughtfully before answering, "There was a big head-bone, but it didn't look like the horse ones I've seen, or the ice lion one my Da killed, although the teeth were kinda like an ice lion," he reflected. Then his little face crumpled, and the look of guilt coupled with the tear that leaked down his round cheek nearly broke Camus's heart, "He told me not to touch anything sir," he whispered, "but I touched the head-bone, even though I shouldn't have! There was light, and it hurt, and then I woke up here," he finished quietly, not meeting Camus's eyes.

"Thank you for telling me," he said gravely, "I know it can be hard to tell the truth about something you shouldn't have done." The Maegi pulled the softly sniveling boy into his arms. "I am going to make sure you are okay one last time. It might feel a little funny, but I won't hurt you, I promise."

At the boy's nod of ascent Camus delved in with his magic once more, relieved to find the child seemed to have suffered no ill effects from whatever power he had disturbed in the subterranean library. *No ill effects my magic can detect at least*, Camus thought uneasily. But who knows what knowledge had been lost since the library had been sealed? He had never heard of a magical library in the Holm, meaning it was likely a remnant from the Age before Memory, and the few Relics that the King's Academy held from that time were guarded jealously by the Demandron. He had never been allowed to study the artifacts, but had heard disturbing tales from his peers about their strange attributes, and how they seemed to preform outside of the universal rules of magic as the Trewal knew them.

Sending Kaur on his way to find his parents and assure them of his safety, Camus began the descent from the tower at a much more sedate pace than the hearty child's headlong plummet. There was much to consider before venturing down to the library. He would need to make a stop in the Jorgen's study for one of the larger sapphire Augments the ruler kept there. Its stored magic would reinforce his own powers, hopefully keeping the danger of being left powerless at bay. If the library had a Renaldis charm set upon it, which would effectively drain any power-source activated within the room, then the stone would allow him to magically explore the room, even if his own magic had been dampened.

Mind awhirl with defensive magic and countering methods, Camus gathered his supplies - augments chalk full of stored magic, various books of methodology, and a strong young serf to carry it all down to the warrens for him. He found Torman with the map maker,

Lear, in the secondary larder, where the corridor young Kaur had found was being guarded against entry. Scholarly weapons in hand, they plodded down the hallway to the dripping maw of the newly discovered stairway, leaving strict orders to not be disturbed behind them. Meeting eyes grimly, the old Maegi and the young ruler began their wary descent.

Chapter 5

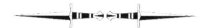

Sylvia

She awoke to the insistent flutter of nausea in her stomach. The flutter morphed into a flailing beast in her gut and she struggled to sit up before disgracing herself, but the bolt of pain the movement caused had her lying back down as gently and as quickly as she could. She tried to bring her hands to her head, to soothe the abominable ache in her temple but discovered they were tangled in scratchy cloth at her sides. Her muscles were too weak to break free. Struggling to open gummy lids she found only soft darkness little different from the blackness behind her eyelids.

What the hell? She racked her brain, trying to come up with the where's, why's and how's she so desperately wanted to know. Could she be back home? The last time she had awoken in a strange place with no memory of how she had gotten there, was upon her arrival to Prium. She thought back to the last thing she remembered, a giant hand grasping her calf, her terrified escape from the tent, her headlong dash towards the forest at the edge of camp. And then nothing.

The twinges of an all too familiar panic twirled a riotous dance in her stomach, adding to the nausea that seemed to wax and wane with her heartbeat. She struggled upright, finally managing to pull her hands free of the tangling blanket, and promptly threw up, her head swimming. Sylvia flopped back onto her side and retched again, bitter bile burning in her throat.

"Ugh!" Syl froze at the disgusted sound. "You could have just told me before making such a mess! I would have taken you outside." It took a moment for Sylvia to translate the feminine voice speaking in stilted Layette, and by the time she figured out what the woman was saying the blindfold was being roughly unwound from her head.

She blinked her eyes, willing the blurry vision before her to clear into more understandable shapes. A Trewal woman dressed in soft green was folding the blindfold busily, standing at what appeared to be the side of the cot she lay in. Sylvia groaned, stopping abruptly as she realized the pain in her head was from the vibrations of her own voice. The woman leaned over her, her face broad and brown, blending seamlessly into the mousy color of her hair, the fawn coloring was interrupted only by the shiny black horns curving downwards from her head to intermingle with her frizzy locks. Her wide lips parted on words Syl thought she should be able to understand, but could not quite grasp the meaning of. The brown woman gently touched her sore head, her fingers coming away slick and red, and then Syl lost her eyes in the blur before her, and darkness came for her again.

Tamol

Tamol looked down on the bleeding girl and shook her head at the now closed eyelids. Such eyes! The blue was frightening in its intensity, not the gray-blue of the few Hinterlander's eyes who were born as such, but a swirling crystal blue akin to the sapphires mined deep in the northern Skypeaks. The Morgal needed to know, and quickly, before Pralick returned to claim his spoils of war, and realized just how valuable an item he had carried home across his horse's withers.

The raid two days before had been successful. The Trianti had killed more soldiers of the Holm in one attack than they had in the last two years combined. Tired of useless forays to the Wall of Jorgenholm, where the losses were never made up for in spoils or enemy deaths, the Morgal had hatched a new type of plan, one focused more on weakening the enemy than on any actual gain in their ages old war. But even though killing the enemy had been the main purpose, the raiders had found the tents of the lowlanders laden with spoils. The men had returned with a hoard of new weapons, jewelry, paper, writing implements, ink, and women.

Their Autumn camp now swarmed with *kurianit*. Lost women, confused, beleaguered, and taken from everything they once knew, set to tasks they had never done, and beset upon by the very warriors who had slain their fathers, sons, and lovers. Tamol hated the series of punishments and lessons these women went through on their entrance to the Hinterland way. She wished her people didn't take women from the Holm for this use. *Kurianit* captured from the other tribes knew the way of things. They settled into their new Name to await the cleansing, the *Cetrian,* and then they would gain yet another Name, *Ianit,* if they chose to stay with the tribe after their internment.

Every *kurianit* the Morgal had brought back from his countless raids remained with the tribe, even those taken from Jorgenholm. She should know, as she had been one of them. But now she was *Tamol Ianit*. She had been made *kurianit* very young; and after two years serving the Morgal she had had no wish to leave her new home, and no ties to her old tribe beckoning her back. So she had remained, apprenticing with the tribe healers upon the Morgal's blessing. But not all of the *kurianit* were so fortunate in their masters. Pralick, a fearsome warrior and a veteran of many raids, for all of his deplorable personality, had captured nearly as many young women as the Morgal, despite their age difference. But not a single one stayed beyond their *Cetrian*, choosing to leave, even if they were forced to abandon a child of their own body, which their master claimed as his own.

In the aftermath of the raider's return to the mountains Tamol had been busy, cleaning wounds, stitching skin, keeping the tribe's few Maegi's, whose magic hadn't been depleted in the raid, hopping from patient to patient to keep the worst alive. She had seen the limp form of the girl hauled from Pralick's horse and into his tent. Knowing he would not care for the girl's wounds she had snuck in after night had fallen, when the bonfires had been lit, and the pyres built for the dead. In the midst of the feasting her presence was not missed, and the brute who would claim the girl on the morrow was getting too drunk on mead to perform any act of possession that night. The girl would be safe until the morning, and by then the Morgal and his followers would have come up with a plan to deal with this political viper's nest.

Pralick had been slowly gaining friends and supporters from the outcasts and loners of the tribe. He had been currying favor with those who were disgruntled with the Morgal, and his less than aggressive raids on the Jorgen stronghold. He talked ceaselessly of the Bloodhunger and the spoils it had gained them, but never of the costs. Slowly but surely Pralick was splintering the tribe, tearing families asunder with his poisonous talk. This blue-eyed girl would be the last token of power he needed to challenge the Morgal.

She finished cleaning the girl's head, wiping crusted blood from the edges of the gash. Pralick's pommel had opened a good sized cut amidst the coal black hair. The flesh oozed blood, tinging her wet cloth with rusty red streaks that reminded her of the iron streaking the rocks inside the caves of Orr. The Trianti will bleed like those walls, she knew, if the Morgal fell. Pralick would lead the men she chose to be her blood, her sons and brothers and fathers, to break like a bloody wave upon the thorny Wall of the Jorgens. He would break her people, until they were nothing but corpses for the unnatural vegetation of that hated barrier to drink dry.

"We are of blood and bone." She uttered the ancient words under her breath, her hands absently stroking through the girl's heavy hair where a serf's clipped antlers should have sprouted.

"Blood is iron." The sapphire eyed girl twisted fretfully in the cot.

"Bones are stone." Blood pumped into her rag sluggishly after the thrashing of her patient. Tamol's soft voice hardened, became lethal even in its low volume.

"We are iron and stone."

Lessoran

The tribe was celebrating. Their merriment filtered through the dense trees covering the lowest slopes of the Skypeaks, the sounds of drinking, dancing, and love making bounced off of the lacy boughs of the Listenbarks, and seemed to fracture in their weblike configurations of needles. Words became simple noise. Names broke into pieces only recognizable by the emotion they were uttered with. From his perch on the outskirts of the nomadic settlement, it could have been mistaken for the chaos of battle, for the cacophony of death.

Les rarely felt as alone as he did after a raid. In that time where his brethren let loose and indulged in life-affirming acts of excess and pleasure. The isolation always ate at him as they piled their dead upon high pyres in preparation for *Traumek*, the long cold journey their fallen brothers would embark upon once the flames took them forever from this world. The women of the tribe were more often than not with child after a night like tonight. He could hear the joyful sounds of coupling from the dense brush surrounding the camp, from the skin shelters of the warriors, and even from the darker corners around the fire in the center of the celebrating settlement.

The gross dichotomy of the act of creation stemming from the completion of the funeral pyres made him break out in goosebumps. *Death should come after life,* he thought, *life should not be born of the death of kinsmen.*

The warriors of his tribe forgot the trauma of battle so readily, but he could not shake the events of this raid so easily. In his rational mind he knew his magic was the reason raids appeared so differently to him than to his peers, but in his heart he could not comprehend celebrating of the butchery which had taken place today. The lives lost, the families grieving, the bodies, nearly identical to their own, maimed and torn. He had tried to speak of his unease with the other battle Maegi, but tradition held them firmly in its grasp, and they shied away from his dislike of battle as unnatural.

As the head Maegi of the Trianti, he could not escape the battles. He was the major force behind the death of their enemies. His magic boiled the water in their bodies, drowned their lungs with the moisture in the air of their own lands. He felt, witnessed, and was a part of each death his magic made happen. He knew first hand that the deaths of their enemies felt no different than the deaths of the people his magic fought to protect. Each was a waste. A horrible, needless, pointless, waste of potential.

His ribs throbbed dully, the slash in the skin over his rib-cage was not too serious, but the sturdy bones beneath the layers of muscles had been grazed by the spearhead, and he knew the deep pain would linger for days. He had been cleaned and wrapped and poked and fussed over by the Healers upon returning from the raid, but had still managed to stay in the Healers tent to lend his magic to the wounded, even though his skills in that area were not great. Tamol had tried to shoo him from the tent too many times to count, mothering him as if she was not rebirths his junior.

He had finally relented, making his way through the throngs of celebrators towards the ice cold creek they had been living by for the last few fortnights. The water took a sharp turn at the western side of the little canyon, curving to the east before continuing its headlong flow downhill, and out of the Skypeaks. Decades of water cascading into that sharp bend had carved into the rocks forcing the water eastward. The resulting pool was deep and wide, with a sheltering overhang of speckled granite. He washed the smell of death from his body under that overhang, the flecks in the rock looking like the sparkle of stars in the torchlight. He wished there was a way to let the cold rush of the mountain waters into his skull, to scour him clean of the images of the men of Jorgenholm he had killed. And now here he was, damp and shivering, hunched in on himself on top of a rock near the bathing pool, those very same images he wished to wash away the barrier keeping him from joining his friends in celebration, keeping him from honoring the kindred he had failed to bring home safely.

He shook himself like a dog, his long uneven hair throwing droplets in every direction. *Enough moping around.* The melancholy of a battle was hard to shake off, but he always did it. Eventually. Usually it was with the help of his close friend Courit, and a large quantity of old man Horout's strongest wine. But he had seen the too-pale face of his friend amongst the tangled limbs atop one of the pyres. He had seen his face, and closed the bright green eyes with his own fingers, struggling against the death stiffened eyelids.

Tamol might be done in the healer's tent by now, maybe she would want to settle down in his tent with a jug of wine, lend him some comfort with her soothing hands and soft body. She had never questioned his sadness on nights like this, only offered kind smiles, understanding lurking in her eyes. Maybe tonight they would break all tribe traditions and actually talk about the wrongness of their ancestral customs, maybe they could talk about how it *should* be, if his people were able to let go of their stranglehold on the past.

Movement caught his eye on the beaten path leading to the bathing pool. The short, round figure of a woman clothed in a Healer's pale green cyn picked her way across the uneven shore. She shaded her eyes, leaning out over the water, searching, and her voice finally reached his ears, "Les? Lessoran! Are you here?"

Tamol's voice had an edge he hadn't expected. He pushed his tired body into higher gear, scrambling off the rock and towards the light of Tamol's torch. Her face was pinched, worry etching lines into a forehead that was usually smooth. "What's wrong Tam?" She gripped his hand hard and began drawing him along behind her, pebbles skittering noisily out from under their hooves.

"Tam? If someone needs Healing, my magic is worn out, I can't do more than produce a globelight after today..." He let his words trail off as she towed him not towards the Healers like he had expected, but towards the warrior's tents.

"Shut your mouth and move quicker Les, the day is not over yet, and things are not looking up," she said tersely, "now keep your head down."

Without another word she ducked through the hanging flaps of a tent, her curled horns scraping against the hide flaps, her firm grip on his wrist tugging him through the rank skins with her. He waited for his eyes to adjust, but did not immediately see what could have caused that frantic tone in her voice. There was a shape upon the bed, small and vulnerable, had a child been hurt? With a groan he dredged up as much magic as he could find within himself, struggling to keep even that paltry amount under Control, and suddenly the tent exploded into clarity.

The owner of the tent was a pig. That became obvious rather quickly, aside from the smell of the place itself, there were weapons strewn around, clothing interspersed liberally, and more than one warrior's fair share of wine jugs adding a particularly sour note to the overall odor of unwashed body. Upon the filthy looking blankets, a young woman lay unmoving, her head swathed in pristine white bandages, likely the only clean cloth present in the tent, the girl's own clothes included. Seeing nothing in dire need of attending to, he turned to Tamol pushing a hand through the damp hair between his antlers, "Can't this wait? I'm exhausted Tam…"

Muttering under her breath, his friend dragged him closer to the bed, "Use your eyes *romkin*, and maybe knowing that this is Pralick's tent will perk up your absent sense of curiosity! This girl does *not* belong here. She *can't* be here; this could ruin everything."

Tamol's voice muddled on, but he stopped hearing actual words when her calloused hands peeled back one eyelid fringed in sooty black lashes, and a sliver of intense color became visible. He felt like something made a very physical impact with his chest, as if suddenly all the oxygen in the world was not enough to let him breathe. But then her hands were traveling down to the ragged hem of the girl's robe and he tuned back in enough to hear her say, "And then there are *these*! The lack of antler's is nothing new on someone wearing a serf's robe, we all know they allow their children to be mutilated by the Jorgen's men at birth, but this? What is this?"

Realizing his mouth was open, he shut it with a snap and looked into the face of the woman beside him. The beginnings of hysteria were lurking in her usually warm eyes, and he quickly pushed the robe back over the girl's strangely shaped appendages. He grabbed Tam's hand in a rough grip, pulling her away from the edge of panic. "This is Pralick's tent? Are you sure?"

"Positive." She bit the word off angrily. "I can't approach the Morgal with everyone watching, but he needs to know, *now*." She gestured helplessly to the prone figure, "I don't even know how to react to this, Les. We need to handle it very carefully. Things were already so bad. I thought we had a plan for every contingency, but how could we have foreseen this? Why didn't the Ancients foresee this? Do you think they *want* the Morgal to lose his Name? I can't even breathe right now Les, how can this be happening?" The words tumbled from her lips gaining force and momentum.

"Tamol! Get a hold of yourself!" His harsh tone brought her tangled words to an abrupt halt. "One thing at a time, the Morgal needs to know. We can ask all the other questions afterwards." He let go of his Control, and felt the magic within his chest extinguish, guttering out tiredly. In the soft dark of the tent he took a fortifying breath. He could be tired later, but now he needed to spread the word of this imminent danger to the correct ears. "You need to go find Horout and Courit," Tamol's face blanched at the latter name, and Les wished he could pull it back into his mouth, just as he wished he could pull his friend back into life. "Sorry." He dropped his head into his hands, taking a breath, "Find Horout, Jamae, and Breanne. Tell them about 'Eyes' here, and whose tent she's in, but leave the rest out." He looked down at the end of her robe again, "Tell no one about the rest."

Tam nodded her head absently, glad to have a mission, glad to have someone else telling her what to do in this precarious situation. "We'll need to meet. The usual place? An hour before dawn?" she asked. At his nod of ascent, she bustled out the door, short legs kicking up the hem of her robe in her hurry, and she sped off into the night in search of the Morgal's few truly loyal supporters.

Sylvia

Things had gotten worse. So much worse. She had thought her arrival in Prium, the long trek to Jorgenholm, and the even longer days of servitude marching away from Jorgenholm had been bad. The events in this world had tried her spirit and her stamina. It had all tested her sanity, and her belief in what could and could not actually exist. But this, this was evil. This was *wrong*. Her adventurous dream was quickly devolving into nightmare. She wanted out, and she wanted out now.

The giant, hulking, beast of a man standing before her backhanded her again, this time on the left side of her tender face, and the world spun crazily around her. Each blow he rained down made the wound on her head throb and pulse in time to her heartbeat. He repeated his previous words slowly, almost gently.

"Take off, your clothes."

Her thoughts raced. If she undressed, something bad was going to happen, she knew it from the smirk on the large man's angular face, from the stink of alcohol on his breath. But if she didn't undress for him, she was afraid his next blow would knock her unconscious, and then she would be utterly powerless to stop anything from happening after that. At least if she retained consciousness she could take advantage of an opportunity to escape. The beast's lips twisted up on one side as she delayed, his amusement at her indecision evident.

"Make it easy on yourself little blue eyed whore, let me fuck you and I will be gentle, you might even like it," His head tilted, eyes raking her body consideringly, "if I want you to."

Rage flashed hot across her vision, it tilted her range of view, blurred the hellish scene in front of her with its intensity. She began taking off the outer layer of her robe with shaking hands, fingers questing subtly for the knife sheathes secreted about her body. By the time the robe fell from her shoulders the shaking had intensified, fear this time, rather than anger. He had her knives, all of them.

This can't be happening. The beast swayed closer, his eyes glued to her breasts beneath the thin shift which was her only remaining protection. His stale breath fanned across her face, the fumes of wine almost overpowering. *Nope, not happening, it's time to wake up, it's time to be home again.* She let her eyes shut, blocking out the horror in front of her. She focused on an image of her parents in their kitchen. The feel of her cat Sammy's soft belly fur, anything to block out the noises of the man in front of her moving slowly closer. *This place isn't real. You can't be assaulted by a man of another species, because another intelligent species DOESN'T EXIST!*

A fist bunched in the light fabric of her shift and pulled, hard. Her eyes flew open at the sound of tearing cloth and then she was fighting, screaming. His fists were everywhere, his hold on the gaping front of her clothing pulling her arms in tight to her body, constricting any chance she had to get in a full swing. Holding her at arm's length with one hand he used the other brawny arm to hit her, over and over. The taste of blood was metallic in her mouth as her lip split upon contact with her own teeth.

He began laughing. The sound came to her as if from under water. Her head was in a state beyond agony, the sensation making her sick. The need to vomit almost blocked out the pain of him gripping her shoulder in his powerful hand. She tried to dredge up Torman's calm voice, tried to remember the training he had so painstakingly taught her. But the Beast spun her suddenly, and she found her face pushed against the fetid tangle of blankets on the cot she had woken on. Too strong hands ripped the tattered shift off of her. She tried to wiggle out of his hold when one of his hands began to explore her body rather than hold her down, but he simply pushed down harder on the back of her neck with the other hand. The wandering hand paused in surprise as it trailed down her thigh, the barbarian catching a glimpse of her legs and feet for the first time. She kicked out, hoping to catch his unawares, but he simply crowded closer, locking her legs between him and the cot, dismissing her strangeness in lieu of other pursuits.

Syl labored to breath. *No, no, no, NO!* She struggled, not sure she could believe this was actually happening, that this *could* happen. Suddenly she saw the situation as if from outside herself, the tiny naked girl on the bed had no chance against this giant. She had no chance to escape. Black started to edge in on her line of sight as she failed to pull oxygen in through the pressure on her throat. With the last bit of breath she could pull in, she screamed again.

The cry died in suddenly bright air. Light and fresh, cool air streamed in from her left, engulfing her bare flesh, but her face was still being held forcefully to the right. The Beast was illuminated clearly, the look of surprise on his rough features slowly morphing into one of anger. Dust motes swirled above his head in the morning sunlight from their struggles, and his antlers gleamed bright as the sun spangled off the hammered metal adornments. His thick top lip curled upwards in a sneer, golden whiskers highlighted, and he ran his free hand down Syl's body, dipping into the curve of her waist before possessively grabbing at her ass, never taking his eyes off whoever was in the open entrance to his tent.

"Lessoran," he said, "care to join me while I break in the Tribe's new Mage? She looks like she will be a much better ride than

I could have ever hoped for from any of the current Maegi." As his gaze traveled scathingly up and down Syl's rescuer, the grip on her buttock tightened and the little air she had left in her body whooshed out at the unexpected pain.

The voice of the interrupter snapped out, cracked through the glittering air in the tent like a whip. *"Foraul nu' Groth!"* An electric tingle arced through the small space, like the first warning prickle in your skin as your foot falls asleep. The draped skins of the tent flew out of her sight, and more cold air gushed over her exposed skin. She began shivering in earnest. Hundreds of Trewal circled the tent of her captor. They were clothed in skins and leather, cloth and feathers. Pale green robes like Camus's stuck out at intervals, the light color at odds with the muted shades of fur and hide. Here and there among the crowd she saw women wearing one shouldered dresses, the drab cloth all dyed the same shade of olive green. Each woman kept her eyes trained on the ground, even as the rest of the crowd stared. Every face looked grim and expectant, their muddy and hazel colored eyes trained on the two men, and one very naked Sylvia, facing off at the center.

Keeping his hold on her, the Beast casually looked at the watching tribe, seemingly uncaring of his mostly naked state. He trained his harsh gaze back on the man who had spoken. "You cannot challenge me, Maegi." He spat. "This blue eyed *kurianit* is mine. No contest, I dispatched her in battle, and now she belongs to me." The anger in his eyes faded a bit, overcome by a tide of satisfaction. "She will outrank you and your Water magic quickly." His hand stroked down her butt and thigh, eliciting a squirm of revulsion, "My little Mage."

"I wasn't challenging you, Pralick." The man called Lessoran spoke calmly. "I was informing the tribe that the Morgal has called you out. This has nothing to do with the *Kurianit. He* has called for the *Foraul nu' Groth* simply because he believes you are no longer fit to live among his people."

The Beast, Pralick, guffawed loudly. "His people? The Morgal should talk to 'his people' more often, then he would know these men think him soft! Soft and old. This tribe needs a *real* leader, someone who is not afraid to attack the Jorgens!"

"Where did you find this girl, Pralick? Was she wandering in the woods? Or did you claim her during a battle with the Jorgen's soldiers? A battle planned and lead by the Morgal?" Lessoran's voice grew nearer to Syl's bent over position, and she flexed beneath Pralick's vise-like grip on her nape, testing his concentration on her captivity.

"You think one raid will appease our God?" Pralick thundered, spittle flying in an arc highlighted in the bright sun. "You think our tribe is happy playing farmer in the woods? Jorgenholm should be OURS! And yet the Morgal plays at politics with the other tribes, politics that would be nefarious if we could capture what is rightfully ours, and then bring the fractured tribes of the Hinterlands under our rule!" He heaved in a great lungful of air, and the pressure on Sylvia's neck lessened the slightest bit. "The Trianti are withering and growing old under this Morgal, when we should be dying in bloody glory fighting the war Freyton calls us to fight!" Pralick turned slowly, with Syl as his focal point, searching the faces of the surrounding Trianti tribe. "How can we continue to allow the Morgal to lead us when he defies Freyton himself? It is time for this Morgal to die, and for the tribe to send a new leader to the Caves of Orr, to bring us forth from the ashy ruin we have become. Then we will rise! We will flame the embers of our faith and Bloodhunger, and rush across the Skypeaks like a tide of flame to consume the Jorgens!"

A weak cheer erupted sporadically from the crowd, and the focus of the entire gathering was abruptly split, as mothers looked on in surprise at their sons voicing their support of Pralick. As brothers made eye contact across the circle, one with his mouth open in furtherance, one shut tight in furious disapproval. The small pockets of those in the tribe inflamed by Pralick's impassioned speech drew tighter together, and began eyeing the astonished persons to their rights and lefts with distrust.

Syl felt the focus shift. *It's now or never,* she knew, and with a big inhale she threw herself into a violent twist, using the weight of her hanging legs to propel herself towards the disembodied voice of the Maegi. Pralick started in surprise and attempted to clamp his hand down on her neck again, but only managed to leave four deep gouges as his nails scrabbled across fragile skin. Syl hissed in pain, her initial momentum carrying her into a roll that was abruptly halted as she crashed into a pair of strong legs. Lessoran grunted at the impact and his surprised face peered down at her. From her ungraceful heap on the dusty ground, Sylvia shakily climbed to her feet and skittered around behind the Maegi, placing his impressive bulk between herself and her would be rapist.

Pralick looked livid, and the volatile crowd began to surge forward and sideways and backwards as he lurched towards Sylvia and her newest favorite personal shield. Through the dissonance a voice rose, and with it thunder rumbled and the sky boiled in a mirror image to the turmoil below. Syl clutched the folds of the back of Lessoran's cloak as the Maegi grew eerily still, his eyes dropping closed, much like Ryland's had when he had used his magic to open a pathway through Jorgenholm's living Wall. Recognizing the tingle of magic, she backed off just enough so she was not touching him, and cautiously peered out at the figure striding into the middle of the conflict.

The Morgal was a large man, just past his prime. The silvering of his hair and beard leant him an air of wisdom that clashed boldly with the deadly intent in his eyes as he approached Pralick. His antlers were some of the largest she had seen in her time in Prium, and his neck and shoulders were built powerfully to support the cumbersome tines. Syl saw the Maegi had his eyes open now, fixed on his leader, and at the barest of nods from the great shaggy head Lessoran's body tightened, he held his breath, and brought a great bolt of lightning down at the edge of the clearing filled with tents and Trewal.

The resulting thunder was deafening. Fights that had begun stopped just as suddenly. Those locked in combat separated slowly as the last of the noise rumbled off. Into the silence the Morgal spoke calmly, "Pralick, I have called for the *Foraul nu' Groth.* We will meet at the common fire at midday, and this conflict you have brought upon our families will be resolved." He turned, making eye contact with all of those who had jumped so readily into the skirmish, "It will be resolved for everyone, and our tribe will be whole again."

He turned again, giving a nod here, and a twitch of a smile there. The crowd shifted guiltily, like children caught fighting by their father, but they did not disperse. He held them all captive with his gaze. Even Pralick seemed unable to turn from the imposing man's lazy perusal. As the Morgal turned towards the Maegi, Sylvia tried to melt into the drape of his hanging cloak, her face heating as attention was focused her way. But the Morgal simply gazed at her briefly, eyes barely flickering at her nakedness, spending more time gazing at her feet than the areas her hands instinctively rose to cover. Then he spoke into the pregnant hush, "We are of blood and bone."

The tribe joined their voices to his solemnly, quietly. The murmur a deep sonorous echo, "Blood is iron, bones are stone." The Morgal turned to face Pralick directly, his eyes on the younger man's, and this time the words resounded from the crags and the throats of the tribe alike.

"We are iron and stone!"

Lessoran

Still tired from his magical antics during and after the raid, Les let go of Control with a grateful sigh. He immediately missed the invigorating hum of the water droplets in the air, of the charged energy of the storm he had magically 'encouraged', but today the relief of relinquishing Control was as great as the joy of his magic. The warm bundle pressed up against his back stealthily pulled a little more of the fabric of his cloak to the back of his shoulders. He stifled a chuckle. Modesty was not a feeling you could afford to harbor in a tight knit tribe like this one, where bathing, cooking, fighting, and, more often than not, fucking, was done communally. Yet it was a trait that all *kurianit* taken from the Holm exhibited. He released the heavy silver cloak pin at his throat and turned with his cloak partially in hand, trying to wipe the amusement off of his face as he confronted the young woman who would eventually replace him within his tribe.

The little glimpse of her eyes he had gotten in the dim tent was no comparison for the actuality of her face in full morning sunlight. The rest of her features faded to nothing as he allowed himself to get lost in the glorious color. It was too intense to be called navy, too vibrant and speckled with lighter shades for the title of midnight. They were azure edging into topaz, dancing on the line of cerulean, and flirting with the barest hints of indigo and sapphire...

Her abrupt grab for the rest of the cloak they were both partially holding catapulted him from his musings on the correct color to assign to her eyes. Shaking his head at himself he gave her a much more practical and brief going over, allowing a smile to break through at her hurried dive beneath his thickly woven cloak. She was young, and very small compared to Trianti females, but maybe her people were all of smaller stature. Her features were as tiny as the rest of her, with a slightly too long nose flecked with freckles, dark slashes of eyebrows in sharp contrast to her pale face, and long, slim fingers. *Not bad at all, were it not for her age, he had always preferred woman his own age. Well, her age and those, whatever they are, on the ends of her legs where hooves should be.* From the brief glimpse he had gotten, her lack of hooves was her only true anatomical difference, other than unique sizing, a much slimmer stature, and some stunted ears.

A heavy hand struck his shoulder and pulled. From the fear that suddenly leapt up in Blue Eye's gaze he knew Pralick had turned his attention back to his latest *kurianit*. While Pralick propelled him backwards with his harsh grip, Les grabbed the hand on his shoulder by the wrist, and with a simple tuck turned his backwards momentum into a turn, compelling the larger man to swing in a wide arc around him. Les ended up back between the warrior and his prize, and he couldn't help the grin that split his face at the consternation upon the bully's grim countenance. Most Trewal, be it the Jorgen's men, a rival tribe, or members of the Trianti itself, saw his lack of weapon, and Maegi's robe, and thought him completely reliant on magic to protect himself. He kept up rigorous physical training just to see that look of confusion on their faces when his physical body defeated them, rather than his magic.

"Move Maegi!" Pralick spat, "You sully the pure magic of my Mage just by being near her." Les felt his grin grow wider, *baiting this hulk just never got old.*

"Don't you think if she was the great Mage you believe her to be, she would have avoided capture by someone like you? And now, do you think if she could have frozen you in place she would have let you manhandle her like you were when I so politely knocked at your door this morning?"

Pralick looked taken aback, but fumbled forward anyway, "Her eyes are blue, that means she is a Mage of all of the magics, not just one paltry element." He marched forward, slamming his broad chest into Les's shoulder. The move tugged brutally on his barely healing wounds, and Les had to concentrate on breathing through the fiery pain for a moment before he could focus back on the goings on in front of him.

Pralick had Blue Eyes in hand again, and was rapidly tying her hands together with a long leather strap as she struggled against him. Les's favorite brown cloak hung off her shoulders, nearly a full two feet of it dragging in the dirt due to their height difference. The loose, flowing garment gaped lewdly in the front now that she could not hold it together, and pale flashes of her delicate breasts and stomach were visible.

Sighing, Les shook his head sadly, "Logic never was your strong suit, Pralick. Everything you said is true; you just haven't figured it all out yet." The brief flash of confused worry on the giant man's face made him feel like gloating, but he continued on. "She *will* be a Mage, once she learns how to use her magic, which she obviously has no idea how to do at the moment. And so, until then, regardless of the *Foraul nu' Groth,* I will be this tribe's head Maegi. And I will be the one to train our little Blue Eyes here, however I see fit."

Pralick's beady eyes narrowed, and a flush of red suffused his face. Fighting back his obvious anger he rounded on Les, causing the girl to tumble to the ground with his abrupt movement. He smiled down at her cruelly, and casually grabbed a metal stake from the debris of his tent. He put one large hoof down on the spread fingers of her right hand and slowly worked the spike through the knots of the leather thong between her wrists. Leaning over put more and more of his weight onto her hand, and Les heard a terrible crackling noise as some of her fingers broke beneath the unforgiving pressure.

The little whimper she let out nearly broke him, but he remained still. The truth of it was that he had no say in her punishments, which were for her *asodin* to decide. But he would need to train her, and during the daylight hours when he was not needed elsewhere she would be in his custody, completely in his control, and safe from Pralick. He just wished the bastard wouldn't have ownership of her every night. Pralick had a sick mind that was far too proficient at twisting his *kurianit* into shells of the women they once were. He had seen it firsthand. He had watched the vibrancy fade from Chrisyne's lovely chocolate gaze, until he barely recognized the fearful creature she became.

Rising from his crouch on Blue Eye's hand Pralick casually backhanded her, leaving her unconscious, sprawled ungracefully in the sandy dirt. Her hands tethered securely to the earth, the cloak tangled around her, baring her odd limbs and the rest of her body for any passerby to see. Facing Les once again Pralick smiled a hard smile, and put into words the fears roaring through Les's mind. "I guess we will just have to see who she listens to after her *Cetrian,*" He nudged her legs farther apart and stooped to run a possessive hand over her rump and between her legs.

"It will be a contest, the same contest I won the last time…Who can train a woman better? Who will she answer to? Who will she obey? The man she fears? Or the man she does not?" His grin was pure poison.

Les watched him walk away, observing the bulk of hard-won muscles sliding underneath his smooth skin as he stooped to retrieve various weapons from the ruins of his belongings. The Morgal had looked like that once, when Les was very young. But now the once smooth skin of his leader hung looser, and the brawny muscles were sinewy rather than bulky. He was a great leader, but he was not young anymore, and Les feared this *Foraul nu' Groth* would be the death of him, and the beginnings of a civil splintering within the tribe.

He knelt next to Blue Eyes and covered her, taking special care that her legs remained hidden, and desperately trying not to let his eyes linger in places they should not be. *If I had fathered any children, they could have been her age by now*, he admonished himself, even as he tucked a lank tendril of soot dark hair back from her face. He untied the water skin from his waist and left it near her bound hands, after grabbing onto Control one more time to right her broken fingers as best as he could with the trickle of magic left inside. He needed time to recover, days if possible, before he could use his magic safely again.

He could only hope she was stronger than Chrisyne, just as he could only hope his friend and Morgal did not die today. If the Morgal won, if he killed this challenger, then the new Mage would be safe. Then his tribe would be safe from falling back into the old ways. But if Pralick triumphed, then all of the hard won victories and revolutions the Morgal had brought to his people would be swallowed by the Bloodhunger again, and Lessoran would be expected to sully the pure light of his magic once more, with the taint of blood.

Sylvia

Was this her life now? She thought dully, as she once again awoke from unconsciousness, wondering where she was, her body hurting. Dried blood flaked off of her face as she grimaced, pulling futilely at her hands which were bound in front of her. She took stock of her surroundings noting with horror that her hands were tethered tightly to the ground, and she was still naked but for the tall Maegi's cloak. Her fingers looked fat and purpley with angry red and white areas where the leather was brutally pinching the skin. The pain emanating from the fingers of her right hand throbbed dully. Strangely, she could still flex the digits that she was positive the Beast had broken before she lost consciousness.

She sat up, the pounding of her concussed head becoming more familiar by the minute. Curled in on herself she was small enough that the cloak shielded her bare bottom from the cold ground and still protected most of the rest of her skin from the chilly wind blowing through camp. But there was not much she could do about the edges of the cloth yawning open at her front when she couldn't move her hands more than six inches from the ground. She shook lightly with shivers and huddled down into herself further.

She was staked out in the area Pralick's tent had been erected, but now it was bare ground strewn with his belongings. She had originally thought she was alone among the forest of skin tents, but tiny movements at her periphery alerted her that she had company in the form of several small children, raggedly dressed in pieced together hides that looked blessedly warm.

"Do any of you have a knife?" They shied back at her accented Layette, eyes going wide, as if they didn't expect her to be able to speak. "Better yet," She addressed the largest child, who seemed the boldest as he moved in closer to her position. "Can you just hand me any one of those knives?"

The gleaming collection of Fen Torman had gifted her with lay scattered amongst the array of pristine weapons that had been revealed as the activities of the morning unrolled a tightly woven rug. The various knives and hand axes stood out in stark contrast to the squalor of the rest of the warrior's effects. They were obviously well cared for, and, if luck had it, incredibly sharp and good for cutting leather. But the large, dark eyes of the children's ringleader did not move from her at her mention of the knives, instead he moved closer still and plopped down a few feet from her.

"*Kurianit* don't speak to children" he said solemnly.

"They do what they are told." Another child chimed in, plunking down behind his cohort. A tiny, androgynous toddler tottered out after the second boy and he pulled the squirming child into his lap absently. The remaining kids seemed unsure of how close to her they could safely get, and remained standing in a rough semicircle behind the two eldest boys.

"Well that's fine then, because I am not a, whatever you just said...A curranit?" She smiled winningly. "My name is Sylvia, and I am just trying to go home to my family. Will you help me get home?" Her voice nearly broke on the last word, *did home even exist anymore? Had it ever existed?* She felt like she had been living this hell for years.

The gathered children shifted uncomfortably, and the first boy shook his head disgustedly. "You will learn." He admonished,

"*Kurianit*. Don't. Speak. To. Children." He spaced the words out carefully as if afraid she did not comprehend their meaning. "They obey. Or they are punished." With a mercurial shift a sudden smile broke out over his serious demeanor and he looked at the gap in her covering pointedly. "Show me your hooves! Jerra says you have funny hooves!"

Syl shrunk in even further, horrified. The kids weren't going to help her, they thought a young woman secured to the ground naked was par for the course. What kind of people were this so called 'tribe'? Earlier she had begun to hope that rescue had arrived and her brutish captor was acting out of the norm. But now the tall Maegi who had interrupted one of the most horrific moments of her entire life was nowhere to be seen, and she was on display like some sideshow for the curiosity of the young tribe members. Tears began to trickle down her cheeks and she was as helpless to stop their flow as she was to escape this hellish hallucination.

The tiny toddler had eyes glued to Sylvia's face, the little face pinched up in a joyous smile, tracking the bright globes of Syl's teary blue eyes. It reached out, cooing, and began to climb from its perch towards Sylvia. The instigator stood and scooped up the youngling as Syl reached her hands out to the toddler as much as her tethers would allow. He shook his dark head once again.

"You will learn. And then you will show me your funny hooves." He leaned in closer, like he was going to impart a very important secret, and as he adjusted the little child on his lean hip he whispered, "Learn fast," his brows quirked up in apprehension and his gaze darted around the clearing in the sea of tents, "as fast as you can." And with that the children melted into the tents, their skins blending in with the stretched hides seamlessly as the entire tableau wavered wetly from the unshed tears welling in her eyes.

Chapter 6

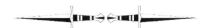

Ryland

He had been standing in front of his father's camp desk for nearly a quarter of an hour, and still his father did not speak. The Jorgen's face was paler than usual. Tension evident in the tight line of his lips and the careful way he sat, with his chest held rigidly upright by the bandages that swathed his left pectoral and shoulder. The wound was not serious, but it was one more reason for him to be angry with his youngest son. He had been forced to release Ryland's magic before the battle was truly over, and had lost the Arrowcatch that would warn him of incoming projectiles which Ryland's magic had been fueling. The Jorgen had faced the decision of releasing Ryland and leaving himself vulnerable, his own magic long used up, or burning out his son's magical capabilities for good. Ryland wasn't sure he was grateful for his father's decision. Life without magic seemed a whole lot safer than an audience with an especially irritable Jorgen.

Ryland tried for patience, knowing it was just the pounding in his head, and the worry that he had not been able to get away to check on Sylvia that was making this wait agonizing. His father wanted him off balance. He was tempted to tell the Jorgen that he needn't have gone to the trouble, his balance had been shoddy since he woke. He had barely been able to stand without additional support as he was led to his father's tent.

After Ryland collapsed, the Jorgen had taken an arrow. And now, Ryland looked at his sire's bowed head, now he worked. He read missives, sent out orders, received reports and decided how to handle each new situation. Each new crisis. Because this was a crisis, Ryland knew, the Hinterland tribes had never attacked this far south. They had never shown anything but a single minded ferocity towards Jorgenholm itself. They would take the opportunity to raid the settlement sprawling outside of the Wall if it seemed easy pickings, if the winter was hard and they needed the supplies. But their true, full throttle attacks, had always been on the Holm itself.

The Jorgen family held a special affinity to the God Garrin, brother to the Hinterlander's God, Freyton. Their battle was in essence a religious war that had been waged for centuries. The Hinterlanders were nomadic, and their obsession with the ancestral home of the Jorgen's had always seemed strange to Ryland. He had done extensive research at the Academy concerning his family's past, and not a single textbook spoke of the Jorgens without mentioning the Hinterlanders also. The two groups were always linked. But the farther back he had looked, the less clear their history had appeared. They had been at war forever, but no matter how deep into the stacks of the Academy Library he had dug, the why's and the how's of the initial quarrel remained a mystery. It had bothered him then, as a puzzle that left his research hanging by a thread, and now, when he had faced these men in battle, when he had seen them die, had his people die by their hands, it seemed a much more practical puzzle that needed figuring out.

He knew some of the secrets of Jorgenholm were only known by the ruling Jorgen. There had been mention of secret passages in one obscure tome written by one of his ancestors nearly a hundred and fifty rebirths past. That same book had also spoken of a secret laboratory, the work-space of some powerful Mage from the Age Before Memory. But it was hard to put any credence in ancient books, especially since that particular Jorgen had a tendency to over-boast about his importance and power. Plus, Ryland mused, he had spent his entire childhood in those halls with his brother and sister, exploring the depths of the Holm from dank underground warrens to dusty attics. He doubted there was a corner of that place that they hadn't explored on their unending quests for adventure, and their frequent gambits to escape their father.

His eyes found his father's dark head again, still bent over the latest missive a messenger from Seaprium had brought into camp. The messenger's eyes had been wide above the garish uniform he wore as he took in the wreckage of the Jorgen camp. He did not envy his father the compulsion to explain what had transpired here to his Majesty. Ryland brought his eyes back to the man in front of him again, fidgeting a little in the silence. *What enigmas hid behind those inky eyes?* Maybe his sire knew of the secrets of their shared history with the Hinterlanders. Maybe that was why he always held such hatred for them. A fury and frustration Ryland and Torman had never understood, or shared. Suddenly out of patience he opened his mouth to ask his father about the strange actions of the Hinterlanders when the Jorgen's harsh voice lashed out across the room, freezing him, mouth still gaping.

"Are you a man yet Ryland? You have weathered your first battle. You had a woman in your bed when the fighting began. But are you truly a man?"

The Jorgen still hadn't lifted his attention from the piles of papers on the camp desk, but Ry could feel his focus trained upon him, and knew without a doubt that answering this question incorrectly would be a grave mistake. He also knew these trivial matters were not what his father was working up to, he was just testing the waters, testing his son, like he had for Ryland's entire life. In the past he had always been found wanting.

"If those are your standards for being a man, then yes I am," he replied cautiously. That was the truth really, Sylvia *had* been in his bed, just not at the same time as him. Thank Garrin for euphemisms. Jorgen had an uncanny knack for sniffing out lies. Torman and he had perfected the art of lie by omission, and the twisting of truth through vague wording, at a young age.

His father finally looked up, and their eyes met. "Because I can respect a man who keeps secrets for his own purposes, as reserves for a future battle," he continued as if Ryland had not spoken, "but I cannot stand a boy who keeps things from his father because he is afraid." Ryland tried to hold his body still as a wave of chills swept up his spine. Jorgen's voice was so cold, so full of loathing. What had he ever done to deserve such disdain? Ryland had only one option. Show his father he was a man, or reap the consequences of being a pawn in his father's eyes for the rest of his life. He would aim for his father's respect. He always had, and always would. But this was the first time in Ryland's memory that it had ever seemed within reach.

"You didn't need to know the full extent of my Control, father," he dredged up the arrogance he had seen in his friends after their return from a whorehouse, he tried to imitate their swagger. "My magic is my own, regardless of your use of it, it is mine alone."

His father's eyes hardened, and the granite expression on his face pulled the skin taut over the wide-set brows and high cheekbones that were mirrored in Ryland's own face, making the Jorgen appear years younger, and eons angrier, as the fine lines of age were brutally smoothed by his intensity. "Wrong" he spat, "Any power within the Jorgen line belongs to the ruling Jorgen, to use as he sees fit, to extinguish if it pleases him." He stood and moved out from behind the desk, facing his son squarely, and Ryland was astonished to find himself looking at his father from an almost equal height. "You are mine, Ryland, do not forget it. This transgression shall be forgotten, but only because I am pleased you have finally shown the merest hint of a backbone. You belong to the Jorgen, whether that is me, or your brother, it matters not. You exist to serve. If you wish to belong to yourself, well then," a mocking smile broke out over his face, and his next words took on the semblance of a dare, "you need to become the Jorgen."

The Jorgen

They would reach Seaprium within the day. It had taken his army, with its tag-along group of nobles, serfs, and traders, an additional four days to make the journey due to injuries and losses during the skirmish with the Hinterlanders. The missives the King sent from the capital were increasingly impatient and angry, making Jorgen wish he could drag his feet even more, just to avoid the childish temper of the monarch. Delay was unavoidable after any battle, and this battle had come completely out of the blue. He knew he was a harsh ruler, but he prided himself on his understanding of what was logically possible. He liked to think that in the King's position he would push for haste, but not unleash unwarranted anger upon his right hand man, when he had done everything in his power to correct an unforeseen flaw. Sometimes life had other plans than the ones Trewal made.

But he was not the King. No, the King was his childhood friend who had never grown out of his childishness. While he had been ruling his lands with an iron fist, his Majesty had been indulging in the Demandron's harem, drowning himself in fine wine and Dreamweed, consuming copious amounts of the dark magic that was harvested within that sinister place.

He was still shaking off the lingering touch of that same magic, which he had used to siphon off his son's power, wielding Ryland's stunningly potent Earth magic against the Hinterlanders when his own had dwindled. He shook his head ruefully. *His son*. He had almost lost hope that either of his offspring would show any hint of the grit and strength of character so prevalent in the Jorgen line. But then he finds his conniving youngest child to be lying to him, and quite convincingly. He allowed a brief flicker of pride to surface before tucking it away again, before the emotion could make itself known on his face.

Ryland rode beside him complacently, a faraway look in his dreamer's eyes. Jorgen had always supposed the child was too lost in his thoughts, too involved in the tomes of times long past. It was a trait he had found endearing in his late wife, but an unseemly devotion for a man. Maybe there were plots and plans floating around in that head which he did not suspect. Maybe ambition was sprouting within, finally a sign of his seed, rather than the womanly caring of his long dead wife. The Jorgens believed the seat of the Holm should be earned. Inheritance did not denote worthiness, which was why in the long history of the Holm nearly every succession was achieved through assassinations, clever politics, or societal traps proving dishonor to the ruling Jorgen, making way for the next hungry son of their ancient lineage.

He would be keeping his youngest child close from now on. To watch him, to examine his motives, and possible attempts at a bid for power within the Holm. In all honesty he was surprised at himself, for the knowledge of his descendant's cleverness and deceit was a welcome element. It filled him with fire and gratification at bringing such a deserving adversary into the world. If his son could overthrow him, he would rejoice from the Afterlife. But that did not mean he wouldn't fight tooth and nail to stay Named as the Jorgen. The kindness of his beloved Cara had been evident in all three of their children from the beginning, regardless of how he tried to harden his sons after her death, and that component would make

Ryland a leader loved by his people; but it was the Jorgen's cunning, hard hearted mind which would allow his son to make the hard choices, sacrifice willingly, and demand loyalty like a truly great leader needed to be able to do.

The air was crisp and salty here near the coast. The sting of Autumn in the Skypeaks tempered by the warm air riding the tide in from Saerin. He could taste the faintest hint of fish on the air, a sure sign that they neared the Palace by the Sea, Prium's seat of power. The city sprawled for miles, and the smell of the myriad types of fish that were caught and sold in its bay could be found everywhere except in the manically polished palace itself.

The King wanted his army to set sail within the week, in order to use the darkness of the moons on the solstice to raid the shores of the Sareth Isles. *But why this fixation on the Isles?* He wondered. They were rich in many things, but trade across the Blitherly sea was prolific, the commerce beneficial to not only the people of the Isles, but also to the entire Kingdom of Prium. Goods and items not found on the mainland made their way from the Isles to port in Seaprium and then were dispersed throughout Prium. Along with the more traditional stock from the tropical Isles came the even rarer, exotic artifacts brought West by the smattering of brave merchants who traversed the Galeshorn Ocean from the unknown lands beyond. The tight lipped traders spoke in broken Layette to sell their wares, dealing only with the Merchant Triad, the three wealthiest trading families in Saerin.

The treasures of Sareth were many, from basic metals and minerals to the fantastical jewels mined from the catacombs beneath Mount Qee. The tropics of the island produced exotic fruits the gentry in the Palace by the Sea consumed by the bushel. The skins of the mysterious creatures dwelling within the steaming depths of those same jungles set the trends and pushed the boundaries of exotic fashion among the elite living in the capital of Prium. Trade had been good, relations even better, with the offspring of each royal family coming of an age to marry. He himself had met the King and Queen of Saerin when they had crossed the sea to formally sign the marriage contract, and had seen the strength of character in the foreign monarchs. The future had looked bright with a marriage to cement the two nations together as one extended family. But the King, damn him, had gotten greedy. In all negotiations the Saerin royalty had outright refused to pay into the Demandron's harems with the children of their land, no matter the benefits of the magic pulled from the suffering therein. They wanted no part in the dark magics of the Circle, and instead of parleying for an acceptable compromise, his damned fool cousin Gartlan was throwing it all away by taking what he wanted without permission.

The Reedwood forest thinned around his forces and ahead of them a long spit of land jutted out into the Blitherly Sea. In the mists from the water he could just make out the sprawling mass of the city proper, and the dark smudges of the shantytowns inhabited by the common folk snaking outwards from that more solid mass. Above the fog, bright purple and green pennants flew from the multitude of clean white spires sprouting from the main bulk of the Palace, announcing the presence of the Royal family, and the Galmorish forces from the south. Soon the blood red banners of Jorgenholm would fly from the heights alongside the others.

Jorgen loosed the stranglehold he had on the reins. With a lessening of his rider's tension the Galmorish stallion he rode calmed his flighty prance back into the smooth gate the breed was known for. With a deep breath he tried to shed the build of frustration, striving for serenity. He would need it to face the King in an hours' time. It was not often that he had to leash his temper, being the ultimate authority within the bounds of Jorgenholm. But he had a sick feeling about this trip to the capital, and that feeling taking root in the pit of his stomach bade him use caution. Something deeper was affecting the currents of the nobility, something large and dark was stirring the social waters of Prium and he was astonished to find it bringing to life within him the faint tinge of fear.

Ryland

The view from the bathing tub upon the raised dais was opulent in ways he had never seen living in the Holm and the sparse dormitories of the Academy. The room he had been shown to upon their arrival at the Palace by the Sea was covered in Jorgen red, from the thick velvet drapes at the windows overlooking the Blitherly Sea, to the gauzy red hangings which could be pulled around the entirety of the massive four poster bed. Even the intricate carvings on the bed frame and headboard had been embellished with the blood red of Jorgenholm. The eyes of each hunting hound shone baleful red, while the lithe body of the *flaix* that the hounds were pursuing in gory detail throughout the carvings was finely shaded in beautiful shades of crimson. He wondered if the King kept rooms decorated in the colors of Jorgenholm and Galmorah all year round, or if the room had been decorated to his family's colors when word of their arrival came. The faint reek of oil paint beneath the cloying smell of incense made him think the room had been modified recently.

A young serf approached the tub with another pitcher of steaming water to rinse his hair of the dust from the road. He tried not to stare at the girl's nearly diaphanous shift as she stretched her arms above her to pour the water for him. Her attire did not leave much to the imagination; the sweet blue of the thin material was so light that dusky nipples were just visible through the cloth. He had barely managed to keep her modesty intact, at least from him. He had not, as of yet, glanced to see if other, equally dark, secret areas of her body were on similar display.

Many of the female serfs he had seen while treading through the halls of the Palace had on the same exhibitionist uniform, leading him to believe that it was the designated attire of all the chambermaids within the Palace. After that startling epiphany, for the first time in many days, he was glad Sylvia had vanished. The Palace staff might have tried to dress her in one of those see-through excuses for a dress, and then the game would have been up. The strange angles of her legs, and her feet themselves would have been far too conspicuous beneath the flowing garment. It would have been discovered she was not all she seemed to be.

The young woman stepped back and set her pitcher upon the shelf near the tub, picking up a soft cloth and complacently asking, eyes still on the floor, "May I wash your back my lord?"

"I can manage on my own, thank you," he replied, before quickly lowering his face into the water as she approached to hand him the washcloth. The apex of the girl's thighs was at the same level as his head as he sat in the tub. She held the cloth out to him with a small smile on her face. He groped blindly for the cloth, which the smiling serf stubbornly held in the same place, just before her, until he gave up and used his eyes to find the proffered item. His gaze got caught, without his consent, on the slim body visible through the gathered cloth, just behind the washcloth she was so innocently offering him. *Trollit! I told myself I wouldn't look!* He chastised himself, dunking his flaming face back into the rapidly cooling water of his bath.

With a soft titter he heard the serf turn and exit his rooms. He heaved in a breath gratefully, glad to be truly alone for the first time in nearly twenty days. *No, not glad, not truly.* He wished Sylvia was here, just so he would know for sure, one way or the other, if she still lived. He had grown to rely on her lightening his foul moods in the evenings, after dealing with his father each day her genuine curiosity and quick wit was just the distraction he needed. He had been looking forward to showing her about Seaprium and the King's Academy, seeing the big city through her eyes would have been rewarding. She always seemed to pick up on details that slid past his familiar gaze, and asked questions that had him pausing to reevaluate everything he thought he knew.

But she wasn't here, she wouldn't even want to be, with him sitting naked in his bath, ogling the chambermaid! He shook his head at himself once more. He was tired of his body's endless fascination with the female form, tired of the blushing and embarrassment. He could barely interact with a pretty girl without turning into a bumbling fool when his mind inevitably wandered. He wished the whole ordeal was over with already. He wanted to snap his fingers and not be a virgin anymore, but without having to be witness to his own fumbling, insecure actions, the love making of a rank amateur.

But here he is again, his mind in the gutter when he had so many other things to think about. So many important, dire things. There had been no sign of Sylvia, nothing to tell him what had happened to her other than his shredded tent. No blood. No tracks. Just shredded canvas on two sides of their little haven. But every time he allowed himself to hope, logic asserted itself and he knew if she still lived she would have found him during the delay after the fight. Which meant she was either dead, or taken by the

Hinterlanders, which could, in actuality, mean the same thing either way.

He had failed. Failed to protect her fragile beauty in this world of his, the one she didn't belong in, the one that was trying to kill her at every turn. He was at a loss for how to tell Torman and Camus. He had received Torman's letter early in the day, the messenger had reported to the Jorgen's tent first, and then slipped the tightly rolled parchment to Ryland with a wink and a grin as he exited the Jorgen's presence. While the letter had been written and signed in his brother's hand he could tell from the wording that Camus had had a say in its construction. It was brilliant really, seemingly a normal correspondence between brothers who cared about one another deeply.

My dearest brother Ryland,

I truly hope this letter finds you, my favorite young friend, in good health. When I learned of the attack; so many innocents dead! So many of our young serfs taken! I was immediately concerned for your health and safety. I wonder if our Lord Father will be keeping a close eye on you during your time in the Capital? I fear the trouble you could get into if you return to your previous haunt in the King's Academy.

If you do end up back in that Library, it may be wise to keep better track of time than you used to. Maybe Lana could find a chambermaid willing to accompany you, despite the boredom she will no doubt endure. That way you will have someone there to measure the hours you have wasted among those ancient tomes.

I would like to keep a regular correspondence going between us while you are away. One of the Holm messengers, Chir, has informed me that it would be of no trouble to him to carry an extra letter when he next returns to the Holm. That said, please write to reassure me of your good health, and to let me know of the going's on in Seaprium.

Ever Yours,

Torman

Ryland could read between the lines. He knew Torman was desperate for information on Sylvia's wellbeing, and also worried about the two of them poking about in the Academy Library, looking at the oldest of all the old books, and the attention that may garner. Still dripping from his bath Ryland wrapped a large towel around his hips, marveling again at the blood red color of the bathing accessories, and slightly worried the lurid tint would rub off onto his skin. He wandered the room, finding both parchment and ink in the delicate writing desk that lay opposite the colossal bed. Thinking hard, he began to draft a letter to his brother.

Brother Torman,

I am, indeed, in good personal health. I made it through the battle at our father's side, and fared no worse than a headache from my prodigious use of magic. I mourn desperately for the losses we suffered that day, and sometimes I feel at a loss for what to do next. I find myself wishing you were here in Seaprium also, to lend me support.

As for a serf to accompany me to tell the time, I hope you find it amusing that I actually asked Lana for such a girl, and she was unable to find one. She mentioned she could think of only one young chambermaid who would have happily accompanied me, but sadly, she was among the missing after the Hinterland attack near the Crossroads. Alas, I shall be venturing into the Library alone.

Our father will indeed be keeping me close while we reside in the Palace, I do believe he fears for me, after seeing me in action during the battle. Sometimes I fear he will want to keep me so close, for my own protection of course, that I will not have the time to lose myself in the Library! Hopefully matters of state will soon consume his energy and I will be left to find diversions more suited to my nature than politics.

I know you will be writing Father to keep him apprised of the activities within the Holm, but please, continue to pen a word or two of our home to me, I crave knowledge of our home and your safety. With the Hinterlanders showing such initiative I worry about my brother and loved ones within Jorgenholm.

Ever Yours,

Ryland

There! He finished his signature with a flourish. The letter read benignly enough, and he was sure Camus at least would understand Sylvia had disappeared after the conflict with the Hinterlanders. He also had tried to convey how at a loss he was for how to proceed. His father kept him firmly at his side ever since their conversation in his tent following the skirmish. Ryland did not foresee that being any different now they had reached the capital. Even if he found the time away from the Jorgen to research Sylvia's predicament in the Library, how would he be able to help her? How could he tell Torman and Camus whatever arcane secrets he unearthed, or where Sylvia's home lay, through a simple letter that was likely going to be read by their enemies? All the codes and ciphers he and Torman knew they had been taught by their father, and with the distance between them too far for Camus to farscry, working out a code was all but impossible.

There was a soft knock on the door and the serf from earlier entered the room subserviently, "Would my lord like help readying for dinner? All guests must be seated before the King attends."

From the girl's slight agitation Ryland surmised he was running late and he gladly accepted her help. The dress doublet his father had requisitioned for him upon learning they would journey to the capital was form fitting, with laces running part of the way up his lower back, a design which made it impossible to do up himself. He missed the more comfortable dress of the Holm, finding the current trends here in Seaprium restrictive and ridiculous. He remained lost in thought as he dressed and followed the pretty serf through the halls to the dining chamber. The wonders of the Palace by the Sea slid by unnoticed as his mind was consumed once more with visions of what could be happening to Sylvia at this very moment. The pale stones of the Palace floors were covered in thick carpets throughout the halls that connected to the guests' chambers, so not even their footsteps were loud enough to disturb his turbulent thoughts, or the horrible deeds being done to his friend in his mind.

The Jorgen

After the formal supper, a quiet affair which his Majesty failed to attend, he was escorted to the King's personal study in the easternmost tower of the Palace. His childhood companion stood with his back to the door as Jorgen entered, facing the huge, floor to ceiling windows of the room. *The glass for these showy windows alone must have cost more than it would to feed the entire Holm for a month,* he noted angrily. The sun was setting over the Blitherly Sea, bathing the round study in rose, tinging the white stone of the Palace to a delicate pink.

Gartlan's shadow stretched long over the thick carpeting, a dark bar in the otherwise illuminated room. The King turned towards him and smiled a sickly sweet smile at his cousin, crossing the room with arms outstretched to engulf the Jorgen in an overlong embrace. "Cousin! How my heart sings to see your face! You have been too long hidden away in those cold mountains, I should have ordered your presence here years ago if just to ease my yearning for your company," he jested falsely.

Jorgen executed a formal courtier's bow, just low enough to appease the haughty monarch, but not an inch more. "Your Majesty, I apologize for our late arrival, extenuating circumstance delayed us, as you must know."

"Ah yes, your mountain barbarians. Decided to have a little going away battle did they? I hope you spanked them and sent them back to their frigid peaks with their tails between their legs!" The King guffawed loudly, clapping the Jorgen on the back and leading him to a pair of chairs placed before a neatly laid fire in the mammoth hearth. "Have some wine old friend, tell me of the goings on in the mountainous regions of my realm. All the dirty details mind you, I want to know everything! All the fucking and fighting, all of it!"

Jorgen settled into the wing backed chair, resting his head on the high back to ease his tired neck muscles. Riding always made him ache these days, a common occurrence in middle aged Trewal males as the hefty weight of their antlers became cumbersome after hours of jostling on horseback. The King busied himself pouring wine as red as blood from a crystal decanter laying on the small table between them, giving the Jorgen time to study the face of the man he once thought he knew as well as he knew himself. Gartlan's eyes were over-bright, pupils huge and dark in the light spilling from the fireplace and the dying sunlight, nearly overtaking the russet of his irises. The skin of his neck hung looser than he remembered, gravity pulling down on the skin to form a wattle beneath the royal chin, a chin that seemed permanently thrust out in a petulant sulk that would have been more fitting on a young child.

Ruling has not been kind to you cousin, he thought to himself as his eyes picked up more signs of softening and age in the man before him. Twinkling rings crusted with sapphires and rubies hung loose on his fingers, singing as they clicked gently against the crystal he poured from. As Jorgen inhaled, the faint stench of Dreamweed reached his nostrils, accounting for the guileless look in Gartlan's wide eyes, and the pallor of his skin. He nearly shook his head in disappointment. What a ruin of a once bright man, destroyed by overindulgence and ease. He was appalled to think that the creature before him was his blood. The thought that the skinny King was one and the same with the hearty lad Jorgen had once known was disheartening to say the least.

"The Holm stands strong." He stated simply, "My eldest fortifies the Keep against the Hinterland tribes as we speak, as per my instructions, and they have made no further attacks upon us other than the skirmish in the Reedwood forest. My youngest is here in the palace, I shall be keeping the boy close so I can continue his magical training, along with instructing him on the ways of the court."

The King rolled his eyes expressively, "Same old Jorgen, all facts, no details to liven it up. Fine! If you don't want to catch up, *friend,* we will get down to it." His voice lost its jolliness, becoming brisk and businesslike, bordering on unfriendly "There is much to be done, and little time to do it in. I need you to clear up a few…

unpleasantries, here in the capital, and then you will sail for Saerin, and war. I wish you to lead the Imperial army," he said, referencing the conjoined forces of Seaprium, Galmorah and Jorgenholm.

"What of the betrothal?" Jorgen asked, still aiming to talk Gartlan out of his planned war with the Isles.

"What of it?" The man spat, "It stands still, and I will honor it! My Fragon will wed that Sareth whore, as soon as I behead her parents! Then the islanders will have a new queen, one who will belong to *my* son. We will buy the loyalty of her subjects by letting her remain in 'power' and they will submit to our rule without question!"

Jorgen wiped spittle from his cheek, keeping his distaste firmly in check and his face outwardly calm. "Why waste resources fighting when you will have the same scenario if you wait but ten years? The King of Saerin is old and will die, leaving your son to rule the Isles. You only have to wait. Or if you must push the time line, wed your son to their daughter and then conceal an assassin among his personnel, poison the King and Queen if you desire their deaths sooner than the Gods decide." He fought his temper down fiercely, striving for a calm and even manner, but some of the fire of his temper slipped through as he spoke. "Patience is hard to practice, but often the greatest weapon in the game of politics!"

Silence fell upon the pristine study as the King glared, his eyes seeming clear of the Dreamweed for the first time that night, as if his ire had burned the last traces of the drug from his system. Jorgen glared back, finally releasing the stranglehold he had been keeping on his temper and letting his anger shine through in all its hard glory. Seconds ticked by and neither man backed down, a silent battle of wills was taking place, one which could affect the fate of two kingdoms.

Slowly the King's face fell into friendlier lines, until he gave a small chuckle, thawing his cousin's grim countenance also. Soon the men were laughing wholeheartedly, savoring the untouched wine in their glasses now the initial tension was broken. "You always were a straight shooter," the King said, "and it never failed to piss me off! The games of subterfuge are played for a reason, Jorgen, and you are just too blunt for your own good sometimes. It's no wonder you spend all your time hiding in the mountains. You would be fighting a duel a week living in the Palace." They chuckled some more, helping themselves to more of the wine, a dry red, imported from the hilly fringes of the Sacred Plains.

"I am aware of the need for patience cousin," the King continued, "but there are things you are *not* aware of which lead me to these hasty actions. I know you think me a fool, but things are not always what they seem in the capital. There are currents and powers playing here that are likely to tear this kingdom apart if I do not act."

Gartlan's words bore an uncanny resemblance to his own thoughts of dark currents as he rode towards the deceptively pristine Palace by the Sea earlier in the day. The coincidence sent a shiver down the Jorgen's spine. At his continued silence the King began to look uncomfortable, as if he regretted his dramatic statement. Jorgen spoke abruptly when he saw the King draw breath to speak again, "Tell me Gartlan" he used the King's former name in hope of eliciting some of the closeness they had shared before he had been Named King. "Tell me what drives you to these extreme measures. The city does not want this war; the people do not want this war. I could hear the fearful whispers and angry words from nearly every commoner's mouth on the ride through the outer city. Help me to understand so I can be the Captain of the Imperial Navy in truth, rather than another mindless minion." The King's mouth opened and closed multiple times before he was able to find the right words to continue with.

"No." His face fell into a sad smile, "I know what you ask, and I wish I could give it. But times are not what they used to be. We are not *who* we used to be. But know that I wish we were. What I wouldn't give to be Gartlan and Dourith again, before we were Named, before the world went mad, plotting our rise to power in the hidden corners of Jorgenholm." The King straightened in his chair, finishing off the wine in his goblet with a flourish. "But some loyalties are mightier than blood, and some duties must be performed regardless of what you, or my subjects, think of them, Jorgen."

The King stood and ushered Jorgen towards the door, "Enough of catching up, you need rest after your journey. We will convene with the Circle on the morrow and clear up those few tasks I have for you and your son. Then the War Council will meet." The King's saccharine smile was back, his pallid face once more a mask that effectively hid the boy Jorgen once knew from view. The Jorgen looked back through the open door of the study as he made his slow way to the stairs, to see a cloud of gray-blue smoke curling around the King's thin antlers as the monarch faced the vast Sea once again.

Ryland

They had been in the capital for six days already, and the only time he was not forced to his father's side was when the War Council met, which he was never invited to join, and after dark when his father retired to his chambers. The infrequent freedom had left him little time to research in the Library, but at least he could be honest with his desires to visit his old home with no one the wiser for his true reasons. Those who studied at the Academy often wished to return. Some never left at all. It was the greatest center of learning and largest collection of knowledge in the known world other than Saerin's famed University. Anyone with a scholar's heart longed for time there. His father dismissed his frequent pleas for a visit to the Library as boyish yearnings, and forbade him from wasting time there when he had so much to learn of magic and court politics.

Ryland sat stiffly on a richly brocaded chair that faced the delicately decorated sitting room of one Lady Elaine Herrion, a girl who looked about two rebirths his junior, fair of hair and as vapid as anyone he had ever known. He made her acquaintance at dinner his first night in the Palace, as they had been seated next to one another. He had been pushed into her company at every opportunity since. How his father arranged for the War Councils to take place at the exact same times as the court's insipid meet and greets he didn't know. But unfailingly, when the Jorgen took his leave of his youngest he would order him to attend one of the court's events; recitals, plays, balls, or social hours, where he would be beset upon by the Lady Elaine.

She was unshakable. He had at first tried subtlety, a polite disinterest in her, to try to escape her clutches. But she followed him everywhere he went, joined every conversation he was a part of and intercepted him each time he tried to make an escape. He had begun to think his father had employed the damnable woman as a spy, to keep tabs on him when he could not. Her thin face haunted his dreams. The big green eyes wide, her rosebud lips endlessly moving, but only a high pitch whine audible, the powder so thick upon her hawk-like nose that even her endearing freckles were covered up.

She turned to him now, vacant, pale green eyes lighting upon his nearly empty wineglass, "Why Lord Ryland! I do apologize for the poor service you are receiving; I'm embarrassed your glass has remained empty!" She exclaimed brightly, only to level a furious glare at a nearby serf attired in her family's colors of deep maroon and buttery yellow.

He covered the rim of his goblet quickly as the serf approached in a rush at her master's overly loud exclamation. "No please, I don't need more wine. You have no need to be embarrassed, I have not been accepting the refills your serf has proffered," he offered quickly, glad to see the brief flash of relief his words brought to the round face of the young woman who had been chastised by Elaine's words.

Elaine's green eyes zeroed in on the wordless communication between Ryland and her serf and her painted lips pinched together tightly, white lines appearing unattractively at the pressure. "Well she failed to refill my glass!" She snapped shrewishly, thrusting her mostly full goblet beneath the poor girl's nose. Ryland sighed, he was constantly amazed at how poorly the nobility in Seaprium treated the serfs under their protection. The serfs of Jorgenholm were indentured servants, bound to the Holm and subject to whatever use was required of them, but he knew they were important members of the household, performing essential duties. They were treated accordingly by everyone in the Holm. With respect at least, if not always kindness. He sighed again as the Lady Elaine launched into yet another comparison of her favorite flowers and the benefits or shortcomings of each. His mind wandered as her voice whined on.

The previous night, he had passed by his father's room while making his way back to his own chambers to change, after spilling wine on his doublet. The Jorgen and a stern, matronly woman had been visiting in his father's sitting room, the door left open as was proper when a lady of the court was unaccompanied in the presence of a nobleman. As he trudged by, slowly so he could delay his return to the mind numbingly boring recital he had left, Ryland had caught his name on the lips of the strange woman.

"Jorgen, my dear, do you think it wise to keep your Ryland in the dark concerning this matter? I see the wisdom of keeping the happy news from the court until we wish it to be known, but surely you may trust your own son to stay quiet? It hurts my dear Elaine's heart that he treats her like any other young lady in the court because he knows not that they are betrothed!"

The words themselves were of the politest sort, but the venom and disdain in the woman's voice were unmistakable. She was there to demand the Jorgen tell his son, not to plead with him. Her voice was sure, the words crisp, and not a hint of embarrassment tinged her melodic speech. She had no doubts her wishes would be carried out.

The few sentences she had uttered brought him to a sudden, heart pounding halt in the plush hall. Betrothed. *Betrothed? He couldn't be betrothed! Not before his brother!* While not necessarily a rule, the eldest married first. Maybe she had mixed the two brothers up and was actually referring to Torman. His frantic mind searched for a way out of the net those few words suddenly cast about him. But she had said Elaine, and there was only one Elaine he knew, the girl who, mere minutes before, had been so enthusiastically talking to him that she had bumped the hand holding his wine glass and sloshed the ruby red liquid onto the newest doublet his father had commissioned for him from the Palace seamstress.

Upon his return to the recital he had paid closer attention to the words the Lady Elaine spoke, reading behind the lines to see the excited young girl behind. After each bout of quiet which reigned while a new debutante took the stage with their chosen tale or spoken ballad to tell, with varying degrees of success, Elaine would grip his arm and chatter away. She fancied herself a master of love, and spoke often of the glorious union of marriage with such guileless hope in her glassy eyes. Previously he thought all young ladies of the court were this intent on marriage and had read no further into her topic of choice. But after the snippet of conversation he overheard, her talk of table settings and whom she would want as her ladies in waiting felt like nails being driven into his coffin.

Since then he had done some quiet investigating among the serfs of the Palace, who, in general, seemed both surprised and a little thrilled he chose to speak to them as individuals rather than simply demanding obedience or information. From the cooks in the kitchen he learned of supply requisitions almost fit for a royal wedding, even though everyone in the realm knew that Prince Fragon would wed the Saerin Princess on Saerin soil in the spring.

The young girl apprenticed to the seamstress, her rosy cheeks endlessly smiling as she dropped off yet another stiffly starched outfit for him, happily told him of the unusually large amount of white and gold embroidered brocade she had been asked to commission from the weavers. Sparkling emerald eyes seemed to laugh at him as she peeked up from her properly lowered stare to add with a chuckle that the amount of white silk her master had purchased from Galmorah was also in excess of the usual court wedding season.

The more serfs he spoke to the more he realized that while he had been in the dark, most of the Palace was already aware the King had arranged for the youngest of the Jorgen's children to marry the daughter of the most disgruntled of his noble subjects, the honorable councilman Tager Herrion. The betrothal was a move engineered in order to gain support for the war with Saerin. A marriage tie with one of the most powerful families in Prium like the Jorgens was highly sought after, and afforded the family joining the Jorgen line a huge rise in status and power here in Seaprium. Unfortunately, *he* happened to be the youngest son of the ruling Jorgen, and the simpering maid whose sitting room he currently decorated, was destined to be his lady wife.

Ryland had been raised with the knowledge that his marriage would be arranged, regardless of his feeling on the matter. His mind flickered briefly to Sylvia, wishing that the young woman sitting with him held even half the allure of his human friend, and then gently, but deliberately, he pushed her image from his mind. He had been ill prepared for the actuality of his marriage as he had always figured Torman would get married first. Looking at the situation now he knew he should have been warier, the Jorgen and Torman had been fighting about marriage for the last five rebirths, ever since Torman first asked permission to marry his lover Metra, a commoner employed at the Holm as an agriculturist. Metra could grow anything, aided as she was by her Earth magic, and her Windthorn roses of astonishing color and scent sold at top price throughout the realm. But she was still a commoner for all of her worth. Jorgen had refused on the grounds that the first son's duty to the Holm was to marry a noblewoman of good stock, and to carry on the peerless line of the Jorgen's. His father insisted the Jorgen line would not be polluted with common blood on his watch, no matter how worthy the girl may be.

Elaine's voice broke through to him suddenly, her question eerily paralleling his own thoughts about Metra as she asked, "The Windthorn roses, the ones with that divine smell, aren't those grown in Jorgenholm dear Ryland? I do love how they smell, and their color! So unique, but they never last as long in my vases as the Galmorish Lily, or the Datura and trumpet vines we get from Saerin! Oh how I wish I could get my hands on a shipment of those when I wed!" Her slightly sweaty face beamed at him, the sheen of perspiration clumping the powder on her nose in the crowded and overly warm room.

"The Windthorns are from Jorgenholm" he agreed politely, "Our agriculturist Metra bred them for those very attributes. It was a long effort to create blooms that both smelled as they do and looked beautiful. It is likely they do not last as long because of the journey they have to make to the capital, it is a longer one than from Galmorah, or even from Saerin if the ship is a swift one."

"Well, living in Jorgenholm must be so lovely then! Fresh roses in every room!" Elaine exclaimed slyly, slanting a coy look his way. He winced, maybe she was smarter than he was giving her credit for, her comments seemed innocuous enough, but with the knowledge he had gained from his eavesdropping, conversations with her had been taking on new meanings. "Tell me about your home Ryland, is it true the Greathall of Jorgenholm is as large as the

Palace banquet hall? And are their truly Ice lions roaming close enough for you to see them from the Keep?" She asked with a delicate shudder.

He kept up the inane conversation with half his attention, while letting his mind wander back to Metra and Torman. The arguments between his father and brother had been harsh and frequent the first few years, making marriage a topic nearly everyone in the Holm was afraid to broach when either man was near. The strangest part to Ryland about the family feud, was how adamant his sire was, even though he, much like his oldest, had exhibited a soft spot for the talented Metra. Before his sister Fria had been taken by the Demandron she had tried to explain to a young Ryland why their father was so against his son marrying a woman he obviously respected. But to his young mind the puzzle had never made sense. Metra was a beautiful woman, kind and compassionate to the serf and common children alike, who aided her in the gardens. Her smile lit up the Holm much like the peaceful scent of her Windthorn roses perfumed the air, making everything seem lighter and brighter for her presence. He knew she would make a fine wife for his brother, and a proficient wife of the Jorgen when his brother eventually took that name. But his father denied the request to this day.

There was a stir in the sitting room as a group of new guests entered the already populated room, and Elaine let her words trail off as Ryland's father made a beeline for her and his son. The girl shrank back as the Jorgen's powerful presence seemed to draw the oxygen from the room. He looked at Ryland commandingly, sketching a perfunctory bow to his host before locking his onyx eyes on his son and saying in his gravelly voice, "Please pardon my son Lady Elaine, I have need of him. Ryland, come with me, we have matters to discuss." He was already walking away as he finished speaking, sure Ryland would follow dutifully after. With a quick word of farewell, and a bow to his betrothed, Ryland grudgingly did.

The Jorgen

His son trailed after him in the hall leading to their chambers, his long strides kept time with Jorgen's swift pace easily, making him grind his teeth in irritation. Not so long ago the boy would have been half running to keep up with his father's longer legs, but time was gifting his youngest with well-muscled legs and a powerful, if lean, frame that would likely dwarf his own in a few years. Jorgen's smallish stature had always been a sore point, and the fact that his sons were both going to outgrow him did not sit well. He had been pleased when he first met Cara's father, a giant Galmorish Councilman who easily topped him by a foot, happy to have such genetics for his offspring, but now that the Galmorish blood was beginning to show in Ryland he found himself cursing that large jovial man for giving his sons what his own line had not provided to him.

He pushed the door to his chambers open with more force than necessary and winced slightly as the heavy wood crashed into the pale stone of the wall behind it. Schooling his face to stillness he breathed deeply, once, twice, searching for his self-control. This whole place set him on edge, with its pretty surfaces barely concealing the fetid filth running behind. Ryland shut the door softly behind them and turned to him, an obstinate look on his face, one that set Jorgen's teeth to grinding again.

"Did you bring me here to tell me of my betrothal father?" Ryland said mildly, even as the red of anger flushed his face.

That would never do, the child must learn to control his features! "Do not dishonor yourself by taking that tone with me boy, your face betrays you. If you are angry be angry, own it. If you wish to play games, then at least have the forethought to learn how to do it in both voice and body." He said harshly, tucking away the surprise he felt at his son's knowledge of the agreement he had made with the King to think upon in privacy.

"Fine" Ryland spat, "How dare you not consult me, how *dare* you withhold knowledge which directly concerns me!" The red spread down from his cheeks to flush through his neck, contrasting luridly with the blue of his doublet.

The Jorgen smirked in satisfaction at his son's loss of control. Ryland still had much to learn. This absurd marriage would be an excellent teaching platform for his youngest, however much they both despised the union. The King had him backed him into a corner, he could not openly defy the throne without dire repercussions to his lands and peoples, along with his standing in the court. In these times of war his standing was possibly even more important than his other responsibilities. If only he could sway enough of the powerful nobles in Seaprium to oppose this unwarranted attack on the Isles! He had been forced to agree to this marriage to keep any hope of that end alive.

The Jorgen strove for the opposite of the heat of his son's temper, making his voice ring out icily with his next words, "You didn't need to know. Now you do. You will marry Elaine Herrion in two weeks' time, securing her family's support for the King, and with it the many lesser families who are tied to their line. And then, according to the King's plans, if he has the majority support of the Council, we sail to war." The Jorgen paused gravely, "The Herrions are a powerful family, their influence may be just what I need, Ryland" he said, trying to impart the importance of the marriage.

Ryland gaped like a fish, and his eyes began to bulge as he failed to take in air. Finally, he sputtered, "And you think I didn't need to know this? You think the first impression I make on the woman who will be my wife is unimportant? How can I marry when Torman has not? How can you possibly expect me to act accordingly if you don't tell me what to expect?" The questions built and built, and Jorgen let them stack up carelessly, knowing Ryland would eventually run out of breath and think about it logically. "...I am not a horse to be sold! An asset used to tie an unruly noble to your old friend the King!" He finished, gasping in the breath his long string of queries had denied him.

"Are you finished? I would like to think we can discuss this as men rather than have you scream your petulance at me until you can barely draw breath." He saw Ryland's mouth snap shut with some measure of pleasure before he turned to take a seat in one of the armchairs sitting before the cold fireplace. He rarely returned to his rooms before the evening, so the staff had not bothered to light it, he saw approvingly, at least some people in this damned Palace knew how to do something other than needlessly waste.

"It is a necessary arrangement; one the King has asked for as a personal favor. And it is the wisest course of action I can see now that I know the state of the court here in Seaprium." He conceded to

Ryland's plea for knowledge, then added sternly, "You *are* my asset to use as I please, Ryland. Your marriage was never to be anything other than a tool. Now I have used it. What you make of the rest of your marriage is up to you." He strove for a gentler tone as his sharp gaze picked up the tattered edge of despair in his son, "I hope you come to find some amount of happiness in it. But it is done."

Silence fell in the chilly room as father examined son. He did want his son to be happy. He knew he had been fortunate in the woman his own father had arranged for him to marry. Cara had brought a light to his life that he had never experienced before, and had never seen since her death. They had grown from strangers into a united front through their marriage. He hoped that same light and companionship would touch his son's life; he had been made better for it, and was now all the stronger since its passing. Ryland's head finally came up and he straightened in his seat grimly.

"Am I to sail to Saerin with you?" He addressed the other life changing scrap of information the Jorgen had loosed in the room.

"Yes," he said, feeling an uncomfortable surge of pride as he watched the young man visibly pull himself together and harden his exterior to the torrent of emotion that had been evident in him just minutes before. "The betrothal will be announced to the court at dinner tonight. You will be seated with Elaine; I suggest you dress appropriately for the amount of attention that will be focused on you two this evening. You will be approached by the entire court as they wish you well. Have you any questions of etiquette?"

Ryland paused, mentally scrolling through the dog eared pages of one of the large tomes of etiquette he had been assigned to read in his studies. Then his bright eyes focused back on the Jorgen, their disquiet now the only visible sign of his earlier upset. "No, father," he said as he stood. He gave a short bow which slightly muffled his next words, "If there is nothing else, I would leave you to prepare."

Jorgen took to his feet also, grudgingly bowing in response to his son's sudden formality. "Ryland, you must know that the commoners and many of the merchant families do not want this war. Once the announcement is made everyone in the city will link you and your lady wife to the start of this attack, and it will not make you any friends." Ryland's face remained blank at the statement and the Jorgen sighed in disgust, *did the boy not understand that he was warning him of potential danger?* "You must not venture anywhere alone, especially outside the city. If this wedding can be stopped, the war may just come to a halt also." He let the words hang in the air darkly until Ryland gave a curt nod, as the boy turned to leave he had a worried look on his face, much to the Jorgen's satisfaction.

He stood there long after Ryland shut the door behind him with a firm click. *How did he know about the betrothal?* he wondered. In his negotiations with Tager Herrion they had both agreed on the need for secrecy until the details were hammered out, and Tager had the time to secure his followers on and off the Council. If he announced a sudden marriage to the King's closest ally the many lesser nobles who had begun to flock to him due to his resistance to the King's warmongering would likely throw their support behind someone else. So they had agreed to their terms, and kept the contract under wraps until Tager had a chance to speak to every one of his cohorts, to wean them onto the idea of war with Saerin. Only now that a sufficient number had proclaimed their continued alliance were he and the Herrions free to announce the betrothal of Elaine and Ryland to the entirety of the court.

But how had Ryland stumbled on this information? His son continued to surprise him with his wiles, even as he made him despair with his soft manner and passive ways. The dual emotions of elation and foreboding irked him to no end and he wished to be on even footing with his youngest son, rather than this uneven landscape they had reached as Ryland edged into manhood. Torman had not been so difficult. The older boy had never given him anything to be proud of other than his strong body and competence as a warrior, which were traits to be expected rather than praised. Torman had challenged the Jorgen at every turn, but never with the intelligence and forethought that Ryland now was. Torman came at a problem head on and tried to knock it down with brute strength of will, an attack the Jorgen could easily counter. Ryland, however, was coming at things from a direction he could not seem to anticipate, and that made him dangerous.

The girl. He thought suddenly, the damned Herrion girl must have tipped him off. Her mother had all but told him her daughter knew of their intentions to wed the two, it had been her main reason to come and speak to him as she had. Her daughter's feelings were being hurt by Ryland's ignorance. "Pathetic," he snorted scornfully. Actions should be dictated by logic, not trivial emotion. He finally broke into motion, becoming aware of the chill in the room and his need to prepare himself for the coming festivities. The kitchens had been notified even if the court had not. Tonight's dinner would morph into an impromptu engagement celebration, shortening the timetable until the two young nobles could be properly married by cutting out a separate engagement celebration. There would be no need for a lengthy and expensive engagement ball, all planning would instead be put to use on the wedding itself so it could happen as soon as possible. The King was anxious to send his army off to war, and even more anxious to receive the bounty of their victory.

As he pulled his finest doublet of Jorgen red from the lightly scented wardrobe he shuddered, finally acknowledging the horrible deeds he was condoning with this marriage if he could not stop the coming war by persuading the Council. He generally chose not to think of it, now that it had become obvious that he could not sway the King's mind on the matter, because that shudder, that visible reaction he could not stop his body from having could ruin everything if seen in public. Only here in his private suite dared he think of the conversations he had been party to in the War Council meetings, of the crazed words that came so blithely from the mouths of the Circle as they sat like shadows stretched out on both sides of the King.

He had tried to talk himself out of recognizing the darkness seeping out from the cowled figures of the Demandron, but the shadow they cast over the King as he sat among them was impossible to deny. Their inky magic suffused the air around them, making their robes a purer black than was ever naturally conceived, and blurring the edges of their profiles. When he dared to look, tendrils like smoky tentacles broke off and curled loving around the emaciated body of his old friend Gartlan, their nearness enhancing the look of vacant bliss that the Jorgen had originally attributed to the Dreamweed the King used so heavily. With regret he finally had to admit to himself, the King was indomitably addicted to the heady power the Demandron offered. There was no return from such addiction, he knew, only farther to fall.

Chapter 7

Tamol

High noon was upon the Skypeaks. The sun beat down strongly, but only produced a weak heat to combat the chilled mountain air. Autumn burned through the forest, transforming the trees into showy flames of gold and orange and red. The shadows of the gathered Trianti were sick and stunted things, living almost completely under the hooves and trailing cloaks of each individual. They mixed grotesquely with the neighboring crowd members. Only two shadows stood in stark relief, laying proud upon the sandy ground in the clearing at the center of the funeral pyres.

The pyres would be lit after the *Foraul nu' Groth,* to send their loved ones on *Traumek.* But first they must add another body to the piles. One of the proud shadows in front of her would fall and remain stuck to the earth, to rise again only in the form of ash upon the winds. Les put a large hand on her shoulder, seeming to sense her desperate sadness, knowing exactly when to pull her out of her thoughts before they could collapse in on her. He left his hand there as the Morgal and Pralick began stripping down to their britches, and were each handed their weapons of choice. The Morgal took up the huge broadsword *Ilyria* he had claimed when he defeated the previous leader of the tribe in a combat similar to this one, years and years before. His challenger would be able to claim that great length of iron if he won today. But for now Pralick took into hand two wickedly sharp axes of differing lengths.

Across the circle of bystanders, the blue eyed Mage stood, slightly hunched over as the new lead line tethering her hands to the ground was too short for her to stand at her full height. Pralick had left her naked again, forgoing the traditional *Kurianit* one shouldered dress as he sensed, as Tamol could, that the vulnerability of her bareness left her timid. Tremors shook her frame and Tamol pulled her own fur lined cloak tighter in helpless commiseration to the girl's obvious cold.

Tamol hated her. She knew it was irrational, but if this young woman had not been brought into her world it would not now be falling apart around her. She may be just a pawn in the politics of the Trianti, but the girl was still the instigator of this *Foraul nu' Groth.* She was the precipice, the reason Pralick finally felt he was in a strong enough position to challenge the Morgal. If the Morgal fell today she wouldn't even feel sorry for the torments Pralick would foist upon the young woman. She would be too busy herself, trying to avoid the torments of a tribe ruled by Pralick.

The Bloodhunger would come back to the Trianti. No matter how sweet a disposition a warrior was at heart, when he returned from battle the Bloodhunger did not just disappear. It waned slowly. And slowly, agonizingly slowly, a man would once again emerge from the beast he had become, but not before the animal's desperate violence and rutting had been forced upon any woman unlucky enough to catch the beast's eye. This tribe she had come to love and have a respected place in would devolve. The women would turn against each other, all vying for the strongest warrior to bed them, so they would be protected by that man's inner demons when the other demons in the tribe came out to play.

Men coming down from the addictive rush of the Bloodhunger were possessive creatures, and they would fight to the death for something they considered theirs, be it a weapon, woman or a haunch of meat. The Morgal had slowly weaned his warriors off of the filthy magic, starting the minute he gained the support of the tribe and took the name Morgal in the caves of Orr under the watchful eyes of the Ancients. But many of the tribe saw the savage success of the other Hinterland tribes, saw their ferocity, their total domination of their respective territories, and felt weak. It was these Trewal Pralick courted, that he belittled the Morgal to. He fed them hatred and dreams of glory, when the young men were barely old enough to remember the horror of warriors returning home from battle, unable to stop fighting. The terror of a tribe tearing itself apart.

Les's deep voice boomed out from behind her as he said the ceremonial words to begin the challenge by combat. Pralick sprung into sudden motion, darting with speed surprising for such a large man. He set his axes spinning, using their momentum to save strength, one always in front as a block while the other whirled around behind. He came at the Morgal with a gigantic swing of his right hand, which the Morgal easily evaded. Then Pralick followed up with a quick jab with the ax in his left hand, held close to the head so the entire force of his quick punch was behind the blade aimed for the Morgal's midsection as he evaded the first swing.

The Morgal slapped the punch away with the flat of his sword, the blow ringing like a gong in the silent clearing. They danced around one another in tight circles as the crowd moved back from the erratic patterns the fighters were drawing in the dusty ground. The two men seemed evenly matched. The flurry of movement when they came together was nearly too fast to follow, and every time they parted Tamol raked her eyes over the Morgal, desperately searching for wounds, hoping there were none to be seen.

The Morgal made a sudden push, forcing Pralick back on his heels as he retreated. *Ilyria* sang as it arced through the air over and over, and the crowd held their breath as one. It could end here she knew, this could be the triumph they needed, a victory for the status quo. Pralick was driven backwards and the tribe fell back with him, mimicking his withdrawal, clearing more space for the battle to move into. But one of the pyres stood directly in the path of the retreating warrior. Right before Pralick would have stepped back into the solid stacked wood at the base of the pyre he lazily hooked the blade of his ax around *Ilyria* as the Morgal completed a leftward swing meant to cleave open his opponent's chest. With a mighty yank on the long shafted ax Pralick pulled both man and sword forwards while he agilely slid out and around, placing the Morgal's back to the wall of firewood and fallen kinsmen.

Tamol knew the Morgal could not possibly disengage quickly enough to get his weapon up to defend. And in horror she shut her eyes, unwilling to witness the death of the first man she had ever trusted in the tribe. But as the gathered Trianti gasped like they shared one set of lungs she could not help but glance up, just in time to see the Morgal execute a diving roll out from underneath the whirling ax she feared was going to take his life. His broadsword lay gleaming upon the ground by the pyre, and the Morgal, weaponless, warily circled his adversary, breathing heavily.

Les's hand was a painful vice upon her shoulder, but the pain seemed secondary to the fight unfolding before her. She grasped at his hand, seeking any measure of comfort her old friend could offer. Les drew her in close to the front of his body and whispered in her ear, his breath tickling the fine hairs at the nape of her neck. "Stay here Tamol. If the Morgal dies I'm going to take the Mage and run. It's the Morgal's orders. We don't need Pralick having the extra power. I need you to stall, any way you can. The longer before the tribe casts their votes, the longer I will have at the Caves to convince the Ancients to help us."

She had barely brought her chin back down from her nod of ascent when his comforting warmth disappeared. She tracked his progress through the crowd by the absentminded shifting of the distracted onlookers. And then the glaring white of the girl's pale skin was engulfed under Lessoran's cloak as he drew it around her, and the wall of spectators was once more a homogeneous blend of dull brown and forest green caging the fighters into their dueling arena.

Sweat was running down the bare torsos of both combatants, even in the crisp mountain air. The Morgal had acquired *Ilyria* again but his parries were beginning to slow, his guard dropping lower every time he had to raise the heavy broadsword to block one of Pralick's weighty blows. The huge sword began to seem cumbersome in comparison to the agilely spinning axes and the Morgal's two handed grip left gaps in his defense he was no longer quick enough on his feet to close with movement.

Pralick struck the first true blow, a glancing cut on the Morgal's thigh when he was not quick enough to bring the sword back up and around to block. Blood dripped down his leg, the red a startling contrast to the dusty men and women serving as a backdrop to the battle. Pralick's mask of concentration broke into a feral grin at the sight of his enemy's blood. And he began to press harder, coming at the Morgal in quick bursts of movement meant to tire the older man.

The Morgal wavered in her vision drunkenly, and Tamol drew in a heaving gasp, realizing she had forgotten to breathe. Dashing the moisture leaking from her eyes she focused once more, willing the Morgal to make a sudden come back, praying to Freyton to take care of his chosen son. But it was a losing battle. Pralick cut into the flesh of the Morgal twice more, a long gash across one bicep, and a jagged nick from the hammer of his ax along his left pectoral. And then it happened, the Morgal's injured leg gave way, and he fell heavily to his knees in front of the other man.

Pralick stepped forward, one ax to his enemy's throat, the other raised behind him in readiness for a killing blow. He made quite the figure. Boisterous vitality seeped from his pores, the sheen of sweat covering his muscled torso made him glimmer like a polished statue. He looked like a leader, like a God amidst the mundane figures he stood before. He was Freyton himself, with four point antlers proud upon his wide features, and the glint of murder in his eyes. But the killing sweep of the ax never happened. The fallen Morgal eventually raised his eyes to look at Pralick, strangely calm in the face of his demise, simply curious as to the delay. Pralick kicked *Ilyria* out of reach and relaxed his stance, keeping the ax at the Morgal's throat in a clear command to stay put, but swiveling his head this way and that to pull in the crowd.

"This is how we have lost ourselves." He stated boldly. "This weakness is why we are the least of the Hinterland tribes, when we were once the greatest. We have let this old man taint the wildness that lives in the heart of the Hinterlands. But look at him! Know his frailty! Witness his feebleness!" Pralick swept the ax down from the Morgal's neck and the fluttering pulse there and buried the head in his bared stomach, gently, almost reverently. "This is not something we want to find waiting for us in the Afterlife. His fragility dishonors us, and so I dishonor him." The ax left the Morgal's body with a sickly sucking noise, and his life's blood flowed bright and fluidly from the gash.

"I do not give you a warrior's death, I do not send your soul on to live with our forefathers in the next chapter of the world. Fire shall not touch your bones to bring rebirth. You will not ascend to the Gods in the Afterlife as ash upon the mountain winds." The ceremonial farewell was twisted and defiled by Pralick's hatred, the wonder and excitement of the next life seemed dulled by his warping of the sweet Hinterland wish for a loved one to pass peacefully onto the next.

Pralick then looked directly at her, his cold, cold eyes freezing her to the core. "No one will tend his wounds. He will die slowly, as he has killed this tribe slowly. He will rot in this forest for eternity, as he would have had us rot in austerity."

He finally stepped away from the Morgal and the older man fell to the side, unconscious, but still living. Pralick prowled to the gathered Trewal, snatching up *Ilyria* on his way. "Light the pyres, and talk to your brothers. We cast stones upon the Morgal's last breath. And then *Ilyria* will have a new master." He stalked from the clearing, knocking Tamol out of his way in passing, and leaving a sea of whispers in his wake.

Lessoran

He had just reached Blue Eyes when the first blood of the *Foraul nu' Groth* was shed. And as his mentor's blood came spilling out in a fitful rush he snagged the girl's shoulder and drew her slowly back towards him. At the tug of her tether he drew a slim ribbon of magic from his chest, grimacing at the strain it caused him, and gathered moisture from the air to coalesce around the iron stake binding the Mage's ties to the ground. The stake rusted through slowly, and Les watched the fight with half of his attention, as it turned from a battle to a desperate struggle for survival.

The girl squirmed against his hold and her restraints until the weakened stake snapped at ground level and she tumbled back into his chest, the air leaving her lungs with an audible wheeze and a frankly adorable squeak. He checked the faces of those in the crowd around him and with relief saw that no one was paying them any mind; all eyes were on the two men dancing with death at the epicenter of the clearing. He banded his arm about her middle, his forearm banging into her ribs to keep her close when she jerkily tried to move away. "Stay calm Mage, don't attract anyone's attention. I am going to get you out of here," he breathed in her ear.

Her taunt body relaxed marginally, and he snuggled her in closer to his body, drawing his second favorite cloak around them both. He doubted the cloak he had left with her earlier in the day would ever find its way back into his possession. And it was a damn shame too, that cloak was soft without losing thickness, and pliable without losing warmth. A fantastic cloak for the cold months in the mountains. *Not that it would matter if the Morgal lost*, he mused. *Then the only thing that would matter is how fast he could run from Pralick's wrath.*

The girl's head barely came to his sternum. Her lithe form was easy to conceal beneath the folds of his cloak as long as she stayed flush with his body. He began inching backwards, letting the sway of the crowd ebb around them naturally so that their departure was gradual and unremarkable. He focused on breathing in and out, trying not to look at the dueling Trewal regardless of the gasps from the crowd around him.

He knew the Morgal was lost only when Pralick began his venomous speech. They were nearing the back of the gathered Trewal by then and from his periphery he could see tents and beyond them, the tree line that would mark the official start to their flight. He could no longer see what was happening in the middle of the crowd, and he was startled to find tears trickling steadily down his face. As one who wielded Water magic, tears came easier to him than many, but at this point in his life it was a rare occurrence. The Morgal had been his pillar of morality, the unbreakable stone that turned his life from being drenched in blood to one of light. His unconscious mind was grieving. *I have no time for that right now*, he thought, dashing the tears from his cheeks with a swipe of his hand.

When he had made his way to the Morgal's tent with the dire news of a budding Mage in Pralick's control, the Morgal had been adamant. He had been absolutely unbending. Regardless of the cost, the girl was to be taken to the Caves in the case of his death. There had been true fear in the older man's face when he told Les that Pralick could not be allowed to touch the young woman with the strange appendages and brilliant eyes. He had tasked Les with getting her to the Ancients unscathed, and then he had spent twenty minutes digging through his tent, examining this pouch and that crevice until he thrust into Les's hand a small but heavy medallion. The circular charm had what he assumed was the likeness of Freyton stamped upon one side, and on the other was a strange looking crown of sorts, sporting its own set of antlers. The silver of the necklace was so old the gleam of metal was nearly lost amidst the tarnish.

Now, with girl and medallion, he stood at the edge of camp, at the edge of his life before, and whatever would happen next. He was completely inclined to cut the girl's hand free and give her a nice solid pat on the rump to send her off to figure out her own destiny. But the Morgal had given him this one last undertaking. The man who had freed him of the Bloodhunger had beseeched him, who was he to refuse?

"What now?" The small voice roused him from his reverie. Behind them Pralick's voice reached a rousing crescendo, then cut off, and before them the golden forest of the Skypeaks lay quiet and serene.

"Now we run." He stated simply as he cut her hands free with his belt knife. He rummaged through the rucksack he had stashed in a friend's tent nearby and pulled out one of his extra tunics for her. "We'll go to the Caves of Orr, where the Ancients can decide what to do with you, and Pralick has no power." He glanced behind again, back towards his tribe. "And we need to go now."

Sylvia

They were being hunted. The Maegi, Lessoran, had said the journey to the Caves took a two weeks on horseback, and more like three on foot. They had been scrambling over the rough terrain in the foothills of the massive mountain range for six days now. Always looking behind, always fearful. The tribe was coming for them, for reasons she still wasn't quite clear on. Just like the Maegi had helped her escape, for reasons she wasn't quite clear on. And they weren't allowed to make a fire during the freezing cold nights, for reasons she wasn't quite clear on, and she was stuck in this bizarre hallucination…for reasons she wasn't quite fucking clear on!

What *was* clear to her, was that she was losing her sanity. This little side trip from her real life kept dragging on and on, and it was beginning to weigh on her mind that something had gone horrifically wrong in surgery. Was she allergic to the drugs they had given her? Or had the anesthesiologist accidentally overdosed her and that is why she hadn't woken up yet? Things were so real here, the experiences so new and random that she had often been tempted into belief. But fantastical events like this only happened in books, or movies, and not to girls like her. Things happen to the orphans, and girls with tragic pasts who needed redemption, love, something they didn't have before. But her? The only thing that had been missing in her life was a knee! A whole and working knee, which should have been fixed by now.

And now, now she had been trained to fight, befriended and made enemies of an alien species, essentially learned a new language, been kidnapped, beaten... and the connections began dropping into place. One by one the 'random' occurrences had slight connections to her life, and the world her subconscious had built around her began to seem a little more translucent.

The realization had come crashing down as soon as her heart-rate and churning mind had calmed after the near rape Lessoran had interrupted in Pralick's tent. At school they had just finished up a segment in health class, concerning rape. The rest of her peers were to turn in the research paper the week she was missing due to her surgery, so she had turned hers in early. With all of the statistics she had read, all of the firsthand accounts and psychological profiles along with how the trauma effects victims rattling around in her brain, it was just too convenient that she would be faced with the same events herself.

Pralick was a textbook rapist, using the act for power and domination rather than anything sexual. And her? Her mind was taking all of the information it had filed away, and was applying it to these little scenarios in an artful portrayal of medieval life on a foreign planet. Weird? Yes. Most definitely. Maybe she was destined to be an author, or a screenwriter, something where her obviously overactive imagination could be put to good use. For now, though, she just wished it would shut down and let her back into control of her body and mind. Of her *life*.

Her bare and battered foot skidded out from under her on the edge of the trail they were climbing, the one that lead back and forth across a nearly vertical cliff. From behind the Maegi's hand rudely cupped her left butt cheek while the other captured one pin-wheeling arm, effectively settling her back onto the steep pathway. Syl shook him off with a huff, and abruptly decided she had given him enough of the silent treatment. He had rescued her after all, sort of, and even if he was maddeningly close mouthed about her situation and his knowledge of, anything, this tense silence was not exactly comfortable for her either.

"Who are the Ancients?" She decided to start with the impersonal questions first, he seemed a little more open about things that did not concern him directly, when he was willing to talk at all that is.

"They are Seers." He stated blandly, his hand once more hovering near her waist as her foot slipped the tiniest bit.

She slapped the offending hands away and glared. "Stop touching me and talk dammit!" A slight twitch at the corner of his mouth prodded her ire further, and she whirled around to face the smug bastard head on. But then the twitch turned up the corner of his mouth, morphing it into a smirk of amusement, and she wanted to hit him for being so irritatingly good looking when she was trying to hate him. "What is going to happen to me?" she fired off. "What will the Ancients do that you can't? Why won't Pralick be able to hurt us once we get there?" She poked a finger into his chest, "And no evading me this time, mister! I deserve to know what is going on!" She pressed so hard into the firm wall of muscle that she threw herself off balance again and the loose scree her feet had been resting on top of sucked her in to her ankles, sending her into a backwards fall that would have doubtlessly ended up with her on her butt in the sharp rock. But once again, Lessoran's hands were there to catch her and with a yank she was pressed up against his chest. His very firm, and enticingly warm chest.

Hormones really are quite annoying, she thought, feeling his pecs flex beneath her hands as he effortlessly lifted her out of the scree to slightly more stable footing. I mean really, how was her mind finding the time and energy to keep thinking of the big Maegi like this when she had barely slept in six days? When her every step was a study in concentration since the blow she had taken to the head, and Pralick's subsequent beatings, had rendered her vision in a constant swimming state. She rested her forehead against him for a moment, taking a big breath, and reaching vainly for balance, for her anger of seconds before, for any feeling but tiredness. But the world, already in a constant lazy spin behind her closed eyelids, tilted even further as Lessoran casually picked her up like a bride, *or a baby, dammit!* She had never felt as helpless as when she was around this man, but maybe that was the concussion talking. She felt like a child next to his larger frame, and his careful treatment of her was absolutely infuriating! She was a capable young woman, everyone who knew her would agree. She was competent, and hardworking, and quick to learn new things. If her mind was going to conjure up a handsome stranger to save her couldn't she at least pull it together enough to behave like less of a drooling idiot?

"We'll make camp at the top of the hill." Lessoran said as he began steadily plodding up the hill, ignoring the equally steady beat of her fist hitting his chest as she protested being carried.

"I can walk" she said as it became obvious he would not be beaten into letting her down.

"Your balance gets worse every day, and I can see you squinting. The light hurts your eyes doesn't it? You need rest, and I need to rest if I am going to recover enough to Heal you with my magic." He shifted her about a little as they rounded yet another switchback in the trail, and she pressed her face into the blessedly dark crook of his arm as the lurching motion of his stride continued on and on in her stomach.

He continued, "We haven't seen any trace of the tribe in more than a day, likely thanks to me exhausting my magic in confusing our trail, it should be safe to slow down just a little today."

"What if they catch us?" She asked quietly.

"Not an option."

"I'd say it is a completely feasible option. One we should have a plan for, you know, like if we see them, then we split up and meet somewhere safe? Or maybe if you just let me look at that map of yours then I can get to the Caves on my own and meet you there." She looked hopefully at the rucksack on his back where the coveted map lay.

"I can't afford for you to run off and try to get back to wherever you came from. If you see the map you'll know how to get back. I've seen you walking these last few days, you leave a trail behind you a child could follow. The tribe would pick you up in a second if I wasn't there to cover up the traces." He paused to take a few breaths, laboring a bit as the trail turned into a series of rocks so steep it resembled a set of stairs more than a hiking path.

"Pralick *cannot* have you. It would be the end of everything the Morgal strove for. The end of everything good in the Trianti tribe." They had finally crested the top of the small peak, and hundreds more crags rose up like a forest of mountains in front of them. He swung her down and held her steady, his grip tightening as his voice built, tension and frustration evident in his tone. "He *died* for you. Died *because* of you!" He raked a hand through the loose waves of chestnut hair between his antlers, tugging in vexation. "And you couldn't care less" he spat, "Don't think I don't know why you want to get your hands on the map, you want to get home, no matter the cost to the Trianti, no matter what the Morgal sacrificed for you, or that I have given up my entire life to get you away!"

She glared at him for a moment, stunned at the hypocrisy of his words. "Of *course* I want to get back home! Just like you want to save your tribe, or whatever it is you are trying to do, no matter what it is costing me! You're trying to do what you need to do just like I am trying to do what I need to do! Unfortunately, we seem to be at cross purposes." She took in a great lungful of air and then the words started coming forth again, great heaving buckets of words that had been stoppered up inside for days as events kept buffeting her this way and that. "Do you think I want to be here? That I planned to get hit on the head so hard I'm still seeing stars? That I wanted that awful man to drag me back to your camp to rape me? That I wanted to come to these frigid mountains to freeze my ass off with a grumpy stranger who blames me for coming in and ruining his life? This is ruining my life too! I shouldn't be here! I don't belong here! I really,

really don't belong here, far more than you know, and I just want to go HOME!"

The tirade tapered off into sniffles, much to her horror, and she whirled away from his stunned face, tramping off into the woods with a muttered, "use the bathroom" before the dam could truly burst and she cried all over him. When she had fled a safe distance she hunkered down behind a tree and let it out. Sobs, snot, spittle and all. *How dare he think she was out to ruin things for him, that she didn't care if someone died for her!* Her outpouring of words had been cathartic, but she already regretted it, no matter that she felt like a little bit of the terrible pressure inside of her had been released. *It doesn't really matter what the Maegi thinks, he doesn't really matter,* she tried to remind herself, *this whole place doesn't matter.*

She kept searching for the oddities always present in dreams, the strange juxtapositions. Trying to reassure herself that this was not real. But did you feel the gnawing of hunger in a dream? The annoyance of a splinter? Where were those strange moments where events flowed from one seamlessly to another? It would be comforting to be able to identify those little cues, to pinpoint a moment where she positively *knew* she was dreaming. But instead she was stuck with long treks over mind numbingly boring miles of forested mountains. And awkward silences that could stretch for an entire evening as she and Lessoran begrudgingly huddled close, back to back for warmth, waiting for the sunlight.

She just needed to relax and continue on with the ride, practice some patience and wait until she woke up again. Maybe try to enjoy herself more, like she had when she had been with Ryland and Torman. If she was stuck here she might as well enjoy it, right? Lessoran was certainly nice enough to look at, regardless of the fact that he was multiple years her senior. Maybe with an attitude change she could prod this dream to more fantastical heights, enjoy a little flirting banter, see what the depths of her mind could procure for her to enjoy. Feeling more resolute she stood, and with a deep breath straightened her shoulders and tried to will away the constant aching in her head, focusing instead on the emptiness of her stomach. Syl picked her way back through the quiet Listenbark trees to where Lessoran had set up camp in the dusky light.

Lessoran

Les strung a sturdy rope between two young Listenbarks, coiling the excess to the side in the hopes of it staying dry through the night, the less wet items he had to repack in his bag the next morning the better. He would rather not lug around any extra weight in water regardless of his affinity to the element. Mechanically, he began draping the wool blanket over the taunt cord, weighting it down on the sides with rocks, checking the wind once again to make sure their shelter for the night would be a wind block rather than a sail. His body on autopilot, his mind was left to churn over the deluge of words that had come spouting out of his companion's delicate mouth.

Delicate, ha! he snorted to himself. Some of those words had been anything but 'delicate'. But curse words aside, she had said some things that painfully pinpointed how very one sided he was approaching this entire debacle. He hadn't stopped to consider the ramifications of their little adventure on her life, only the fact that it likely meant the end of his own way of living. The end of his inclusion in the tribe that had been his family for the entirety of his life.

He was a selfish bastard. Yep, that was the title for him, one he had been given a time or two before, from other beautiful women with less than delicate mouths. He smiled in fond remembrance. He didn't even know the Mage's name, preferring to call her Blue Eyes in his head, and had rebuffed any of her attempts at true conversation. Anything deeper than, "Are we stopping here for the night?" or "Any more of that dried meat stuff?" had been met with his silence. He was essentially holding her hostage; the least he could do was treat her like a person rather than annoyingly talkative baggage.

He could hear her picking her way back to camp, and gave himself a mental slap to the face. He would do right by her from this point on. She seemed nice enough, even in her innocence. He had even been impressed with her dogged perseverance, despite what must be a severe concussion. He tried to put a welcoming smile on his face, but it fell halfway through, the feeling foreign and so painfully fake in the wake of the previous week of his life. He would just have to work up to the smiling, try something simpler first.

She took a seat under the lean-to without looking at him once. The awkward quiet pressed down on him until he couldn't bear the pressure any longer and he threw himself down next to her. When they were both gazing into the misty crags they would be faced with in the morning he said simply, "Sorry."

She grunted in response. A little "huh" of air escaping that seemed almost as much surprise as acknowledgment. And then she slanted those eyes in his direction, one brow lifted in a gentle arch. He raised his own in imitation, shrugging his shoulders, unwilling to put more words into his apology, reluctant to offer a deeper explanation. She held his eyes for a second and then nodded her head in agreement, shrugging her own thin shoulders, one of which was bared by the neckline of his large tunic no matter how tightly she tied the lacing.

"I have one question for you, and then you can ask me whatever you want to know," Les said slowly, conscious of her simplistic use of Layette, and frequent lapses into the old scholar's tongue, which he knew from the texts all the Trianti Maegi learned from. Her eyes were back on his face in an instant, surprise evident. "And I'll even answer." A ghost of a smile pulled at his lips, and he hoped one day he would be able to truly smile at her. Tamol had always said his smile could melt ice, and Courit had joked that a smile from him attracted the girls like bees to honey.

"What's your name?"

She turned to face him, folding her legs into an impossible knot beneath her, a position she seemed to favor, even though it made his joints ache just looking at it. "My name is Sylvia Eldritch," she said, and then with a hesitant look she continued in her slow Layette, "I can ask you anything?"

"I will tell you the answer if I know it."

"Fair enough." She grinned at him impishly, "How old are you?"

He stared, flummoxed at her odd choice of question. There were many, many questions she had asked in the last few days, but this was not one of them. This was not even pertinent to her at all. But his question hadn't been all that pertinent either, he supposed. Hostages didn't need names, but he liked that she had one, and such an odd one at that. "I've seen twenty-six rebirths of the seasons," he said.

She looked more confused by the new information than satisfied. "Dammit," she breathed, a word she used quite often, but one that held no meaning to Lessoran. "That means nothing, does it?" She switched unconsciously back into the scholar's tongue, and he pieced together her words with difficulty. "Even if you have seasons like back home, what if your days are longer? What if there are more days in a year? Dumb question I guess." She gazed back out towards the mountains. They were gathering the darkness to them like a shawl, blanketing the panorama in monochrome, leeching the silver from the low hanging clouds and feeding that light to the stars instead.

Loria, the largest moon, bathed Sylvia's features in that same silver, as she tipped her face upwards to consider its pocked surface. She spoke in his language now, her words slow and careful, but steady. "It's easy to forget where I am, sometimes. So easy that it scares me." She turned her head to him again, and he could still see the incredible blue of her eyes even though the night had stolen most other color out of the world around them. Her gaze arrowed in on his face after lighting briefly on Sorret, Loria's smaller sister, resting in lavender glory on the horizon.

"Why do you call me a Mage, Lessoran? I know blue eyes mean magic to the Trewal, but I'm not Trewal, and I have no magic."

He considered the question, stumped for a moment at her denial of being Trewal. "If you aren't Trewal, what are you? And where did you come from?"

Sylvia rolled her eyes at him, "I thought I got to ask the questions here," she challenged.

He grimaced, *right, he was answering questions, not asking them*. "There is nothing in the Hinterlands, or Prium itself and the world as we know it beyond that kingdom, that has blue eyes, at least not that I have ever heard of, except the Trewal. I guess I just assumed that you were Trewal, maybe just from very far away, where things had gone a little..." he eyed the tangle of her legs and the awkwardly situated lumps of flesh resting at the ends of them, "...differently," he finished.

Les watched her untangle herself, and pull her knees into her chest where she could wrap her arms around them. "Fair enough assumption I guess. Does knowing that I don't have any magic change things for you? Maybe enough for you to help me get back to where I was going before?"

The emotions on her face were easy to read, and he hated to dash such earnest hope, but magic was a fickle thing, sometimes not making itself known for much of a person's life. "You could still have magic Sylvia," he said carefully, adding in her name, "and just not know it yet. Some Trewal don't show any magical abilities until they are far past puberty, which is when the majority of us find out we have magic, and begin learning Control. The later a person comes into their magic, the stronger it usually is."

"Oh," she said in a small voice, head bowing under the weight once more at the loss of that brief spark of hope he had seen. "And why are you taking me to the Ancients?"

Trollit, this was much harder than he anticipated. He had assumed she had a basic understanding of the tribe, its politics, and customs. But she was completely in the dark. He really was a selfish bastard. She had no concept of what had happened back there, her part in it, or if he was even helping her, rather than leading her into yet another horrible situation. He opened his mouth to try to explain, shut it again, then opened it once more, "It's complicated," he began, waving off her look of exasperation. "The Ancients come from all seven of the Hinterland tribes, and while they don't rule them, they definitely have a say in what is happening in each of them. Morgals have no power in the Caves of Orr, only the Ancients do, because that is where Morgals are reborn to their Names. So Pralick will abide by whatever they decide to do with you, regardless of whether the tribe casts their stones in favor of him, or not."

He paused for breath, to consider. That was all true, and good reason for them to head to the Caves, but why was he taking her there truly? In all honesty it was because the Morgal had asked him to, as simple as that, coupled with that foreign look of hard desperation in the old man's eyes when he bade him do it. But she seemed to be happy with the answer he had given, once she had clarified what casting stones meant, what a Morgal was, and he was grateful to not have to dig into it too deeply; some things she just didn't need to know.

"I don't suppose you know what the Ancients will say about me? Oh never mind, I can already see you don't," she huffed, squinting at his face in the light of the moons. "Do they know anything about magical travel? Or maybe places really, really far from here?"

His mind reeled from her quick change in topics, but grasped onto the last question in sudden understanding. "Are you from very far away? Do you not know how to return? The Ancients would be who I would ask for help with such things." He was pleased that his task might actually be in her favor also, a traveling companion with a common goal would be much more pleasant and helpful than a prisoner who he had to watch at all times for fear of her escape.

"Very, very far away. An entirely different world." She said in a small voice. Her shoulders shook with little shivers and before he could examine the impulse, or put a stop to it, like he had been doing for the last three nights, he pulled Sylvia to him, settling her between his knees with a satisfying squeak on her part. She remained sitting, bolt upright between his legs, body tense and eyes wide. He parted his cloak, opening it invitingly and couldn't help the little flash of triumph he felt as she settled back against him, her back to his chest, and proceeded to melt into his warmth, her shivers fading as their combined heat reverberated and grew within the confines of the coarse fabric and fur.

She wriggled around a bit, until her head rested comfortably on his breast and she had tucked every last bit of herself under the trailing ends of the cloak. Then her next question came. "Do you dream Lessoran?"

"Of course I dream," he responded in surprise, and as an afterthought added, "most people just call me Les."

"Les then." Her voice had gotten quieter, slightly muffled by the cloak. "Ever wonder why you dream what you dream, like where it is coming from? Is it all there in your head already?" She turned a little to the side so she was nestled up against his shoulder, and he tightened his arms around her despite her brief stiffening at his movement, tucking her silky head under his chin.

"I guess I don't think about my dreams much. But I suppose they are made from things already floating around in there. People I know, places I've been, things I've thought about doing." He bent one knee slightly in the hopes that it would make it less obvious what his body was thinking about doing at *this* exact moment. But as the silence after his last words stretched on and on, he realized she had fallen asleep. Les smiled to himself, perplexingly happy that the expression didn't feel as alien as it had earlier in the day. He decided not to wonder why the warmth of the woman sleeping on his chest made the weight of events from the last week seem light enough to allow a smile to slide through the cracks in the stone wall the trials of his life had made of his heart.

Cirillia

The mantle of pain came with the Name, Ancient. But she hadn't anticipated the donning of a new Name to make each of her years feel like it was etched upon her skin. The pain of age was now written on her bones, inked in tiny excruciating letters in the fibers of her body. She was the youngest of the Ancients, the most recent to arrive. She hadn't known, as she aged, whether she would be called to the Caves, or left to wither into nothingness. But one day, not long ago, she had heard the call. The call no one else could hear, and so she had made her slow, steady way to the Caves.

No one was sure in her tribe, whether an Ancient was replaced only if they died, or if it was something else that decided when the elderly Seer's usefulness was over. But there was only ever seven. Seven Ancients, one from each of the Hinterland tribes, Trianti, Rishal, Proult, Diarmas, Baroun, Kla'routh, and the shy Verie. The Seers were said to speak with the Gods themselves, to enjoy prolonged life, and Sight beyond this world. But here she was, an Ancient now by Name, by rite, by the blood she willingly spilled from her own old, tired, veins. And she was still unsure what exactly an Ancient was, where they drew their power from, or how they lived to be so old. She could feel the power her body now held, as if that rite performed at the peak of the night had leached her old life from her, replacing it with magic, a magic that burned like live sparks within her skin.

She had thought her days of social drama and politicking long past when she passed her eightieth rebirth. But the seven elderly Seers living in the Caves whispered and gossiped and plotted as if they were still young men and women, like their years had made them no wiser in the fleeting nature of power. Maybe they did not fear death, did not find futility in power plays, maybe they still saw something she did not, even though now she could see things that no Trewal should ever be capable of seeing, with her milky Seer's eyes.

Turning her new eyes upwards she pulled her cloak in tighter. The stars were bright above the entrance to the Caves of Orr, and she often came to sit here, just outside the tall, carved archway that led into the heart of her new home. The fanciful whorls and detailed vines carved into the stone of that framed doorway looked almost alive in the moonlight. She was sick to death of stone, but stone that looked like living things was better than the hard walls awaiting her inside the Caves. The rocks encircling her bedchamber had the eerie tendency to look like they were bleeding, as the moisture from the underground streams rusted the iron streaking through the caverns, making it weep red rust down the walls.

The whisperings were not as loud out beneath the stars, but her memories were. It was like the ghost of her former life could overpower the Sight when she went outside, a thing the other Seers rarely did. They chose to stay cloistered in their tunnels, dreaming their Dreams of what was to come, listening for the voice of Freyton. They preferred overseeing the goings on in each of the seven tribes, and manipulating the holders of power, the users of magic within each group, while she wished for younger days, for the sweet warmth of a great grandchild in her arms.

Maybe Freyton had chosen wrong. Maybe she was not meant to be a Seer and he should have left her to die among her family and tribe. Some days she wished she had been left alone, or that she had ignored the terrible voice urging her to make her way to the Caves, the voice she could hear, very faintly, somewhere in the back of her mind, even now, out under the stars where she almost felt like herself again. But this 'gift' was an honor among her people. It was distinction of the highest caliber, the secret hope of each and every Hinterlander born to magic; that they would be chosen by their God.

The Caves had been abuzz with heightened activity since this morning and she had not been sure she would be able to slip out; but getting away from all the fuss had become priority number one after hours and hours of preparation and talk. Freyton has come to them, all of them at once, which was a rare occurrence. He usually spoke to one Seer at a time, and had them all working at separate plots that each Ancient tended to keep to themselves. Their own God played them against one another. At least it seemed that way to her, that they were all working at cross purposes, no one with enough information to get a good idea of what the whole picture actually was.

But now they were all set upon the same mission. She wondered sometimes about the other Gods, and why she heard whispered words sometimes, with different voices than the severe Freyton, but could never quite make out the words meanings. She shook herself, *enough musing for one night, old woman.* Standing, she shook the creaks from her limbs and stretched her hands up towards the stars, and with a deep, fortifying breath she knew her respite was over; it was back to plots, back to manipulation and communication by Dreams. She had a tribe to coax into the right decision for leadership, a whole host of people to sway back to the old way of thinking, the way their God wanted them to think. She grimaced in distaste for her task, a tribe to bring the Bloodhunger back to.

Sylvia

Syl woke to find her left leg had slipped from beneath the covering of the cloak, and hastily pulled it back into the confines of her nest. Over the past week she and Les had fallen into a comfortable rhythm of waking and walking. Once he had recovered enough from overusing his magic, he Healed her concussion, which had been an incredible experience. She thought back to that day, her sitting cross legged on the rocky outcropping they had found shelter in, Lessoran facing her, hands gently cupping her temples. A warm sensation emanated from his fingers as he rubbed them slowly this way and that, and following the warmth was an electric tingling that had almost made her giggle. But then the tickling sensation grew into something vaguely akin to the uncomfortable pins and needles felt after a limb had fallen asleep, and waves of dizziness hit her, so that when Les withdrew his hands she was left gasping and exhausted. They had both slept long that night.

Now she was much surer on her feet and they covered ground in great leaps and bounds, while every night they rolled up together under his cloak to share body heat. Their combined warmth combated the ever growing chill as they moved higher up into the Skypeaks, and as autumn slipped closer to the coming winter. They had their first freeze the night before last, and getting up from the warm cocoon of blankets and limbs had been the very last thing she ever wanted to do that cold morning. But faintly, very faintly, they had both heard the jingling of a horse's harness, the ring of hoof on stone. And their complacent traveling became a hectic rush once again.

The Trianti were close behind them, their horses making up time that her sore feet and Les's healing body could not compete with. With their head start failing them, their only saving grace was the portion of trail they would reach today, what Les called the Skycastles, huge spires of rock jutting out into the open sky, towering above the winding, maze-like trails between them. Their pursuer's horses would have to be led along the bases of the Castles, as the trails there were largely made up of shale chipped off the great towers of stone above, and the combination of rider and mount would erode the delicate paths. Between the Castles, Les had told her, were steep gorges that flooded with torrential waters when the snows melted each spring, and when the rains came every autumn. In the drier times of year, the creeks and rivers dissecting the Castles would be slow moving and shallow, making the danger of a fall into a ravine all the more treacherous. With the coming terrain lessening the advantage the tribe and their horses had previously enjoyed, the safety of the Caves would soon be theirs. But they had to make it into the labyrinth of rock first.

Above her there was just the hint of light in the sky, *time to get moving,* she acknowledged. With a groan Syl flopped over onto her stomach, loathe to leave the warmth, but knowing she needed to wake Lessoran and that they should spare no time in getting into the low valley before them. But she rarely had any peace like this, rarely had a second to think with their breakneck pace of travel, didn't she deserve just a moment where she was warm and comfortable, and the unsettling tension she felt between herself and her companion was not sending butterflies fluttering in her stomach? Les lay still beside her, the little puffs of his faint snores producing clouds of steam in the morning air. She could barely believe how their interactions had changed in just seven days.

He's a fantastic pillow. She smiled to herself, cuddling into the crook of his body, her stomach and chest flush with his muscular side, his arm curled around her like a heat producing blanket. *Was this wrong?* she wondered, sleeping with a man older than her? Or did the 'wrongness' require all the things *other* than sleeping that 'sleeping together' alluded to? To be deemed a slut in her school was a social death sentence in some ways, and an elevation in others. Girls would shun you, but the boys jockeyed to fill the holes, no pun intended. Or maybe pun intended. She rolled her eyes at herself silently. The whole question of sex was hard to wrap her mind around here.

The temptation was there, it had always been there, even back home, like when she made out with David Granger on the swing on her front porch after homecoming. But there were so many consequences, so many aspects to consider. She had never been able to shut off that rational part of her brain long enough to actually enjoy any of it. Instead she worried she wasn't kissing very well, that there was too much tongue, and where were her hands supposed to go again?

But here those questions seemed inconsequential. Larger worries filled her mind, like the fear that the guy she might have a crush on was a different species. Was sex even possible? Or how about the fact that this might just be one big delusion? That was actually an addition on the "go for it" list if she was quite honest with herself. If you had sex in a dream half of the consequences disappeared, no one at school could ever find out, no chance of pregnancy or disease, and the fear of the first time not being 'perfect' wasn't applicable if it wasn't real.

But all these thoughts always lead back to the same place, the question of reality. How could she decide to pursue something with the grumpy but charming Lessoran if she didn't know if he was real or a figment of her imagination? She generally didn't examine that overarching question in great depth. It was too big, too real. She was rather fond of some of the nice parts of this dream. She liked the eye candy dressed in antlers and muscles. She liked Ryland and Torman and their brotherly banter, and she liked being something special, someone important in this world. If she and Lessoran were together and her mind came up with a blank on what sex was actually like, would the bubble burst? She was growing attached to him, and it would hurt to know he wasn't real, it would be like she lost a real friend, a real person in her life. Conversely, if she allowed herself to entertain the thought of this being her new reality there were a whole host of issues to face. Ones she was not ready for. Ones she didn't think she would ever be ready for.

Pushing on his shoulder she tried to wake Les, tired of her brief 'moment of peace' which had quickly devolved into the chaos of her mind. "Les wake up, it's getting light. We need to go." She flung the cloak off of them, letting the chilly air in.

"Mmphfff!" Les woke with a start, sitting bolt upright at the shock of the cold. He handily reached out with one long arm and snagged her around the middle from where she had been kneeling, pulling both her and the warmth of the cloak back down to him. "That wasn't very nice" he growled in her ear.

From her new position laying on top of him, the answer to the question of their anatomy being incompatible became shockingly obvious, and the blush that sped up her neck to her face felt twice as hot as usual due to the frigid morning air. She scrambled off of him hastily, horrified to find herself babbling in a mixture of English and Layette, "We should get going, yep! It's that time, the time where we need to go. Pursuers you know. Tribe following us, they have horses, we have feet..." Her eyes followed his body, down long legs to dusty hooves before darting away, "-ish." She let the embarrassing outpouring of words hang there in the air for a second before whirling away from his perplexed face and busying herself with packing up for the day's walk, mind still churning. *The question of sex doesn't even matter,* she chided herself, *when at the first hint of an actual penis you turn into a manically talkative tomato!*

To her relief Lessoran seemed to shrug her strange behavior off quite easily, as he did most of her moody outbursts, slipping off into the small trees surrounding their camp to relieve himself before taking up the bag she had meticulously packed. They turned from their small hilltop camp together, facing the trail which lay ahead. The panorama was breathtaking. The clarity of the morning pinpointing details her tired eyes had failed to see the night before when the view had been shrouded by dusk. The Skypeaks continued to soar ever higher in the distance, their tips dressed in snowy white; while directly below lay a long, wide valley that funneled into the forest of rock towers that the Hinterlanders called the Skycastles. She could see why they had acquired that name, the formations looked almost carved, and she wouldn't have been surprised to see inhabitants swarming out of the arches and caves dotting the grove of stones.

Dark fissures in the ground ran between most of the rock formations, which was where the danger of this beautiful landscape lay, she reminded herself as she and Les began picking their way down the hill and into the valley through sparse vegetation. Those cracks in the earth were deep and sheer. A fall when the snow melt made them fill with rushing water was sure death, as the water drained beneath the Skypeaks somewhere, traveling for miles under the mountains, or maybe collecting in a great underground sea that resided beneath the entire mountain range, Les said no one knew for sure. But the water went somewhere, through unfathomably deep cracks that they would soon reach.

"So no one has tried to explore the canyons in the Skycastles when the water is low?" she queried.

Sounding a little startled Les replied, "No, everyone knows if you go down one of the ravines, especially the lowest ones where the water falls forever, that there is no coming back. I've never heard of anyone descending of free will."

"Huh, how cool would it be to be the first people to go down there and figure out where the water goes?" she mused, ignoring Lessoran's nonplussed gaze.

"I imagine it would be quite cool, cold even, verging on freezing, especially since you would undoubtedly get wet, even in the driest months."

"No no no," she backpedaled, stumped once more by English slang not translating correctly. "Cool meaning neat, or exciting and... praiseworthy."

Les shook his head negatively, "I think it would just be death, like it has been for the entire memory of my people. Some things we are not meant to know. What would it benefit us anyway? Knowing where the water goes? We don't need more water; the sky provides that," he stated simply.

Interesting, Sylvia thought, maybe the Trewal didn't possess the curiosity that drove human beings to the edges of their known world, down into the depths, and up into space, just to see what was there. But that didn't seem right, she knew, because Lessoran had proved to be a very inquisitive companion, one who asked questions born of curiosity, and tried to glean information about her in order to figure out why she was so far from home, why she appeared so different than all the Trewal he knew.

As they approached the first towering sentinel of rock, the sound of water reached her ears. It was deep and rumbly, a bone deep vibration building in her chest as they crested a small hill leading directly to the first 'Castle'. It was huge. Much larger than the view from above had suggested, perhaps seventy-five feet or more of the same speckled granite she had seen all over the Skypeaks. Portions of the spire were worn smooth by the elements, leaving the polished sections to wink brilliantly in the sunlight filtering through the overcast sky. Looking into the stone forest before them, she wished for more sun. The Castles would be magical on a clear day, they would shine and glitter like jewels.

Bringing her gaze down, she saw Les had forged ahead to stand by the first ravine; the plume of water spray that wafted up from the opening dwarfed his tall frame as he peered down at the maw of the earth. As she approached him she saw in surprise that he was not getting wet from the spray, even though he stood close to the edge on the slippery rocks. Dashing through the curtain of mist to him, she clung tight to his back for a moment, marveling at the small dry space they seemed to be standing in. But then through her grip on him she felt the resonance, the energetic tickle of his magic, followed by the deep rumble of his voice, "Water magic has its perks in the rainy seasons."

He grinned at her before pulling her in front of him, retaining a tight grip on her shoulders as she leaned closer to the edge of the abyss. The water bubbled and swirled down the narrow channel through the rock to this lowest point, where it broke against a solid rock face, the one they were standing upon. As the angry waters surged against the barrier, she could see it being sucked down into a whirlpool, and occasionally, when the water ebbed, you could see the chasm it dissipated into, a dark pit that swallowed the water in an endless stream. She leaned out a little farther, mesmerized by the ever moving water, and got a face full of spray as her head breached the small sphere of Les's magic.

"Whoops" she said, spitting water. Wiping her face, she tried to stem tears as her eyes watered from the gust of wind that had so kindly brought the water which now ran dripping down her hair and into the collar of her tunic. Lessoran ran the edge of his cloak over her hair roughly, ruffling the black tresses into a snarl as he pulled her to face him, laughing the whole time. Over his shoulder, through the mists surrounding them, a group of riders galloped down the slope towards them. Syl let out a gasp that was swallowed by the noise of the water, just like the noise of their pursuers had been concealed.

"Les they're here!" She screamed, clutching him as he whirled to face the oncoming warriors. They were close enough she could see Pralick at the head of the group, fierce concentration on his face as he brutally heeled his big boned mount to greater speeds, his sharp hooves leaving bleeding gashes in the poor beast's soft belly. Tearing her eyes away, she followed the tug on her hand as Les led them into the shadow of the Skycastles. Skirting the first monument, she could feel the ground loosen beneath her feet, and the sharp bite of rock shards on her now calloused feet.

They fled headlong into the maze of rocks, kicking their speed up to a run when the trail allowed and the danger of a fatal plunge was minimal. Eerie echoes of water and the shouts of men chased them as they made their way farther and farther into the labyrinth. Paths branched out from theirs but Les never hesitated, and after yet another fork in the road she finally saw why. Symbols were scrawled upon the rocks near the split in the trail, guiding them in the right direction.

"Les," she called tugging at their tightly gripped hands, "Les! Can we erase the directions? Can we change them?" If they could just get far enough ahead of the tribe following them they could slow down, take their time over the dangerous terrain, and hopefully avoid dying here amid the towering cairns.

"Brilliant!" he gasped, and still gripping her hand Lessoran tugged her to one of the faces of rock containing a written note. They ran their hands over it frantically, scraped at it with bits of the loose rock at their feet, only to turn in defeat and start running again as the cacophony of pursuit grew loud behind them.

"Carved too deep," he panted.

"How about magic?" she asked, equally winded from their flight.

"Would take too long, water eats stone, but slowly. I would need Earth magic." He shrugged helplessly, "Just run! The Caves are at the other side of the Castles, we just have to make it there and then we'll be safe." He vaulted up onto the top of the broken body of a fallen spire, reaching a hand back to hoist her up. Her knees scraped painfully against the rock as she scrambled, one handed, up the side of the mammoth stone. Half climbing, half falling down into Les's arms on the far side she realized they had left the beaten path of the marked trails, instead following one of the rough game trails zigzagging through the Castles.

"Do you know where you're going?" she asked as the trail they followed suddenly snaked back towards their hunters.

Les tossed the words out over his shoulder as he foraged on, "Not really, but if I don't know where I am, maybe they won't know either."

All roads lead to Rome, she shrugged to herself, *at least I hope they do.* The Skycastles were undeniably beautiful, but here, under their feet, she saw that they were also inhospitable. This would not be a good place to get lost. Water was present but inaccessible, and other than these game trails she had seen no signs of wildlife or edible vegetation. They had little to no preserved food stores left, and had been hoarding what remained, eating off the land as much as possible in preparation for the two-day trek through these stone Castles. But Les had been here before, she knew, maybe he could lead them through, the long way around.

"I know the Caves are roughly below that peak, the Crooked Mountain," he continued, pointing at a steeply sloped mountain that was now to the right and behind of them. "The one with the chunk missing out of the top. If we just keep choosing trails heading in that direction I think we'll get there eventually."

The noise of the Trianti hunters behind them had faded a bit, so they slowed their pace marginally, trying to walk quietly despite the clink of stone on stone. Pausing for breath they both held still, listening, as the faint sound of voices sounded off far behind them, and then an answering call came from the left. "They split up," she breathed.

With a nod, Les held his fingers to his lips, listening again. To her horror Syl heard the shifting of stone behind them and as one she and Lessoran turned to see a Trianti warrior step carefully out from behind the spire they had rounded seconds before. He smiled grimly, a bow trained on the slowly retreating duo.

"Teegar," Les began calmly, his hands held up pleadingly, "just let us get to the Caves, we can let the Ancients decide what to do. The Morgal ordered her taken to the Caves, untouched by Pralick. No one needs to know you let us go, we're the only ones here. We won't say anything to Pralick..." Syl felt the ground shift dramatically behind her as she stepped back, and she halted their slow retreat by pressing her hands into Lessoran's back, arresting his next step.

Glancing around she let Les handle the man, trying to reason with him. There was no good escape route in sight. They had a deep gorge at their backs, and the trail they were on veered sharply left to follow the great crack in the earth. To the right was another fallen spire, this one reduced into a pile of boulders. Leaning close to her companion she whispered, "Our only shot is getting to the cover of that broken Castle." Les nodded while still speaking to his tribe mate. *Clever man,* she thought even as she saw the Trianti warrior shake his head in denial of Les's pleas.

"On three then, to your right Les, as fast as you can." Again the tiniest nod, an assent from the man in front of her, "One," She began, the words barely more than breath leaving her lips. "Two." She wrapped her hands in his cloak, ready to push him in the right direction with her next word, trying not to notice the shaking in her hands. "THREE!" she screamed, throwing herself into violent motion, tugging Les along, desperately trying to get them behind the outcropping of stone and away from the range of the bow. She dashed through a slim opening between two massive slabs of rock, as Les grunted close behind her. She tried to turn, to make sure that the thud she had heard, nearly in tangent with the grunt of her companion, was not what she feared it was, but mid turn the world fell out from beneath her, and she tumbled through the air, Les close behind her. Down, down, down.

Chapter 8

Torman

"We've been over this place ten times Camus; I don't think there are any more booby traps to find," Torman said wearily from his seat on an overturned bucket. The ancient pail creaked with every breath he took, and Torman knew he shouldn't be trusting his bulk to the tired item, but by Garrin's bones he didn't think his poor hooves could take his weight again. He had been walking around the library, and the mysterious dead end passage forking off from its entrance, for about as long as he could handle.

"How exactly are you still going old man? We've been searching high and low in this moldy cave for nearly ten hours. The tension is about to kill me! I've been primed for action and holding my magic for longer than any battle has ever lasted!" Torman glanced again at the tall Maegi, who had returned once again to study the yellowed cranium of the long forgotten creature Kaur had disturbed.

"Mmm?" Camus straightened with an audible crack. "Oh! Torman, silly me. You don't need to worry about more magical traps, the place is clean, no need to hold onto Control."

Torman turned to his mentor, a deceptively mild look on his face, "And how long have you known this?"

Camus closed his eyes as his fingers gently explored the skull before him but at Torman's question he looked around owlishly, blinking repeatedly in the bright glare of the globelight above his head. "Hours ago," he said sheepishly, "Didn't I mention that?"

"Scholars!" Torman threw up his hands in disgust. He stood with a groan and a glare, and not a moment too soon as the pail that had been his seat finally gave up on holding its shape and crumpled, falling over with a clatter. He kicked the offending object out of his way and strode up to Camus. Gentle even in his irritation, he took his arm, saying firmly, "Bed! We should have been there hours ago! There will be plenty of time to study the contents of this library in the morning!"

Camus's eyes strayed back to the shelf and the skull sitting there with its layer of grime, he fluttered the hand still free of Torman's grasp at the younger man, "You go ahead, I want to poke about here for a while longer. I find I don't need as much sleep as I once did." His attention was already back on the contents of the library, and Torman stood, forgotten, amidst the relics of another time. With a befuddled sigh he made his way out of the library alone, leaving instructions for a soldier to join the Maegi, to keep watch in case of any incident, or if the old man finally came to his senses and needed aid finding his bed.

Upon emerging from the dark hallways under the Holm he found they had passed the entire night in the cold cavern. The sun was breasting the horizon with the promise of another clear day. He made a beeline for his rooms, hoping to get a few hours of sleep before the day truly began. But his escape was interrupted four times before he could even reach the stairs that would lead him to his bed. First the acting Captain of the Guard, the capable man he had promoted to his usual position while he and Camus took charge of the Holm in his father's absence, needed his approval to promote new squadron leaders. More squads were required to handle the increased sentry duties both inside and outside the Wall.

Next was the head cook, Gambria, her rotund face perpetually red and sweaty from the ovens. She was rumored to have a soft spot for the children under her tutelage in the kitchens, keeping aside sweets and special treats for them, especially in this, one of the kitchen staff's busiest times. But he had never seen this gentle side, even when he was a child. Looking at her stern frown above the wobbling of her double chin, he couldn't remember the thin lips ever smiling in his direction. But then again she had probably still not forgiven him for filching that blueberry pie she had made specially for the pregnant wife of Councilman Jeston when he was ten.

Gambria handed him a sheaf of papers delineating the numbers from the harvest thus far, and put one last paper on top with a stern look and a waggle of one plump finger, saying, "This is what I need from the next trader; if he doesn't have it, order some, or we will be eating tasteless gruel for every meal once the snows block the roads!"

He was then accosted by the man he had put in charge of building new residences inside the Wall, who towed along the surly blacksmith, both arguing in loud voices Torman thought quite unnecessary at this hour of the morning.

"My Lord! Sir, you need to talk sense into this good for 'nuffin metal worker!" the irate carpenter said heatedly.

"Sense? *Sense?* It's the Lord's own *sensible* orders you're asking me to go against! He was the one who requested an overhaul of the armory and replacements for any weapons as are too old for use!" retorted the smith in his deafening bellow.

Torman quickly sorted out the men's grievances, keeping the blacksmith and the majority of his journeymen busy making sure the Holm's weapons and armor were both plentiful enough and in good repair for any upcoming battles with the Hinterland tribes. The carpenter he appeased by convincing the smith he could spare one Journeyman to watch over the apprentices at the forge while they made more nails for the carpentry detail to use in their building.

Lastly, just as he approached the last corner which would lead him away from the common areas of the Keep, the quiet, melodious voice of his lover called for his attention. Metra approached him, her smile a welcome balm in a morning already fraught with upset and arguments. He wanted to take her hand in his and whisk them both away to his bedchamber in order to forget the world for an hour or two. But even she needed something from him as the Holm's agriculturist. From Torman the Lord, not Torman the man.

With the increase in the Holm's interior population, the gardens had become something of a retreat for those common folk and serfs looking to escape the hustle and bustle of the Keep's main courtyard. But unwary feet had tread upon Metra's fresh seedlings getting ready to bring about Fall collards and vegetables. And idle hands and mouths were picking off the produce destined for winter stores. She wished to requisition a fence for the Holm gardens, for both the health of her plants, and for any unrest rationing might cause later in the winter when fresh food was in low supply. Torman tiredly agreed to her forward thinking plan, agreeing that the orchards on the far side of the Keep from the gardens would be a much better place for any in the Holm to seek out should they need a moment of peace. The pears, coreps, apples and terns there were almost completely harvested by this time of season.

With a kiss he left her, the feel of her soothing hand on his cheek fading as the day's problems and requirements tumbled messily through his head. By the time he stood facing his bed in his chambers he knew the time for rest was long gone today. With a groan he turned instead to his father's study, and the newest set of missives waiting for him there. He had seen the messenger, Chir, wearily entering the kitchens earlier, so he knew in the pile of petitions, tallies, reports and correspondence was word from the capital, and hopefully from his brother.

He dug through the stack impatiently; word about Sylvia and Ryland would save this day from the pit it had begun in. He'd been having trouble sleeping since learning of the Hinterland attack. His worry about Sylvia and the relationship between his brother and the Jorgen lurked in the back of his mind during the busy days, then came out into the open to torment him when he retired for the night. The general loss of sleep on top of the completely restless night spent in that cursed ancient library had sunk him into a black mood. He could use some good news.

He found the letter he sought, his brother's seal unbroken. He would have to find a way to properly thank the young messenger. Chir had been as good as his word, delivering letters under the radar rather than selling the brothers out to the Jorgen, which would have been very profitable for him. Maybe this next letter could be a little less circumspect, he never was any good at riddles; he would leave that for Camus and Ryland, who both seemed to come alive when faced with the cursed puzzles.

Skimming the contents of the letter, his heart fell. He didn't need to be good at puzzles to figure out Ryland had lost Sylvia in the battle, but he could not confirm her death. He ran a hand through the curly hair between his antlers, stopping to finger the hammered silver Terling that encircled one tine of the rugged horns. Ryland's antlers sported an identical ring, one that had previously graced the much smaller horns of their elder sister. Fria had given Torman the Terling the midwinter before Ryland was born, a token of sibling solidarity in the face of their father's harshness. Years later, not long after their sister's suicide, the twin of his ornament had appeared on the budding antlers of his baby brother. They had never spoken of it, but Torman secretly liked the idea of Fria's youthful notion of camaraderie living on in the remaining siblings.

Torman set Ryland's letter down with a sigh. That poor little girl. Trewal or not, he had liked Sylvia, with her copious amounts of fierceness and humor, all boiled down into one tiny little package. He could only pray to Garrin to keep her safe somehow. Maybe she had run off into the woods during the battle and was making her way back to the safety of the Holm. He would have to have a word with one of his more trustworthy sentries to keep an eye out for anything unusual in Jorgenholm's vicinity.

The alternatives didn't bear thinking about. They were completely out of his control while he was stuck here ruling in his father's absence. Captured by the Hinterlanders was a harsh enough fate, to become both slave and child bearer whether she wanted it or not; but if the Demandron had gotten their hands on her... A shudder wracked his body as his fingers once more toyed with Fria's Terling before curling into a tight fist to slam down on the desk with a thump. He hadn't been able to save his sister, and if *they* had little Sylvia, well he wouldn't be able to save her either. His head dropped heavily, despair dragging his proud stature downward in a rare show of depression.

Kaur

Due to his involvement in the discovery of the underground library, Kaur had been allowed to continue his exploration of the place under the guise of aiding Maegi Camus with his categorizing of the books and scrolls housed there. It was dusty, dirty work which made him sneeze often and the cold damp in the room had undoubtedly been the cause of the deep, dry cough that wracked his body even when he was tucked warmly in bed. His duties for the Maegi were infrequent, as the man spent an inordinate amount of time leafing through each separate book he had Kaur take down from the shelves. Kaur's duties were of the fetch and carry sort, along with cleaning each item removed from the shelf they were working on, and dusting the shelf itself when it was clear.

From the frequent sidelong looks Camus gave him he suspected that his help in the library was not the only reason the Maegi had chosen him for this task, but an excuse to keep an eye on him after his first strange experience here. He noticed no difference in himself after the pain and light had engulfed him when his hand touched the skull. The item in question leered at him from the shelf next to the one they were currently working on. He refused to touch it, even at the Maegi's insistence that it was completely harmless. Once was enough for him. He had learned his lesson. Regardless of the reasons for his new-found rapport with the Big Lord and the Holm's Maegi, this job had increased his standing among the other children aiding in the explorations, and he had never been prouder.

Camus set aside the book he had been examining to make a note in his journal, muttering to himself as he scratched away with his quill. "...detailed account of medicinal herbs found in mountains called The Teeth. Most all plants are ones I recognize from the Skypeaks. Could the Teeth and our Skypeaks be the same? Or a distant range of similar climate?" Kaur eyed the man with interest, intrigued by the idea that the landmarks of his world were old enough for people to have forgotten they were once called something else. He stayed still so as not to disturb the man, hoping he would continue his musings, but instead Camus turned to the boy and said, "Kaur, the next tome please, the one bound in leather will do."

Kaur picked up the giant book with difficulty before gently scrubbing the dirt from its thick cover with a damp cloth. The pages of the book were almost as large as his torso, and the brittle leather of the cover was stamped with an intricate pattern resembling vines. He polished the metal clasp with a flourish before handing the awkward burden to Camus.

"Ah!" The Maegi exclaimed happily, lightly tracing the title of the book with one gnarled finger, "an atlas! This should answer my questions about that mountain range if it's from the same time period as the last book." Kaur looked longingly at the cover as Camus flipped to the first page, but the squiggles and connected lines Camus had so happily read meant as little to the boy as the decorative vines curling up the spine of the book.

"What's an 'at lass'?" he asked tentatively, hoping to gain Camus's attention before this book captured him as firmly as the last had.

Camus looked up with a smile for the boy, "It's a book of maps and charts that detail the lay of the land. The maps can be for as small an area as a single village, or as vast as all of Prium and whatever lays beyond our borders. If there is a mountain range named The Teeth here, I can compare it to our own current atlas to see if the Skypeaks are one and the same. Come here and see child." Camus patted one knee invitingly, settling the small boy on his lap in front of the large pages of the book before them.

Kaur gazed at the spidery drawing before him in awe. What would it be like to see the world like this? Laid out flat and distant below him, as if he viewed the terrain from a perch upon a stalkwing's back. The wandering path of a river looked as small as a game trail as it trekked through the small drawings of trees, only to peter off into spiky lines that must represent a field of long grass which looked to be the same size as the entirety of the mountain range where the river had sprung from.

"I don't recognize any of these names" Camus fretted, his breath minty as it ghosted over Kaur's shoulder. "Aha! There are 'The Teeth'" he said in triumph, pointing to the tiny lettering amidst the craggy lines of the mountains Kaur had been looking at. Kaur squinted at the writing, and a feeling of shame flooded his body. He slid from the bony lap that held him, wishing his parents were smart enough to teach him to read, as Retcha's mother had. But a hunter had no use for letters, and a scullery maid's hands were too busy with pots, pans, and platters to bother with the utensils of learning. He moved restlessly to the half empty shelf they were making their way through, wishing, for the first time, to be back to his old task of exploring empty rooms rather than standing amidst hundreds of books that were all but meaningless to him. There was too much standing around, too much time to think, too many things surrounding him that were never destined to be a part of his simple world, no matter how they fascinated him. He plucked the next book from the shelf, a small thing, thin and worn. When he turned to find his rag so he could wipe the cover free of dust, he was met by the watchful eyes of the Maegi.

"Do you know how to read, Kaur?" Camus asked softly, "You are a bright boy. Even if you don't know now, with your mind it wouldn't take long to teach you." His brown eyes were soft as they searched the child's face. Kaur hunched his shoulders self-consciously, gazing down at his feet as he fidgeted under the direct attention of his elder.

"Ma says I don't need to know. I'll just be a hunter like my Da, and he hasn't read a word in 'is life. It's a waste of time sir." The last words were spoken like a mantra, as if he said them out of habit rather than felt their meaning.

Cocking his head to the side to ease muscles tired of the ponderous weight of his antlers, Camus considered briefly before speaking. "Do you want to be a hunter?"

"It's a good job," Kaur responded defensively.

Camus nodded in grave agreement. "A very good job, and immensely important. But it's not for everyone. I myself did not take up my father's trade; I had a different path. And I think that I have been much happier being a Maegi than I would have been as a trader."

Kaur's eyes widened, "Your father was a trader?" he asked incredulously.

"Indeed he was. But my future wasn't to be the same as my father's. I had talents in different areas than he, and my family was wise enough to know that. Have you ever asked your father if he could find you someone to teach you to read and write? I have always thought the Holm would be much better off if all of its children could learn their letters, rather than just a few."

Kaur looked at the old man consideringly before launching into speech. "It would be more fair," he said quickly, as if afraid Camus would interrupt him at any moment, "We could help more if we could read and write down numbers instead of memorizing." He paused as he drew in breath, eyeing the man before him to see if he would be allowed to continue speaking. When Camus simply looked at him with the same kind regard, he barreled on. "If everyone learned, we'd all have a fair shot at being something better. My father could make maps of the game trails while he hunts, the cook could record recipes for us to learn rather than teaching everyone what to do each time, my Ma could draw up patterns for clothes rather than having them all fitting different."

The boy stopped speaking, his eyes weary as he searched Camus's face for anger at his speaking out of turn. But the man simply smiled. "Those are many of the same thoughts I've had, which just proves me right about that sharp mind of yours," he added with a wink of one heavy lidded eye. Kaur smiled back at him tentatively, completely thrown that such an important man not only took the time to hear him out, but actually seemed to think he was on to something.

"That's it!" the Maegi said determinedly, "This winter when the snows fall and the children, serfs and common folk are left to darning socks and feeding fires, I will begin basic lessons. The Jorgen is not here to dissuade me, and I know Torman will approve." The Maegi's grin had turned fierce at his proclamation, and Kaur recoiled a bit before the man's face lightened and he beckoned the child closer. "Enough of future plans, I have so many questions about the past. Kaur, in my tower there is a rolled map of the Skypeaks and Jorgenholm, it will be marked like this..." He scratched out two sets of symbols on his blotting paper for Kaur to examine. "That reads 'The Skypeaks'; can you please fetch it for me? And we will find out if these so called Teeth are one and the same as our Skypeaks."

Kaur fled the library gratefully, keeping the image of the words Camus had shown him firmly in his mind. It was nice to have someone talk to him so equally, but it was also stressful. He desperately wanted Camus and the Big Lord to think him smart, but it made everything he said and did in their presence so important. It made him afraid to say anything at all for fear of disappointing them. This menial task of fetching a scroll was simple, there was only one way to complete it, and no 'above and beyond' to achieve. In some ways he thought that was better. His life had greatly improved since finding the forgotten passageway, but in some ways he missed the simplicity of the life he had enjoyed before.

He sped through the upper halls of the Keep to the spiral stair leading to the Maegi's tower, pausing to catch his breath before he began the long upward climb. Kaur pushed through the thick wood door with difficulty, preferring to leave it cracked just enough to emit his slight form rather than wrestle with the heavy thing. With the aid of a shaft of light from the closest arrow slit, he shuffled the various rolled maps aside, searching for the markings that matched Camus's earlier drawing. "Aha!" he said aloud in triumph as he pulled a long roll of parchment from the tightly packed basket. He fingered the two lines of letters, they looked much like the ones Camus asked for, but slightly different. He looked them over carefully one more time before deciding the differences were slight and his memory was sure. This was the map the Maegi had requested.

He scampered back down through the Holm, dodging serfs with lowered heads as they went about their tasks. As he sidled back into the stairwell that lead down to the library he eyed the other passage that broke off from the main one. He had gone down the hall that took him to the library, many times since the first time when he and the Big Lord had unsealed the corridor, but he had never seen what lay at the end of the other fork. Torman and Camus seemed completely uninterested in that second passage, focusing entirely on the library. The looming dark called to Kaur each and every time he passed it.

Knowing his headlong sprint to the tower had him returning much quicker than Camus would be expecting, he raced back to the top of the stairs to pluck the torch from the entrance and then ran back as fast as the flickering flame would allow. Leaving the rolled map propped up against the wall he stalked quietly down the hall until it banked sharply to the right and then peered cautiously around the corner. He let out the breath he had been holding in anticipation in a gusty sigh. "A dead end" he said aloud, and then giggled at the sad tone of his voice. Well of course it wasn't something exciting, Camus and Torman would have been exploring it if it was as interesting as the library. With one last look at the bulging tumble of rocks that blocked the passage, he turned around to deliver the map to Camus.

Camus

The library was as fascinating a place as it was confusing. For every discovery he made, like that whoever had stocked this library had known his Skypeaks as 'The Teeth', there were ten bewildering manuscripts he couldn't puzzle out. He found himself wishing for Ryland's company, he would have taken as great an interest in the tidbits of ancient history as himself. Instead he was kept company by the bright, but unfortunately illiterate, child who had discovered the rune that opened the stairwell to the library. He had a feeling the small boy would be in his presence for much of the next few rebirths, considering what Torman had told him about Kaur's ability to smell the old magic permeating the book filled cavern. Kaur would need magical training soon, and before his magic ripened Camus planned to have him fully versed in reading, writing, and basic maths. *Poor boy*, he thought with an inward grin, he doesn't know what studious torments he unleashed upon himself when Torman brought him to my attention.

Camus and his young helper were slowly cataloging the collection of books down here, making a note of each tome and scroll's original position before sorting them into an order his mind could comprehend. The tall shelves by the door were being filled by anything that was written in old Galmorish, while the extensive central shelves that blossomed off of the pillars dripping from the lofty ceiling were beginning to brim with the books penned in Layette. Far in the rear of the Library he had Kaur shelving those books he couldn't make heads or tails of, which far outnumbered those he could decipher. Kaur was attempting to keep them in groupings of like languages, the ones with similar looking symbols staying near their fellows. It was a task well suited to the curious boy, and one his inability to read had no effect on.

One long, curving wall at the left of the entrance to the room was outfitted with a deep workbench that had been scattered with the devices of potion-making and various other instruments Camus could not identify. Kaur had slowly been filling up the extra-large, waist high shelf with the objects scattered throughout the library, items Camus knew the uses of at one end, and the ever growing array of mysterious ones at the other. Camus had had to move the huge skull that Kaur had so unfortunately interacted with that first day. The boy would not go near it. It now lay among the artifacts of a forgotten time, snugged up to a box of smooth blue metal with no discernible way to open it, and on the other side of the skull lay a slim rod about as long as his forearm and made of a material strikingly similar in color to the yellowed bone beside it. He had been dumbfounded when Kaur had accidentally dropped the rod as he transferred it to the bench, and the clatter it had made was not the dry rattle of a bone, but like the chiming of a bell.

So many mysteries to unravel, so much information to be gleaned! He wished he were a younger man, because there was no way all of the secrets of this library would be discovered in his lifetime, maybe not even in Kaur's lifetime. He sighed heavily, shutting the book he had been looking over with a snap before adding it to the precarious stack of unreadable books for Kaur to shelve at the back of the library. Pulling the next tome towards him from the pile of unsorted books, he fingered the stamped leather cover with interest. His gnarled fingers moved over the raised image of a seal, divided into four segments, each bearing a sigil, one for each of the Gods. "So the Gods outlived this fallen civilization" he said, his eyes lingering on the bow and arrows that represented the Jorgen's God, Garrin.

Flipping to the first page he grinned, *finally!* A book in a tongue he could read, and one that might shed some light on the religious aspects of the Age Before Memory. He had always suspected the Gods and their fickleness had been a factor in the fall of the ancient Trewal. It was a theory dismissed by his peers, even though he had pages and pages of notes gathered from the ruins of ancient cities to back up his idea. Something dark had happened in those cities, and all the scraps of information he had found seemed to pinpoint Garrin, Jeale, Freyton, and their dark brother as a part of that black force which began to interpose itself on the artwork and buildings left from that era. But his view on the Gods had always been less than flattering, a belief picked up from his roots in Galmorah perhaps, or more likely from his unique position as a *Weiring*.

The soft sounds of Kaur moving around the library faded to the background as he began reading eagerly. The book was written from the perspective of a traveler, detailing his adventures. The first page bore the detailed visage of a snarling ice lion, the mark of the Hinterland God Freyton, and also the crest of the Jorgens of Jorgenholm. He quickly zeroed in on the portion of text where Freyton's name was evident in hopes of gleaning any useful information.

My journey began in the cold northern province of Fallon where I was born, amidst the snowcapped Teeth and their jagged stones. From a young age my tendency to wander was evident, much to my humble mother's terror. She was constantly fetching me back from locations unfit and unsafe for a meandering toddler, but no matter her adroit diligence and wily plots to confine my free spirit, I would manage an escape to explore the world around me, beginning within the confines of good Freyton's stronghold. Soon the walls of my Lord's Keep could not confine me and as a young boy, the densely wooded slopes of The Teeth began to sing their siren's song, summoning me to endless hours spent walking in silence but for the whisper of the wind, the rustle of wildlife and the austere beauty of my homeland...

Interesting, he mused. He had no knowledge of a stronghold in the Skypeaks belonging to the Hinterlanders and Freyton. They were largely nomadic, he knew, each tribe keeping to their own land except for raids against one another, and Jorgenholm. It would be strange to find out that the Hinterlanders had a Keep like Jorgenholm hidden away in the north of the mountain range. It would rewrite history as Prium knew it! Also strange was that this ancient Trewal seemed to refer to his God as a ruler. His finger hovered over the passage that mentioned, 'my Lord's Keep'. The presence of the Gods must have been much stronger in those times, rather than the vague nudges and dreams that the Gods communicated with in the present. Camus flipped a few pages, scanning the elegantly penned words for facts rather than the personal musings of the rather pompous explorer. He stopped on a new page, this one topped with the bow and arrow of Garrin.

It took years of wandering and many, many, footfalls for me to consider my home province fully explored and mapped, but soon after I had witnessed nineteen rebirths of the seasons my roving feet fell onto Duronti soil where the Lord of the Hunt roamed the gentle woodlands with his brightly attired court trailing after him like a string of lesser gems behind the sparkling center pendant. I found little to capture my interest in the woodlands of this region, excepting my encounter with Garrin and his hounds as they thundered by in pursuit of a great boar, but I found my joyous love for new sights rekindled by the utterly entrancing expanse of golden grass that the people in these parts call the Ocean of Grain. This endless stretch of gently waving stalks yields up most of Duronti's wealth in the form of grain and weave-able fibers, but to me it afforded a burning need to see the great expanse of water it was said to resemble...

The abrupt clearing of a throat at his side jerked Camus from his engrossment in reading the flowery account of what he knew must be the Sacred Plains, bordering the Reedwood forest to the south of Jorgenholm. He twisted his head to see Torman standing by his side, one eyebrow raised bemusedly at the lengths he had to go to, to get the Maegi's attention.

"You with me now Cam?" he asked, laughter lurking behind the words. "I've a letter from Ryland in the capital, news from the here and now." He brandished a letter in Ryland's distinguished hand under his nose until Camus marked his place in the traveler's journal to take it from him and read its contents. Casting a glance around the library to locate Kaur, Torman spoke on with a lowered voice after seeing the boy busy with a stack of scrolls near the rear of the cavern. "Sylvia isn't with him, she disappeared during the battle, but was not among the dead."

Camus struggled to rid himself of the vague notions and tentative connections that had been forming in his mind as he read the long dead explorer's words, bringing his mind back to the present, and the problems he actually had a chance at helping with. "I can try to farscry her location," he said slowly, "It's really our only option, but it is by no means a sure way to find out what happened to her." His heart ached for the young girl, lost in this world she knew nothing about, and he sent up a silent prayer to any God willing to listen, *regardless of my qualms about your benevolence, protect that girl child that you have dragged into this mess of a world. Whichever of you wanted her here, you owe her that much!*

"Any information we can get that might set my mind at ease would be welcome," Torman said, rubbing eyes dark with the smudges of sleepless nights. "Ryland seems to be handling things alright other than that, although he hasn't managed to get to the Academy Library to figure out how to get Sylvia home," he paused before adding morosely, "if we ever find her again."

Camus touched Torman's hand in commiseration. His tender heart had never done well with events beyond his control. He was a man of action, and when faced with a danger he could not take up arms against, it ate away at him. "Find me an escort Torman, I will go now if it has the chance of putting you at ease." Torman nodded his head gratefully, striding from the room to arrange for a group of soldiers to guard him as Camus fought his joints to gain his feet, following at a more sedate pace.

Torman

Torman could tell that Camus's trip outside the Wall to farscry had been unsuccessful from the second the Maegi stepped back into the Keep's courty ard. From his vantage stacking bales in the hay loft above the recently finished stables, he saw the disruption the small squad of soldiers made as they escorted Camus back into the Holm and then broke away from the tall man to return to their other duties. Camus remained where he was standing, parting the flow of busy people crossing the courtyard like a tall, thin, boulder in the middle of a river. His face was turned upwards, eyes roving the facade of the dark stoned Keep in front of him, his mouth a disappointed slash and his bony shoulders hunched just a fraction more than usual.

With a sigh Torman tidied up the last bale of hay he had been slinging into place and then descended the ladder to the packed dirt floor of the stable, earning himself a multitude of splinters from the green, un-sanded ladder that had been constructed just this morning. Weaving his way through the animals being led into their new home, he met Camus in the courtyard, greeting him with a simple, "No luck?"

"No luck," the old man agreed, "I found her, but all I can see is a blinding light of ever changing colors, it blocks out everything else, her surroundings, her companions, everything. All I know is that she lives, and the Gods still have her in their hands, all four pairs of them."

Torman started at that last bit of information even as he took the Maegi's arm to help him into the Keep and in front of a fire. Camus's claw-like hands were frigid in his own warm ones from his prolonged time outside. *All four Gods,* he thought? He remembered Camus mentioning the Gods likely had some part in Sylvia's presence in Prium, in a conversation that felt like it took place seasons ago, rather than a mere month. But he hadn't taken the time to think on the details of *all* of the Gods having a hand in her being taken from the home she knew. The Gods did not work together. They guarded their worshipers jealously, the only exception being in Galmorah where the people tried to appease all of them at once, and then ignored their existence afterwards. If all four Gods had a claim on the human girl, they were fighting over her. He shook his head in vexation. *What was so special about Sylvia aside from those blue eyes?*

Camus spoke as they entered the Keep and Torman's feet automatically propelled them towards the stairs to Camus's tower, making Torman realize he had been lost in his own thoughts for too long. "I'll go to the library I think," Camus asserted, tugging vainly at his large escort. "I found the writings of an explorer from what must be the Age Beyond Memory. In his time the Skypeaks were called 'The Teeth', and the Sacred Plains the 'Ocean of Grain'." His tugging stopped as Torman obligingly turned back towards the kitchens, and the path that led to the underground library. "The traveler also speaks rather familiarly of the Gods, as if in that time Garrin and Freyton walked among their people, rather than speaking to them through Dreams, Mages, and Seers."

His tugging started up again as Torman stopped them in front of the kitchen's largest hearth where the head cook Gambria stood testing the feel of a batch of bread. "Gambria," Torman said with as much respect in his voice as he would have afforded a visiting Councilman. "Can you spare a snack and some hot tea for Camus? He wants to go back down to the warrens, but after his trip outside the Wall I fear he will catch his death down there in the damp." Torman lowered his eyes from her face, the ultimate sign of deference.

With a "humpff" and a glare for Torman that held less venom than usual, Gambria took Camus in hand, whisking him to the fireside and a convenient stool positioned beside its warmth. Soon his red knuckled hands were wrapped around a steaming cup of spicy Kercha from the Sareth Isles, and a thick slice of bread so hot the butter Gambria lathered on it melted immediately, rested on his knee. Torman thanked the grumpy woman, hiding his small smirk of satisfaction with lowered eyes once more.

Coming to lean against the wall near Camus's perch, he smiled in truth at the old man's contented sighs as the heat soaked into him. When the bread had disappeared Torman prodded him gently. "So a traveler's account huh? You really think the library has been sealed off since the Age Beyond Memory?"

"Yes!" Camus said enthusiastically, and Torman was glad he had strong-armed him into a little recuperation before he descended to the cold library again, as he saw the fire's warmth loosen his movements and the angry red of his visible joints fade. "There was also a peculiar mention of a stronghold in 'The Teeth' belonging to Freyton, which may mean we have been misrepresenting the Hinterland tribes as nomadic for centuries when in actuality they have a Keep just as we do!"

Torman stared at Camus in shock. If the Hinterlanders truly did have a central base, then the wandering tribes were more akin to raiding parties than familial groups as his ancestors had always believed. His mind reeled for a moment with the new knowledge, but then his training in battle mechanics asserted itself and he said breathlessly, "If we could locate the Keep and capture it then this endless war would finally be done with!" The concept was one he could barely grasp, a life without the fear of a Hinterland raid? No more needless deaths or casualties among the innocent? A Holm where the commoners could spread out and grow without the constant threat from the barbarian tribes?

A sudden thought occurred to him that brought his growing elation to an abrupt halt. "I thought all Relics from the Age Beyond Memory had to be taken to the Demandron in Seaprium?" Torman asked, suddenly wishing the treasure trove of ancient books and artifacts had been left to rot away under the Keep.

"Yes, well..." Camus said uncomfortably, "I can't be sure that is the time they're from, you see, so it seems silly to bring their attention down on us when it may not even be something they are interested in..."

Both men sat in contemplation for a moment before Torman spoke abruptly, "We should double the guard on the warrens, and limit the number of men that guard the entrance rather than rotating them with the sentries on the Wall."

"Yes we should," Camus agreed.

Without further discussion they stood and made their way down to the larder where Lear still toiled away on his maps of the warrens with his miniature army of children. A handful of the little ones stood around Lear waiting for their turn to report to him, the serf children discernible from the commoners only by their filed antlers. A hearty coating of dust covered each child, hiding the finer quality of the commoner's clothes. Passing the man with a nod, Torman handed Camus off to a solidly built boy so the old Maegi could have assistance down the steep stairwell to the library, while he stopped to speak with the guard posted at the entrance to the Northern hallways.

When he had finally sorted out the rotation of the guards with the man, he continued down to the library himself, content he had only the most trustworthy of soldiers working at guarding the secret room. He felt confident he could trust the six men he and Johan had selected to keep any unwanted visitors, and any potent information from slipping by. Each and every one of the handpicked men had family who had disappeared into the Demandron's harems, never to return. They had every reason to keep the information the secret library held to themselves, and away from the black robed Mages.

He made his way into the now familiar hallway, passing the dead end corridor with barely a glance before reaching the brightly illuminated library to find Camus back at the books and Kaur faithfully working his way through the piles that needed to be re-shelved. "Camus!" he boomed, startling both man and boy from their pursuits. He quieted his voice "I would like you to make finding the location of your supposed 'Hinterland stronghold' your main focus from this point onward. If we can begin gathering information on the lay of the land around this Keep before the heavy snows hit, then I will have all winter to devise a plan to take out the tribes once and for all."

"The Hinterlanders have a Keep like Jorgenholm, sir?" Kaur asked in amazement. "Then why do their women and babes wander round the mountains with them all the time?"

Camus and Torman exchanged a quick glance before Camus jumped in with an explanation for the boy. "That's why he said 'supposed' Kaur. I found some mentions of a Stronghold under the Hinterland God's sway in this journal here. If what I am gleaning from this man's rather rambling account from times long forgotten, is true, then what we thought we knew of the Hinterland tribes could be wrong."

"Is that the man who calls the Skypeaks 'Teeth'?" Kaur had made his way over to the table Camus sat at to finger the small leather bound journal. He turned a page and ran his finger under the first line, his tongue making an appearance out of the corner of his mouth as he concentrated on the words.

"Can you read it, Kaur?" Torman asked in surprise. The young boy had only been taking lessons with Camus for a short time, and the language of the ancient diary was stilted and old fashioned enough that he himself might have trouble puzzling through it.

"Only a word or two." Kaur responded, defeated. "I wish I could help more! Not just putting books on shelves and cleaning, but finding important things like a way to stop the Hinterlanders from killing my friends!" Rare frustration colored the competent child's voice and Camus reached out to rest a hand on his shoulder in consolation.

"You being here is a great help, Kaur," the old man said, drawing the boy closer to his side for a one-armed hug. "I need you down here to look after me, and soon enough your young eyes will be better at reading than my own! Then you will be the one discovering ancient secrets and mysterious northern strongholds from a time where people thought mountains were the teeth of the land!" Camus's attempt at levity fell flat as Kaur frowned in sudden concentration.

He picked up the journal again and then shyly looked up at his elders, "If he wrote it so long ago that the mountains were teeth rather than peaks then maybe the name of Freyton's keep was forgotten too!" At the considering looks that appeared on the adult's faces he continued on, "Maybe it was years, and years, and years ago and even the Gods forgot whose keep it was and it is someone else's now," he finished.

Torman locked eyes with his mentor, and found sudden clarity in the mystery Camus had unearthed. "What if indeed, Kaur. I think you may be on to something there young man. We will need a fresh sheaf of paper to transcribe the journal, can you fetch some for us?" Torman waited until the youngster had scampered out of earshot before putting his thoughts to words.

"Camus, what if this Hinterland keep is Jorgenholm? What if that is why the Hinterlanders plague us unendingly? They war to regain the stronghold of their God!" Such a simple solution, yet it seemed impossible to him that the root of a centuries long conflict was as uncomplicated as that.

"It does seem feasible..." Camus drew the last words out as he considered. "It *would* explain the green Hinterland magic, the touch of Freyton that I saw in Kaur when you two opened the library. In my Sight, Freyton's touch is always that same green, it flickers over some of the Hinterlanders during raids, just as it flickers around Sylvia."

The two men grinned at one another, pleased by their possible discovery. Then Torman spoke, a little sadly, "Ryland would love this. He would love this library and he would love discovering its secrets. But hopefully he will be happy to simply hear of our findings. When Kaur gets back with that paper we shall write to him of this, all of it."

Chapter 9

Cirillia

Something was not right. Never before had the Ancient's foresight been this wrong. They had all seen the same image in their Dreams. But the strongest foretelling in any of the Ancients' long memories had not come true. Each detail she and her peers had Dreamed was recorded and compared, the similarities unmistakable. The timing exact. She had only to close her eyes to recall the vivid vision. Most times she Dreamed a Seer's Dream the images were cloudy, the faces of the important players blurred or shifting so quickly she could not identify them, objects in their hands morphing as if the future was uncertain. But that morning had been different.

A young woman, a Mage, blue of eyes and hornless picked her way through the last few turns of the path through the Skycastles. Her face was dirty and pale, her thin frame angular beneath ill-fitting garments. The clarity of the vision was such that Cirillia could almost smell the unwashed state of the girl's body, and feel the grit in her lank hair as she swiped some loose strands back away from her face. She walked with a strange grace, her hips rolling as if the ground beneath her was the deck of a ship rather than the solid earth of the Crooked Mountain.

Behind her a shadow flickered, tall and broad one moment and almost nonexistent the next. Sometimes she could make out the tines of a glorious rack of antlers. Or the glint of the dying light on a high cheekbone and the furrow of a darkly brooding brow. But the shifting of the figure's form was so extensive she could tell no more than that it was a Trewal male. The full belly of Loria was paired illogically next to the glowing orb of the sun as it descended towards the horizon, behind the approaching Mage, marking the time of arrival clearly.

As the girl drew closer, Cirillia saw a long knife appear in her hand, its blade worn and chipped from use. It disappeared in the next breath to be replaced by a crumpled standard, the blood red color making the pale gray insignia of the Jorgen's stand out in stark contrast. She tore her eyes away from the nauseating fluctuations taking place in the Mage's hand, focusing instead on the strange crown perched precariously on the girl's dark head. It came and went like a flame in the wind, making the details hard to pick out. A wide silver band settled itself loosely on her forehead, twin antlers shining metallically as they sprouted from the heavily ornamented band to tower over her fragile features. Delicate filigree twined around the crown to hang down at elegant intervals, shining brilliantly against the midnight backdrop of her hair.

From every crack and crevasse of the stone towers behind the Mage, Hinterlanders appeared, decked out for war, weapons bristling in every hand. The tide of Trewal followed her straight towards Cirillia at the entrance to the Caves. The Mage appeared as if she didn't even notice the destruction she was leaving in her wake, the madness of war. Cirillia's special spot, her peaceful getaway from the stuffy underground tomb her God had called her to, perfumed with the sweet smell of Windthorn roses, was now ringed by the combined fury of all the Hinterland tribes.

She could pick out the individual tribes, their colors vivid even as they intermingled with the group next to them. The green of the Trianti with their towering antlers forking majestically, complementing the delicate blue sported by the Rishal, and their similarly delicate horns. The iconic black Steelskin leaf of the Proult butted up against the crossed arrows worn by the Kla'routh, their horns of opposite sizes heavily intermingled. The deep purple of the Diarmas stood out from the gray and white ice lion pelts that were the only mark of the reclusive Baroun, only to be swallowed by the huge number of bodies covered head to toe in brown, their antlers filed down to small, wickedly sharp stubs among the tightly braided blonde locks of the Verie.

Her people united behind the strange, ethereal woman as she toiled towards the Caves, the wispy shadow-man closer to her than her own shadow, which stretched before her for what looked like miles, as if the small female was actually a giantess, dwarfing the Skypeaks themselves. The majesty of the gathered Hinterlanders

nearly took Cirillia's breath away, the bloodthirsty cries of the seven
tribes co-mingling with purpose rather than antagonism until her
vision was swallowed by the growing howl of war cries that had
been sounding among the Skypeaks for centuries.

She shook herself, pulling her consciousness from the
powerful vision as it sucked her in again. She and the other Ancients
had prepared the Caves, they had prepared themselves for the Battle
Mage all of their visions foretold, the one who would finally unite
the splintered tribes into the great nation she knew the Hinterlanders
could be. But instead of a powerful Mage on the eve of Loria's
fullness, a group of angry members of the Trianti had ridden in from
the maze of the Skycastles with the dying sun, their tempers as red-
hot as the sky.

The leader at the forefront of the group was a mountain of a
man, beefy muscles stacked on his shoulders and chest like slabs of
rock, the hateful look in his eyes just as unyielding as his hard body.
Cirillia looked past him to the shifting group of young men he had
led through the maze to reach the Caves. Some of the warrior's eyes
were as hard as their leaders, but sprinkled through the crowd were
shifting feet and uneasy glances at their fellows. Most of the looks
were directed at the man facing off with the Ancients, but a good
number were being cast at a stocky archer with unfortunately uneven
antlers standing stoically in the center of the crowd, his gaze fixed
unwaveringly on the Ancients.

The large man spoke formally, his eyes flickering among the
seven elders before him ceaselessly. "I am Pralick of the Trianti. I
come to the Caves of Orr as my ancestors have come before me, to
cast off the name my mother bestowed upon me when I woke to this
world. I will enter the Caves Nameless. I will enter the Caves
weaponless. I will enter the Caves with only the stones of my tribe
for succor and life, and I will emerge Named once more, or never
again." The ceremonial entreaty felt flat coming from him, anger an
overlying tone that deadened the usual awe, hope, and fire that came
with a young man asking entrance to the Caves to seek the name
Morgal.

Kon, a wizened little man who had been living as an Ancient
at the Caves longer than any of the others, stepped forward after a
brief glance at the rest of the Seers. That one look spoke many things

to his fellows, the milky white eyes conveying both confusion and resignation at such unexpected guests. These were not the faces they were expecting tonight, but tradition must be upheld; the Trianti needed a Morgal, and the Ancients now had a supplicant to prepare for his Naming.

Kon's thin voice rose into the fast falling darkness, "Pralick of the Trianti you are no more. Enter the Caves, Nameless, bring us the stones of your people that are the hope in their hearts, bring us your blood of iron, bring us your bones of stone. In Freyton's name we will scour you of all you are until a new name blooms from the wreckage. Enter now Nameless, and face your destruction so that you may be Named by the people once more."

The gathered Ancients intoned the next words together, their tired voices strong only in their unity, "We are of blood and bone, blood is iron, bones are stone," the members of Pralick's tribe chimed in, strong male voices overshadowing the reedy vocalizations of their elders, "We are iron and stone."

They ushered the Nameless inside the Caves, escorting his bulky frame through endless tight passages to the large chamber that lay at the heart of their abode, deep underground. The room was stark and bare but for the two doors on opposite ends of the oval enclosure. The first, they stopped just inside of, was plain and unadorned. Dual heavy timbered doors fitted with a hefty iron bar that would drop down on the outside, locking the Nameless in. The other opening was not wood, but some sort of very hard metal Cirillia had never seen the like of outside the Caves. Its bluish surface rippled with waves like those seen on the fabled Relic blades from the Age Beyond Memory, recovered in the ruins that was now the city of Saerin. The expanse of folded metal was smooth to the touch, except where a detailed etching loomed at the center, split down the middle by the seam of the double doors.

The image depicted confounded her. These Caves were sacred to Freyton, and no other God was worshiped within its catacombs. But here, on the entryway to their most sacred ceremonial rite, was not a fearsome replication of their God, nor even an image of the warrior deity's chosen weapons, but the split carving of a man and a woman, gloriously proportioned in their nudity, each only half of a being, their other side represented by the opposite gender. Both figures' hands were raised with flat palms, holding two different objects of the same size, maintaining the overall balance of the artwork. The male held a carrion crow with wings outstretched, sharp beak open, while from the female's hand a seedling sprouted, mimicking the same shape as the bird, but staying true to its own nature. The woman's delicate face was framed by flowing hair that looked to be stirred by a teasing wind, whipping it up and around her head and horns to occupy the same space as the male figure's huge rack of antlers. At the base of the etching the tangled brambles of Windthorn roses climbing the female figure slowly gave way to the pile of bones the man's hoof stood upon. It was undeniably beautiful, but it always caused a sense of unease in the pit of Cirillia's stomach. The man in the door could be her God, the fierce warrior who brought to her people the strength of the Bloodhunger. But Freyton would never share his worshipers with a woman, or with any other God. He was a jealous deity.

The Nameless's muscled form suddenly blocked her view of the doors as he moved lithely into the center of the room. As she gazed at the mysterious door, her fellows had stripped him of his garments and outfitted him with the only items he would take with him on his full day sojourn behind the door. He moved to kneel before the door at Kon's instructions, and then lifted a hand to take the rough iron knife the old man proffered. Before him he scattered the white voting stones of his tribe, their number sufficient to seek his new Name, but not plentiful.

Kon looked to Pernal, a small woman with frosted eyes set deep in her wrinkled walnut face, and she gazed skyward, seeking the fissure that ran along the ceiling of the cave. She breathed in the air deeply, scenting out the correct time for the Nameless's vigil to begin. Silence held sway for long minutes in the chamber until her grizzled head swung down once again, signaling the rise of the moons and the start of the Naming rite.

"While the moons hold sway you will contemplate all that you were so you may fully cast it off." Pernal said in her wispy voice.

Tall, skeletal Folt spoke next, "When the birth of the sun pierces through the ground you will rise and enter the Caves beyond the door. Take only that which you have been given."

Cirillia stepped up to the man, taking the knife the Nameless one offered her in hand. "With the blood your mother gifted you," she sliced into his palm with the rusted blade to free his bright blood in the chill air, "the stones your tribe entrusted to you as their hope," she stooped to pluck a small round stone from the grouping before him, then placed the rock directly on the cut she had made, curling his large fingers around the pebble before returning the knife to his uninjured hand. "and the iron your God grants you, rise with the sun to seek your Name among the bones of the Nameless, or join them in their endless sleep."

She made her way back to the gathered Ancients, and they filed silently out of the vigil chamber. As she turned to shut the doors, she had one last glimpse of the young man, his hands by his sides in tight fists, blood dripping slowly from the left, while the right clutched the cold iron of the ceremonial knife. *Would they be entering the dark tunnels beyond the chamber to fetch that knife from his corpse tomorrow night,* she wondered? Or would this warrior wield his anger as well as his weapon to triumph over the demons sequestered in the lowest Caves? Only time would tell, she knew. She had seen only two Namings in her brief time as an Ancient, and both men had staggered through the strange metal doors to live Named once again. Pernal had spoken only once about the time she had been sent to retrieve the iron knife from behind those imposing doors, when one of the Nameless had failed to return. The horrors she had seen were evident in her milky eyes, even if her mouth spoke benignly.

Without speaking the seven Ancients made their way back to the entrance of the Caves of Orr, to speak with the tribe that waited there, to gather information, to seek the whereabouts of their Battle Mage. It took the seven of them more than an hour to sort out the tangled stories the Trianti brought, and by the time she had all the facts from the various warriors, a horrible suspicion had taken root in the back of her mind. The Mage was not coming this night. Something terrible must have happened to change a fate that had seemed so unshakable. The clearer a Seer's Dreams were, the more likely the event foretold was to happen. The intensity and clarity of that vision should have meant the Mage's arrival was all but set in stone, that the power of the united tribes was already written in the fabric of the future. *What future awaited them now,* she wondered?

Lessoran

Water, darkness, and pain were the only things he knew for what felt like an eternity. But the pain revived him, kept him conscious, when he might have drifted off otherwise. When they had first plummeted off the edge of that cliff into the turbulent waters below, he and Sylvia had found each other, and he clutched at soaked clothes and slippery limbs to stay with her. Syl had yelled over the roaring of the river, trying to get him to let go, telling him to float, feet first, like he was sitting on the ground, so their combined weight didn't pull them down and drown them. Her tactic worked surprisingly well, so they hurtled along the raging waters for a time, hands joined and heads mostly above the water.

Just before he lost her hand for the last time, he had the presence of mind to reach for his magic. The ribbon of power seemed to twist and turn in his grip as his Control was eroded by the pain of the arrow in his side, and by the panic of his head being dunked under the water as the rapids worsened. With frantic effort he wrapped a tendril of his magic around Syl's lungs, reaching through the connection of their hands to give her every chance of survival that he could. Now she wouldn't be able to pull water into her lungs. The danger of dying from lack of oxygen was still very real, but she would not drown. After doing the same for himself and slamming a binding on top of the power he had released, he lost his grip on his magic. The reverberation of his power snapping back at his loss of Control was agony, sending a blinding flash of light ricocheting around inside his head, but the actions he'd taken would stay in place due to the *Starsh* binding.

They must have traveled miles, all of the ground they had covered since the morning passed in minutes. They were unable to halt their progress or gain a hold on the steep cliff sides that rose above the narrow passage. He periodically heard Sylvia yelling for him, but could not spare the concentration to look, too focused on riding the waves of water without harm. He scraped past rocks and banged into the sides repeatedly, but was still miraculously alive when he spied a solid wall looming in front of him, then there was a shift in gravity, and all was darkness.

He felt the same falling sensation as when he was sucked down into the maw of the earth a few more times, after the darkness enclosed him, but was unable to see where he was, or if Sylvia had made it down with him. The fight to keep his head above water became difficult as his weary body struggled to tell up from down, and he was buffeted about in the current. Finally, the water around him seemed to calm, and he lay completely flat, floating with arms outstretched, greedily sucking air into his starved lungs.

When his breathing slowed enough he called out, "Sylvia?" Echoes bounced back at him but no answering voice sounded. Taking in more oxygen in an attempt to stop his body's shivering, he tried to relax, seeking Control, trying to push aside all of the sensations he was experiencing so he could produce some light in this underground tomb. His globelight flashed into being above as he grasped the blessedly warm Water magic, and his surroundings were revealed in the harsh light.

He was floating in a huge expanse of gently rippling water. Far, far above him he could make out the ceiling of the cavernous room, jagged with tooth-like projections of glittering stone. Sending his globelight higher he could make out the messy tumble of great quantities of water feeding the underground lake, his entrance he assumed. He stuck out towards the nearest shore, needing solid ground under his hooves, needing to catch his breath before he could call to Sylvia again. He allowed himself some time, collapsed on the stony bank he chose as his resting place. But then turned to face the lake once more, unable to relax when the fate of his companion was still unknown, despite his own weariness.

"Syyyyylviaaaaa!" he called, the name bouncing and reverberating in the cathedral-like space. His heart, which had calmed after his struggles in the water, began beating faster the longer he heard no answer. Fighting his way to his feet despite the arrow shaft protruding from the meat of his side, he scanned the water to no avail. Les sent his globelight out, leaving himself in darkness as it scanned the edges of the massive cavern. The far side of the lake was indiscernible even with illumination, it was simply too far away. Frustrated and scared for the young woman, he called out again, "SYLVIA!"

Faintly, very faintly, what he thought to be an echo of his own voice distinguished itself as a separate call, "Les?"

"SYL! WHERE ARE YOU?" he cried, splashing back into the water, only to freeze, trying to tell which direction her answer came from.

"I'm here Les! Can you hear me?" He oriented himself towards the faint sound of splashing as the cave played tricks with her voice, throwing it this way and that.

"KEEP TALKING SYL! I'"M COMING TO YOU!" Wading deeper out into the water he pushed himself off of the rocky bottom, only to abort the attempt to swim as soon as he raised his arm. The arrow in his side pulled atrociously, and he was glad he hadn't make it very far out as his body protested the abusive treatment it had received. Weakly he floundered back to standing, chest high in the lake, calling out to his companion once more, "SYL? SYL I CAN'T SWIM, CAN YOU COME TO ME?"

The sounds of splashing paused and her faint answer floated over to him, "Yes, just show me where you are with the light! I'll swim to the light!"

Calling the globelight back to hover over his head he waded out of the lake, examining the ledge he exited the water on. It ran along the lake, narrowing almost to the point of nonexistence as the cave curved over to the waterfall they had entered in. To his left it widened to roughly the size of a road. Lifting the globelight higher with a thought, he saw the lakeside "road" continued on into the gloom outside the radius of his light. Looking down at the edge of rock he had clambered over to get to the flat ledge, he could make out various signs of change in the height of the lake. At its highest the road would be covered in water, he saw, from the dark line a few hand spans up on the wall and the debris littering the 'floor' of the road.

Tracking the sounds Sylvia made, he could just make out her form as she swam into the farthest reaches of his light. He breathed a sigh of relief, she was okay, thank Freyton, and back in his sights now. Feeling the drain of adrenaline as his body slowly came down from the horrific experience and fear of their ordeal, he slid down the smooth wall to sit at its base, watching Sylvia swim closer as if mesmerized. It was cold down here, and they were both soaked to the bone in the frigid lake water; getting dry would be difficult but it was essential, he knew, or they would die of the cold.

Sylvia emerged from the water, shaking, and flew straight into his arms. He gave a grunt as the impact jostled the arrow, but wrapped his arms around her, still unable to quite believe they were both still alive. Pulling her closer still, on his side that was not acting as a pincushion, he kissed the top of her dripping head, saying wonderingly, "We're alive Syl. We made it. It's going to be okay."

She leaned back, searching his face, then sending those blue, blue, eyes over the rest of him, causing an outbreak of shivers all over his body. "I thought I heard..." she began, then started running her hands over his body on the same path her eyes had taken. It didn't take long for her to find the shaft protruding from his side. The turmoil in the water had broken the fletching off at some point, and the arrow didn't extend all the way through to the front, the head laying inside of him. She gasped, "No, no no no. Oh Les, I'm so sorry. This was my stupid plan, and I ran us off a cliff! Oh my god, what do I do? How do I get it out?"

Her voice had risen as she talked, the last words evoking a wince from Les as the high pitch noise bounced back and forth off of the landscape of stone and water. "Its fine," he placated, "I've been shot before. The arrow needs to come out, but we need some fire first, the wound will need to be cauterized." They both glanced around at the unending expanse of non-burnable elements. He pulled her down beside him, and they huddled together, shivering. "But we can catch our breath first. Are *you* okay? I can Heal *you*, just not myself."

189

"A few bruises, nothing too serious." She played off the rough treatment of the water. But he had seen the care with which she swam as she had approached him, "Syl," he admonished, tipping her head back with a sturdy grip on her chin. He met her glaring eyes with what he hoped was a firm, fatherly look, but he supposed the way his thumb was gently stroking along her jawline somewhat spoiled the illusion. The relief he was feeling at having her back at his side was disarming, and he needed to get a grip on himself, quickly. He needed to remember that she was his responsibility, not a potential lover. Her eyes had softened from affront into something else entirely, he saw with surprise, and he moved quickly to remove his hand from her smooth skin before that smoldering look snatched away what remained of his will power.

Her whispered, "Oh, fuck it," was the only warning he got before her hand cupped *his* face, and those brilliant blue orbs grew impossibly big in his sight as she brought her lips to his in a frenzied kiss. He remained motionless for a moment, lost in the shock, but before he could give his body the command to retreat, instinct took over and his lips moved against hers, tasting her softness, his body ravenous for more of her warmth. All thought stopped as the kiss continued, the only thing he was cognizant of were the sensations, his entire world confined down to the point where his mouth met hers.

She broke away, breathing hard, and red suffused her cheeks. He chuckled at her bashful retreat, loving the dichotomy of fierceness and self-doubt she consistently displayed. He zeroed in on her lips, a little plumper, a little redder for the kiss they had shared, and he felt a zing of satisfaction at her mussed features and panting breath. His eyes made their way from her lips back to her eyes, and all at once he realized his mistake at the hurt he saw there, the embarrassed anger. He had laughed at her, after she put herself out there, he had laughed. Or that was how it must seem. In *his* mind that little laugh had been full of appreciation for her sweet passion and enthusiastic inexperience, but the look on her face as she whirled away from him told him she had not heard the undertones.

He struggled to stand, to follow her and explain, to throw desperate words at her until that look was chased off her delicate features for good. He needed to kiss her until she couldn't even remember he had put that look on her face in the first place. But his body, steady and resilient as it had been throughout the trials of the day, failed him. He slid back down the water-smoothed wall of the mammoth lake cavern in agony, scrabbling to remain conscious as the movement pulled at the stiff shaft of the Trianti arrow inside him, and warm blood seeped down his side. Through failing vision, he watched her retreating form, pulling just enough strength from the colossal power of the lake to send his globelight floating dutifully after her.

Sylvia

The little ball of pale golden light tagged along behind her like a puppy as she fled from her embarrassment. Its light had dimmed somewhat as she walked farther from its power source, although the burn of Lessoran's laughter remained strong. But even through her chagrin Syl's mind drifted back to their kiss. *That kiss!* It had surpassed any of her other explorations by a landslide. The fumbling kisses she and David Granger shared had been awkward and, frankly, slimy. But Les, when his lips had finally moved beneath hers, was soft and sweet with a building fire underneath. She wanted to see that fire rage. Never in her life had she been so tempted to let herself be consumed.

But then that *laugh* as she pulled away for breath. It was like being plunged into the icy river in the gorge all over again. She knew she was young and inexperienced; she just hadn't thought that would matter to Lessoran. She thought he genuinely liked her. They laughed together, they survived together. He was her ideal man, her strong protector, patient teacher, the fantasy hidden in her subconscious. When she finally got up the nerve to make her move, shouldn't he have responded by pushing her up against the wall of the cave, and kissing her like he just couldn't survive without touching her a moment longer? *There should have been some life affirming making-out, dammit!* she thought angrily.

The light following along behind her was still fading, her shadow growing darker before her, blocking her sight of where to place her feet in that bar of darkness. In the faint light she could make out a shape before her and bent to explore the strangely familiar object with her hands. "A wagon?" she asked out loud. "What is a wagon doing next to an underground lake?" Her hands and eyes worked together to give her a clearer picture; the wagon was old, slick with algae growing up the lower portions. The large wheels were broken, the cart bed sitting upon the ground. She began breaking apart the dry portions of the wheels for firewood, amazed at their luck. *If a cart got in,* she mused *then we should be able to get out of here!*

Sylvia filled her arms carefully with the spokes of one of the wagon wheels, and turned back towards where she had left her companion. Her left arm hurt like the dickens, it had gotten smashed against a rock early in their unanticipated river 'float'. And she was pretty certain the bone in her forearm was broken. She had learned quickly what motions were still pain free when trying to swim across the lake to Lessoran, but luckily carrying the even-lengthed spokes was easy enough, mostly one-armed. With a fortifying breath she placed one foot forward, following up with the other until she was walking without hesitation back to Les. *I can be an adult about this. I'm just going to act like nothing happened. Move on.* It became a mantra in her head, *move on, move, on,* each word punctuated with the slap of her bare feet hitting the ground beneath her.

With her back ram-rod straight and her chin held high, she stomped back to where she had come ashore, dumping her armload of wood in an untidy pile near Lessoran where he slumped against the wall. Without deigning to look at him, she got to work on a fire as Les's light continued to fade slowly. His silence slowly ate away at her facade of nonchalance, until her emotions were boiling once again. *How dare he keep silent! SHE was the only one who had the right to give the silent treatment. HE should be apologizing!*

Reaching a breaking point, she realized her arm would not be able to handle lighting the fire with friction as Torman had taught her. She needed Lessoran's flint, which should still be in the pouch he kept around his neck. She whirled to face her companion, and her ire deflated abruptly as she saw the pallor of his face, the awkward angle at which he lay. Her hands rose to her mouth in horror, *this was no silent treatment, this was unconsciousness!* Rushing to his side, she frantically checked his neck for a pulse and sucked in a relieved breath. It was slow, but steady, beneath her trembling fingers.

"Okay, okay. What now Les?" she spoke aloud to him, the sound of her voice tempering the fear she had felt when she saw how very dead her companion appeared. The light floating above them gave a fitful flicker, deciding for her that the next step should be to get the fire going as quickly as possible. Digging around underneath Lessoran's tunic, she pulled his small travel pouch out and set to striking the flint with a shard of the stone littering their resting place.

The air around her was moist with the water confined in the cavern and it took her a long time to get the old wood to catch, but finally she had a merry blaze eating away at the bones of the wagon. She moved on to Les without hesitation, the light above was barely producing illumination anymore, and she had this terrible fear that when the light went out, Les would be dead. She tried to arrange his bulky frame in a more comfortable position, her hurt arm protesting his weight as she slid him down the wall so he lay prone upon the floor.

From this open position Syl could clearly see the dark stain spreading down his side, wet with fresh blood, and she gingerly pulled his tunic up until the soaked cloth lay bunched under his armpits. "Oh Les!" she said with a gasp, the fingers of her good hand gently touching the arrow shaft protruding from his bloody skin. "You said it needs to come out, but you wanted the fire to umm, umm, cauterize it! Yes, okay..."

She knew basic first aid from the class she had been required to take before starting her lifeguard job from last summer. Unfortunately for Lessoran, in the case of impalement with a foreign object they had been taught to leave the object in the body until an ambulance could arrive, as the object could be keeping blood loss to a minimum. But here and now, there would be no ambulance. She was the only help Les would be getting. Resolutely she pulled Les's knife from its worn sheath on his hip and cut a few long strips of cloth from the over-long tunic she wore; the trailing end had been annoying anyway, she told herself grimly. Laying the cloth out flat, close to the fire to dry, she then plunged the knife into the heart of the small blaze, and turned to stumble her way back to the wagon for more wood, the barely lit globelight limping along behind.

With the fire stoked, bandages at the ready, and the knife glowing red hot, she was ready. *Ready, right,* she scoffed, *ready to rip a hole in my only friend's side and then burn him horribly.* With a grimace she shut down her thoughts, trying to focus only on Les, on gripping the arrow with her good hand so she could pull it out at the straightest angle and cause the least amount of damage with the arrowhead. "Here we go Les," she spoke to his prone figure, "on three, one, two, THREE!" With a great heave the arrow slid grudgingly from his body. Thick blood poured out of the jagged hole. Quickly wrapping a bloody hand in the edge of Les's cloak, she grabbed the knife and pressed it onto the wound, wincing at the smell of burned flesh, but intensely grateful the alarming flow of blood stilled with cauterization.

Syl checked his pulse incessantly as she cleaned up their makeshift camp. First she washed the majority of the blood from his skin before carefully wrapping her less-than-clean bandage around his middle. Then it was cleaning the knife of Les's charred flesh in the gently rippling water of the dark lake, and ringing their small fire with the largest rocks she could find in the vicinity. Finally, at a loss for what to do next, she huddled in close to his still body, adrenaline fading from her system, cold settling in. They needed to get dry she knew, especially Lessoran, when he was so weak. But everything they owned was wet; the pack, which had somehow remained with Les through their wild river ride, was still seeping water near the edge of the lake.

Touching Les's hand, she shook her head at the clamminess of his skin. He needed out of these wet clothes, now. She allowed herself one more moment of rest, her body was tired and in pain. All she wanted was sleep, and maybe a couple of ibuprofen to dull her aches. Instead she forced herself to her feet once more. "More wood, less clothes, lay things out to dry, and sleep is yours Sylvia" she spoke to herself encouragingly, trying for motivation. Taking a flaming spoke as a torch since the ghostly globelight barely cast any illumination anymore, she made the trip to the broken wagon twice more for wood before laying out their stock of supplies.

They had one blanket, oiled to keep out water on one side, but sopping wet on the other. They had an inky ruin of a map, flint, some soggy jerky, rope, one loaf of travel bread that was a complete loss, Les's knife, the clothes on their backs, a water flask, the smallest cookpot, and half an arrow. She had lost her makeshift cloak, Les's extra tunic, in the river when it had snagged in some flotsam; but Les still had his, which she gingerly took off of him and lay out to dry next to the blanket. She also shed her cloth pants, taken from some small member of the Trianti tribe, as the coarse material had begun to chafe as it slowly dried. She relieved Les of his bloody shirt and dragged him gracelessly closer to the fire, draping the blanket, waterproof side down, over him. Looking around, she couldn't think of anything else productive to do, not with weariness dragging her down, so she slid beneath the sodden blanket with her unconscious companion and snuggled into his bare torso, hoping she could keep him warm enough that he would eventually wake up.

Lessoran

He was dreaming of swimming with Chrisyne. It was almost clear enough to be a memory, but small inconsistencies tinged the scene. They were floating lazily in the clear water of a mountain lake the Trianti had spent most of the last summer of her life near, but the water stung his naked body with cold as if winter had the Skypeaks in its grip. Her lovely face was blurred; his eyes could not quite bring her into focus. She was a ghost beside him, a wraith born of mist with plump red lips, a glimpse of rosy cheeks, and honey colored hair a cloud of lightness in the darker water.

Chrisyne, I miss you. He spoke to her, unsure if the words ever made it off his lips, or if they only reverberated through his head. She continued her splashing play as if she could not hear him. Her laugh was clear and joyful, she dove down into the water like a playful otter, twining her warm limbs around him as she surfaced, shaking droplets of water like diamonds onto his face where they clung like icicles. He brought his hands up to cup her body closer to his, walking them from the water to lay her down on the grassy lakeside. Her sweet giggles made his heart hurt, a sharp ache mirrored by a deep cold in his body that the sunlight of memory was unable to thaw.

Her small hands hurried him down to meet her in the grass. As he joined with her she sunk sharp fingers into his side, digging deep as if her pleasure bade her seek something that was lost within him. Reaching for the peak of his own body he lost sight of her face, the laughing hazel eyes coming into sharp focus just before slipping away in a shaft of brilliant sunlight. He reached blindly for completion but a sudden darkness blanketed his lover, and as he looked up the shade of his enemy stood over them, a spear pinning the writhing body beneath him to the ground.

Lessoran retreated in horror and Chrisyne's hands slid from his body with an agonizing tug. With a glance down he saw she had dug a gaping hole into his side before reaching upwards to grasp his heart. It lay next to her clutching hand as her body's thrashing slowed, as the shadow warrior's spear drained everything that was light and innocent and good from his life. He screamed at the silent figure as it killed his lover, at the pain piercing his side, at the hollowness he felt living without his heart.

The noise woke him with a start. Closing his gaping mouth, he stilled to pinpoint the origin of the raspy noise, only to find it had ended when his lips came together. The pain from his dream lingered in his side, along with the bone deep cold. He attempted to sit up, only making it to a reclining position as the slight weight of Sylvia weighed his exhausted body down. She lay entangled with him much like Chrisyne had been in the dream, but the lingering heartache made her embrace feel like a trap, and he longed to free himself from the potential pain she could bring him.

His movements woke her and she disentangled herself from him, hurriedly pulling away from his bare torso. "Glad you're awake. I had no idea if you were going to make it." Her face looked drawn and pale, "You had a fever, and I could barely get you to drink any water." Sylvia busied herself adding wood to the small fire contained in a ring of stones, and had yet to look him in the eyes. "I moved us over here, there's a wagon to use as firewood, although this algae burns well too, if it's dry enough. I think it might be edible, but I didn't have the guts to try it." She paused uncomfortably, "I'm sorry but I ate most of the food, I saved you a bit, but you have been unconscious for a long time, and I wasn't sure you would be waking up."

He peeled away the cloth wrapped about his middle, noting it seemed to be pieces of the tunic she wore, and saw the burn marring the skin of his side. She had taken the arrow out, and cauterized it. By herself. Regardless of the fierceness of spirit he had seen in her over their days together, she was frighteningly unaware of how to survive out in the wilds, and strangely timid when it came to necessary tasks like hunting and fishing. Yet, she had managed to save his life despite her naivety. He looked up, catching her eyes before she could look away, "Thank you for saving me."

"Of course," she broke the eye contact hurriedly "I'm really glad you're alive, this is *not* a good place to be left alone in." They both turned to look out over the lake, its waters looking almost solid as the firelight reflected off the inky surface. Her eyes moved back to him, a hint of terror present in the azure depths, "Les," she hesitated, "I think there's something living down here... I don't know what, but I've," she glanced at the dark water again, "I've heard it."

Les used the stone wall at his back to help him stand, suddenly unable to ignore the call of nature. "Guess I won't go too far from the fire to relieve myself then," he joked weakly. He immediately felt bad as Syl's face pulled taut and angry. He tried to backtrack, "I believe you, I just really need to..." He motioned off into the blackness. At her nod of understanding he stumbled off to the edge of the firelight, berating himself, yet again, for his poor handling of the situation.

His bladder blessedly empty, he continued to stare off into the dark, wondering why they were always at each other's throats. He couldn't seem to say the right thing around her and the pain in her eyes from his words left him feeling wretched. She had been through enough since she came into his life, without him adding to her burdens with careless words. She was Chrisyne all over again. Her brightness and cheer so similar to the first girl he had ever loved that it was frightening. But this time he wasn't going to play, he didn't think he could bear the pain, not with Sylvia. Not when her future was so uncertain, not when his was. She was too fresh and optimistic, while he felt old and tired. He didn't deserve her, just as she deserved so much more than him, and he refused to sully her innocence, her bright and beautiful spirit, with the scars he bore.

For her sake, he would be hard. He would save her from himself, even if she hated him for it for the rest of her life. He needed to be her captor again, and she his prisoner. His job was, and had always been, to get her to the Ancients at the Caves of Orr. He had lost sight of his promise to the Morgal somehow, getting tangled up in the allure of her eyes, the warmth of their shared laughter and reliance on one another, and the mysteries of her strange past. He touched the medallion that still hung safe around his neck, glad he had kept it close to his person. She would be safe in the Caves and he could walk away, wash his hands of the whole situation. His mind shied away from thoughts of after. There likely was no 'after' for him, no tribe that would welcome him and no one to turn to. *But she would be safe, and my last task completed.* He told himself that was all that mattered.

Trying for businesslike, but feeling a bit wobbly, he returned to the fire and took stock of their position, asking Sylvia to tell him what had happened while he was out, and what she had heard to make her think there was something lurking in their subterranean abode. Her hands moved animatedly as she talked, bringing his attention to the deep bruising on her forearm. She continued on about dragging him on a plank from the wagon bed so they could be closer to their source of firewood. He tuned her out, reaching within himself for the warm glow of his magic. Being so close to the water as he lay healing had bolstered his body's resources, and recharged his magical reserves as he slept; he was surprised how quickly he had recovered. Blue magic brimmed within him, its power a comforting warmth.

"...that's when I figured out burning the algae would make the wood last longer. Hey! What are you doing?" She tried to tug her arm from his grip, but ended up doubled over in pain from the instinctual movement.

"I'm going to Heal you," he responded mildly, and as his magic flowed into her skin he marveled at her resilience once more. The bone was broken in two places, the worst fracture a gaping fissure where her continued use of the arm had ground the bone nearly to dust. Dragging his much larger body would be hard for a female her size, regardless of injury, and yet here they were. His power flowed over the break, and Sylvia gasped before slumping into his arms in a faint. Les smiled grimly, he knew the immediate drain Healing put a patient through. His magic was the catalyst for the process, but it used up her body's resources also, forcing weeks' worth of healing into a few seconds. She would be out for a while.

He laid her down on the blanket near the fire when he finished, feeling a bit woozy from using his magic while he was hungry and weakened. Control was hard to hold on to with distractions like pain and hunger. Dreaming of Chrisyne made him feel raw, and it was hard to hold fast to the promise he made to himself, to keep his distance from Syl, when she was awake. He was drawn to her like a moth to flame, his hurt needing the balm of her wholesome energy, especially when Chrisyne lay so close to his thoughts.

Munching on a stick of dried meat he wandered the camp, nodding in approval at Sylvia's set up. Half of the wagon bed had been propped up over the blanket, creating a cozy enclosure that helped to hold in the heat given off by the fire. Much of the rest of the old wagon had been torn into pieces and stacked close to the fire and bedroll for easy feeding. A few longer, sturdier portions had been wedged against the wall with their rope strung between, there most of his clothing hung drying. Pulling on his tunic carefully, Les also noticed a couple spokes of a wheel had been sharpened, laying near their bed. *Busy little bee*, he thought.

Feeling stronger after eating something, he pulled on the deep well of his magic again, sending a fiery globelight as far up in the big cave as it would go. The light ate up the darkness, sending it scurrying for hidden corners and underneath overhangs. The cavern was huge, a great cathedral, a temple of water and stone that left Lessoran feeling small and insignificant at its fringes. Orienting himself Les saw the cascade of water where he and Syl had been dumped into the lake at his left. The cave was not nearly as wide as it was long and he could see the far side of the lake from where he stood. To the right the water stretched on and on until it turned a corner and all he could make out was stone walls. Out in the middle of the stretch of water, something jutted from the surface, remarkable only in that it was the only place the glass-like surface was marred.

Looking at the waterfall, he knew there would be no escape from this underground grotto that way. The water rained down from a large crack in the rock that was nearly horizontal. Searching for another route his eyes followed the road they had made camp on as it continued around the perimeter, disappearing with the lake as it turned in the distance. They had little to no choice when it was time to move on, but at least the road was an easy trail to follow for their abused bodies. He stooped to gather some of the streamcress that grew prolifically here underground. It was a common strain of algae in the Skypeaks, and edible if not very tasty. *At least we won't starve*, he thought.

A sudden splash made him drop the streamcress he had collected and grope for the knife that should have been in the sheath on his hip, but it was empty. He brought the globelight down from its lofty position in order to examine the water more closely, remembering the fear he had seen in Syl's eyes when she spoke of hearing something else in the cave with them. He fumbled blindly for the sharpened spokes he had seen earlier, keeping his eyes on the water, constantly scanning for movement, but he saw nothing. Not even a ripple other than the slight current flowing from the waterfall in the distance. The hair on the back of his neck stood at stiff attention, and he felt the weight of unkind eyes on him, regardless of the emptiness surrounding them. Sylvia was right, he knew, they were not alone down here.

Sylvia

They had come to an unspoken truce of sorts, soon after Syl woke from her faint, one that rested solely on the laurels of silence. She felt much restored after her forced nap, and pain free, but ravenously hungry. Lessoran had some of the gooey brown algae bubbling in their small cook pot over the fire along with part of a very large fish he admitted to magically "encouraging" onto his sharpened stake, since they could not spare any of their scant supplies to use as bait. What remained of the big white creature was fearsome looking, with long spines spaced evenly along its bony back, a jaw full of jagged, needle-like teeth, and large, milky white eyes she assumed it didn't use in the darkness of the cave. Contrary to its frightful appearance, the aroma of it cooking set her mouth to watering immediately.

A few hours after she first woke Sylvia found herself wrapped up in the blanket, huddled beneath its damp folds close to Les, her belly full for the first time in far too long, and 'The Kiss', as she had come to think of it, in capitals, an unspoken cloud hovering above their camp. The silence was not especially comfortable, but survival had a habit of looming larger than small dramas. Hunger overshadowed anger, and the need for warmth canceled out the discomfort of touching the one you were hurt by. But now that her immediate discomforts and needs were taken care of, her treacherous mind wandered back, examining the event in detail, turning it over and over, adding "what if's", and "if I had's". She didn't want to be the one to bring it up, and determined to wait him out even as the desperate need to know how he felt about her fluttered madly within her chest. She felt short of breath and a little panicky sitting this close to him, a feeling that was escalating at an alarming rate until Lessoran spoke, shattering the quiet and the buildup inside her in equal measure.

"We should get a few hours' sleep, then pack up and see where this road leads. If we're lucky we'll find a way out of here before too long, and we won't have to backtrack too much to reach the Caves."

Right, the Caves, she thought, *that's totally the most important thing going on here, nothing else we need to talk about, nothing at all!* Her mother would have given her a long hard stare for the sarcasm, with an added 'watch your tone young lady!' for good measure. The picture of her mother steadied her, she realized, grabbing onto the image as she nonchalantly replied to his businesslike statement with a nod of assent, "Sounds like a good plan, I'll just get a little sleep then." She lay down calmly, her back to Les's warmth and her arm pillowing her head from the hard stone beneath.

She breathed, trying to make each breath even and exactly as long as the last. The picture of her mother's exasperated face was as clear as day in her mind's eye, and she grabbed on to it, expanding the moment, adding details and circumstances until the scene behind her tightly shut eyelids was more real than the darkness surrounding her physical body. *A dream,* she reminded herself, trying to ignore the tinge of desperation in the thought, *the cave is just a dream, Lessoran is just a dream.* She zeroed in on her mom again, *THIS is what is real.*

If she could just get the picture right, add every detail in, then maybe reality would reform around her. But the niggling sense that she was deluding herself kept interrupting the process, forcing her to start over, beginning with her mother, adding in the kitchen in her house with the cat bowls her dad was constantly tripping over, and the red checkered hand towel hanging from the fridge door. But that fear, the small stones digging into her flesh, Lessoran shifting against her, and the abrupt crack of a piece of wood in the fire dragged her back again and again until she gave up on the thought of sleep. Sliding from the makeshift bed she began picking up camp, quietly tying their remaining firewood together into a bundle with the rope, and starting in on repacking the rucksack as neatly as possible.

Les sat up, "I can't sleep either," he said quietly, "let's just go."

He rolled the blanket up after seeing her nod, adding it to the pile of "in the pack" items lying before her, before he moved on to preparing the gutted fish for travel. As they worked he spoke again, "I heard something while you were out, just like you said. There must be something living in the cave, pretty big from what I heard, but I haven't caught a glimpse of it yet."

"I think there's more than one of them, whatever they are," she replied, "Thought I saw something down the road right as I woke up, the first time I slept down here, but then I also heard a splash in the lake, like something swimming away. So I figure there are at least two."

"Seems to me if they were dangerous they would have attacked by now. It's probably some sort of animal that's just curious, not a lot of travelers passing through..." he joked lightly, his smile falling a bit when she didn't reply.

She swung the pack up onto her back resolutely, meeting his eyes full on for the first time since they kissed. "Let's go. Can you manage the wood? I figure it will be easier for you than the pack, since you still have a hole in your side." He stared back at her for a moment, looking a little lost, and Syl fought her immediate urge to comfort him, then he nodded and swept the bundle of firewood into his arms before taking the lead, globelight bursting into being above his head to light the way.

They traveled that way for what felt like hours. Les occasionally sent the globelight out over the lake when they thought they heard something, or to see what lay ahead when they stopped to rest for a minute. As they neared the bend in the lake that would take them out of sight from their original campsite, he sent the light out to hover around a strange rocky protrusion far out in the water. They both faced the odd outcropping, toes hanging off the rough edge of the road over the still waters below, squinting to make out the fuzzy details.

"It looks like..." She searched for the word in Layette, finally falling back into English, which Lessoran sometimes understood, some of his Maegi training having come from books stolen from the lowlanders, passed down from Maegi to Maegi in the Trianti tribe. "A church steeple," Sylvia said in confusion, looking over at her companion in time to catch his puzzled expression.

"Church? I don't know that word. But it looks like the spire of a temple to me, is that what you mean?"

"Yeah, temple is another word for church," his head cocked to the side in consideration, "Mostly," she amended, suddenly unsure of her the definitions of words in her own language, and looked out over the lake again. "Why is there a temple at the bottom of a lake?" They both shrugged after a moment, contemplating the strange sight, then turning as one to begin walking once more, knowing there were no answers to be had from the silent expanse of water.

"I wonder if your Ancients know about this place. They're Seers right? Couldn't they look back and figure out who built a temple down here?"

Les was quiet for so long she thought he was just going to ignore her, but then he finally answered, "The Ancients are Seers, yes, but they usually look forward and see a tribe's future. Sometimes they remind us of the past, so we don't make the mistakes of our ancestors, but I don't know if those are things they See or just things they know from all of their years."

"Huh, so the Ancients actually are... ancient? How old are they? Are they born Seers?" Most of the truly old people Syl knew were not really in their right minds, and were definitely not the people she would seek guidance from. She had originally thought 'Ancient' was just a title, regardless of their actual ages.

"They are old," Les chuckled a bit, "Some of them are *very* old. But they're not the same after they come to the Caves as they were before." There was a pause as he caught his breath, hunching slightly over his injured side, then he continued, the words coming slower, more consideringly. "I could have been an Ancient. If I lived long enough. Every Ancient was first a tribe's head Maegi, although not all of the Maegi's are called to the Caves when they age."

One of his words stood out to her, "*Could* have been?"

He glanced back over his shoulder, a lock of hair falling over his eye until he tossed it off his brow impatiently, "Ancients come from the tribes, always, and I don't seem to belong to a tribe anymore." The words were matter of fact rather than self-pitying.

She wanted to tell him she was sorry for causing him pain, but it didn't seem right to apologize for her own kidnapping, nor did the new tone of their relationship lend itself to heart to heart talks. So she held her tongue, focusing instead on the road in front of them as they finally breasted the curve they had been walking towards. The lake narrowed at the cave's turning, the current picking up so it gradually morphed into a deep flowing river. The road continued alongside it, rising steadily so it lay about fifteen feet from the water's surface. They continued on for about fifty yards before a large gap in the dry stone brought the travelers to a halt.

Syl and Les looked down at the broken road. A large stalactite had broken off the ceiling, far above the road, and crashed down on the flat ledge, crushing it to bits. The water below was strewn with bits of rock and larger boulders, and the far side was a good ten feet away. They contemplated in silence for a while, walking this way and that, searching for possible routes across.

"The little bit of ledge that's left looks too unstable to try," Les said from his vantage point near the wall.

Syl gazed across the chasm, "Too far to jump, but we could toss our pack across easily enough." She moved towards the river, gauging the likelihood of them scaling the cliff falling sharply to the water.

Les sat down abruptly, "We camp here for now then, we can eat something, sleep for a bit, then figure out a way to cross to the other side."

Sylvia plopped down across from him, automatically making a pyramid of kindling for a fire, "Yes sir," she said blandly.

Lessoran

They elected to swim around the gap. It was not an appealing idea, but after much contemplation it seemed the route least likely to maim or kill them. With his globelight they'd spied a promising section of rough rock some fifty yards downstream that was less steep than the majority of the rest of the cliff between river and road. He was nearly certain they would be able to climb back up to the road from there. To that end he and Sylvia were packing their bag with extra care, to sling across the gap so their possessions would be dry after the swim.

With a heave Syl sent the tightly tied firewood sailing across to land with a thwack on the other side of the road. Turning to him she said brusquely, "Close your eyes."

Les shut his eyes hurriedly, holding out the bag so she could stuff her clothes in once they were off. *What was I thinking? This plan may be logical, but it's also torture!* They had both agreed that it would be best if they tossed their clothes across with the bag, securing the lighter garments that might not have made it all the way if thrown without the weight of the pack. But all that rational thinking had led them here, to this awkward moment. He kept his eyes closed as she stuffed her tunic and breeches into the bag and as the scuff of her soft feet on the rock moved off to his left. When her movements were lost in the quiet trickle of the water and he heard a soft yelp echo through the cave as she entered the water, he opened his eyes and quickly stripped down, tossing the bag across nimbly before scrambling down to the water himself.

"Brrrrr!!!" Syl chattered as she swam a frenzied breaststroke, a sentiment he repeated as a gasp when the dark water eased over his bare stomach. Their movements in the water refracted the globelight's radiance, creating rippling lights along the cliff side. He sent the light farther ahead, to their exit point, leaving him and Sylvia a semblance of privacy as they skinny-dipped their way to the bobbing light.

"Ohmygod, ohmygod. So c-cc-cold!" He couldn't help the chuckle that escaped his mouth like a series of bubbles at Syl's unending string of complaints, but he tried to keep his amusement to himself as his longer arms and strong strokes bridged the gap between him and his companion.

By the time they reached the slab of rock they hoped to use as an escape from the river, he had pulled ahead of her, and he called breathlessly over his shoulder, "I would tell you not to look, but I honestly couldn't care less as long as I get out of this water!" Pulling himself into the circle of light, he gazed up at the fifteen-foot climb ahead, wincing at what the reality of the view from below really would be. Putting the uncomfortable thought from his mind, he glanced over one shoulder to check on Syl's progress, swinging around fully in horror as he failed to find the familiar dark head at the surface.

"Syl?" He summoned the globelight down, searching the rippling surface to no avail. He was already shivering, but a fresh crop of goose pimples broke out all over his body. *Where was she?*

"Sylvia?" His voice broke hollowly halfway through her name and before the thought had fully formed, he found himself splashing back into the frigid water, his globelight close by his side.

There. Les froze, what was that noise? The high pitch whine was abruptly interrupted as the surface in front of him broke into a mass of air bubbles. He plunged downward in a dive, pulling the globelight into the disturbed water with him as an afterthought. He struggled to decipher the scene before him as the water blurred his vision and his eyes fought the invading liquid. But slowly, the violently thrashing mess of limbs and scales sorted itself out, painting a picture more terrifying than any nightmare he had ever had.

Sylvia struggled in the clutches of a creature three times her size, its body a confusing tangle of scaled coils and frighteningly commonplace Trewal features. The giant head hung nearly motionless but for a slow tilt as it cocked its head from side to side, examining the naked girl before it with first one eye, then the other, as if it was unable to see directly in front of itself. Its powerfully muscled chest looked much like his own, but the arms sprouting from the torso were overlong and ended in a splayed hand webbed between the fingers, and at the end of each digit a nastily sharp talon protruded.

Syl released a string of bubbles from her mouth as she fought, but her movements were weakening the longer she went without air. The monster played idly with the bubbles of escaping oxygen with one hand as it manhandled the slight form of its prisoner with a seemingly never ending length of tail. The scaled appendage was a mottled green and blue, the green ranging from toxic neon hues to a darker green akin to the leaves of a Steelskin tree. The underside of the tail was a deep blue, so dark, even with the globelight illuminating the scene, that it appeared black.

Les groped instinctively for his knife, but only wet skin met his fingers. *Trollit! He couldn't use magic when the beast was so close to Sylvia!* He vented half his breath in a scream of fury and swam closer with powerful strokes, ignoring the growing burn in his lungs. Kicking out with his right leg, his hoof hit the scaled beast solidly, the sharp edge deflected by the tough scales, but the force behind it still bruising. The thing recoiled in dismay, obviously expecting little resistance from its experience with the defenseless Sylvia. The lake monster swam backwards, dropping Syl like she had burned him. Les saw with pride that the hand it had clasped around her neck now trailed a smoky stream of red blood through the water where she had bitten it.

He drew on the power of the water around him, feeding the magic contained within his chest, and sent lances of boiling water after the beast, harrying it away from them as he and Syl both swam frantically for the surface and fresh air. They broke the churning surface with twin gasps before Sylvia began coughing and hacking, her head barely staying above water as she struggled with the symptoms of hypoxia. He got his arm around her, under her arm pits to help keep her head above water and began a slow crawling stroke back towards solid land, his eyes skimming the surface around them constantly.

"I can- I can swim," she croaked after finally catching her breath, just as they reached the rock jutting out near their escape route. He slung her towards the projection, helping to push her exhausted body from the water to start the long climb up to the road, and then faced the water once more.

"Can you climb?" he asked when he didn't immediately hear the sound of her ascent.

Her shuddering breath was his only answer, until he turned to look and found her cradling her hands to her chest, smears of blood on the rocks before her. He divided his gaze, turning his head frequently to keep both Sylvia and the open river in his sight. "What's wrong? What happened to your hands?" He reached deep, struggling through cold, adrenaline and fear to retain Control. Healing magic sparked from his fingers before she could even answer, and he took both her hands in his.

"Donno, scales must have cut me," she said dully before a tremor shook her from head to foot as his magic rushed through her.

He turned back to the face the water, "Try to climb now," he said shakily. He could hear the sounds of her hands on the rocks and her heavy breathing grew farther and farther away, easing the tension in his body ever so slightly now that she was out of reach of the creature. His own breathing was finally evening out after the tussle, and he wished she would hurry up; he didn't know if he could make the climb up the steep face when his adrenaline finally subsided.

"Okay, come up Les, I'll watch the water. The climb isn't too bad." Her voice drifted down to mingle with the slight water noise surrounding him.

His thick hooves skidded off the unforgiving rock multiple times as he climbed, and it seemed to take him much longer to reach the top than it had Sylvia. By that time his arms were shaking, the burn in his forearms abominable. His hands felt like they were going to cramp at any second as his head breached the level of the road. He had always pitied Syl her soft and tender feet, having seen firsthand the pain their travels caused her. But now he envied the nimble appendages his companion sported. They seemed to make climbing much easier, acting like a second pair of hands.

Sylvia's hands locked under his arms and helped heave him up over the crumbling edge of the road, until he lay spread eagle on blessedly solid, dry land. She pushed at him gently until he turned his head to look at her. They were both filthy. Bits of rock and copious amounts of dirt streaked her body from her intimate encounter with the cliff. And looking down, Les saw that he was in much the same condition.

"You okay?" She sat abruptly, curling into a ball to try to keep in body heat. "Les what *was* that?"

Mimicking her posture, he replied, "I have no idea. And yeah, I'm okay. Did it get you anywhere else? Or was it just your hands?"

"I honestly can't tell, I'm too cold to feel anything. But I don't think it wanted to hurt me." She continued in a puzzled voice, "It just pulled me under and kept turning me around, looking at me, like it was trying to figure me out... I don't think it knew it was killing me. I saw these slits on its neck, like gills. If it can breathe under there, how would it know I can't?"

"You're too nice for your own good," Les said with a groan. "Let's get our stuff and warm up. Then I want out of this God's forsaken cave!" He dimmed the light as they limped back along the road to where their pack lay next to the firewood, even though the awkwardness of their mutual nudity had faded in the face of the attack.

They took turns scrubbing off the grime with Lessoran's cloak before dressing in their cloths once more. Keeping their voices low, they discussed the strange turn of events their morning swim had taken, and cautiously picked their way down the road, each listening wearily for the splashes that would herald the monster's return.

"What I don't get," he said in a whisper, "is why it looked so, so Trewal. It was like it was part man, part serpent, part beast." Chills broke out over his body as he cataloged the strange attributes of the creature again. "Trewal chest and arms, but the hands were wrong. Trewal head, but the nose was more like a snout, and it had to turn its head to see straight ahead. Then there was the forehead, I'm not even sure what to make of that...Did it have legs, Syl? Hooves? Or just that tail? I didn't get a chance to see."

"I was a little busy drowning," she said with a sniffle.

Les started in surprise, abandoning the mystery of the denizen of the Lake cavern for the moment when he saw glistening tear tracks on Sylvia's cheeks. He slung an arm around her shoulders, alarmed to find them still shaking even though they were now mostly dry and clothed again. *I can comfort her without losing myself, can't I?* He thought a little frantically, the sight of her tears tearing him apart bit by bit. *It's just part of the job, getting her to the Caves in one piece, physically and mentally. It doesn't mean anything.* The thought rang sour even in his head. But as more tears slid down her freckled cheeks, he pushed his misgivings aside, tucking them away with his dream of Chrisyne in some dark corner of his mind.

"Hey now little one, you're okay, *we* are okay." He halted their progress to bring her into his arms properly, hands rubbing up and down her back to warm her up. She leaned her forehead against him, a solid weight pressing into the hollow just below his sternum, continuing to cry almost silently until his tunic sported a large wet patch from the tears.

"I'm just so tired, Les" she said brokenly, wiping her eyes with the sleeves of her own shirt. "I don't know if I can keep doing this."

He pulled her to his chest tightly, holding her until her arms snaked up around his back to return the pressure of his hug. There was no need to define "this" -he knew exactly what she meant. He had felt the same hollow tiredness before; after battles, while trying to Heal a friend too far gone to save, when he had cradled Chrisyne's lifeless body in the same arms that now held Sylvia. Everyone had a breaking point, a limit to what they could endure. Years ago, in one of his first battles as a Maegi he had seen two brothers' a few years his senior fighting side by side. The men had been inseparable since the day they left the womb together, and they fought like separate pieces of the same whole, short swords darting and blocking in tandem. Even as he had marveled at their prowess one of them took an arrow to the chest as they strayed too far from the reach of Les's Arrowcatch to be shielded. Tren had knelt frantically, checking his brother's pulse, tearing the arrow from his flesh and attempting to stem the blood loss. The blood stopped all too quickly on its own, and Tren's horror transformed to calm in an instant. He had knelt down by his brother's head, pulling it into his lap with a sad smile at Lessoran before dropping his weapon and bowing his head in acceptance as an enemy warrior approached. He simply gave up.

"You *can* keep doing this," he said with conviction, "because there is nothing else to *do* but keep going. It's the only thing I know for sure in this life; keep going, even when we feel like there is nothing for us in the future but more of the pain, loss, and fear you feel now. The sun will still rise tomorrow, and the moons after that. Life continues on no matter what we endure today."

Her crying slowly tapered off in the silence after his uncharacteristically profound statement, and she broke the circle of his arms to wipe her face once more. Taking a deep breath, she said, "Okay, let's walk."

They turned and gathered their things, still cautiously quiet, waiting for any hint of the lake beast's return. As they began to make their way down the road Les reached out and took Sylvia's hand in his, wishing the warm clasp could tell him whether she believed him or not, whether she was ready to keep going, to keep fighting their way on, or whether she was too far gone, and had already given up.

Chapter 10

Ryland

"Lord Ryland?" The interruption was a whisper, highly tinged with frustration. Looking up Ryland found the thin young soldier whom he had entrusted his last letter for Torman to, suddenly at his elbow while he had been immersed in his reading.

"Chir?" He asked in confusion, "What are you doing in the library at this hour?"

The messenger had dark circles under his eyes and mud still splattered his light green trousers and fawn colored boots, making Ryland wince at the tracks he must have made walking through the immaculate King's Academy to reach this deserted corner. Chir rolled his eyes in a manner that would have earned him a sharp reprimand from the Jorgen, but elicited only a chuckle from his youngest son. "Sorry, stupid question. You just got back from the Holm?" He took the tightly bound scroll Chir held out, "And you sought me out to make sure this didn't fall into the wrong hands." Ryland rubbed at his eyes to clear vision bleary from hours of reading before focusing back on the man before him.

"Lord Torman said it is in code sir, but I figured it's best if you were the one to receive it anyway," he ducked his head to hide a small smile, "I've witnessed the good Lord's attempts at riddles" he finished with laughter coloring his tired voice.

"Thank you Chir," Ryland said earnestly, "I don't know what my brother or I have done for you to deserve such loyalty and dedication, but I am endlessly grateful."

Chir grinned before saying, "I'd say the fact that you thank me is reason enough, don't know if those words have ever left your Lord father's lips to my knowing. If you've word to send back, I leave at dawn." And then he turned around smartly, following his muddy trail back through the scattered reading tables and towering shelves to seek his bed.

Ryland set the scroll aside for the moment and stood to stretch the kinks from his back that his long hours hunched over a book had earned him. He had finally found the time to visit the Academy's Library without an escort or watchdog of his father's dogging his every move. Unfortunately, it meant losing sleep as he hadn't managed to escape his rooms undetected until a very late hour. He had been forced to make numerous false trips as he found himself with a tail the first three times he attempted his escape. He had visited the kitchens for a snack, spent time in the communal bathing rooms soaking in a vat of hot water scented with lavender, and took a long walk in the shadowy Palace gardens. After each outing he 'retired' to his rooms for the night, only to wait for a small period of time and exit once more. On his fourth try there was no serf tailing him and so he sped as quickly as he could through the Palace grounds to the King's Academy. The familiar sights of his youth made his late night escapade feel like coming home, despite the nerves he felt after the Jorgen's warning of unrest from the commoners who opposed the war.

Then he had been faced with the daunting task of beginning to research the human race, where they came from, and any way to get Sylvia home. It was a discouraging undertaking without her sunny presence and dogged perseverance, especially since he had no way of knowing if any helpful information he came across could ever be relayed to her, or if she was alive to continue her search for home. Regardless of the negative thoughts circling in his mind he had pulled all the books on magical travel and accounts of travel to distant lands from the many, many, large shelves populating the library, in hopes that he could figure out where Sylvia had come from, and how to get her back there in one piece.

He drew in a deep breath, relishing the scent of this place. Even the slightly unpleasant odor of mildew made him smile. Some of his favorite memories had been made here, among the nearly silent stacks and the furious scribbling of scholars, searching out some forgotten detail in a book ten times older than he was, with only a quiet "Aha!" for celebration when an answer was found. Other than the first years of his life when Fria was still alive, he had never been as happy and carefree as his time studying in here. But even when his sister's loving presence had made everyday life in the Holm an adventure, the cloud of his father had hung over the three siblings. This place was the only escape from the Jorgen he had ever enjoyed.

With one last tendon snapping stretch, he settled back down to his table, pocketing Torman's letter to read when he got back to his room. He began to tidy up his notes on all the possible ways Sylvia could have been brought to Prium from her mysterious 'Oregon'. It seemed most likely that magic of some sort had brought her here, as he could find no mention of humans in any of the numerous traveler's accounts the Library housed. No one, no matter how far they had traveled, had come across a land that was populated by humans rather than Trewal, although there were a few discreet mentions in three separate books of a Sareth scholar, one Pealer Grunswer, who had traveled widely and discovered a land where they spoke only the ancient scholars tongue. But all of the books that scholar had ever penned were housed at the Saerin University, and the details of his discoveries disappointingly thin. Even knowing he had read about humans before in the library did him little good, he had read too many books to be sure of where to find the reference. If he continued hitting dead ends here in the King's Academy, he would have to take his search for Sylvia's origins across the Blitherly Sea to Saerin.

From his carefully disguised notes taken from Sylvia's narration of her home, he knew that the Trewal were not even known of there, antlers only adorned the heads of animals in her world, which made her fascination with them understandable. So this 'United States' must either be unimaginably far away, or accessible only by magical means. He was betting on the latter, so he had spent the last portion of his time in the Academy Library focusing on the art of magical travel.

He opted to put away the seven or so books he had been looking at himself. The Library scribes usually performed that task themselves, so visiting scholars only had to place the books in one of the return bins strategically situated around the reading rooms. But the titles of the books he had picked out earlier in the night were far too telling to leave lying about. Even without his father watching his every move, the scribes might be interested enough in who had been reading *'The Hazards of Teleportation'*, *'Lands Far Away and Beyond as seen by Cinsul Garson'*, *'Magic at its Most Powerful'* or the ominously titled, *'A Dark Grimoire'*, to attempt an investigation into his late night excursion.

After shelving the last book and covering an enormous yawn with his hand, he made his way furtively back to his rooms. He found the Palace by the Sea a much more convenient place to sneak about than Jorgenholm. Its pale stones caught the two moons' combined light and reflected it back into the night, alleviating the darkness he moved through to such an extent that he strode forwards without fear of tripping or losing his way without the help of his magic. The open breezeways and often glass-less windows here were in stark contrast to the enclosed halls of the Holm, where even if the moonlight had been bright enough to cast shadows, no windows were present to allow the light entry.

He peeked cautiously around the last corner before the long straight hallway his rooms lay off of, and nearly groaned aloud in frustration. A colorfully attired serf sat dozing against the wall opposite his door, effectively blocking him from his bed. With a grim smile he realized he was at least in the clear with his earlier escape. If the serf was watching his door, then for all his father knew, he was still inside.

He considered backtracking through the Palace to reach the small ornamental gardens one story below the balcony off his bedchamber. But the climb to reach the ornate balustrade would be impossible without the use of his magic to encourage unnatural growth from the clinging ivy that straggled up the sheer wall. He discarded the idea impatiently. He could use the ivy to ascend, but had no idea how to shrink it back down to a normal size after he fed it Earth magic. The abnormally large vines would be an obvious sign that he had not been in his chambers for the entire night. His shaggy head cocked to the side as he suddenly realized there was a large gap in his magical training. He could perform many seemingly impossible deeds with his power, but generally had no idea how to reverse said actions.

Resolving to add that to his list of topics to research on his next Library trip, he poked his head around the corner once more to see the sleepy serf's head bobbing up and down like a gull on the waves of the sea. At the far end of the corridor he spied a decorative glass bowl filled with polished stones supporting a variety of hardy succulents from the deserts surrounding Woletor's Crater. He smiled triumphantly before breathing in, and reaching towards the warmly beckoning ember of his power, waking it to glowing life with a nudge of his mind and a tug at the distant vegetation from the garden beneath the visitor suites. With closed eyes he reached down the length of the hall, his magic unerringly seeking the green life at the end. The stunted little plants there reached desperate roots into the smooth rocks, seeking endlessly for the water pooled in the bottom of the bowl. With a light touch here, and a slight redirection there, he guided the roots down to drink deeply of the stored water before asking the now water heavy vegetation to grow, and grow, and grow.

He opened his eyes in time to see the serf's head snap to attention at the sharp crack of the over taxed glass bowl. The serf's mouth dropped open as the smooth rocks tumbled in a loud stream from the delicate table, then he clambered to his feet and stumbled down the hall as quickly as his sleep filled limbs could carry him. Ryland tiptoed down the lush carpets, eyes firmly fixed on the scrambling serf as he attempted to stop the rocks from their raucous descent.

Ryland shut his door with a soft click before slumping against it with a chuckle. Poor man, he would have to make sure the diligent serf didn't get in trouble for the broken bowl, but he had a feeling that by morning the mess would have been cleaned away and a new decoration would have already taken its place. He loosened his cloak before stirring the softly glowing fire to life once more. Then he drew Torman's letter from his pocket and knelt by the hearth to enjoy both its heat, and the illumination it provided. He scanned the letter once, and then re-read it another two times, unsure if what he was reading could possibly be true.

An ancient library found beneath the Holm? And he was stuck here in Seaprium about to get married? A sharp longing for the cold stones of Jorgenholm struck him abruptly, like a cramp had seized the muscles about his heart and squeezed until he could no longer draw breath. To spend his hours in the mysterious new library with Camus, unraveling the secrets of a previously unknown language, or assembling tidbits of knowledge to an astonishing new view of their world! Why, they might even uncover the secret of Sylvia's home in the library there! Rather than being trapped here, listening to his besotted wife-to-be ramble on about cake flavors and napkin rings.

Biting his lip until the pain brought him back to the present, he pursued the letter once more. He cataloged the discoveries Camus had already made with growing excitement: an atlas of Prium so old that all of the landmarks were called by different names, objects made of materials entirely unfamiliar to the knowledgeable Maegi, accounts of a time when the Gods themselves may have walked among their people! Ryland considered the implications of this hidden trove of knowledge, picking up on what Camus must have intended him to conclude, but had been too cautious to write, even in code; this library must have survived countless years beneath the ground, hundreds upon hundreds of years. All the clues pointed to it being from the Age Beyond Memory.

With a start Ryland realized a golden ray of light had edged its way onto the sheet of parchment, easing his tired eyes as they read the letter yet again. Morning sunlight now streamed through the window of his sitting room, and the fire lay all but cold at his side. A sudden knock on his door had him hastening to answer its summons, each and every muscle in his body seeming to protest the torment of movement after his sleepless night. The door opened to reveal a serf in the colors of the Herrions, the buttery yellow and dark maroon complementing his thin face and reddish beard handsomely.

He gave a bow before saying, "My good lord Ryland, my Lady Elaine Herrion has requested you join her for a repast this morn." He brandished a beribboned note under Ryland's nose that gave off the distinct odor of the Lady Elaine's favorite perfume, a pleasant mixture of lavender and rose that quickly became overpowering in the copious amounts she tended to apply to her person.

Blinking owlishly at the waiting serf, he took the note and read the brief missive all but demanding his presence in Elaine's sitting room for breakfast; it was penned in a neat hand but sported atrocious misspellings. With a groan he asked the courier to summon him a chambermaid to aid in donning one of the cursed fashionable doublets that was impossible to put on by one's self. Then he turned to his bedchamber, all the excitement and fire Torman's letter had lit in him abruptly drained at the prospect of another tiresome day of wedding planning and court functions at the side of his betrothed. Splashing water on his face, he absently tucked the letter away at the back of his wardrobe with his dusty saddlebags, for safekeeping, before beginning the process of readying himself for the day ahead.

The Jorgen

The largest of the Palace by the Sea's Greathalls had been scrubbed floor to ceiling, to a pristine white so polished you could see your reflection in the glossy surfaces of walls and floors. The family colors of Jorgenholm and Herrion adorned every spare surface and draped in heavy velvet streamers from the highest reaches of the ceiling. The co-mingling of familiar red bearing the stylized ice lion of the Jorgens, and the yellow and maroon sigil of the Herrions lent the hall a festive air, but set the Jorgen's teeth on edge as his ancestral coat of arms was diluted by another of the noble family's colors.

He thought back to his own wedding, an affair so drenched in Jorgen red it was almost bloodier than a true battle. His timid bride had swept into the hall wrapped up in white lace and silk, with a crimson cloak to keep her warm as she walked through the Holm's unheated corridors to reach him, a bouquet of winter Windthorns overflowing her slim fingers. It had only been the second time he had seen her, his Cara, as the marriage arrangements were made primarily by letters between Galmorah and Jorgenholm. He had thought her beautiful, it was true, her sweet rounded cheeks rosy and flushed, dark lined eyes seeming to leap off her face they were so cleverly enhanced with paints. And then she had raised those big eyes to him as they met in front of the Greathall, and the timidness was consumed by the fire behind. He smiled fondly at the memory, Cara had played the dutiful wife to perfection in public, but had given him no quarter once they were alone. He had fallen in love with the fierceness of her fragile beauty, and never wanted their marriage to be any other way.

He looked around again from his position at the long high table where he would watch his son wed. This *travesty*! When a member of the Jorgen family wed, tradition held that the new wife shed her own family's name to take up the coat of arms of her husband. The celebration was always held in the Holm before a disciple of Garrin, where the deep red of the Jorgens dominated the scene, and the cloak of the bride to be was as red as the matrimonial sheets were expected to be. But the Herrions had demanded equality in representation at the very public binding of their families, breaking with century old tradition by dangling their support for the King as leverage for a wedding exactly as *they* wanted. Engineered to make the court as a whole see their family as equal to the rulers of Jorgenholm. The King, of course, had forced the Jorgen's hand when he would have liked to fight tooth and nail to uphold the honor of his family.

No amount of logic had made a dent in the King's plan. He wanted Saerin, and in order to get the minimum number of votes he needed from the Council to sail to war, he needed Tager Herrion. As much as this wedding rankled, the Jorgen could not refuse. There was no reason to at this point. The match was a good one, even if the girl seemed somewhat lacking in wits, and tying Jorgenholm to one of the most powerful families on the Council is what he would have attempted to do with Ryland's marriage in a few years anyway. But he didn't like being forced. And he didn't like being used as a means to an end. Especially an end he did not support and had been trying desperately to find a way to put a stop to.

He had seriously considered derailing the wedding simply as a means to put a stop to the King's obsession with having power over the Sareth Isles. But the damage that would do to his family name, and to Jorgenholm itself, was too great a risk. The Herrions owned a huge amount of trading houses here in Seaprium, with strong ties to Galmorah. If he angered them trade between his home and the other two great cities of Prium would be greatly diminished, putting his people at a disadvantage. So his son would be wed, earlier than he had imagined, and to one whose breeding stock was not ideal, but in truth this alliance would make Jorgenholm prosperous if the coming war was successful.

He would have to find another way to stop the King's mad plan. His stomach tightened at the prospect. He had already exhausted himself trying to rally Seaprium against this war, and while the people or the city itself were violently and loudly against stabbing their allies in the back, too many of those in powerful positions saw opportunity for wealth in the Isles.

He locked eyes with his son as he stood awaiting the Herrion girl in front of the high table. *Stop fidgeting.* He thought at him furiously, hoping to convey the command through the connection their eyes shared. For all his twitchiness, his youngest son cut a handsome figure in the white brocade tunic, accented heavily in red and with brightly winking gold buttons marching up the left side under his arm and then up the outside of the arm itself. Yet another senseless deviation from tradition that no one in Seaprium seemed to care about.

Would the boy ever stop growing? The tunic had been altered yet again this morning after Ryland had tried it on a final time, needing more room for shoulders that seemed to have sprouted more width in the space of a night. He released his anger at the mockery his family was a part of today, to let a shiver of pride into his heart. That powerful young man standing straight before the gathered nobility, the one with hard muscle hidden beneath his elegant clothes, and callouses on the hands clasped tightly before him. The one in such sharp contrast to the softness and utter uselessness of the other noble men his age. That was his son.

Ryland broke their locked gaze as the somber musicians in the corner struck the first notes of 'A Blessing from Garrin', and trained his eyes on the open entryway his bride would be walking through at any moment. Jorgen felt a moment of regret, knowing there would be no fire behind the eyes of the Herrion girl, no steel sheathed in silk to keep his son on his toes and challenge him to push farther, try harder. Elaine Herrion was not of a bloodline he wished intermingled with his own, she was not someone his wife would have chosen. The fond smile came back to him, and Ryland slanted him a strange look as he saw the unfamiliar expression on his father's normally stoic face. But how could Jorgen not smile picturing the epic fight he and Cara would have waged in the privacy of their bedchamber, and the inevitable making up afterwards, over the unsuitable marriage he had arranged for their son? He wiped the look off his face with effort, as Ryland's attention remained fixed on him even as his bride first stepped into the room to the excited tittering of the crowd.

He barely contained an eye roll at the pretentious dress nearly concealing the homely girl cocooned inside it. Yard upon yard of frothy white lace ballooned out from a waist cinched so tight he was actually impressed with the girl's tolerance for pain. His eyes narrowed at the veil embellished with yellow and red rosettes that were complemented by delicate slippers of the same design, just visible under the hem of the full skirts her chambermaids held up so she could walk without tripping. Weaving her way between the many tables where their wedding guests stood to honor her entrance, the girl's eyes darted to Ryland at the front of the room.

The Jorgen flicked his eyes to Ryland also, seeing the tight expression on his face slowly turning to a stiff, welcoming smile as Elaine approached him. The smile didn't reach his wide eyes, but the Jorgen could tell without a doubt that the girl would never notice such a subtlety. Her self-satisfied grin nearly split her face, and her heavily painted eyes were too busy flashing triumph at the row of her peers seated strategically close to where the ceremony would take place, likely just for the bride's gloating pleasure.

A heavily cowled Demandron that the King had demanded wed the two young persons stepped forward, and Jorgen had to close his eyes at this last and most grievous break from hallowed tradition. It should have been a devotee of Garrin, clad in only the bounty of the hunt as befits the disciples of Garrin, antlers strung with fresh Listenbark, and a crown of prickled holly heavy with red berries on his brow. But instead the Demandron stepped forward, dragging his dark cloud of magic behind him to cast a pall over the gaily lit affair. Even the smug bride shrank back from the black clad figure, looking away from the gaping hood, propped up to an impressive height on the tines of the man's unseen antlers, as if she was afraid to see what dark thing lay beneath.

It was impossible to tell if this was one of the various Demandron he had met in the War Councils. Each was identical to the last, excepting height and the shape of the antlers beneath their hoods, their genders concealed fully by the enveloping robes, but he rarely saw more than one together to compare their differences and to get an idea of who was who. The anonymous man's voice rang out harshly, tinged by the tumultuous thunder of the unnatural magic hovering around his person. Jorgen let the ceremonial words wash over him, tempted to close his eyes in remembrance of his own wedding day in order to escape the horror of this one, but the strange timbre of the Demandron's voice kept him firmly in the here and now, banning even those few pleasant thoughts from his mind with its strangeness.

Both bride and groom flinched as the unnaturally pale hands of the officiant placed their hands one on top of the other to knot the red silk cord around their joined wrists. And not even Jorgen could fault the young people their revulsion. The man's hands were barely Trewal, impossibly long and slim, whiter than a corpse and tipped with thick yellowed nails that had been allowed to grow to an astonishing length before being filed to sharp points. In the silence holding sway as the knot that would remain in place all evening was tied, the audience winced as the nails snagged repeatedly and audibly on the corded rope, pulling fine threads from their tightly woven braids to frizzle messily around the intricate knot. The pale hands then picked up an ornate hammer to seal the matching, solid gold Terlings at the bases of Elaine and Ryland's left antlers. The rings pinged metallically against the hammer, releasing a stench of magic as they sealed.

The Demandron moved on unconcernedly, voicing the passage binding husband and wife under the eyes of the Gods, and with dread Jorgen felt an icy prickling in the jet stone hanging, as always, around his neck. This was exactly what he had feared, ever since the King insisted a Demandron preside over the ceremony. His Majesty had no reason to wish The Circle involved in Jorgenholm or Herrion affairs. But the Demandron, with their proclivity of worshiping the dark and lesser known God whose name the common folk would not even utter, rather than Garrin, would wish to have a say in the binding of two families known for their dedication to the God of the Hunt.

The stone grew colder against his chest, and the darkness

around the Demandron standing next to his son grew closer, thicker, somehow even more malign. Jorgen snuck a look at the throne where Gartlan slumped, propped up with cushions on the huge chair, attired entirely in royal purple that hung garishly on his emaciated frame. The man's eyes rolled back slightly as he watched, sallow eyelids fluttering in time to the cold pulsing Jorgen felt from his chest. Contempt flowed through Jorgen suddenly, overpowering the pull of the magic as he saw the King languishing in the sick pleasure the Demandron magic afforded him. Jorgen grabbed onto that contempt like a lifeline as the actions fueling the magic played like a grotesque performance behind his eyes.

A young girl struggled against bonds that trapped her arms up above her head. Beautiful blonde hair streamed free, and her tears ran just as freely as the clawed hand of a Demandron smoothed the locks back from her face tenderly, to gather it at the nape of her neck, baring her naked torso to the fearful eyes of the two teen boys standing before them, a too white hand clamped hard on each of their shoulders to anchor them in place.

Jorgen summoned forth a vision of his daughter's face when his contempt could no longer distract him from the greedy suction of the dark magic's siren song, superimposing her round face over the lusty and violent images that always accompanied a Demandron's use of the gem around his neck. Through will power alone he changed each detail of her lovely face, so like her mother's, to how the Demandron had left her. *Sunken cheeks,* he thought harshly, *pale as sour milk,* he could see the lewd smile curling Gartlan's lips in his periphery and he flinched away from the scene that put it there, *dead, used up eyes.* He let out a low growl when the images broke through again, and he tried to place Fria's face over the young girl's, trying to keep his distance with revulsion. Struggling to not be pulled into the arousal of the magic.

The swirl of sensation and chaotic press of the images abated abruptly as the Demandron spoke the last words of the binding, "And you shall belong only to one another, under the eyes of the Gods."

"We shall belong only to each other," Ryland and Elaine spoke together, both obviously shaken by the power suffusing the air, but prompted into action by the prolonged silence after the officiant's last words.

Gartlan staggered to his feet, adjusting himself surreptitiously before clapping his hands giddily. "I love weddings!" he cried out as the Demandron made his way back to the King's side. His Majesty absentmindedly reached out to finger the man's cloak as he passed, petting it lovingly even as he rambled on. "And the best part of weddings is the feasting! So let us feast so these two love birds can get to the best part of *their* night all the quicker." He gave a huge wink to Ryland and laughed bawdily as Elaine blushed heavily enough for it to show through the paint upon her face. "Feast I say! Feast!"

Serfs began streaming into the Greathall, carrying platter after platter of gourmet food and enough pitchers of beer and wine to drown a small city. And just like that, whatever dark compulsion the Demandron had forced on his son and his new bride was forgotten by the masses and the celebrations began. Ryland and Elaine were tugged this way and that by well-wishers thrusting drinks into their hands for toast after toast, all the while remaining joined by their tied hands. That bond was tested again and again, as one or the other was pulled away from their counterpart by yet more admirers. They bobbed about in the sea of bodies, never far from one another, but neither were they entirely together.

Jorgen took his seat, troubled beyond words. He had seen the confusion on Ryland's face as the scent of magic grew heavy in the air when his vows were being spoken. He felt a pang of guilt at allowing this to transpire. At allowing, whatever had just happened, to happen to his son and daughter-in-law. His blood, *his* son! Every other person in this room was all too happy to forget the faint scent of blood in the air from whatever evil magic the Demandron had just preformed, but he would not forget. He could never forget, because whatever ploy the Demandron were attempting to put into play was his fault. His doing. He had allowed this to happen, against all of his better judgment.

Ryland

The high pitch giggle he was coming to dread speared

through his head like lightning, setting off sharp pains behind his eyes and at the back of his aching skull. He rubbed his eyes gingerly, cursing his 'friends' at the palace for that last round of toasts which seemed to never end, and always required him to drink in acknowledgment. The noble boys his own age, the Councilmen's sons and young noblemen he had been socializing with since he arrived in the capital didn't deserve the name 'friends' he decided savagely, not after their gleeful grins and frequent toasts had pushed him well past drunk and into a lofty territory of inebriation he had never before reached.

The giggle sounded again, this time followed by a heavy thud that cut the awful noise off with alarming speed. He whirled around to make sure his bride was still breathing, but overshot the turn, stumbling instead into the bed he had just been facing before using it to help him turn at a more sedate pace. His wife lay in an ungainly heap of gauzy fabric before the hearth, bared legs weaving in the air above the fluffy skirts, and arms scrabbling at the thick carpet as she fought to regain air for her lungs. *Likely so she could voice that horrendous cackle once again,* he thought meanly. Ryland sighed, disappointed at himself for the ungracious thought, and made his way slowly to Elaine's side to offer her an arm in getting up.

Leaning over he saw her eyes bulging a bit and her too red lips puffed up into a comical 'O' as she tried to suck air into her lungs. Her arms came up to him entreatingly so he yanked her into a sitting position as carefully as he could manage, ending up kneeling over one of her splayed legs, his knees pinning her skirts down to trap her in the mountains of fabric. He patted her on the back as she swayed and gasped until she was able to take in enough air to start laughing all over again, pointing between herself and him and then the floor. He couldn't help but chuckle a little as well, wincing as his mirth brought the abominable ache in his head back to his attention. She was a strange little creature, not what he had hoped for maybe, not nearly as much fun as Sylvia, but at least she was an entertaining drunk.

Elaine's giggles finally subsided, leaving them in the very same situation which had set off her hysterics in the first place; alone in their marital chambers. She peered up at him breathlessly and he tried to see beyond the smeared cosmetics and miles of fabric to the girl who would be a fixture in his life until either he, or she, died.

The silence stretched on too long as he stared at her and he could see the giddiness of the alcohol wearing thin, a hint of fear showing in her glassy eyes. He plopped back onto his bottom, suddenly feeling a little too close to her.

"Little help?" she asked, turning her back to him so he could see the row of minuscule buttons running down the back of her gown to disappear under her, appearing here and there in the tornado of skirts and underskirts floating up around her seated form. Ryland groaned, urging his drink-clumsy hands up to the buttons in dread. The tiny pearl buttons would be a pain if he was entirely sober, but at his current level of drunk they looked more like torture. He popped one through and felt an absurd urge to cheer at the monumental achievement before he remembered he had to repeat that same move about a hundred more times. Halfway down her back she began fidgeting, squirming this way and that, making his job even harder.

"Oh just rip it off!" she finally said, craning her head over her own shoulder to see how much progress he had made before tossing her head in annoyance. "I *have* to unlace this corset or I think I'm going to die" she added piteously, goading Ryland into action.

He gripped each half of the dress in his hands and heaved, sending buttons spraying across the room to ping and clatter their way to the floor, leaving behind a silence that was unexpectedly filled with his laughter and her breathless giggles. He hastened to the stays of her corset, not liking the raspy tone her voice had acquired and he hurriedly untied them, wincing at the red markings on the skin he unearthed under the device. Finally, the corset and dress gaped open and Elaine drew in a huge breath, blowing it out in a satisfied huff. Ryland reached out tentatively, running his hand over the hot skin of her back, trying to sooth the irritated skin back into creamy smoothness, to no avail.

She shivered a little at his touch and he drew back, remembering that fearful look she had gotten every time one of the less circumspect wedding guests had mentioned the coming wedding night. He backed away from her on all fours, and climbed to his feet once he was sure he wouldn't fall on her if he didn't make it to his feet on the first attempt. Then he made his way to the vanity, pouring a stream of water unsteadily into the bowl while he asked over his shoulder, "Do you want to wash your face before bed?"

There was a lot of rustling and then her voice, finally at a timbre that didn't hurt his ears, spoke from behind him. "Yes please."

He turned, hitching a smile into place before skirting around her in the small space and making for the other side of the massive bed. He peeled himself from his fitted clothes to the sounds of splashing, choosing to keep on his underclothes as he made his way to extinguish the lantern, plunging the room into low light that flickered as the flames in the fire danced from the breeze of his movements. By that time Elaine was sitting up in bed, knees tucked to her chest and the covers pulled up under her chin, watching him. He climbed in beside her, suddenly fascinated by the face of the girl who had spent the entire night by his side.

It was the first time he was seeing her without the face paints she favored so heavily, and the clean canvas of her face took years away from her normal appearance. He suddenly wondered just how old this girl was, for all that she had the curves of a full grown woman, her unadorned face made her look young and vulnerable in the firelight. He settled in to his pillow, turning towards her, intent on knowing at least that much about his wife. The covers were pulled to the side with his movement, baring one naked breast to his accidental gaze, and eliciting a squeak from the obviously apprehensive girl.

"Sorry!" he said, turning over quickly to lay on his back, hating the blush that heated his cheeks. They lay perfectly still for a while, barely breathing into the pregnant silence.

"I, um... I don' think you are supposed to be sorry," Elaine said hesitantly. "My mother said you would take what you are due and that I was to lie here and do nothing to discourage you." Ryland's mouth gaped open at the callous words, but she continued before he could protest the crude advice. "And my eldest sister said you would hurt me, but I'm not allowed to cry, if I cry it will only get worse. And that sometimes, only after the first few times, it might not hurt anymore if you were feeling nice."

He couldn't believe his ears. Her mother told her that? And

her sister? Those women who should have assuaged her fears, and explained what was supposed to happen tonight rather than scare her even more! He could barely form words around the hot anger clogging his chest. Even his father, his notoriously cold and distant sire, had made mention of his duties to the woman in his bed tonight. How a noble woman of gentle birth was no serf, so he had better act accordingly and gentlemanly when she came to his bed.

"Elaine!" he said, more sharply than he intended, and she shrunk back from him, an entirely different person than the bubbly young woman he had known at social events. "I'm not going to hurt you! I won't even touch you if you don't want me too." He shook his head in bewilderment, and he turned in the plush bed to face her again, careful this time to leave the covers in place. "I can't believe your family would say those things to you," he finished quietly, horrified to see tears leaking down the side of her beaky nose.

"It's, it's not, no-ot just them," she stuttered, crying in earnest now, "Its everyone! All the noblewoman hate it, only serfs ever enjoy being with a man!" she wailed. "And if I enjoy it, or desire it, or even think of it then I'm no better than them!" She tossed the covers over her head, effectively hiding from him even as she continued to cry.

He stayed frozen, absurdly perplexed at the outpouring of fear and self-loathing he had just witnessed. He wondered if he might have been better prepared for this situation if his brain was not swimming in alcohol. Long minutes passed with her staying beneath the covers and him staring open-mouthed at the spot she had disappeared from, before the subtleties of her last ringing statement finally penetrated his tired mind. "If you desire it or think of it?" he asked her empty pillow, before a grin spread over his face.

He pulled up the coverlet and burrowed underneath, joining her in the close confines and finding her face with careful touches of his hand. "Elaine," he said gently, "Does that mean you desire me?" A sodden hiccup met his ears, and he laughed, suddenly finding his wife absurdly adorable, a nice change of pace that had him mentally blessing the effects of alcohol. Other parts of his anatomy stirred at the positive feelings he was having towards the warmly naked girl lying next to him.

"Well, you are very handsome," the words came out sullenly, "And so gentle whenever you touch me. But I know you don't like me. I just didn't think it would matter when it came to...*that*. Men will take any girl when it comes to...*that*." Another hiccup followed that little revelation, making Ryland feel like the worst person ever born to have so casually made his wife feel like he didn't like her. He flung the covers back so he could see her face, but had to pause before he spoke to rearrange the cloths to cover her breasts when he found his eyes glued to her chest and his tongue strangely inhibited.

"I barely know you, Elaine. I don't know enough about you to like *or* dislike you, but I hope very much we can change that." He laughed a little forlornly, "If I manage to return from Saerin in one piece, we will have the rest of our lives to figure it out."

Elaine grimaced and fidgeted beneath the blankets, finally turning her head to face his squarely. "Will you return, Ryland?" Her voice had sharp edges that made Ryland feel even more guilty than before for not taking into account what this marriage truly meant to his new bride.

Elaine was being sold off for the good of her family, to a man who would leave her after only one night to sail for war. Many of the men leaving on the morrow would not be returning, and it was entirely possible he could be among the fallen. Where would that leave Elaine? A widow, still young and with a good family that would leave her many prospects for another union, but ostracized by her peers, forced into mourning for a year and a day and unable to attend any of the social functions that she so obviously enjoyed. His death would mean an end to her social life, which is nearly all that the women of the court were allowed occupy themselves with.

Ryland sighed, searching her glassy eyes that had faded from their defiant questioning into drink-bleary tiredness. *There is more there, beneath the surface*, he told himself, willing it to be true. Needing his wife to have some spark of wit and willfulness, even if he never got to see it again, it would sustain her in the lonely years ahead of her if he did not return. "I will try my very hardest to come back to you, Elaine," Ryland said, meaning every word.

She nodded solemnly, another hiccup breaking the serious tone of the conversation, so even she cracked a smile. He wiped the moisture from her cheeks, determined to give her a chance to be someone he could love, he owed her that much. He owed *himself* that much, to give this forced relationship a real try, rather than writing it off before it had even begun.

A huge yawn interrupted his thoughts and he pulled his hands from her face, tucking some stray hairs which had found their way into her mouth back behind her ears as she lay her head down. "We are both too tired and inebriated for any of this tonight. What do you say we get some sleep?" he offered. She mumbled in reply, eyes already closed as she snuggled down into the bed. He flopped back onto his side with an exhausted sigh, more than ready for this unfathomably long day to end.

Gartlan

"I'm done talking about this, Jorgen. We finally have the support of the Council, and the Circle has been preparing this for months. I will not let all that work go to waste. We are going, end of discussion." He waved his hand in front of his face to ward off the haze of Dreamweed escaping from his mouth as he spoke, catching a glance of the Jorgen's murderous face through the smoke. He wished the obtuse man would dissipate as easily as the sweet smelling cloud, but he could tell from his expression that he planned on staying. And talking. And arguing. Again. Didn't he understand the title King? His decision was law, LAW! But there he was, standing in the same spot as before, ready to try to talk him out of this war.

The Jorgen's mouth opened, but Gartlan beat him to the punch and stood abruptly, his anger ratcheting even higher as he stumbled slightly, his head swimming, and he was forced to clutch the arm of his chair in a very un-kingly manner. "Enough, cousin," his voice was weaker than he would have liked, but he shook it off and stood straight before his old friend, his left hand hovering over the arm of the chair covertly. He saw Jorgen's mouth close with satisfaction and the two men faced off in silence for a few heartbeats, allowing the King to get his temper back under control. *This is my oldest friend,* he reflected as he looked at the familiar face, its harsh lines grooved deeper with age, but the sharp mind contained within unchanged. *It's to this man's tenacity I owe my throne,* he reminded himself, pushing down the petulance the Jorgen's unending arguments made rise up within him. He was just not used to being questioned; it was the man's own fault that he had finally snapped.

With a deep breath he dragged his next words forth, wondering idly when the last time he had said this word to anyone was. "Please." He watched the Jorgen's eye twitch with vague pleasure. "Cousin of mine, you sail to war at nightfall. Let us spend these last few, safe hours enjoying one another's company and some fine wine. Let's smoke together and dream of the foolish children we used to be before we ruled the better part of this kingdom." Other than that first flicker, his cousin's face remained impassive, and Gartlan cursed the man's damned control for the umpteenth time that day alone. He was impossible to read.

"Thank you for the kind offer your Majesty, but I have preparations to make and many instructions to send back to Jorgenholm for my son to carry out if I'm to be gone from my duties there for the duration of this conflict." His tone let none of his frustration show, even though the mention of his duties back at the Holm was an obvious jab. Gartlan gave a tired nod of dismissal, suddenly exhausted by the never ending passive aggressive displays of his vassal. He turned to the massive windows in his study before the Jorgen had fully left the room, his scattered thoughts already floating away from the ugly scene that had just played out.

His eyes trailed down the thick glass to the wavy panorama below. Two hundred and fifty-nine ships lay peacefully at anchor in the harbor far below, their black sails furled and all of their oars at rest even as the docks and decks swarmed with activity. Serfs and common sailors loaded barrels of salted fish and fresh water for the journey ahead, and soldiers secured bundles of spears, arrows and swords below-decks, fastening shields along the outer railing of each ship for ready use. From the vantage of his study, the harbor looked like an ant's nest freshly disturbed. Countless persons running this way and that with important tasks, and just as many bodies wandering aimlessly, restless with adrenaline for what was to come.

A contingent of black robed figures made their way towards the ships, easily spotted as the surrounding Trewal parted to give them a wide berth, and the pale beige of the dock-wood encircled their dark numbers like a beacon. They split off one by one, twenty of them, making their solitary way to each ship in turn, dragging their bubble of solitude with them as they checked the magic imbued in the vessels. The entire contingent of Demandron had been taking shifts sleeping at the docks, a wise precaution they had suggested to dissuaded any vandalism to the warships. The Mages had stopped five separate attacks on the vessels since the announcement of the Herrion/Jorgen wedding.

A shiver raced over his body and he felt his desire rising as he thought of the long nights to come. The Circle was sending the ten disciples in training under them to guide his ships to Saerin by night, calling on their magic for the long hours of darkness, so their movements would be concealed from the Sareth Isle's farscryers. He fingered the large dark stone hanging beneath his cloths to dangle at the top of his stomach, grinning wolfishly at the hardening in his body that he could now only achieve when the Demandron drew on the stone nestled close to his skin.

The price for such pleasure was well worth it to his mind. A little of his life force for unimaginable satisfaction. A sympathetic ear for The Circle in return for a sea of indulgence in his darkest fantasies. And the coming pleasures would last for entire nights at a time. A high pitched cackle sounded through the room; he whirled to see what depraved soul dared to interrupt his solitude without leave, only to find the sound abruptly cut off at his turn and the room left achingly empty behind him. He laughed again, a little timidly, to find the strange noise repeated from his own throat. He shrugged in discomfort, reaching for the still smoking pipe of Dreamweed to distract him from another of the increasing instances of unintended outbursts that came from his own traitorous mouth. *It's worth the price*, he reminded himself, *it will always be worth the price.*

He brought the Dreamweed to his mouth for a languorous pull, only to abort the move when his rings clacked together and one slipped from the tip of his finger, nearly making him drop his expensive and incredibly delicate pipe. "Trollit!" he cried, placing the smoking instrument down gingerly before tearing all the overlarge rings from his hands and hurling them across the room. He leaned with both hands on the windowsill for a moment, breathing hard, his head hanging low, before he decided a nap was in order. He would need his strength for the long ride down to the dock from the Palace, at the head of his army. A palanquin would take him back to his residence once he saw the forces off, but he needed to be seen leading the procession down. He needed his people to see him in his rightful position of power. The King turned from his window and drifted listlessly towards his bedchamber, his hand stealing unconsciously under his loose robes to caress the stone secreted there as he climbed into his bed.

The Jorgen

The wind edged beneath his cloak with icy fingers, but the chill paled in comparison to the cold he felt from his pendant. The Demandron drew upon his life force like a leech to guide his fleet safely into the pitch black of the night. Beside him he saw his son's eagerness fade bit by bit from his face, to be replaced by a sickly green cast that made him want to howl with laughter. Brave, powerful, serious Ryland, being taken to his knees with seasickness. Garrin must have a sense of humor after all.

He reveled in the bob and weave of the deck beneath his feet, made all the sweeter by Ryland's weakness. There was a sharp tang of salt in the air and heavy clouds misted his face, making the lantern light feel close and intimate, even under the vastness of the night sky. In the future they would travel without even the scant light of the lanterns to see by, but this close to Seaprium they could risk it as the cloud cover made it almost impossible for them to be spotted with farscrying. The night was alive around him, and he felt like monkeying up the rigging as he had as a boy, like screaming with abandon into the oncoming wind, pulling in every ounce of magic he could hold just to feel alive at its burn. He was even tempted to speak aloud the name he had discarded all those years ago, just to feel the freedom the boy named Dourith had once enjoyed.

He stoppered up the wild feelings stirring in his chest, wondering at the uncharacteristic urges taking up residence in his normally controlled mind. From the corner of his eye he saw Ryland stagger suddenly aft on unsteady feet, making it to the rail, but failing to turn far enough downwind to avoid his own vomit being blown back onto him. Jorgen allowed himself a quiet chuckle, easing the pressure of the building outburst inside nominally. The boy had a lot to learn still. "Don't puke into the wind, idiot! You clean up any mess you make on this ship!" he called to his son, unsure if the words made it to him before the wind snatched them up and away, but not particularly caring if he had heard or not.

When had events gotten so out of control? he wondered idly. He knew it was since coming to Seaprium that he had been getting this fluttering feeling of panic in his chest. But the more he examined the people around him, the more he realized the calmly sailing ship he saw as his life had been listing, unbeknownst to him. How long had his sons been lying to him? And were they keeping back more than just the impressive amount of magic Ryland Controlled? His own blood plotting behind his back was almost reassuring in this family. But with that new knowledge he had been forced to realize that Camus, his own right hand, was also keeping important information from him, in favor of his children. *So what else didn't he know?*

Then there was the debacle of events forced upon him once he reached the capital. The wedding, with its sinister magic. The King, and his slow decent into madness no one seemed willing to acknowledge. The secret war being waged despite his Majesty's promise of peace to the Saerin royalty. And lastly his loss of control over Jorgenholm. Having to leave his home in the hands of Camus and his son stung worse than any other slight. He let out a tense breath, the pressure was back in his chest, beating in time to his pulse and making him move about restlessly, a show of nerves that infuriated him even though he could not still himself. He tried to blame it on the swirl of Demandron magic, faint but present in his mind, casting even this sleeping ship in a lustily violent light to his mind. But he knew the unrest grew from deeper within, just as he knew there was no way to stop its creeping advance.

Jeralt, the captain of this ship, and his second in command over the entire Imperial fleet, came to stand with him at the bow. He glanced at the grizzled warrior, trying to find his measure by mere appearance. The old sailor was common born, making his high rank all the more impressive as it was not awarded by blood, but hard work and a slow climb through less worthy men. He kept his face cleanly shaved but for the very tip of his chin from which sprouted long silvery hairs, tamed into a braid. The rest if his hair was sparse, kept closely cropped to his head in defiance of the courtly fashions, but likely much safer in both sailing and battle. Dark eyes met the Jorgen's, and one heavy brow quirked in amused understanding of his perusal.

"You might not 'member me," Jeralt said, his speech still holding the roughness of the lower warrens, the depths from which he had clawed his way to the Palace by the Sea. "But I 'member the boy you were, always up in the rigging of ole Gustus's fat tub, urging the crew for speed that the poor boat didn't have in 'er." The Jorgen squinted at the man, trying to see in the wrinkles a younger man he might have known from his year apprenticed aboard one of the older model ships, under the command of the previous Imperial Commander, Gustus.

Jeralt continued on, unfazed by his intense scrutiny, "Full of piss and vinegar you was. But a man had to look in yer eyes to find it. Even then yer face was more rock than flesh. Like your Ma had forgotten to connect the muscles of yer little face to all the others when you lived in her body with her." He turned his gaze to Jorgen from the sea, a self-deprecating smile gracing his weathered face. "Still don know me, eh? Guess the years've been harsher than me mirror has been telling me."

That spark of good humor finally pinpointed where he had known the younger Jeralt from, and it was not from the crew of the 'fat tub' he had served on as he had originally assumed, but from the slip where they berthed when in harbor. "You fished me out of the harbor when Gustus would have left me to drown for sneaking his good rum," he said in amazement. The memory of the actual event was still a blur for obvious reasons, but he remembered that same toothy smile beaming at him from the face of the fish boy who had saved his miserable life, when the rest of the world had been laughing at his drunken fall into the water.

Jeralt laughed loudly and clapped him on the shoulder,

"Now ye've got it," he said, "I knew we'd meet again one day, an I'm glad tis today. With you on the deck o' me ship and me captaining the flagship of yer fleet," he finished comfortably. Coming from anyone else the familiarity Jeralt spoke with would have been grievously insulting, but Jorgen couldn't help the smile that came to his lips as he compared the boys they had been with where they were now. He could not grudge the man his ease, not when it suddenly felt meant to be that they were meeting here, so many years later. Like the Gods had planned the reunion the second they had met by chance in their youth.

"I'm glad to be *on* your deck Captain Jeralt, and it does seem fitting you are my second in command. The Gods seem to be toying with my fate of late. This at least, is a happy occurrence." Jeralt raised that eyebrow again, and coupled with his slight nod it seemed like he raised a cup to the strangeness of their mutual Gods.

"We got a few days' journey ahead, but I was thinkin we could get a start on the battle plans. Fancy a cupp'a in the galley?" he said, rubbing his hands together briskly to warm them.

The Jorgen nodded, slipping his own chilled fingers into the fur lined pockets of his tunic, as they turned to search out some libations and a clear space to map out the coming naval assault of Saerin. They passed by the slumped form of his youngest, his long body draped bonelessly over the rail, now safely angled aft to avoid any spatter. He and Jeralt skirted the mess he had made on the deck, and Jorgen paused long enough to forcefully nudge Ryland's motionless foot and growl, "This deck will be clean before you seek your bed or you will find yourself sleeping with the bilge rats, boy."

Turning back to the short walk to the galley, he heard Jeralt chuckle at his threat. The small room they entered was filled with light and blessed warmth. The heavy scent of fish stew and rich dark Kercha permeated the air, with faint undertones of body odor and sweat that took him back to his days aboard a vessel very similar to this one. Jeralt moved to the galley stove where the perpetual pot of Kercha sat, never empty and rarely left so long as to cool completely. Jorgen plopped two cracked mugs of thick ceramic down on the scarred table, so the Captain could pour for them both, and then sat in quiet contemplation as Jeralt retreated to his stateroom to fetch the maps.

"That boy o' yers must have a mighty big stomach," he said as the wind blew his sturdy frame back into the room. "I'm guessing he din't spend the time on a boat that you did?"

Jorgen snorted, "No he did not." It stung that Ryland was so woefully unfit for the voyage they were undertaking, especially when a respectable sailor like the Captain took notice.

"He's a good looking boy anyways, he'll find 'is sea legs soon enough. We all had to." The silence after his statement turned awkward, as Jorgen clenched his jaw on an angry retort to Jeralt's kindness. "I bet the boy's a fine warrior on land. An with the way the words roll outta that mouth, 'is mind's like as strong as 'is body," Jeralt ventured, sensing Jorgen's discomfort but not knowing how to set the man at ease again.

"He is weak," Jorgen spat.

"Looks hale 'nough." Jeralt sat down across the table from him, spreading a map out with sure fingers while his eyes stayed on his commander's face.

"His weakness is not of the visible kind. He was a mouse as a child, unfit for the harsh life of a warrior of any kind. I had to cart him off to the gutless scribes at the King's Academy just to wean him from the tit!" Jorgen was aghast at how quickly he spilled his innermost thoughts to this near stranger, even with their shared history. Something about the captain elicited honest responses from him he wished had stayed unsaid. He brushed a speck of dirt from the map, changing topics drastically in his unease. "You have sailed the bays of the Sareth Isles before?"

"Aye Commander."

"Good." He upended the small wooden box of figurines they would use to mark their approach on the maps.

"Pardon me ifn' I speak outta turn Commander, but Ryland don't look like no mouse to me sir. He looks like a son I'd like to have." The old sailor said bluntly, looking Jorgen straight in the eye as if daring him to confront the conflicting emotions he had about his son. "Seems to me that on the eve o' war a man should be at peace with 'is own blood. I made me own peace with me good for 'nothin son afore leaving. A young man should know where 'e stands in 'is father's eye at least once afore 'is father aint here no more." Jeralt cleared his throat and broke their eye contact, knuckling his lumpy nose in embarrassment before deftly lining up the tiny ships in a fleet just outside Saerin's harbor, splitting off smaller groups to position at the two smaller harbors north and south of the largest one.

Jorgen added some of the boats he had taken north back to the main fleet with a heavy sigh, letting Jeralt squirm in the fear he had completely overstepped with his newly appointed Commander. He had of course, but Jorgen knew truth when he heard it. Part of his unease over the last month came directly from the clash of pride and disdain he felt for his son. He couldn't afford to go into a fight with distractions unsettling his thoughts, not when the lives of every single man aboard these nearly three hundred ships were at stake.

He pinned the man across from him to his seat with his eyes, seeing with satisfaction the utter stillness that came over him. "You do speak out of turn, *Captain*, even if you speak in truth. A good second must tell his commander the truth always, even when he doesn't wish to hear it. That is what a second in command is for." He let the relief wash over Jeralt's face before putting him in his place with his next words. "However, I only require my second to question my decisions in battle. In all other topics, including that of my son, I am the better. I am the leader. I am the Jorgen. You are warned to keep your sentimentality to yourself."

Jeralt reeled for a moment like the words were a physical assault rather than verbal, then he pulled himself together visibly with a small nod and a disbelieving exhale. "Aye, Commander."

"Tell me how you would wage this assault with the resources we have at hand," Jorgen started in briskly, watching the man settle back into a lesser role. His every word, and even his posture became one of respect and deference. A situation that left the Jorgen much more at ease than the companionable talk they had shared just moments before.

Chapter 11

Sylvia

There had been no further signs of the beast from the lake, or its brethren. But Sylvia had noticed encouraging signs that their time in the caves was coming to an end, which couldn't come soon enough for her. Among all her other, numerous complaints, she hated the algae they were relying on as a food source, and hoped to never taste the chalky stuff again, even though any sustenance was preferred to starving. The air in this section of the caves was clearer and less damp. When she had asked Les to extinguish the globelight as they made camp, they had both been surprised to find they could see one another in the faint light suffusing the little alcove they were stopped in.

Fresh air and sunlight. Or at least fresher air and diffused sunlight. They were surely close to an exit of some sort. She just hoped it was one they could get out of, rather than a crack in the earth too small, or too inaccessible to use. It was impossible to tell how long they had been down below the ground, without the sun to mark the days; but as they walked she had Les extinguish the light often, trying to figure out what time of day it was, to no avail, as the faint light always seemed to be present. The road had taken a sharp turn away from the river shortly after they broke camp, and unless she was mistaken, they were slowly climbing uphill through a tunnel so regular in shape and size it had to have been man made. Just the faint hope that the changes in their surroundings brought had lightened the mood of the travelers considerably. The rift between them had been bridged somehow during that brief underwater battle, and even though they hadn't talked about things, they both seemed content with the status quo.

Sylvia had decided not to examine the tangled emotions she had about Les. She was tired, completely exhausted by the weeks of turmoil she'd endured in this strange place. Considering her growing attraction to the Maegi, or the bigger question of why she was experiencing these trials in Prium in the first place, was simply too much to handle. Surviving was challenge enough. She preferred to stay in the numb state that had settled over her after the monster's attack, living completely in the moment, without examining either the past, or what was in her future. Just survival.

It made for a much more comfortable life now that she was able to accept the succor Les offered, without tagging on any complications in the form of "what if's". After he had taken her hand that day, they had walked for hours connected by the comforting grip. And now each time they camped she crawled under their blanket to welcoming arms. He was the lone source of warmth in this world of hard stone and damp earth. His was the only voice she had heard in days, possibly even weeks, to assuage the loneliness she had felt since her time with Torman and Ryland. Les's dry humor and sarcastic nature paired with his protectiveness and confidence appealed to Sylvia in ways that the boys in her high school never had. There was give and take in their conversations, honest answers without the usual 'pretending to be greater than you actually are' that riddled the interactions of teenagers jockeying for the attention of the opposite sex.

They had been to death's doorstep and back, hand in hand. They had saved one another numerous times, and likely would again in the future. Her heart had accepted her love of the grumpy man, evident in the sense of peace she felt in his embrace, even if she was too stubborn to put a name to it.

In contrast to her determined lack of reflection, Lessoran fixated on the strange creature they had encountered, and had even gone so far as to sketch what he could remember of the beast's anatomy on the back of their washed out map with charcoal from the campfire. The sketch looked much like her memories of the encounter, but neither she nor Les had seen enough of the thing's lower half to complete the drawing, leaving a large gap between the detailed torso and head and the gigantic tail below. The gap seemed to bother Les, a worry she didn't share until he explained that if the monster had hind legs it could potentially follow them onto land, while if it only sported that monstrous tail, they would know for sure they had left it, and any others, behind in the underground lake and river.

After that enlightening conversation Syl had trouble sleeping, jerking awake at every imagined sound, sure the beast had come back to finish the job it had started at the mouth of the river. But it never was, the sounds were only in her head, and the creatures contained to her frequent nightmares. Other than disturbed sleep, their accustomed pattern of wake and walk formed once more; she and Les worked together seamlessly to make and break camp, as familiar with the other's needs as with their own.

The monotony of the regular tunnel was broken every so often by side passages, more often than not smaller and rougher than the main path they followed. Sylvia took to placing small round pebbles at each opening. If the pebble rolled down the passage they continued on in the larger tunnel, as it was still heading uphill. The latest passage they stopped at saw her round stone rolling backwards to stop with a clink at her feet. She was so surprised by the event she simply stared at the rock for a moment before turning excitedly to Les. "This one goes up!"

His smile was tired, and his face had smudges of dirt across the forehead where he frequently swept his hair from his face with less than clean hands, but the excitement in his eyes mirrored her own hopes. Hopefully the new pathway would lead them from the catacombs.

"Let's try it," he said, stooping to scratch a shallow X into the ground of the passage they were leaving. "Just in case we have to come back," he explained at Syl's questioning look, "We'll know this is where we turned off the main passage."

"Good idea," she agreed. It had been easy thus far to remember their path, as it was the largest tunnel, and there were few other options; but if the new passage they were going to follow forked, they would need to leave themselves instructions on how to get back in case of a dead end.

They hadn't been walking in the new tunnel for long before it opened up into a small chamber light enough for Les to get rid of the globelight which had been their nearly constant companion. A shaft of light speared through the dusty air in the center of the space to pool in glorious gold on the uneven floor. Sylvia walked directly to the sun beam to stand in it, blinking, eyes watering from the unaccustomed brightness, a huge smile on her face as she felt the heat of true sunlight on her skin for the first time since their plunge into the depths.

Les's deep voice interrupted her basking, "There's a hole way up there, but we aren't going to be able to get out through it."

"Shut up and enjoy the sun, you negative Nancy," she called from her brilliant spotlight. She couldn't see anything of the surrounding cave, blinded as she was with all of the light spilling down into the earth. She felt like it was filling her up with radiance, reawakening hope she hadn't noticed she'd lost.

"You barely look real standing there like that." Les spoke from behind her now, the words tickling the small hairs at the nape of her neck, bared by her high ponytail.

She whirled around to grab his hands, "It's the sun Les, the *sun!*" She did a little dance, wiggling in a circle as Les swung bemusedly after her. "It's real and it's the *SUN!*" Les laughed, following her joyful dance obligingly. The smile on his face growing to proportions she had never seen, dimples appearing in his lean cheeks that she hadn't known were there. Infected by her excitement, he suddenly scooped her up and twirled her around in his arms, her feet flying out in a wide arc, high off the ground until he halted the spin and she wrapped her legs around his waist to keep from sliding down. And then his hands were urging her closer, his tan face, bathed in light, taking up her entire field of vision as he brought his lips to hers.

One large hand cupped her hips close, while the other brought her chest flush with his. Their usual height difference absent, she felt her nose bump awkwardly into his repeatedly until he guided her to tilt her head to the side, never breaking the kiss, but settling it into a more comfortable position. They were drunk on sun, giddy with the prospect of life lived on the surface once more. The kiss continued until her smile grew too big, and she leaned her head back into that beautiful light as Les kissed his way down her throat to the tender crook of shoulder and neck, where he buried his face with a chuckle.

How long they remained there she didn't know. The relief of returned hope was so potent that they clung together tightly, sharing the rush of emotions. Her heart beat against her breast like it was trying to get out of its prison of flesh. Les lightly kissed each of her closed eyes before letting her slide limply down his body until her feet rested on the ground. She kept her grip on his arms, feeling a little wobbly now that she was holding up her own weight.

"If that's what happens when we see the sun," she said breathlessly, "I might just spontaneously combust when we finally get back to the surface."

Les nuzzled the side of her head, that same low chuckle from before spreading goosebumps across Sylvia's skin in a tingling rush. "I think that's the idea," he said lazily.

Oh. My. God. He thought I meant- oh god- I think I meant! Syl buried her head in his tunic, hiding her suddenly flaming cheeks as Les's chuckle turned into a full laugh. She could feel the vibrations of his mirth in his chest and helplessly began to laugh a little herself. *How ridiculous, I should know better than to try to flirt. It always ends up this way, me blushing and stammering and the boy laughing,* she berated herself.

But this time, unlike after 'The Kiss', she was laughing too. Red cheeks seemed a small price to pay for the bubbling, giddy feeling being this close to Les brought to life in her. Embarrassment was such a small emotion now, on the scale of the trials she and the Maegi had endured, and the riot of emotion that had come along with their misadventures.

His laughter halted abruptly and he pushed her back from him, leaning down a bit so he could look into her eyes. "You know I'm not laughing at you, right?" he asked hesitantly after searching her face for one seemingly unending moment.

A self-deprecating smile turned up her lips as she lightly punched him in the chest with one fist, "Yeah, I know. You're laughing *with* me this time. Now let's get out of these damn caves!"

Les grabbed her hand with a mock bow, "After you milady," he deadpanned, a smile breaking through the facade as she sailed past him, nose in the air and one hand flicking the long tresses of her ponytail back over her shoulder imperiously.

"Thank you my good sir," she said haughtily before giving voice to one of the numerous questions that now clamored in her head at the prospect of escape from the tunnels. "We obviously aren't the first people to come down here, how does a whole tribe of people forget about a place like this?"

Les frowned, "There are many things the Trewal have forgotten, it's not just my tribe," he said, a bit defensively. "There is a whole age that we know little about, The Age Before Memory. Your people can't possibly remember everything that there is to know about your history either," he challenged.

Now it was Sylvia's turn to frown. "I guess we don't remember everything, at least not every detail. And we are still discovering ancient structures and cities that we had no idea existed, but we know what was going on in each time period in a general way, their beliefs, their governing structures, who their enemies were, and where our ancestors came from. We haven't lost a whole age though," she said snidely, even as she was perplexed by how that could ever happen.

"Why would you waste time discovering old places? Or do your people not build your own structures and you need them to live in?" He sounded truly puzzled.

"No, we build, probably more than we should. Every family I know has their own house." She smiled inwardly at his incredulous look, thinking of how magnified that look would be if he was faced with the actuality of her modern home and all its trappings. "We discover ancient places because we want to know how they lived and what they did. It tells us a little more about our own history. Some people dedicate their entire lives to it," she added. "Now tell me everything you know about this Age Before Memory."

They fairly skipped through the adjoining tunnels as Sylvia questioned Lessoran on the few tattered bits of knowledge his people retained from the mysterious Age Before Memory, full of hope from their brief time in the light. But as the day wore on the tunnel forked, and forked again, and their weariness and lack of true food dragged them back down from their momentary high. When the sharply upward slanting tunnel they had chosen to follow at the last fork narrowed to the point that Les's big body could no longer fit through the slim opening, Sylvia let out a growl of frustration.

"This is a dead end, let's go back and try the other one," she said through gritted teeth. Les backtracked with a sigh of relief, rolling shoulders tight from the extended hunch the small corridor had forced him into. They stopped when they reached the crossroads, gazing tiredly down the one path they had not tried in that section of the caves.

"Alright, I'm calling it," Les said, just before sinking down to sit in the middle of the rocky path. "We need to eat, we need a fire, and we need some sleep. We'll find the way out when we wake up." At Sylvia's dejected sigh he continued, "It's better this way actually; we don't know what's waiting for us out there. It would be smarter to face it rested and with something in our stomachs."

She made a face, "I was hoping I wouldn't have to eat that crap again," she said, motioning to the crumbly streamcress Les was pouring water over in their lone cook pot. At Les's eye roll she added grudgingly, "But it's better than nothing," before beginning to arrange the last bit of their kindling for a fire.

Soon enough their bellies were full of food that was at least warm, even if it was neither tasty, nor the most nourishing. They snuggled down under their tatty blanket, close to the wall of the tunnel. The fire was fading to embers, leaving a warm orange glow even after Les put out his globelight. Syl was almost asleep, drifting away comfortably with Les's bicep acting as her pillow, while he rested his head on their rucksack, when a faint noise sounded in the distance.

Her eyes sprung open and she held perfectly still, holding her breath to listen better, but she couldn't hear over the loud breathing of the man at her back. She set her elbow into his side, and he woke with a start. "Listen!" she hissed when he grumbled something about elbows like fire pokers. They both stilled, and very faintly, from farther down the passage they could hear it, like music to her ears.

"Wolves!" they breathed, almost at the same time. She could just make out the smile on his face in the glow of the fire. Wolves may sometimes make their dens in caves, but they needed access to the outside world to hunt; so where there were wolves, there was an exit from this underground labyrinth! They lay back down, Syl now with a smile equally as big as Les's gracing her dirty face.

His arm snaked around her middle, pulling her more firmly into the crook of his body before he threw one heavy leg over hers. She caught her breath briefly, this level of physical entanglement usually only happened after a full night of sleep, or when they did a bit of the kissing they had been practicing all day, and Les generally tried to keep some distance between their, private areas. But now her bottom was held snuggly against his groin. She squirmed a little, testing the confinement of his limbs around hers, easing back a little to see if the bulge she usually avoided each morning was truly not evident.

"Not comfortable?" Les's voice was muffled against her hair as he adjusted them with a small thrust of his hips, bringing their bodies flush again and making Syl's stomach tighten in a pleasant way.

Maybe too comfortable, she thought ruefully, and before she could think it through she tucked her arm around his, clasping his hand and drawing it up between her breasts to rest against her sternum. Now it was his turn to freeze, and then wiggle experimentally. Her grip on his hand bent his wrist at an odd angle, and he very cautiously disentangled himself before letting the hand drift lower, dragging fingers over her breast and leaving tingles in its wake. He cupped her there gently and she knew he could feel her racing heart beneath his grip as he smoothed his thumb over the fabric between them.

"Tomorrow night," he said drowsily, "we sleep under the stars." And within minutes his breathing had evened, his tantalizing grip loosening, leaving her body feeling taunt and hot. Syl feared that sleep would never come.

Lessoran

"Does it seem colder here than farther back in the caves?" Sylvia asked from her huddled position under the blanket. "Because I'm pretty sure it's a lot colder this morning than it was yesterday." White knuckled fingers pulled the blanket closer as she eyed his outstretched hand dubiously, his wordless request for the last item that needed to be packed away before they began the day's journey.

As her big blue eyes continued to stare at his hand and she made no move to unwrap herself from their bed, he said impatiently, "I would think you would be excited to get moving after hearing those wolves last night."

"I was excited. Then I woke up and it was winter, and I dreamed about being eaten by giant wolves all night." She grimaced at his proffered hand one last time before disentangling herself with a heavy sigh. She balled up the blanket and spitefully threw it past his waiting hands so it hit him in the chest before falling to the ground at his feet. Packing away the ragged cloth, he tried to ignore the slight smell emanating from it. They couldn't get out of this cave soon enough for him. He had thought Sylvia felt the same, so where had this uncharacteristic sullenness come from?

His mind jumped back to the night before, when he had pushed the boundaries of their relationship, against his better judgement, yet again. It seemed he was helpless to stop himself, and he was getting tired of fighting their attraction, tired of second guessing the Morgal's demand that she be taken to the Caves 'untouched' by Pralick, and if that meant untouched by him also. Though why that would matter was beyond him. *Had he misjudged her reaction to him?* He shook his head to himself, no, she had been waiting for his next move with bated breath, such an obvious sign of her innocence that it had brought any further advance from him to a halt, regardless of how much he wanted to lose himself in her.

"Maybe you'll sleep better once we are out in the open again," he ventured into the silence before standing up and beginning to lead them down the last unexplored tunnel in this highest section of the caves they had discovered. It *was* colder here than they had experienced at any other time underground. The air held a crispness that spoke to his mountain sensibilities of snow in the air and hard frozen ground. But he didn't feel like feeding Syl more fodder for her complaints, so he kept his mouth shut and set a hard pace for them, both to keep their undernourished bodies warm and to hasten their eventual exit from the caves. He pushed on until both of them were breathing hard, and Sylvia was too breathless to continue expressing her inexplicable bad mood with words.

The tunnel continued on its upward slant for what must have been an hour before it leveled off. The ground here was worn smooth, a much more pleasant walking surface than the debris-strewn paths lower in the caves. They made good time, even if the dark mood of his companion cast a pall over the day. Soon enough puffs of ever colder air were pushing back against them as they strode forwards, and Les extinguished his globelight with high hopes for a sign of the end to their subterranean journey.

"Oof," the air left Sylvia's lungs as she bumped into his back, raising her head from her customary position of eyes on the terrain in front of her, as the globelight went out and their eyes slowly adjusted to the ambient light suffusing the cave. "Give a gal some warning, will you?" she said, even as Les seized her hand in a grip that tightened as his excitement built. He towed her forwards and around one last corner to see the tunnel that lay before them ended in a bright wall of light. He raised his face to feel the harsh bite of a mountain wind raise his lank hair off his forehead, letting out a wordless cry of triumph.

"Aahhhyeeee!" he cried. He swept his reticent companion up off her feet and swung her around, oblivious to her quiet response to the end of their captivity. "Daylight has never looked so good!" He kissed Sylvia's forehead absently, setting her down only to grab her hand once more and move them both towards the light at the end of the tunnel. "Where there is daylight there is game, and where there is game there will be kindling for a fire. Put the two together and we can finally eat again!" Sylvia's lips finally rose in a smile at the mention of food, and her reluctant pace sped up to match his own, until they were trotting along the last hundred feet, shielding their eyes against the unaccustomed brightness beckoning them onward.

They broke through into full sunlight only after Lessoran stopped to draw his knife and they held their breaths, listening for any unknown enemy lying in wait outside. But then the sun was on their faces, and even Sylvia's mood lifted. He glanced sideways, the full force of her exultant smile hitting him in the chest like a battering ram. Her face was tilted up to the sun, just like it had been when they found the 'Sun Room' a few days before. She stood now, her shoulders back and her tangled hair blowing back from her face in the wind, a mirror image to that day when she had stood so still, bathing in light. He had felt like an intruder then, like a lecherous old man spying from the shadows. But he had also felt a desperate need to be close to her beauty, to feel any part of the joy springing unfiltered from her features. She was so, *alive*. So much emotion and excitement spilling from her at each new experience, it was a heady thing to be around, an addictive one. So he had approached her, even as his rational mind told him he should keep his distance. But he couldn't stay away. She had opened her wondrous blue eyes, pinning him to the ground more firmly than any shackle, and extended her hands to him, selflessly asking him to join her in the light.

Some of the wonder from that day spilled over into him again, and his lips kicked up into a grin as he remembered her breathless admission of lust following her easy acceptance of him, and the glorious flush of red that had swept up from her chest at her boldness. He wanted to find out how far downwards that blush spread, he had wanted to since the first time she smiled at him and then looked away in embarrassment, that pretty red tinge rushing to the surface of her pale skin. The falling sun in the here and now bathed her skin in a red light much like her frequent blushes, but with more colors, and more depth to the hues, lending an ethereal glow to her skin.

"You're staring," she said, having finally turned from her sunset basking to find him lost in her image and his memories. When he didn't answer right away she glanced away, eyes seeking the craggy peaks the exit to the caves had left them facing. He turned to the view also, eyes seeking any familiar landmark to show him where they had ended up. He continued to look in dismay. Nothing. Nothing familiar, just the long, low valley of the Skycastles fading away in the distance to the east and west, cradled between the peak they had exited on, and the ones they faced. But there was no sign of the Crooked Mountain, the one marking the Caves of Orr.

"Is that the mountain you said was right above the Caves?" Sylvia queried, and Les swung his gaze hopefully to the far, far, right of their view.

The familiar broken peak was much farther away than he had thought possible. They must have traveled for longer under the ground than he anticipated. But he didn't truly know how long he had lain with a fever after that first day, so his rough calculations must have been thrown off. The distant peak was unmistakable, even at this great distance. It stood like a beacon, far to the east, a beckoning finger raised crookedly into the sky. "That's it," he replied, and the uncertain future before them suddenly came to a head, embodied by that distant representation of the Ancients and their Caves.

"Les," Syl began in a fretful tone, "we have to talk about what's going to happen next..." Her words trailed off as he turned to her, suddenly fierce.

"No. No, we don't. Not right now. Not tonight." Quite suddenly he knew why she had been dragging her feet this morning, what she had been afraid was waiting for them outside of the caves. It was this, this change in their relationship, this twice-damned journey swinging from simple survival to the complex situation he was propelling her towards. He stepped into her, his large frame crowding against her so much that she tried to move back from the abrupt intrusion, but his hands were there, urging her back into his arms, tilting her head back so he could taste her lips.

He tried to gentle his touch, to ease the hint of panic clouding his mind and making him greedy for the touch of skin on skin. She was an innocent, it was evident in every hesitant caress of her hands, each tentative stroke of her lips on his, and from each of their brief interludes in the caves where she had contentedly left him in agony, unaware of the need her kisses and nearness woke in him. But when her small hands slipped up under his tunic, pressing against hot skin to urge him closer, the neediest part of him was suddenly nestled against softness and warmth, and his attempt at restraint crumbled.

With a low growl he swept her off her feet, settling her down in the damp grass outside the cave entrance, the open rucksack serving as a crude pillow for her head. They needed food. They needed to build a fire to combat the fast encroaching darkness. They needed fresh water. But he pushed all those thoughts aside, consumed by another need, a need for her so encompassing it seemed to have swept her up in its fevered turbulence also. She pulled him back down to her, straining her body upwards to reach his, raining light kisses on his neck and throat as he reached back to pull the itchy cloth tunic from his back. She ran chilled hands up and down his chest, eyes wide and dark as the sun faded. But the cold didn't seem to touch him, his body was an inferno of heat that was stoked ever higher as her hands drifted down his stomach, lightly grazing the mostly healed arrow wound to weave a tantalizing pattern just at the low hanging drawstring of his britches

"Sylvia," he said in warning, aware that his voice grated harshly, and his muscles all tensed in the fear she would heed his cautioning. A self-satisfied smile quirked her lips before she pushed against him gently, a silent demand for some space. He backed off grudgingly, focusing on his harsh breathing, trying to tell himself it was for the best. But then her smile widened and she pulled her own tunic off over her head and lay back once more, the expanse of creamy skin bared to the awakening moonlight an invitation that needed no words.

Sylvia

She was sore. But from the accounts of numerous of her rugby squad friends that was to be expected. She had also expected pain in those first dizzying moments of intimacy, a unifying trait of every 'first time' tale she had heard, but other than a brief pinching, her night had been filled with only pleasure. She moved about experimentally, finding yet more places on her body that ached with the familiar pull of sore muscles, except these pains were located in areas of her body she hadn't previously known contained any muscles at all.

Les appeared, trudging back up the slope to their camping spot from his hunting excursion down to the Skycastles. The sun was up, but its light was weak as it struggled against the clinging fog surrounding them. Lessoran was back-lit by its light for a moment as he approached, looking impossibly tall and entirely inhuman with the various Terlings hammered around his large antlers, winking in the weak light. With disappointment she saw he was empty handed. For all of their excitement to exit the caves and eat solid food once more, they hadn't seen hide nor hair of any game other than a lone bird far up in the sky. Her stomach grumbled unhappily as he squatted down next to her, warming his hands by their fire before pulling some bark and other withered vegetation from his belt pouch.

"I found a game trail, but it looks like it hasn't been used in a month or so," he said apologetically, handing her a small, hard tuber to gnaw on, as he added the bark to the pot of water already simmering near the flame. She got to work on the onion-like bulb, a hardy winter plant Les called a Cheerum. It disappeared all too quickly, but appeased her stomach marginally while they waited for the bark to steep into the water so they could have some bitter tea.

"We should pack up and follow the trail into the Castles today, there might be more game taking shelter down there." She nodded in agreement, moving to him happily when he lifted up the edge of his cloak in an offer of shared warmth.

"We need water in any case, and I don't think we'll find it up here," she added, looking around at the bleak landscape. It was beautiful, frost icing each bare branch and every blade of roan in crystal glory, as the cold, wet fog added to the perpetually growing carpet of ice. But aside from the occasional Listenbark sapling and tufts of roan between bare earth and exposed rock, there was nothing for them here at the entrance to the depths beneath the Skycastles. They'd sheltered in the mouth of the cave last night, after their extracurricular activities, only to be woken by the eerie howl of wolves early in the morning hours. Their ghostly shapes stirred the fog shrouding the hillside. She and Les had frantically burned through their entire stock of firewood in an attempt to dissuade the hungry predators from thinking of them as prey. At one point she peered through the leaping flames, finally out of wood to add to the blaze, to see the shaggy canines prowling just outside the cave entrance, steam streaming from their open jaws like plumes of fire in the cold air.

Les pulled her closer at the shiver the memory sent racing down her spine, and she smiled, burrowing farther into his side, her hands wrapped around his solidly warm thigh. "You know I had always wondered if we could..." she winced, but continued on doggedly, her blushing cheeks bringing some much needed heat to her cold face. "If a Trewal and a human could, umm, well, you know..." She shrugged helplessly.

Les laughed amiably, smiling down at her from his greater height. "We are not so different," he nudged her foot, wrapped up in torn strips of their blanket for warmth, with his hoof, "not different at all in *that* manner, I think." His grin turned devilish as he delved his hands under her clothes to find warm skin, making her twist away with a shriek because his fingers felt like icicles on her sheltered flesh.

She settled back into him after she captured his hands in her own to warm them, a new thought about their compatibility rearing its ugly head. "Do you think I could get pregnant?" she asked in a small voice.

He looked down in surprise. "A child is a blessing usually only delivered after a prayer to Freyton for fertility and favor. I said no such prayer last night," he paused and even though she kept her eyes on their joined hands, she could hear the smile in his voice, "or this morning. Did you pray to Freyton?" he asked, seemingly unconcerned even as her heart began to hammer in her chest. How could she have been so foolish! Of course pregnancy was a possibility if they were physically compatible enough to have sex. All the mechanics for producing a kid matched what had happened between them, and she had just blindly participated regardless of the havoc a pregnancy would cause. Why? Because it had felt good. Syl dropped her head into her hands with a groan. *Stupid, stupid, stupid!*

Lessoran moved his big body back from her and the cold air rushed in gleefully, matching the tone of his voice as he said, "Obviously you didn't pray to Freyton." She met his eyes, wincing at the hurt she saw there. "Would my child be so unwanted?" he asked flatly, his eyes hard on her face, his head bowed as if ready to receive a heavy burden.

"Well, yes! But not specifically *your* child," she spluttered, seeing his face fall even further at her words. "I can't get pregnant! That's just it, I'm too young, I can't have a kid now, my life would be over!" Silence reigned as they stared at each other.

"Children are blessings," he stressed, confusion slowly taking over the hurt. "It's hard to conceive and even harder to bring a child to term in the Skypeaks. If a woman is lucky enough to earn the favor of Freyton and birth a healthy child, it is the will of our God."

She looked at him sadly, knowing her next words would likely hurt him even more. "Freyton isn't my God, and having a child this young, it's a disgrace among my people. We can't, we can't do that again. I'm sorry Les, but I just can't risk it." She rose and began packing so she didn't have to see his face after her statement. He was silent and still for so long, that she was packed and ready to go by the time he stood and kicked their stone fire-ring inward to smother the low flames.

Sylvia finally looked at him, ashamed as tears threatened to fall from her eyes. She didn't want this to be over, she liked him, maybe even loved him, not that she had anything to compare her budding feelings for him to. But she absolutely would not risk pregnancy by sleeping with him again, no matter the wonder of their night together; and she doubted a people who so valued and revered children would have a method for contraceptive.

Tired green eyes peered back at her for one endless moment, before he broke the eye contact to sweep his curly hair out of his eyes. "It's easy to forget," he said, "how young you are, when you act with such wisdom through the trials we face. It's also easy to forget we are from such different worlds, because all I know of you is who you are forced to be in *my* world. I have no right to be angry with you, and you have every right to decide not to bed me. I'm sorry to put you in this situation," he finished resignedly.

"It's not that I don't want you," she burst out brokenly, "I do want you!" The threatening tears finally overflowed to slide down her face at his ready acceptance of her dismissal, like he felt somehow unworthy of her. "How do I fix this? I didn't mean to hurt you, but I just can't take the risk! Please tell me you understand," she begged.

"Something must be broken in order to fix it, Sylvia. I don't think we're broken, just caught in a misunderstanding that is becoming clearer ever second." He smiled weakly at her, running a thumb across her cheek to collect the tears there, before taking her hand in his and setting them on the path down to the Skycastles. Before long he cast a coy glance in her direction, but looked back down as he spoke, "You said you want me?" There was a world of hope in his simple reiteration of her words.

Heat spread up her neck and across her cheeks again, but she kept her eyes on his face until he looked up at her again before affirming, "Yes". She felt like her whole world hinged on this one conversation, her entire future along with the state of her heart. His insecurity had flattened her, how could such a confident, capable, and strong man look so lost when someone like her said she didn't want his children? He had just given up. Like he expected things between them to end. Like he felt she couldn't possibly want him. Her world shifted behind her eyes, settling into a new view where her elders were just as unsure and fallible as her. She squeezed his hand, watching his slowly spreading smile with a satisfaction that far outweighed the embarrassment of admitting her own feelings.

He kept their pace leisurely, like they were a couple out for a stroll in the park rather than travelers in desperate need of food, attempting to find more hospitable terrain. "You know," he said, that smile still in place, "there are many things a man and a woman can do that won't make a child." The pleased tilt of his lips turned salacious, eliciting a shiver from her, kick-starting her heart, sending it into a pounding rhythm at the wicked promise held in his eyes.

Sylvia took a deep breath, feeling her heart beating in every extremity. "I think you have a lot to teach me," she said, feeling a bit faint at her boldness, but this time not noticing a feeling of panic that had always accompanied her previous attempts at flirtation. Les tugged her closer to throw an arm around her shoulders and kiss the top of her head, his chuckle a promise of good things to come.

Lessoran

A rabbit sat in the clearing before him, its little pink nose twitching as it gnawed happily away at a bit of roan. Its tawny fur was fluffed up against the cold, and one long ear flopped over comically while the other rose to a tattered point above its head. Les breathed in through his nose slowly, loading his newly made sling as silently as possible with a small rounded rock. He was much better with his bow, but their supplies were so limited that this makeshift sling of rope and torn cloth was his only way to hunt, as he refused to kill for food with his magic. The rabbit munched on, unaware of his presence, until the abrupt whistle of cloth through the air brought its head up and around towards Les's hiding spot behind the bulk of a fallen stone. The projectile hit the furry body with a muffled thump. Tension drained out of both hunter and prey, as the rabbit toppled over lifelessly.

Les clenched his empty fist in triumph. *Yes!* They would have a real meal today. Their escape from the caves had deposited them in some unknown corner of the Skycastles, and food had been nearly as scarce in the rocky landscape above ground as it had been in the one lying below. He and Sylvia were growing weaker from their time away from the sun, with only algae and that first fish he had regrettably coerced onto his line to eat. They had opted to stay away from the water after encountering the monster in the underground lake, meaning that after their subterranean encounter they didn't even have fish to augment their diet.

He stooped to grip the rabbit, hefting the slight body in his hand only to be disappointed by the lean meat coating the bones of the creature. The animal was nearly as thin as they were, but any meat would be a welcome addition, no matter in how small an amount. Using his worn belt knife, he began preparing the bunny for the fire, glancing around in hopes he could find a stick sturdy enough to act as a spit.

Hands busy with the familiar task before him, his mind wandered once again to the road ahead. Pralick and the rest of the Trianti warriors who had chased them through the mountains had no doubt reached the Caves of Orr days and days before, effectively blocking him and Sylvia from their original goal. He supposed the Ancients might still grant them safe passage into the Caves, regardless of the efforts of the tribe. But there was no way to know what wild tale Pralick had told them, to sway them to his way of thinking. As Seers they might see through any lies he told, but Les could not know for sure if safety awaited them, or if they would be intercepted before he could plead his case to the Ancients. If caught, Pralick would push for him to be put to death, likely by stoning, a traitor's death. Sylvia was too valuable to kill, but her fate would be just as grim if Pralick got his hands on her once more. Les gritted his teeth, wrenching his wandering mind away from the torments Pralick would heap upon her if they were caught. He couldn't let that happen. Not again.

He centered his chaotic thoughts with a deep breath, focusing on the memories of a smiling and happy Sylvia he had from the morning. A smile surfaced on his rugged face as he pictured her, and then pictured what had made her smile in that dazzled way. *The night before,* he thought with satisfaction, *and the night before that!* The sweetness of his memory banished the evil thoughts of moments before, like a swift wind sweeping clouds from the sky, until a scuff of stone on stone had him grasping for the knife he had lain aside as he finished up with the rabbit. Syl's musical voice rang out, settling his nerves as she climbed into view.

"You had a funny look on your face, what were you grinning at like that?" She approached from the side, sliding down the broken length of a spire before spying his prize, "Oh thank goodness! You found something to eat!" she cried ecstatically, approaching rapidly. When she was a few feet away she slowed down and then reversed, "Well that's gross," she said weakly, backpedaling away from the steaming skin he had pulled from the now naked rabbit.

He laughed at the horrified look on her face, kicking some loose dirt over the pile of offal to appease her sensitivity. The gaps in her knowledge had been startling at first, but he had become used to her lack of woodland skill. "Come here, I'll teach you how to clean it. It could make all the difference for your survival," he said, his mind straying once more in the dark direction of before. Their future was so uncertain, he couldn't be sure he would be there to help her, so the more she learned now, while he was around, the better.

She inched a little closer, skirting the bloody pile before stopping a good three feet away. "I'm watching," she said, "Skin on".

He shook his head, beckoning her closer with the crook of one blood tipped finger and offered her his knife. "Cleaning, not skinning. It's already skinned, now we need to gut it and get rid of the organs we can't eat." He positioned her hands on the knife and guided the blade to hover over the sternum of his kill. "You want to cut the skin from chest to pelvis, but be careful not to pierce any of the entrails, they can contaminate the meat."

After one more horrified grimace she carefully slid the knife down the bare belly, adjusting as he talked her through the process of holding the muscle and sinew away from the delicate membrane of the intestines and bladder. When the guts were successfully removed she gave a shudder, careful to keep her bloody hands away from the rest of her body. He then instructed her to search through the pile of organs for the rabbit's liver so they could inspect it for white spots indicating disease. Luckily for them the rabbit had been in good health, if not particularly well fed.

They cleaned their hands with a trickle of water from his skin, and made their way back to the camp they had made the night before, their meal bobbing from his hand. Sylvia collected bits of brush and sticks to add to their depleted stack of firewood, as they climbed up and around more fallen Castles back to the cozy nook they had slept in the night before. Before long a merry blaze crackled beneath the spitted creature, and they were sinking their teeth into the stringy meat, hot juices running down their chins as they hastily ate the first solid food they had consumed in days.

Silence reigned as they stuffed themselves with the bounty of meat, but soon enough decisions they had to make clamored to the forefront of his mind, and he broached the subject they had not voiced since leaving the caves. "We have to decide where we are going," he said bluntly.

Blue eyes met his gravely. "Is there an option other than the Caves?" Her question was a challenge, her back straightened and her chin rose a fraction, giving her delicate frame an air of belligerence.

"Pralick will be there, between us and the Ancients, and he'll be eager to get you back." Les kept his voice devoid of emotion deliberately, trying to control the rebelling muscles of his face so his expression would match the blandness he strove for. He had come to the conclusion on their walk back with the rabbit, he needed *her* to decide their next step. He needed her to know she wasn't a prisoner any longer, that he would treat her as an equal. He had thrown his lot in with hers and if she decided to go back to whatever strange quest she had been on before, he would go with her, be her protector.

Because he'd failed his previous task. The last command of his leader, however mysterious it was. *Take her and the medallion to the Caves, untouched, the Ancients need her.* Their journey had gotten the better of him, and he had failed to protect her, and then disobeyed the Morgal's demands by his own actions. He didn't know what plan he had disrupted, or how to fix what his actions had broken. He would never know, because the man who had tasked him with this was dead by now, his reasons and plans taken with him, his body left to rot. Lessoran said a silent prayer for the older man, a plea to Freyton that he would still take the soul of such an honorable man into the Afterlife, even without the release of fire's touch on his body.

No matter his loyalty to the Morgal, and his best intentions to carry out his orders, somewhere along the way the ties of his tribe had been broken. Maybe it had been when he saw Pralick's ax slice into his mentor's belly, or when his own tribe-brother had shot him with an arrow rather than hear him out. Maybe it had been that first night he held Sylvia in his arms, relinquishing the role of captor in favor of her comfort. The exact timing was impossible to pinpoint, and frankly, irrelevant. The truth of it was that Sylvia was his tribe now, she was his companion, his responsibility. She was his, and he felt entirely unwilling to chance losing the last scrap of identity he'd retained through their unfortunate travels.

The Ancients were a tricky bunch; he had managed to keep his dealings with them infrequent, preferring to stay as far away from the view of their strange white eyes as he could. His first encounter with them was when he made the journey to the Caves for approval, as he took on the mantle of Maegi. But after that unsettling excursion, he had done his best to close his mind to the feathery touch he associated with the Seers and their God-given magic. He limited his exposure to them, preferring to feign inability to "hear" their summons, letting the lesser Trianti Maegi make trips to the Caves for guidance for the tribe, and settling as far back in the Morgal's tent as he could when any of the Seven lined faces would appear in the farscrying bowl to speak with the Morgal.

Sylvia had been silent for a long time. When she finally spoke the words came hesitantly, "I've been thinking about the Ancients. You say they have powers, that they can See, and have magic beyond your own." She waited expectantly until he nodded in agreement with her statement, then pushed on, her words surer. "I want to talk to them. If I can, without getting caught up with your tribe again. I want to see if they can tell me why I'm here. And maybe how I can get home, you said they might know."

Ah yes, he thought, *Sylvia's 'home' where only blood ties made you a tribe, children were not taught how to fight, and food was stored in great buildings for anyone to claim.* He would be interested to see such a land, but he could not bring himself to truly believe it existed, no matter Syl's staunch conviction. "They may be able to help." He tried to keep the grudging tone from his voice, searching for his previous neutrality and determination to let her decide their course.

"Then we should go to the Caves and at least see if we can get in safely. We were down there a long time, Pralick might have given up," she said hopefully.

Les nodded his assent, not trusting his voice to keep his feelings from her. Sylvia cheerfully set about striking camp, happy with the decision they'd come to. Les was left alone with his fading dreams of a simple life. He had foolishly built up an internal imagining, a small stone cabin far out in the Skypeaks, hidden from all of the usual tribe haunts. He would hunt and she could learn to garden. They would trade ice lion pelts for the few items they couldn't make or find in the mountains. Maybe they would live out their lives there together, or with a child or two for company when Sylvia thought she was old enough. A little boy with Sylvia's midnight hair, or a tiny girl child with his fawn coloring, but her mother's copious freckles to brighten her face.

With a sigh Lessoran stood to help his traveling companion, banishing his dreams as the folly they were. What led him to believe he deserved such a life of simple beauty? You reap what you sow in this world. He was a Maegi of the Trianti, soaked in the violence of the Bloodhunger, a traitor to his tribe, a failure to his Morgal, a corrupter of purity. There was no world in which he could live that life. He would never claim a title like husband or father, and the woman beside him deserved a man who was at least worthy of that.

Cirillia

It was the same Dream as before, just as powerful and exact in its details, but for one difference. The shadow figure trailing after the Battle Mage was made of shadows no more. Instead he stood tall, his green eyes glued to the Mage before him, dressed in rags but with a stature fit for the silks and furs of a Morgal. Across his handsome face a smear of blood trailed, igniting a deep cold in her heart. Three fingers across his left eye, bumping over the proud, straight nose to end on the flat expanse of his strong jaw. Three dots accented the arch of his right brow. Three streaks, three dots. Three betrayals to be balanced by three sacrifices. One of blood, one of iron, and the other...

She sat up in her bed, hand pressing against her forehead to ease the pressure pounding behind her altered eyes. The tribes knew nothing about this unfortunate side effect of being a Seer. Even the elderly Maegi who traveled to the Caves at Freyton's call to become an Ancient knew nothing of the consequences of their new life. They were left unaware until the first vision came and with it the pain and pressure of Freyton's presence. After her first vision, a small Dream of the upcoming raid between two tribes, Pernal had come to her with a warm wet cloth and soothing mint tea to combat the headache and nausea. Now she fought it off on her own, knowing her fellows were dealing with similar symptoms, as they had likely experienced the repeated Dream also.

She swung herself from the bed, quickly hiding the skinny length of her knobby legs beneath a clean shift, and drawing on a thick robe lined with fur to combat the chill of the Caves. She let her hand trail familiarly over the walls as she walked down from her chambers to the kitchens, her fingers reading the bumps and pits in the stone like a written language she let guide her so her aching eyes could remain tightly shut. The clink of a ceramic mug met her sensitive ears as she made the last turn into the cave they cooked in, and she smelled the welcome scent of Kercha brewing. Opening her milky eyes, she smiled to see petite Aerin and quiet Wertal sitting close together in commiseration on one long bench that lay between the scarred wooden table and the hewn rock wall of the cave.

She scooped up the steaming kettle and another mug as she made her way to join them at the table, topping off their brews from the pot as she poured herself a cup also. "Not just me then?" she murmured lightly, seeing Aerin's pointed ear twitch slightly at even that small amount of noise.

"Our Mage still comes," Wertal's deep voice rumbled out. He bared his teeth in his feral version of a smile, his large crescent horns looking like an armored helmet curving down around his ears. The barrel chested man came from the Kla'routh tribe, and his size and fearsome appearance had terrified her upon her arrival at the Caves. But in her time here she'd learned that for all his tribe's gruesome reputation, a reputation reflected readily in his physical person, Wertal was a gentle giant with a soft spot for the tiny, fey looking Aerin, who seldom left his side.

"Just a month later than expected." Aerin gave a small smile at the chaos and confusion the small detail caused among the Ancients. Some among them had even begun to doubt in Freyton, that such a strong vision had not come to pass. Though none but the irritable Skalin had been rash enough to voice their fears.

Cirillia thought back to the scattered tales she had gleaned from the Trianti tribe that still camped outside the doorway to the Caves of Orr, their newly Named Morgal presiding over them. The girl and Maegi the tribe had chased into the fissures between the Castles matched the Dream too closely to be anyone else; and now that she had seen the face of the Mage's shadow companion, she felt even more sure the traitor Maegi and captive girl were the ones whose arrival was foretold. "To wander beneath the Castles with the demons, and emerge whole once again," she said in wonderment, "what a Mage she must be." Aerin and Wertal nodded in agreement before both their eyes were drawn to the doorway, as someone else entered the kitchens in search of the pain relieving tea they were soon going to need a second pot of.

"In two nights we will have our Battle Mage," Kon said complacently, "It's good to know Freyton still favors us with the Sight." The old man settled in beside Cirillia, wisps of his white hair nearly concealing the bone white spires of his antlers. He cradled a mug as she poured for him. She took up the pot to refill, as Pernal trailed into the room to sit at the table in Kon's wake, rubbing a hand across her brow, soothing away the persistent pain.

"We should farscry the remaining Morgals," Pernal spoke into the companionable silence blanketing the room aside from the sipping of tea and the clink of mugs.

Wertal nodded thoughtfully even as Aerin shook her head in denial. "We can tell them we will need them to come, but we should meet our Mage before they arrive. I have a feeling things may be more complicated than we know." Cirillia nodded, she had the same feeling, had had it ever since the Trianti Pralick discarded his name and took up the mantle of Morgal. That man was hard, hard and mean in a way that bespoke of trouble for those under him. And if the shadow companion from the Dream was truly the Trianti's head Maegi turned traitor, things would be getting ugly before long.

The quiet conversation around her came to an abrupt halt, as a keening cry reverberated from the empty hallway outside their cozy kitchen. Each Ancient in the room stilled, listening hard, and Cirillia took stock of the situation. Only two of their number were missing, Skalin and Folt; no other Trewal was allowed into the Caves without an escort. The cry came again, breaking the motionless tension at the table and sending the entire room scurrying for the door at once. Her hip bounced into the firm meat of Wertal's thigh as they attempted to fit through the open entrance at the same time; she rebounded into the wall bruisingly, only to be steadied by his big hand, a silent apology written on his face as he maintained her balance, keeping her from further injury. She and the big man trailed after the group, following their hurried steps and the grief stricken cry that now seemed to be sounding continuously in the hall, thanks to the echoes the cave produced. They were the last two to round the corner into Skalin's room, where the commotion was coming from. The scene before her nearly stole the breath from her body.

"Ayyyyyeeeeee!" The undulating cry came from Folt's widely parted lips. His head was thrown so far back, she worried he would break his neck despite the cushion of his multiple chins. Rarely seen muscles in his neck worked furiously to push out the eerie sound. Aerin lowered herself to her knees slowly, and threw her own head back to join her voice to the lament; Wertal moved behind her in support, his hands on her so large that her shoulders mostly disappeared.

The thin hands of the potbellied Skalin were clasped tightly in his friend's grip. The contrast between the two Trewal was stunning, the flushed red of Folt's plump appendages banded around the marble white fingers of the dead man before him. All color had fled Skalin's body; his nose in particular drew her attention, ruddy as it had always been. Now the only color on the corpse of the fractious man she had known, was the deep red run of blood falling like tears from his unseeing eyes. Their milky white was tinged pink, and tracks were slowly drying, vivid red giving way to a flaky, rusted brown. Strangely the lack of flush in his face was all she could think about, even as she too dropped to her knees to add her voice to the rising cry around her.

How long they sang their grief to the hard walls of the Caves she didn't know, but eventually Folt's voice cracked and failed and the rest of them trailed off one by one, a shocked silence holding sway over them.

"He questioned Freyton," Folt said raggedly, "He spoke aloud a fear that was in all our hearts and Freyton punished him for it." There was anger in his voice, but reverent fear also. Fear of a God so vengeful as to kill his own chosen Seer.

Cirillia looked over his body again. This was not a natural death, not with the only injury coming from the eyes Freyton had altered when Skalin became an Ancient. It was as if the vision they shared last night had blinded him, taken its fury out on his eyes and ended up taking his life as well. Ancients did die, but usually peacefully, in their sleep, and usually only the very oldest of their members went, rather than one of the youngest among them. Freyton was the only plausible answer, unless one of their own had unearthed a poison known to no other and taken Skalin's life, leaving the blame to fall on their God. She discarded the thought, searching the aged faces around her and seeing only shock, grief, and frequent flares of fear in the eyes so like her own.

"What-" Her voice failed her, so she tried to get the words out in a second attempt, "What do we do now?" She had been the last one called to the Caves of Orr, and had no idea what protocol awaited them, or if there was even a known plan of action for the strange death.

Folt stood resolutely, meeting each person's eyes in turn as if daring them to resist what he was about to say. "We mourn our fallen brother, unless Freyton sees fit to give us a sign to do otherwise." He gently placed Skalin's hands upon his chest, one up high over his heart and the other just below it, before thumbing his sticky eyelids closed. He turned back to them, sadness etching the lines in his face deeper than she had ever seen them. "Then we wait for our new brother or sister to arrive, and deal with the coming Mage as Freyton guides us to."

Chapter 12

Metra

It was one of those peerless, late autumn days she loved so much. The air crisp enough to warrant a cozy shawl, but the sun shining in a sky so blue and cloudless, it barely seemed real. The barest shadows of the two moons hung like fragments of clipped hooves over the Skypeaks; and a playful wind teased her heavy curls from their pins so her tawny locks tumbled down around her, tangling in the tomato plants she knelt by, as she plucked their red and yellow bounty.

The Holm gardens were her domain, the orderly rows and robust vegetation a testament to both her management, and her magical prowess. This busy time of year the laughter of children rang among the rows of vegetables, as the young ones of Jorgenholm aided in the harvest. Metra smiled serenely from the middle of the tangle of tomato plants, as two youngsters tottered past with a large crate of cheerum held between them. Her hand strayed to rest on her gently swelled belly, even as her other hand plucked more fruit from the fragrant stalks surrounding her.

Torman had been as full of joy as she had ever seen him when she shared her news, which was a feat for a man who seemed to spend most of his days brimming with humor and good cheer. She shook her head in bemusement, thinking of the man. So much darkness surrounded him his entire life, and yet he still looked at the world with childlike wonder, searching for the things to laugh at rather than to sorrow over. He was easy to love, and she felt like the luckiest woman in the world to have him to herself these last five rebirths. She didn't care about the gossips, the snide remarks and the giggling of the other women of the Holm; they may call her a whore and shun her friendship, but in her mind the negatives were far outweighed by Torman's rather large presence in her life and bed.

She stood up gracefully, carrying her basket of tomatoes, picking up the other one she had filled earlier in the morning as she made her way to the kitchens. The cooks worked at full tilt, from before the sun rose to long after it had fallen this time of year. The tomatoes she carried were destined for tonight's stew, but the cheerum, apples, terns, coreps, crowberries, endives, chard and turnips being ferried into the Keep's large kitchens had various other destinations. The serfs working under the cooks broke into many smaller groups at harvest time, which was why the meals this season were always less extravagant than at other times. Only a small percentage of the staff actually cooked the food the Holm consumed every day, while the others preserved food by brine, pickling, canning, smoking, and dehydrating.

A skinny young man with one broken antler took her burdens with a nod of thanks, and Metra escaped the mass of noise and smells with gratitude. Her stomach was likely to turn on her at the most inopportune moments these days. She slipped out the less used side door, intent on making her way to the ornamental gardens she kept by the great cliff backing the Holm. The curtain wall hemmed the garden in on one side, the stone Keep on another. At the back the dark stoned cliff radiated heat and captured light for her prized plants even in the winter, if the sun shone. Here she grew a slew of inedible or dangerous plants, rare herbs for Camus's concoctions, and a plethora of flowers not used for anything but their beauty.

The space had previously been the Lady of the Holm's personal garden. Metra had played there as a child, when the plants were all varieties found in Galmorah, and the Jorgen's wife, Cara, had gone there to combat her homesickness. The Lady had found her there, once or twice, and had only smiled and asked her to join her on the stone bench some long forgotten mason had carved with scrolling ivy, even when she had every right to punish the wayward commoner child for straying. Metra remembered those few instances with clarity. Cara had had a way with children. Maybe it was her soft voice, or the small, kind touch of her dainty hands, or the exotic litany of plants Cara had named for her; but the garden had been Metra's place of peace ever since.

After the Lady's passing the garden had been abandoned. Her prized Galmorish flowers died off in the harsh winters of the

Skypeaks, and slowly, indigenous vegetation took their place. Metra had petitioned the Jorgen for use of the space early in her apprenticeship to the Holm's agriculturist. She had been terrified, standing before the Jorgen's giant desk in his study, his dark eyes showing no emotion whatsoever until her plea was made. His surprise was just barely evident, a slight widening of his dark eyes, but he had consented to her use of the space, practicality winning out over any scrap of sentiment he held for his late wife's favorite place in his domain.

In the years since, she had borrowed, begged, extorted, and traded for panes of glass of all sizes to build the cozy greenhouse tucked up in one corner of the space, against the Keep. It was her pride and joy, her work space that made many of the wonders of her small ornamental garden possible in the harsh conditions of the north. Here she nurtured the seeds of plants that would die with the snows, safe in the heated glass room. It was also her space to experiment with crossing strains of flowers with one another, each new seedling a joyful combination of the traits of its parents, or more often than not, an infertile flop which never sprouted at all.

She had brought to life her special strain of Windthorn roses here, by crossing a strain from Camus's Wall which grew prolifically and bloomed nearly all year round, with a smaller strain found in the Reedwood forest that had the most wonderful perfume; but the flowers fell apart easily, and were not the prettiest of their kind. After some time, the two became one strong plant, boasting wicked thorns, plentiful blossoms of a unique burnt red color, and a smell that transported one to the dreamy days of summer. The roses, which grew upon the cliff behind her garden, began gaining popularity among the nobles in Seaprium. Within a few years after their conception, the late summer months saw traders journeying to Jorgenholm specifically to take away wagon after wagon of the fragrant flowers to distribute in the capital and Galmorah alike.

A tall figure dominated the small garden as she entered, gnarled hands full of fragrant herbs. "Hello, Camus," she said, bobbing a curtsy with downcast eyes in deference to his status, even as he waved aside her courtesy, leaves spilling from his clutches as a result. She hurriedly knelt to gather the spilled herbs, as the old

Maegi stopped mid stoop to place a hand at the small of his back. "The freezes must almost be upon us if you are searching out these pain relievers," she said, sorting through burdock root, turmeric, and a variety of nettles which she placed in a handy basket for easier carrying.

"Who needs to mark time in a calendar, when my bones clearly tell me the time of year?" Camus said with dry humor, startling a laugh out of Metra. "I know the harvest keeps you busy, so I hope you don't mind that I came to help myself to your herbs," he said in a more serious tone.

"Not at all," she replied, "I grow them for you, you know. No one else would know what to do with the stranger ones you have me sprouting." She brushed a hand over the large trumpet shaped flowers of the Datura Camus had specially imported from the Sareth Isles for her to grow. The seeds and flowers were highly poisonous, and she had taken extra care none of the children or animals of the Holm strayed into her garden after it successfully sprouted. It was not only this plant that made the sturdy wooden fence and firmly latched gate necessary, but it was the one she worried the most about, since the flowers were temptingly beautiful.

"I can't be too busy since I found the time to come here today," she said ruefully. "I will never begrudge the excuse to come putter here," she added meaningfully, "So it is never a trial to fetch you what herbs you need."

Camus nodded in understanding before stretching creakily. "The movement does me good I think, and so does the sun, as it won't be long before we forget it ever shined here." Such a mundane statement, but true nonetheless. Soon the snows would come and the world would be reduced to shades of black and white. The intense blue of the sky lost to clouds, and the greenery that bloomed about Jorgenholm dead, except for the Listenbarks and magically sustained Wall.

She looked at the man beside her, seeing every wrinkle, every swollen, exposed joint. She and Camus crossed paths very little in the large Keep, but she knew much of him from Torman. Her lover adored the older man, attributing kindness, wisdom, and grace to the Maegi she had often believed could not be true. Her gifts had eased her way in life, but before they had made themselves known, Metra had been made aware of the depths of depravity Trewals hid in their hearts. No one could be wholly good. There was always a point, an action that would tip the scale into selfishness or violence. Even in her. Even in the old man standing next to her. She could only entreat Garrin to let them live the rest of their lives without reaching that tipping point.

Shaking off the dark thoughts winter always bought to mind, she offered her arm to Camus, turning her back on the little garden. "May I walk you back to your tower, Camus? Or did you have another stop in mind?"

"My tower will do, thank you Metra." His long fingers nearly encircled her entire forearm, but the tall Maegi seemed to appreciate the support of her smaller frame.

It's nice to take your time, she thought, watching the serfs hurry this way and that as they made their slow way across the courtyard and into the dim halls of the Keep. She rarely took this much time to get anywhere, and her eyes seemed to appreciate the meandering pace, picking up little nuances she would never have noticed at her usual breakneck speed. The lintel above the doorway into the Greathall had not been dusted in far too long. The flowers laid on Garrin's small altar in the hall past the laundry were so dry they were almost crumbling. Her mental to-do list grew longer by the second.

They rounded the last corner to the base of the spiral stair that would lead Camus to his quarters, to find a young serf couple in a tangle of limbs and lips. Camus coughed lightly and the two serfs sprang apart, looking guilty, bobbing curtsies and bows while their apologies filled the small, echoing space.

"Enough!" Camus said gruffly, "I'm sure you have tasks to attend to..." It was enough of a dismissal that the couple fled gratefully, leaving Metra and Camus chuckling, surprised the two lovers hadn't kicked up a cloud of dust in their escape.

"I can take it from here my dear, thank you for the walk," Camus murmured, taking the basket of herbs from her hands.

Metra opened her mouth to reply, but a brassy trumpeting from outside the Holm sounded before the words made it out. The horn! She and Camus remained frozen in place, waiting for a second set of notes, one that would tell the entire Holm what danger was approaching their Wall. The next string of notes blared out, sending a shiver down her spine, and as one she and Camus moved back the way they had come, kicking up their formerly sedate pace into a hurried shuffle as she took his arm once more.

"Go Metra, I'm slowing you down! Get the garden workers into the Keep, I will meet you in the Greathall!" Camus's voice was breathy and labored from the pace she had set, so she released him and flew through the halls, intent on getting all the serfs under her care out of harm's way. Arrows tended to fly thick over the gardens when the Hinterlanders attacked.

Kaur

He was in the stables when the trumpets began their wild call, backed up into an empty stall as he attempted to avoid the flying fists and kicks the very drunk man facing him flung his way. He had never been so thankful to hear the frightening herald of a Hinterland raid as he was in that moment. The noise distracted the stable-master from the beating he had been giving him, retribution for the scolding he'd received from Lord Torman when he attempted to keep Kaur from reaching him. Kaur was able to limp by the fat man, holding his breath at the fetid odor of sour wine and unwashed body, as he slid under an outstretched arm. He gave the back of the man's calf a solid kick as he exited the stall, finally breaking him from his frozen state and goading him into the actions he should have been taking from the first call of the horn. Kaur was forgotten as the stable master frantically called for his hands to assemble the warhorses in case a foray outside the Wall was needed.

Kaur stumbled gratefully behind a stack of loose hay, collapsing back into the pokey stuff so every ounce of energy left in his battered body could focus on the coughing coming from deep in his chest. He hadn't been able to shake this cough. It had only grown worse as he worked down in the damp library under the Keep, and Camus finally ordered him to take a few days off to recuperate. The old man was happy with the delay, telling Kaur he needed to catch up on his potion-making to stock up for the winter.

He hacked up some globby phlegm, leaning from the pile to spit it on the dusty floor, wincing at the streaks of red visible in the nasty sputum. Kaur breathed in cautiously, loathe to trigger another fit. He didn't know if he could survive the next one. His chest felt like it was on fire, the dry heat of it now spreading up his throat, making him crave water more than his next breath. New bruises the stable-master had given him faded into the background compared to the searing in his chest; so he staggered to his feet and found his way to the nearest horse trough, taking care to keep out of the way of the stable hands and horses now streaming steadily through the crowded barn. He dunked his whole head in the clear water of the trough when he reached it, the chilled water feeling wonderful against his flushed skin.

After drinking his fill, soothing the fire in his chest, he listened intently. Shouts and arguing voices dominated the courtyard as everyone in the Holm hastened to their posts and duties. All of the younger children, women, and elderly were supposed to make their way to the Greathall of the Keep in the case of a raid like this one. That way they would have four solid stone walls to ward off any stray projectiles, and the position was easily defensible by just a few men in the unheard-of event of the Wall and interior battlements being breached. Peering out of the side door to the stables, he could see the door to the Keep, and safety, through the commotion in the yard. But his body didn't feel quite up to navigating the chaos after that last bout of coughing. So he slipped around to the rear of the stables and along the newly built housing there, until he reached the tiny one room abode he and his parents were now calling home.

His mother's sewing lay abandoned by the fire, the bow that usually hung above the miniature alter to Garrin was absent, a sure sign his father was helping to man the battlements nestled behind the Wall. Kaur looked around, a little lost as to what to do. He had thought to find his Ma here, but being pregnant, again, she had likely made for the extra safety of the Greathall. Kaur jumped as an arrow buried its head through the thatch of the roof above the bed. It made a peculiar hissing noise even after it had creased to move, and to his horror a thin plume of smoke eased down through the thick green thatch.

"No!" he cried, aghast that the home they had just been allowed to move into was now likely to burn down, leaving them homeless once more. He ran frantically for the bucket of water kept in the corner to wash hands and faces, then went to stand directly beneath where the arrow had hit, the spreading flames visible only as a layer of smoke filtering through the tightly packed roof. He looked at the bucket in his hands and then back up at the roof, knowing even if he had been tall enough to reach the rafters, splashing his meager amount of water onto the bottom of the flames would do no good. With an anguished cry that rasped through his aching throat he dashed through the space, loading his arms with their few possessions.

Hands brimming with extra cloaks and clothes, the effigy of Garrin his father had carved, and his prized sling, Kaur ran from the house without further ado. Keeping to the edges of the courtyard gave him a pristine view of the now deserted area, bare save for a scattering of bodies which lay unmoving, struck by arrows. He took a brief breather before making his way across to the side entrance of the Holm, watching an arrow thud into the ground between him and safety. He glanced back at their home once, and had to choke back a sob at the merry dance of flames now wreathing the still green structure. He turned back to the options before him resolutely, knowing the newly built housing was beyond his help.

He considered the arrow strewn yard. The orchards hugging the Wall might provide him with more shelter from projectiles, but the unprotected stretch between him and the golden leafed tern and corep trees was equally as long as the one between him and the side door. However, if he went for the side door, then he wouldn't have to make his way through the naked trees to the rear of the Holm and the service entrance situated there. Decision made, he took a deep breath and made for the side entrance with all the haste his small and encumbered body could produce. Much to his surprise he tumbled through the door in a scatter of his family's possessions, and managed to close the door behind him without incident. Sucking in a slow breath he tried to calm his speeding heart, suppressing the tickling urge to cough that his heavy breathing brought to life. By the time he got himself under control a group of children his own age was approaching, gathering the sprinkling of his belongings as they neared his body slumped against the wall.

"Kaur? You hit?" Retcha asked in a whisper, as the two boys with her made a beeline for the door. They struggled for a moment with the large wooden bar set beside it before it dropped into place, locking them safely inside.

"Naw, jus' catching my breath," he wheezed at his friend, taking his sling from her outstretched hands with gratitude that he wouldn't have to stoop to pick it up. His body felt abruptly drained of all energy, and the unquenchable fire in his chest had begun to burn again. He needed water, and soon.

"Lear sent us to lock the door, and we still gotta do the door at the back'a the Holm. Wanna come?" Lourn asked before stooping a bit to peer into Kaur's down turned face. "Actually, you don't look so good. You sure you're not hit?" Three sets of hands patted him down gently when he failed to muster the energy to reply.

"Something's wrong with him," Retcha said, fear making her voice shrill.

"Grab his other arm Saul," Lourn instructed, slinging Kaur's right arm around his own scrawny shoulders, "We better get you to the Greathall; the Maegi is there, he'll know what to do. Retch, can you run ahead? Grab someone else to bar the rear door with you, you won't be able to lift it alone."

Kaur registered the patter of her hooves as she sprinted off down the corridor, but the burning sensation at his core was quickly blotting out his surroundings, demanding the entirety of his attention. The stone walls passed in a blur, accompanied by snippets of whispered conversation going on between his friends. They paused once when Kaur tried to take off his prized jacket, the heat in his body too intense to be contained inside the stifling fur. Still unable to speak, he simply pulled his arms from their grasp and flopped forwards onto his stomach, before rolling onto his back and pawing ineffectually at his sleeves.

"Trollit!" Saul gasped, placing a hand on Kaur's sweaty brow, "He's burning up, get him out of the jacket." Lourn helped to peel the heavy coat off, discarding the damp pelt and the rest of Kaur's stash at the side of the hall, so he could focus all of his efforts on getting the smaller boy to the Maegi.

The cool air rushed over Kaur's skin like a tide of cold water, bringing a brief respite from the furnace his body had become. "Water," he croaked, in his moment of lucidity.

"Almost there Kaur, there's plenty of water in the Greathall. Can you lift up your feet?" He couldn't tell anymore which of the boys spoke, but he tried to pull his feet up from where they dragged on the stone floor all the same, and the trio gained a bit of speed.

"Maegi! We need the Maegi!"

"Help! Please! Get the Maegi! Fetch him some water!"

A burst of light hit his eyes as both of his rescuers began calling out loudly, and he flinched away from the confusing press of light and noise that erupted around him. He shut his eyes to better focus on containing the fire in his chest, lest it burst forth in a cough that would surely consume him.

Camus

The shouting of young voices beat at the edge of his concentration like moths trying to find a way into a lantern, but he firmed up his Control and banished the distraction to the periphery. The soldier under his hands was living on a razor's edge and if he was going to help the young man he needed every bit of his mind focused internally to where his magic flowed into the warrior's thigh. The thick shaft of a Hinterland arrow protruded from two sides of the leg, and inside, with the awareness of his magic, he knew the splintered wood was pressing against the fragile casing of one of the largest arteries in the man's entire body.

His own slow breath sounded like the susurrus of waves breaking on the shore, a calming layer of white noise he pushed between himself and the growing murmur of voices around him. He let his magic flood the leg, seeing from every angle the slight fraying of the artery where the arrow had rubbed the thin tissue, as the man was moved into the Greathall for treatment. If the artery was breached the man would bleed out in minutes. The tear would be too ragged for Camus to hold together with magic and too large for a tourniquet to stem the blood loss. The only chance for life the soldier had was if he could pull the arrow out without damaging the artery any more than it already was.

He pooled his Earth magic into higher concentration where wood met pulsing conduit, easing tendrils between the two in the thinnest possible threads he could manage. The gap slowly grew, until he was able to begin smoothing stray splinters back to lay flat along the shaft, secured by his magic, and all maintained by his Control. When he had most of the debris cleared from the fragile artery, he spoke, his eyes still closed as he continued to hold everything in place.

"Cut off the fletching, as smoothly as possible." He felt movement around him and the slight jolt of the wood snapping. Camus held his breath after the jarring movement, searching throughout the internal area for problems that may have arisen, but found everything holding in the same manner as before.

"I will count to three," he spoke to Metra, his adept helper, "then pull the arrow out from the head. Keep it as aligned with the angle of the wound as possible. And Metra?" He felt more than heard her small questioning exhale, "Pull hard."

He felt a light touch bounce the arrow. "Okay, ready when you are," she said tightly. Camus checked the distance between rough shaft and lightly leaking artery one more time before he began his count, holding tight to his Control as he felt the strain of using magic draining his old body of strength.

"One, two, three!" He clamped down on the shaft with all his might, keeping the sharp splinters of wood from tearing up the inside of the unconscious soldier more than it already had, and with a shaky exhale he found the artery still mostly intact after the arrow's brutal exit. He cleaned up some of the more severe damage with light touches of Healing, and reinforced the damaged wall before retracting his mind and magic from the body, sure that more traditional methods could sustain life now that the arrow was out.

"Good, good, Metra. Well done. Keep pressure here until the bandage is on," he said, opening his eyes and moving out of the way so the other healers could move in with their heaps of white bandaging and wet cloths to clean the wound.

Camus blinked in astonishment at the tense crew of children ringing the table he had been working on. His tired regard seemed to be some sort of trigger for the restless group as they all broke into furious speech at once, getting louder and louder in order to be heard over one another.

"Quiet!" Metra's voice was loud, and cut through the babble satisfyingly. "Camus, Kaur was brought in while we were working. These good folk didn't understand you couldn't stop what you were doing to see to him until now." She glared at the motley group of children, who seemed cowed at her admonishment, but the largest one spoke up quickly.

"Kaur collapsed Sir, he's hotter than I've ever felt a person be," the ragged boy grabbed Camus's hand, heedless of the blood still coating it, and began towing him away from the makeshift surgery bed, "Nothin else wrong with 'im that I can tell, but he won't stop askin for water, no matter how much I bring 'im!" the boy finished as they reached the corner of the Greathall farthest from the massive hearth.

Camus pulled his cloak tighter about himself, feeling the chill off of the stones this far from the flames. He began to kneel, but a sharp pain in his back and a wobble in his legs had him calling for a table to be brought to him instead. Soon he had Kaur up at examining height and was stripping the sweaty boy of most of his clothes to get a better understanding of what ailed him. Kaur coughed weakly as they worked, regaining consciousness only for a moment when his flushed skin was finally bared to the air.

"Water?" he pleaded.

The boy who had forcefully brought Camus to his side moved forward with a water skin and trickled some liquid into his friend's mouth. Kaur swallowed gratefully before collapsing back onto the table, coughing fitfully. The sounds from his chest were worrisome, a deep, wet sounding rattle that made Camus fear the child had lapsed into pneumonia. He reached for his magic, ashamed at how little he was able to hold onto after his exertions with the wounded soldier, and let the power seep gently into the fevered body before him. He snatched his hands and his magic back after a brief moment, shaking his hands out like they had been stung by Kaur's heated flesh.

"Metra, I need Torman if the Wall can spare him," he said shakily, lifting worried eyes to the pregnant woman, "Something is very wrong here. Send one of the guards at the door for him, quickly."

"The guards aren't supposed to leave their posts-" she began, but Camus shook his graying head forcefully, stopping her in her tracks.

"Now, Metra."

She fled with surprising speed, one hand clutched under her belly to support the growing swell of her child. Camus reached for his magic again, spreading his awareness along Kaur's reddened skin, careful to keep the magic from sinking below the skin into the seething green power that filled his little apprentice to the brim with sickening light. *When had this happened?* His Sight had never failed him like this before. He could will the colored lights away with much focus and will power, but they would inevitably creep back in. But now that his magic had touched the mire of power hidden in Kaur's small body, he blazed green in Camus's eyes.

He racked his brain, trying to identify the last time he had scanned Kaur's body magically. He had kept a close eye on the boy after his encounter with that strange skull in the library, but other than that first trace of green there had been no signs for the two weeks following his misadventure. "Stupid," he mumbled to himself, "should have kept checking."

"Should have checked for what?" a shrill voice demanded, and upon opening his eyes Camus was surprised to find a small and very pregnant woman just across the table from him, clutching Kaur's hand to her chest, her teary eyes trained on him.

"Willa, I'm glad you're here," he nodded to Kaur's mother, thinking fast for an explanation that wouldn't cause the fragile woman to panic, "I was just thinking I should have used magic when Kaur first came down with this cold, it has turned nasty." He saw her focus shift back to her child with relief, and an even greater sense of relief flooded over him as he heard Torman's booming voice echoing towards him from the doorway into the Greathall.

"Torman, is all well out there?" he asked immediately as the Lord strode up, one hand holding a snowy bandage to an arrow graze on his arm. He peeled the bandage back to peer at the shallow cut, then clamped it back on as the wound started to bleed.

"They turned tail and ran, like they always do. They just decided to start early this year. Looks like it was the Rishal tribe. There are more blue casualties out there than dead inside the Wall. I sent some scouts out to hasten their retreat and clean up the mess," he finished, keeping his voice loud so all the curious ears listening in could spread the happy news.

"What seems to be the problem here?" Torman asked, his face falling when he saw who Camus's patient was. "Oh, Kaur, lad," he shook his head sadly, scooping up the boy's unoccupied hand and scanning his body for a wound. "No injury. Camus what's wrong with him?"

"Yes Maegi, what's wrong with him?" Willa chimed in acerbically.

Camus barely held back an eye roll at her accusatory tone. "That cough he had, I suspect," he said vaguely, "I'd like to get him up to my tower now the raid is over. Torman, can you please carry him?"

Torman's brows lifted in surprise and it looked like he was going to beg off, having other duties to perform; but Metra choose that moment to swoop in, neatly tying off the bandage on Torman's arm so he could pick up the child. "That's right Torman, just pick him up and we can get your wound cleaned while we are up there also. Two birds, one stone, neat as you please," she said brightly, before turning to Willa and asking her if she would be willing to help setting up the infirmary for the others injured in the raid while her son was being treated.

Camus pressed her hand in thanks as he passed, and then hiked up his robe to better keep pace with Torman's great strides which took them to his cozy tower in a matter of minutes. As Kaur was being settled into the bed, he woke, coughing weakly at first but then the fit grew in strength. "Sit him upright, Torman!" Camus cried, startled by the intensity of the episode and the creeping red stain making its way up from Kaur's chest, through his throat and spilling onto already flushed cheeks. It almost looked like he was glowing, illuminated from the inside out by a sinister red light.

Sputum sprayed from Kaur's slack jaw once he was sitting, and Camus saw that the material was as red as blood, as was the trickle of liquid that ran from the boy's mouth. He was mumbling incoherently now, in between the hacking that shook his body, despite Torman's steadying hands on his shoulders. Camus ran to his worktable, fetching vials and crocks of different tonics and ointments that he hauled back to the bedside. He opened a jar of soothing balm, made with horehound and lemon balm, gathering a good amount onto his fingers before turning to the struggling Kaur. His movements were weakening by the second, and Torman was able to settle him back against the pillows as Camus approached.

Reaching out he spread the oily balm over his chest, only to recoil from the astonishing heat radiating from the child's skin. Camus looked down in shock at his fingers, reddened and burnt from the brief contact, a horrible thought making its way to the front of his mind.

"Camus! What should I do?" Torman asked in an anguished voice. Kaur lay almost completely still now, but for the labored rise and fall of his chest.

"Get back" he said woodenly. When Torman moved towards the bed instead, an incredulous look on his face, Camus roared, "GET BACK!" And Torman retreated in confusion.

The red glow intensified in Kaur's chest, emitting light like embers, spreading visibly up his neck each time he managed to exhale. The boy's cracked lips dropped open, and a tongue of flame licked its way past that last barrier, carried on the poor child's last breath.

"Kaur!" Torman cried brokenly from his side, but Camus only had eyes for the bizarre scene before him. He watched as the few flames from Kaur's now scorched lips ignited with the building heat in his lungs and burst into a greedy blaze. Camus stayed there, utterly still, barely aware of Torman's frantic calls and movements, watching woodenly as fire tore into the small body of his research companion. By the time Torman found a wash bucket and threw the water over the corpse on the bed, Kaur was unrecognizable. His chest was a field of ash and most of his face had burned away, leaving four limbs, mostly whole, on the charred mattress.

Torman stamped out the rest of the scattered flames from the trailing sheets and turned to Camus, tears streaming down his face and a myriad of questions swimming behind his horrified gaze. Camus held out a hand to stop the flow of words he knew would come next, shaking his head in denial. Patting his own wet cheeks with a sleeve, he made his way to one of his overly packed bookshelves, pulling out a thick volume and leafing through it with cold certainty.

"Draconis Tussis" he confirmed, setting the book on his desk and sliding it across to Torman who had followed him.

"What does that mean? What happened to him? Camus?" Torman finally gave up on finding answers in the silent man, and turned his attention to the illustrated page before him. Camus turned to the arrow slit behind his desk, looking out over the Holm, and the hundreds of people busily cleaning up after the early raid.

"It means 'Dragon's Cough' Torman. It is a sickness borne by magic that kills every single person infected by it." He never took his gaze off the bustling yard, but in his mind he killed off every third person that walked by, a conservative estimation of the death toll Jorgenholm would soon be experiencing.

Torman

People packed the courtyard tightly, leaving scarce room to move and filling the space with whispers. Most were familiar faces. There was Kaur's mother Willa, with her pregnant belly, standing next to a heavily bearded man whom he knew he had met before, but he could not find a name for. He spied round Gambria, surrounded by her staff, easily identified by the smears of flour dusting each of them. There was Lear, pulled up from the warrens with his contingent of young ones surrounding him like the waist high grasses of the Sacred Plains. Finally, he looked down, finding Metra's sweet face by his side, her hand gripped tightly in his, a look of shocked disbelief marring her beloved features.

He released her hand and climbed slowly up on a wooden box situated conveniently beside the wall of the Holm. His emergence effectively cut off the riot of whispers and garnered the attention of every soul in the Holm, save for those sentries on the battlements and the party of scouts currently outside the Wall. He knew the silence stretched on for too long, but he found it hard to drag words from his lips in his peculiar state of mind. It seemed to him he was floating, cushioned from reality by a great distance, even though he could feel the heat from Metra's body, she stood so close to him.

"Today we survived a Hinterland raid," he started, feeling disconnected from the familiar sound of his own voice. "But now we face a greater danger, one that cannot be fought so easily." The crowd shifted restlessly and he saw frowns appear on many faces, quickly followed by apprehension. Kaur's mother fidgeted anxiously and glanced towards the keep as if to go find her son and protect him from whatever danger Torman was about to announce. He drew in a big breath, "We are faced with an epidemic, one with no known cure, and extremely dange-" Raised voices cut him off and the mass of people writhed in agitation at his announcement. Willa's face paled and her grip on her husband's hand turned white knuckled.

He tried to speak again but his lone voice was lost to the hubbub, until a contingent of soldiers just returned from a turn patrolling outside the Wall helpfully banged their swords upon their shields, the clangor bringing silence to the yard. "Thank you," he said into the ringing silence, receiving a nod from the patrol leader. "Like I said, there is no known cure and the symptoms can be volatile and extremely dangerous. There has only been one case so far, but we are asking everyone to limit their exposure to others. If you are able to, stay home. If you are not, try to touch others as seldom as possible. A list of symptoms will be posted at the stables, Greathall, and kitchens. If you cannot read, a scribe with knowledge of the symptoms will be stationed by each of those posts to answer questions."

He paused to catch his breath, trying to formulate his next words carefully. He, Camus, and Metra had decided it would be best if the magical nature of the sickness was kept quiet to avoid panic. They had also decided to omit the fact that no one who had shown end stage symptoms of Dragon's Cough had ever survived. He was tempted to not utter that ominous name at all, but Metra had made a good point on the long walk down from Camus's tower.

"People fear an unknown danger more than one with a name," she had said, "and by naming this pestilence we gain the semblance of power over it in the eyes of our people. If Camus is right about this plague, then they will need all of the extra confidence we can give them."

It had been only a matter of hours ago he had watched Kaur burst into flames. The time between had been spent in frantic discussion and desperate research. They had discussed many courses of action, including keeping the sickness a secret altogether; but the incendiary nature of the death throes of Dragon's Cough had led them to decide that the entire Holm needed to be notified, and each victim isolated in a stone room, lest the entire Holm go up in flames. But how could he explain that to the Trewal of Jorgenholm without causing utter despair? He knew the facts, the horror the next few weeks held for them all, and he found himself barely able to move under the weight of it. How could he expect a better response from anyone else?

One of the kitchen serfs broke into a raucous cough, stopping his tumultuous thoughts in their tracks. His eyes sought out the young man, a lanky youth with a smear of flour beside his nose that was made all the more visible by the redness his coughing brought to his face. He looked down at Metra quickly, awareness passing between them, sending her scurrying out into the crowd towards the disturbance. By the time she reached the boy a large circle of empty space surrounded him, and a look of terror took hold over his homely features.

Torman spoke out into the pregnant pause, "A persistent cough is one of the main symptoms," he said with a sad smile to the boy. "Anyone showing symptoms is to report to our Maegi, Camus, in the smaller common room off the Greathall. It will be converted into a medical room of sorts to house anyone who falls sick." The entire assembly watched Metra walk the serf into the Holm before he spoke again.

"It is essential, for the safety of the entire Holm, that you go into seclusion once you show any signs of the sickness. I know a mother may want to stay near her young ones in their ailment, or a husband may want to stay by his wife's side. I won't tell you you cannot, but you *must* come into the Holm for treatment. Do not stay home. Do not continue your duties, or you risk all the lives this Keep holds." He looked around again, at all the people under his care, knowing that he would fail to keep many of them safe, and feeling helpless anger build inside once again.

"That is all," he finished simply, before vaulting off the boxes and heading into the Keep, nabbing three scribes as he went and towing them along behind him until they reached the sanctuary of his father's study. Willa had made a beeline towards him as soon as he stepped off the crates, her bearded husband in tow, but he had managed to lose her in the milling crowd. He didn't think he could handle telling her about Kaur right now. The noise of the masses in the yard below could be heard even through the thick stone walls and fogged glass windows that hemmed in the room. He gave the three men a quick rundown of the symptoms, along with detailed lists, and sent them off to their posts to answer the myriad of questions and concerns doubtlessly awaiting them. Once he was alone, he sank into a chair, wishing for the first time in his memory for his father.

The Jorgen would know what to do, he might even have some magical knowledge of how to combat this epidemic due to his connection to the Demandron. He looked to the stack of blank sheets that sat ready for him to write to his father of this debacle, knowing that even if he explained all of it, the Jorgen might have already sailed for Saerin by the time it reached Seaprium. He dropped his head in his hands, taking the heavy weight of his antlers from his tired neck as he considered. The discovery of the library needed to be explained and the probable link of Kaur tripping a magical fail-safe there that had led to the release of Dragon's Cough among the populace of the Holm. He could juggle the timing about a bit to escape his father's ire when it came to him and Camus keeping the discovery to themselves, but if the Jorgen ever found them out, only Garrin himself could protect them from the fallout.

But the bigger question still loomed. Did the chance that his letter would reach the Jorgen before he left for war outweigh the risk of putting such volatile information onto paper? Codes could be cracked and ciphers puzzled out by their enemies. Torman knew very well it might be their allies that were the most dangerous risk. The letter would spell out their situation very clearly to anyone who read it, that the great stronghold Jorgenholm would be left crippled and all but defenseless this winter, with the bulk of their forces across the Blitherly Sea and the rest battling a fatal plague. Easy pickings for anyone who wanted to make a huge leap forward in the capital, as the rulers of Jorgenholm traditionally held a seat on the Council. It would also be akin to putting out a welcome mat for increased Hinterland raids if the tribes somehow learned of their predicament.

Torman pulled a sheet of paper to him, settling a large quill comfortably in his hand. If the Jorgen could somehow put a stop to the Dragon's Cough, then it was a risk he was willing to take. He fished the book of ciphers his father kept from the drawer, and thumbed through to the back where the most complex codes resided. He was not a gambling man, he had no interest in leaving things up to chance, he never had. He was a man of action, a man of fighting his enemy with his own hands. In this desperate situation he was willing to bet that his father, the steadfast and unfailingly stern Jorgen, could help the Holm through these trials better than he could. He set his nib to the parchment, and began the story of the unlikely events that had led Jorgenholm to the brink of disaster, hoping his words would arrive in Seaprium in time to bring the Jorgen home.

Chapter 13

Sylvia

Days blended together as they trudged towards the Crooked Mountain, the monotony differing only in what they found to eat and the consistent dropping of the temperature each night. As they wound their way lower into the valley dotted by the Skycastles, game became more abundant, sheltering in the slightly warmer temperatures and hiding from frigid blasts of wind which sucked all the heat from their bodies when they had to climb up a fallen pinnacle to continue onward. They ate and walked, climbed and slept, and Sylvia found herself strangely content.

It seemed that with each step she took she was making her way further and further from her true home. Her parents and her cats, her friends and her team, were fading slowly. Replaced by the very solid and real man beside her and the everyday tasks of survival. It puzzled her that she couldn't dredge up the homesickness and disbelief that had guarded her from the fantastical world of Prium when she first arrived. But it was a vague worry, made smaller by the relationship evolving between her and her traveling companion.

Looking back at those days she could pinpoint certain events, but most of them included the things Les taught her. Skinning the rabbit was one. Using a sling was another. But the lessons which came most easily to mind were the ones Lessoran taught her once the sun had fallen and they took to their blanket for the evening. Like the many uses he had for his mouth, beyond the kissing she found she loved so much, and the incredible agility of his nimble fingers. She was so caught up in the experiences that when she woke this morning, with the Crooked Mountain looming over their campsite, she was almost sad to find the Caves of Orr within a day's walk.

"Morning," Les's gravelly voice sounded out from beneath her and she craned her neck around to meet his eyes, not liking the sadness tinging his voice.

"Morning," she said shortly, frowning up at him before wiggling down beneath their covers, intent on wiping that forlorn look off his face by reenacting one of her favorite lessons, one Les said she had damn near perfected. The breath whooshed out of his lungs in surprise and then silence fell in their little shelter. She lifted up the blanket periodically at first, checking the expression on his face, something she found was a good indication on how she was doing, but soon enough she didn't have to disrupt the cozy confines of the blanket as his sleep roughened voice urged her on clearly.

After a while she freed her head from the blanket, a satisfied grin widening her lips as she cuddled up to Les, pleased to see the sadness that had lined his face completely replaced with languor, and a small bemused smile lingering on his lips. This was her favorite Les. The snuggly teddy bear version, with his longish hair in messy curls between his antlers, his green eyes soft. He couldn't seem to stop touching her whenever he got in this mood, smoothing his hands over her skin constantly, playing with her hair, kissing her anywhere his lips could reach. She felt cherished, and strangely powerful, to be able to affect the big man so.

"You have-," he cleared his throat, still a little breathless, "you have officially surpassed all expectations on that front. I'm not sure I have anything left to teach you," he teased.

Sylvia grinned at the praise. "That's all you've got huh? Well I guess we will just have to go back to the beginning and try all of it over again, see if there's anything we missed."

He sprang into sudden movement, pinning her beneath him tightly and trapping her wrists easily in one of his hands. "Back to the *very* beginning?" he asked slyly, nuzzling into her exposed neck, his uneven whiskers tickled her sensitive skin and caused goosebumps to break out on her arms.

"Mmmmm... wait, what?" she asked, his words finally sinking in. "The very beginning," she repeated his words, her mind flying back to the night they emerged from the caves, and a blush flashed hot over her face, part desire and part fear. "Maybe not the *very* beginning" she retracted hastily, "More like the second beginning, or the middle beginning, the beginning after the actual beginning, if you know what I mean."

Les's laugh interrupted her babbling, but his eyes were strangely serious when he looked at her and said, "It's fine Sylvia, I know what you mean. You know I would never make you do anything you don't want to do right?"

She found her mouth gaping open at that statement and her next words popped out before she could reel them back in, "Like dragging me through the mountains as a prisoner when I wanted to get back to my friends?" She clapped her hand over her mouth after the last word was spoken, aghast at the accusatory tone. "Oh no, Les, I didn't mean it like that. I have no filter, I'm sorry, so sorry! Sometimes I just say things even when I shouldn't." She scanned his face desperately, terrified their last day spent entirely alone might now be wasted fighting just because of her carelessness. *When would she learn to keep her mouth shut?*

One of his dark brows tilted up consideringly as she waited with bated breath for his reaction. "No, that was fair," he said after a beat, smoothing her hair back from her face and freeing her hands from his grip, "But things are different now." It was said as a statement, but he caught her chin, forcing her gaze to his, obviously waiting for an affirmation.

"Things *are* different now," she repeated, thinking that she had never said anything truer. She and Lessoran were different. Her perspective was different. Her entire life had changed in the time since she was captured by the Hinterlanders. She may not be entirely sure this was real, or know how to explain what had happened to her, but she could barely imagine going back now, not with everything that had happened to her, everything she had learned and done. The naive girl she was before seemed impossible to reconcile with the person she was now.

"Good," he affirmed, kissing her soundly before straightening up. He stretched, and all her deep thoughts fled as she watched his muscled chest and lean arms. She finally shook herself into action when he settled his shirt over the expanse of tanned skin, and she began helping him ready their belongings for their last day of travel.

"Any idea what to expect when we get there?" she asked hopefully.

"No more than before, I'm afraid. Either my tribe will be there or they won't. Them being absent would be better for us of course, but it's likely we'd be granted access to the Ancients regardless. And that is where our fates will be decided. You need to convince them to help you get home rather than give you back to Pralick. Have you been thinking of what you'll say?"

She bit her lip, "I don't even know where to start," she answered truthfully. "It's so hard to imagine what their response to me will be, and so unthinkable that anyone would assume I *belong* to another person. It feels wrong to have to explain that I don't."

He looked at her silently for a long moment, before motioning her to take the lead on the trail they were following. Syl wondered what he'd been thinking in those quiet moments, his face was so hard to read sometimes; and she hated it when he clammed up like that. They walked for a while in silence, and she grew more and more fretful. Every glance behind her showed Les's tense face, devoid of emotion. Something was happening behind those eyes, and she didn't like it. He was distancing himself from her for some reason. It made her ache for the sleepy Les from this morning. The longer the silence stretched the more she was tempted to tackle him to the ground at the first level space she came upon to repeat her morning performance, just so she could get him back.

As they walked, she thought back over their earlier conversation, and the assertion from both of them that things were different now. *But what did that mean?* It wasn't a promise, or a declaration, it wasn't even a reassurance! Just a fact, things *were* different between them now. But it gave her no guarantee he wouldn't go back to the Trianti once they were at the Caves, or that he intended to stick around to see what the Ancients decided to do with her. Doubts crowded her mind, making her feel jumpy and anxious, so much so that when a quail took sudden flight just ahead, she gave a small shriek and stopped dead in her tracks, her hands twisted over her pounding heart.

"You okay?" he asked, touching her shoulder as his long legs quickly closed the distance between them.

She drew in a shaky breath, leaning back into him and finding with relief that his arms closed around her without hesitation. "I just got startled."

"Want me to take the lead? We should probably get off this trail around now anyway and keep to the cover as much as we can. I'd rather see any scouts that might be posted before they see us," he said, his eyes already scanning the rocky landscape before them.

"Les?" she said, tugging his shirt to gain his attention, and then finding she wished his shuttered eyes hadn't turned to hers, as she saw just how far away he had become during their walk.

"What?" he prompted.

How could he be so close, touching her even, and seem so distant? "Are you okay?" she ventured timidly.

His hands rubbed up and down on her arms absently and his eyes scanned the surrounding landscape, lingering noticeably on the sparse forest creeping down the mountain a few hours ahead to mingle with the last of the Skycastles. "I'm fine Sylvia. We just need to be very cautious on how we approach the Caves. That hillside has a lot of trees to shield us from anyone watching from the entrance, but the forest could also be hiding things from us. I'm going to take the lead now, no more talking and I want you to stay behind me, no matter what. Try to be quiet please."

Syl glared at his retreating back after that impersonal dismissal. *'No more talking', and 'Try to be quiet, please'? Really?* Lessoran kept walking without a backwards glance, sure that she would be just a few steps behind him. But now her ire was up and she stood her ground, stubbornly crossing her arms over her chest to ward off the wind and pettily waiting for him to realize she hadn't followed. They shouldn't be loud past this point? Fine. She would stay here until he returned and then she would give him a piece of her mind, berate the answers she craved out of his stubborn mouth. How could he be okay with this situation? Did his change in demeanor have something to do with his little declaration this morning? And why was he acting like a stranger now, so close to journey's end?

She watched the drab, weather bleached cloak swathing him meld into the surrounding stone, leaving only his dark head visible before he turned around the towering base of a stocky Skycastle and vanished all together. The wind whistled past, blowing a scattering of small stone flakes and dirt onto her from the top of the fallen pillar at her back. She brushed at the back of her neck and her dangling braid, wincing at the coarse state of her skin and hair. Her all-consuming longings for a hot shower and her cozy bed had tapered off after a few weeks traveling; now she simply scraped off what she could in hopes that the sharp shards wouldn't jab into her skin when she began walking again. *If Les ever noticed she wasn't behind him that is.*

Even with the wind a constant murmur, it was strangely quiet without him in the vicinity. She had been so attuned to his presence in their travels, that having him absent felt strange. Even when he would venture off to hunt, or she would seek out solitude to relieve herself there was an expectation of companionship, that constant connection and reliance between them. Here, in this moment, she let herself separate from him. Feel the silence usually filled with his footsteps, his breath, his heartbeat.

The solitude cooled her anger, morphed it into something softer around the edges, but deeper and heavier. The sadness almost dragged her to her knees. She didn't *want* to feel separated from him. Their closeness was her only lifeline here. And that was why she was so angry with him. She wouldn't have survived without his warmth and humor, their sharing of the burdens and comforting of one another when things became overwhelming. And yet he locked it away behind cold eyes like it meant nothing to him, when it was her entire world. He hastened them towards an unknown future without a word concerning what would happen to them.

Les appeared from around the distant column at almost a sprint. Syl smiled in grim satisfaction when he skidded to a halt at the sight of her, standing exactly where he'd left her. Even from yards and yards away she could see his mouth pull down into a frown. And then he stalked towards her, anger evident in every taut line of his body. He was intimidating with that look on his face, his huge frame bearing down on her. She found herself bracing as if for a physical impact, and her unconscious reaction got her pissed at him all over again, sadness be damned. At least she was willing to fight for something she wanted. He just ignored it and gave up, the coward.

"What in Freyton's name do you think you are doing?" he growled when he was a few paces from her.

"Waiting for you to come back where I'm allowed to talk to you," she retorted instantly, watching him reel a bit from the aggression in her tone.

"Fine. Then talk," he snapped right back after one dumbfounded moment.

Sylvia smiled sweetly at him, "My pleasure. I'm just wondering what the hell crawled up your butt between this morning and now?" His mouth worked soundlessly and his face turned an enjoyable shade of purple, as he strove to find words to respond. She pushed on when he failed. "Because you're not the person I woke up with, and I can't think of one single thing that warrants this transformation. Not one single thing that would ever make *me* go from loving someone to treating them like an accessory." Syl heaved in a breath and tried to maintain her 'woman scorned' imitation. But inside she quailed at her word choice. *Loving. Oh god I used the L word. Maybe he didn't notice...*

"You're not an accessory," Les blinked, and she had the horrible suspicion that he was replaying her words in detail in his mind, but thankfully he moved past her slip of the tongue. "And nothing happened, I'm just worried about getting you to the Ancients without mishap."

"Nothing happened? You mean this has nothing to do with the fact that your tribe might be waiting for us? I wouldn't blame you if you wanted to go back to them, Les. They're your family! But I would like a little warning instead of you just cutting me out of your life!" she railed.

This time his face paled alarmingly; she could practically see all the blood leaving his cheeks. "Do we have to talk about everything? Is that a trait of the 'Humans' or simply the curse of all females? We don't know if they're there. We don't know what they want from us at this point, and we don't know if they would even have me back, so there's nothing to talk about." She opened her mouth immediately to reply but he cut her off harshly, "End of discussion, Sylvia. Now come with me and keep quiet or find your own way." He spun on his heel and strode quickly back the way he had come.

Lessoran

The closer to the base of the Crooked Mountain they got, the easier it was to see that the wisp of smoke rising from the entrance to the Caves of Orr came not from one or two fires, as he had originally thought, but from many, possibly thirty or more. His every instinct was screaming at him to get Sylvia as far away from those ominous plumes as possible, but he couldn't bring himself to break the silence looming between them. Even if he spoke up, he didn't think she would heed his advice. He'd never seen her this angry before. She was now single minded in her determination to reach the Ancients and be free of him. Both their tempers had flared red hot, but where his had cooled to annoyance and self-loathing for making a hard situation worse, hers had iced over. It still hung large between them, but now it was cold, cold and frozen in place, an almost perceptible block of icy fury separating them.

He could hear Sylvia breathing raggedly behind him, as they took the hard way around yet another fallen Skycastle. He was plotting a very careful course, trying to keep them out of sight from above, where there were doubtlessly sentries posted to keep the encampment protected. Nightfall was approaching fast, and shadows gathered secretively around them, enclosing them in an illusion of intimacy only broken by the call of voices drifting down from the plateau above. They had been dodging guards for the last few minutes of the approach, and he had seen the colors of five separate tribes, Trianti green included. Les had known it would be likely for his tribe to still be at the Caves, letting Pralick, or someone else if Freyton was feeling particularly kind, enter the Caves to be Named Morgal. But five tribes?

Five tribes at the Caves of Orr. That was unheard of, and nearly unbelievable had he not seen it with his own eyes. Relations between the Hinterlanders was dodgy at best, and between the Kla'routh and Diarmas it often resembled all-out war due to a slight that occurred so long ago, both parties had forgotten why they hated one another so much. But none the less he'd seen the purple of the Diarmas on a young scout, and the distinctive crossed arrows of the Kla'routh upon the tunic of another. He racked his mind for any instance or event in the history of his people that had called more than one or two tribes to the Caves at once, but could come up with none. Something big must have happened, or was about to, he amended, his mind veering to the Ancients and their Dreams of what lay ahead.

"Les!" The whisper was barely more than a hiss of air leaving Sylvia's lips, but its urgency had him turning as quickly and as quietly as he could, to see what she needed badly enough to actually engage him in conversation. He froze as soon as he saw her predicament, and cursed himself for a fool that he hadn't been paying closer attention. Seconds before, he'd ghosted over a small game trail, and must not have checked well enough for patrolling sentries as he let his mind wander. A gray haired soldier bearing the filed antlers, long braids, and brown clothing of a Verie had meandered up the trail between his passing and Sylvia following, trapping her on the other side where there was less cover. To make matters worse the man had paused to relieve himself just up the trail from their position.

Thinking quickly, Syl dropped to her belly and rolled as far under the cylindrical body of the pillar they had been using as cover. In the half light, shadows cloaked her well enough, but he could still make out bright patches of her pale skin. He motioned for her to remain still, and checked his own visibility. The man's back was fully to him, and he was mostly hidden by the feathery fronds of the two young Listenbarks at his side. Confident he was safe, he fished his sling from his belt, stooping slowly to arm himself with some handy rocks. If Freyton was with them, the man would finish his piss and move up the trail, none the wiser to their presence. But Freyton had never been a particularly kind God, so Les readied his lone weapon, hoping Sylvia managed to fish out their shared dagger from where she'd stowed it in the rucksack she was toting.

Seconds passed that seemed as long as minutes, until finally the trickle of urine up the trail came to a stop. The grizzled soldier shook himself off, humming softly under his breath and then glanced down the trail to their position before sauntering in the opposite direction, a tune still merrily falling from his lips. Les could see Sylvia's eyes widen from the corner of his eye as she tracked the man's movements, and heard the sigh of relief she gave when the man rounded a final corner and disappeared. He nearly dropped the sling once the moment was past; his hands had begun shaking as soon as the adrenaline rush ebbed. He looked at his quivering fingers in mild confusion. He was a seasoned warrior, and while he sometimes got the shakes after a battle, this level of physical reaction almost never happened anymore.

His gaze rose to Sylvia as she wordlessly joined him, eyes still huge in her face, the deep blue of her irises drinking in the falling darkness. One of his trembling hands reached out to brush her cheek of its own accord, and her lips quirked up in a half smile in response, before falling back into the neutral lines it had worn since their argument this morning. She jutted her chin out, indicating he should move forward again. He almost, *almost*, stopped to mend what had been broken between them. The urge to take her into his arms was so strong that he very nearly gave in, but in order to figure this out they would need to talk it through. *A reasonable request,* he acquiesced grudgingly, but talking here would place them in danger of getting caught before he knew what they were truly facing. He wanted to walk into the Caves fully aware of the lay of the land, both politically and physically. To do that they needed to get closer, undetected and figure out why in Freyton's name the Ancients had called five, *no six*, he corrected himself, adding the Verie to his mental list, tribes to the Caves all at once.

Not now then, but later, he promised himself. Letting his hand fall Les turned uphill, scoping out a path through the scraggly underbrush choking the bases of the few remaining Skycastles still lying between them and the rocky plateau that held the entrance to the Caves. They started the scramble upwards side by side, separated by the occasional tree as they fought with the tough, winter-bare branches of brambles and the fragrantly needled branches of Listenbarks. From above an undulating cry rang out, and that lone voice was soon joined by others, rising in a song as familiar to Lessoran as his own name. He tossed a glance over his shoulder, and smiled grimly at the hint of Loria's full face peeking over the horizon. Good news and bad, he knew. They were close enough that they might be able to do some reconnaissance while the tribes all sang the moon's praises. But once Loria rose fully above the distant mountains, her shining countenance would greatly enhance the chance they would be seen.

They paused beneath a rocky outcropping that lay just below the encampment; and when Sylvia would have pushed onward, he barred her way with one arm before leaning in close to whisper to her, "I want you to stay here. I'm going to try to see what's going on up there."

Her face blanched and then hardened almost as quickly. "I'm coming too" she said stubbornly.

Les restrained an eye roll. "I'm far less likely to be caught than you. And even if I'm seen, chances are it will be by someone who doesn't know me and they'll think I'm one of them."

He watched her eyes narrow dangerously before the rationality of his argument won out, and she settled back into the cliff side behind her with a huff. "Fine," she said and then resolutely looked away from him.

With a sad shake of his head he rounded the far left side of the little cliff, wincing as his hooves stirred the loose shale to rattle downhill. The song still rang out from above so he moved forward as quickly as he dared, using the sound as cover for his bolder movements. The cliff slowly merged with the surrounding hillside up ahead, growing smaller and smaller to cup the little mesa in the gentle slope of the base of the Crooked Mountain. He spied two rocks that had dislodged from the main body of the cliff, still half a man's length over his head, and wedged his body between them so he could laboriously inch up between, using opposition to secure him in place. He popped his head up over the edge briefly, cursing the thrust of his antlers towering so far above his eyes and praying to his God once again for aid in remaining undetected.

The mesa was over-crowded by people and tents. Campfires released a haze of smoke over the scene and Les had to rub at his eyes a few times in the dusk light before he finally admitted that it was not six tribes at the Caves, but representatives from all seven. Very few women or children were present, and the numbers were far too few to be the entirety of each tribe, but it looked like almost every Morgal was present with an escort of twenty or so warriors each. Far in the back of the gathering, he could make out the towering arch that marked the doorway into the Caves of Orr. Around its heavily carved base, the Ancients sat in a rough semi-circle with offerings from all the tribes laid out before them.

Piles of Ice Lion pelts from the Baroun, with their shadowy patterns of spots and whorls, were heaped next to the sturdy baskets created by the master weavers of the Rishal tribe. Huge platters of roasted deer were the obvious contribution from the Kla'routh, and the small glittering piles he could barely make out among the larger tributes must be priceless sapphires the Verie mined from their northern territories. Reams of paper and pens gleaned from lowland raids were his own tribe's gifts to the Ancients. And he spied a heavily carved Steelskin stump that had likely come from the Proult, sitting next to a dozen or more earthenware jars he knew must hold a variety of teas and Kercha from the renowned healers of the Diarmas. The Ancients laughed and smiled, their ice white eyes setting them apart from the chaotic merriment around them. They talked to one another and chatted amiably with any Trewal who ventured forth to ask questions of them. But they all kept wary eyes on the well-worn trail that terminated at the mesa. It looked as if they were waiting for someone, or something to arrive.

Inching his way back down the stone chimney, he clambered his way back to Sylvia, seeing her huddled shape exactly where he'd left her. He scooted in close to her, ignoring the scowl that darkened her face in favor of adding his body heat to hers. Her nearly constant shivering tapered off midway through his whispered description of the camp above, and by the time he had finished his account, the scowl too had dissipated.

"So you don't know why all the tribes are here?" she asked.

He shook his head negatively, "I've never heard of all the tribes being in the same place at once, not peacefully. They say that in the Age Before Memory we were all one people, but no one knows for sure what happened to break us apart, or if we were truly ever one."

"And you think the Ancients are waiting for someone?" She hesitated, "Could they be waiting for us? You said they can see the future; maybe they saw we would come tonight and they threw us a welcoming party." Her voice was so hopeful he wanted to buy into that naive scenario just to keep them on the strange middle ground they seemed to have reached in the face of making a decision.

"It's possible," he conceded, "but there's no way to know for sure. Either way, I feel like we'll be able to make it to the Ancients without trouble from Pralick-"

"Was he there?" she broke in, fear igniting in her eyes.

Anger washed over him at how quickly she regressed into the terrified girl he had first encountered, so he took her hand as he spoke his next words, hoping to coax the fierce young woman he had come to know, out once more. "He's there, newly Named as the Morgal by my tribe. But the Trianti are positioned at the far side of the clearing, near where the main trail comes to the Caves. We can come in from this side and avoid them altogether. The Ancients will hear you out before letting Pralick claim you, no matter what, and Pralick cannot dispute that right." She nodded woodenly, sucking her bottom lip into her mouth to sink her teeth into it punishingly.

"You can do this Sylvia," he said gently, tipping her chin up so her eyes met his. He wanted to kiss her, soothe away the sting her own teeth had doubtlessly left in her plump lip, give her a bit of himself as reassurance. But he was loathe to break their current rapport by pushing things too far, too fast. So instead he stood and offered her his hand, "Come on, I won't let anything happen to you, not while I still have breath in my body."

Her small hand fit into his and he pulled her to her feet, pride burning in his chest as her chin rose and her shoulders straightened.

She gathered courage to her like a cloak, and with a slight squeeze of his hand and a nod of thanks, she sailed forward, leading them into the night.

Cirillia

It was always surreal to witness a Dream play out, like a strong instance of déjà vu. But she had never before had events like this unfold right before her eyes. She usually only saw the truth of her Dreams come to fruition through the scrying bowl, or by word of mouth. So it was with slight amazement that she watched the Mage stalk through the gathered Trewal towards the Ancients.

One by one they came to their feet as she neared. She was exactly as Cirillia had Dreamed her, but she appeared even smaller than she had first thought, now that she was next to the burly Hinterland warriors. The crowd parted for the Mage, and a silence spread outwards until each and every face was focused on her and her companion as they approached the seven old men and women standing under the arched doorway to the Caves. The girl's eyes flickered between the Ancients, but never strayed to the press of bodies pushing inwards behind her. The Morgal of the Trianti stepped forward daringly, pushing past the respectful distance all others kept, to intrude on the Mage and the Ancients. Kon pinned him in place with a glare before he could truly ruin the moment, but his presence still nagged as Pernal stepped forward to address the young woman.

"Welcome Battle Mage. Freyton told us of your coming," she said simply, studying the young woman's reactions carefully. The girl blinked, but showed no further sign of surprise that they'd been expecting her. Cirillia mentally applauded her composure.

"Thank you," her voice was small and frail, the Hinterlanders at her back pressed forwards as one to better hear, causing her handsome shadow to finger the rough sling at his belt and step into the Mage even more than he was already, his flat chest nearly brushing the dirty tumble of locks that cascaded down her back.

"I have questions for the Ancients," she made it a statement rather than a request and then gestured loosely behind her, "but they are for the Ancients alone."

Pernal nodded as if she had known the Mage would ask for privacy, "Then let us enter the Caves and talk, your companion may rejoin his tribe."

She saw the girl's hand clench convulsively on Pernal's last words, and she read the tiny widening of her eyes as fear. It made Cirillia immediately aware of the connection between the two weary travelers, and she found herself wishing the Mage had kept that little tidbit to herself. As observant as herself, there was no way her peers had missed the clues. *Give away nothing of yourself in negotiations if you wish to retain anything,* she thought at the pretty girl sadly, only to wonder at her immediate mothering of the stranger.

"He remains with me." The Mage strove valiantly for dispassion, but fell short as her body tensed as if screaming in denial of being separated from its partner.

The Trianti Morgal, formerly known as Pralick, stepped forward at this to interject brusquely, "A traitor may not enter Freyton's sacred Caves!" His proclamation stirred the crowd to life, sending a flurry of whispers racing around the clearing.

Cirillia found herself wondering, yet again, how Freyton could have allowed for this beastly man to survive his Naming. His brutish and bloodthirsty ways had been mucking up their carefully laid plans since his arrival, and had nearly incited a tribal war on the very doorstep of the Caves of Orr. Wertal stepped towards the Morgal threateningly, bearing his teeth until the younger man stepped back, despite his advantage of size and youth.

"You've requested your trial, and we granted it," Wertal growled, "Do not push for more than you're deserving of, you ungrateful pup." Cirillia felt a smile sneak onto her face as the young Morgal flinched at the harshness of the scowling Ancient's words. Then she glanced at the Mage and Maegi standing side by side and her smile faded away to nothing. The Maegi's face had paled visibly at the mention of a trial, and the Mage looked sick with worry, tugging at his hand and whispering in his ear with increasing frustration as he remained frozen in place.

Without questioning the impulse, she swept forwards and gathered up the new arrivals like a mother hen, herding them into the Caves as quickly as her stiff joints allowed. They left an eddy of confusion in their wake, as the rest of the Ancients milled around, unsure what to do now that their original plan had been deviated from. The Maegi was supposed to go to his tribe to stand trial, and the Mage was to be distracted by a bath and some clean clothes and hot food while the spectacle played out. She saw consternation on Kon's face as she led the two worn travelers past him, and plain confusion painted Aerin's tiny features. But Pernal stepped back and out of their path with a glimmer of understanding in her eyes. *Maybe,* Cirillia thought, *I have an ally there, one who finds our new Morgal as abhorrent as I do.*

"Where are we going?" The girl slowed her pace now that they were safely in the Caves, and she looked around cautiously, seeming none too pleased to be underground, never mind their close escape from the dangerous Morgal waiting outside.

"I thought you might like a bath after all your travels," Cirillia said, beckoning them onward towards the natural hot springs that warmed the Caves and served as a bathing pool for the resident Seers. Her sharp eyes picked out their joined hands in the dim light of the hall. "I would mention that we have two separate rooms, but it seems that you may not require the privacy."

The young Mage dropped her companion's hand like it had burned her, bringing the trio to an abrupt halt just outside the cavernous communal bathing room. She bit her lip as she considered Cirillia before sticking out her hand in a peculiar manner and introducing herself, "My name is Sylvia Eldritch, and this is Lessoran, Maegi of the Trianti."

Cirillia looked at the proffered hand bemusedly, unsure what the girl was offering to her. With a shrug she took the slim hand in her own and turned it palm downwards, pressing a light kiss to the back before releasing it. "I am Cirillia." She looked into the haggard face of the traitor Maegi, still shocked to silence. "I suggest you use what brief privacy you have here to say a proper goodbye," she told him, and then ushered the two into the room and closed the rounded door behind, taking up a position opposite to await her peers and their furious questions. Sure enough, five old men and women came bearing down on her shortly, each with varying degrees of anger or upset on their faces. Kon came in the lead, as he was wont to do, absolutely livid at her high handed disruption of the events that had transpired outside the Caves.

"Cirillia! What is the meaning of this? We agreed to appease the Trianti Morgal with the Maegi's blood!" he admonished.

She shrugged uncomfortably, "It was not a well thought out action, but one of instinct. I couldn't ignore the impulse Kon. I am truly sorry for acting without the knowledge of all the Ancients, but it had to be done." She tried to keep her voice firm in support of her actions, but inside she quailed at the disapproval on Kon's face. Behind him, only Pernal looked sympathetic, the rest watched the confrontation consideringly, looking for the ulterior motives behind both her actions, and Kon's obvious ire at their original plan going awry. *What plans of his did I disrupt?* she had to wonder. *What deal did he strike with the Morgal of the Trianti?*

"Fine. It's all fine, we can save this situation," Kon said, making his way past her towards the door to the bathing chambers.

As one she, Pernal, and even tiny Aerin blocked the old man's path. "One does not disturb a woman at her bath." Pernal said gently when Kon's face reddened with fury at their interference. "We need this Mage. And even if we have her in our hands now, things will go easier for us if she bears us no ill will. Let them bathe in peace, let them sup afterwards. Did you not see the love with which she looks at him? We agreed payment of his blood, Kon, when it is not ours to give, but we never specified a time."

Aerin spoke, taking up Pernal's words almost seamlessly, "The Trianti will be payed. But we must secure the Mage first. Do you not think she will argue the trial? Do you not think she will rebel? We must move cautiously, and consider."

Slowly Kon's tension lessened, the women's soft words soothing the urgency he'd been approaching the situation with. With a sigh of relief Cirillia urged the cluster of elderly Trewal to move in the direction of the kitchens in search of Kercha. They were now fully engaged in the conversation of how to deal with the young Mage's obvious attachment to her protector, and the promises they had already made concerning him. Looking behind the tight group, Cirillia saw Wertal linger behind. He nodded at her gravely before settling his large frame back against the wall opposite the bathing chamber's door. *Guarding them, or spying on them,* she wondered?

They entered the kitchens and poured Kercha all around, eliciting a moment's respite to the near constant chatter that had taken hold. Cirillia resisted the urge to savor the rich, dark liquid in favor of studying the people around her. It was impossible to know the motives they each moved with, or who, if any of them, had been set by Freyton on some hidden agenda. She knew she hadn't. She had simply felt the pangs of motherhood in her withered womb, and wanted to protect that fragile girl with the blue eyes from the pain the next few days might bring. She could be spared some of that pain she knew, but they would all have to agree to go back on their agreement with the Trianti. It was a dangerous decision to make, one she feared no one but her would be willing to do, as it would be seen as a slight to the powerful tribe.

"How do we keep the Mage happy *and* the Trianti?" Folt spoke out into the quiet chamber once the sighs and appreciative murmurs faded into the slurping of hot liquid.

"Do we *need* to keep the Mage happy?" Kon asked. "We don't know if she's trained in her magic. At her age it wouldn't be unheard of for her powers not to have surfaced yet. If she isn't trained, or is only just learning, she's no threat to us and we can proceed as we originally planned."

His return to their initial plan cemented her inkling that he had made some sort of deal with the Trianti's new Morgal concerning the Maegi, but it lent her no insights as to what Kon could possibly be getting out of the deal.

"And if she's in full control of her powers?" Aerin asked, looking Kon straight in the eyes. "The consequences could be disastrous. I think a trial is not something we can risk until we know the full extent of her training."

"I agree," Cirillia put in, happy that her peers were at least aware of the possibility that their preemptive promise to the Trianti had jeopardized the entire future of their people. "We need her, and are at the disadvantage of not knowing if she needs us, or is sympathetic to our cause. You all saw her strangeness." Heads nodded all around as their minds mulled over the girl's strange legs, stunted ears and hornless head. "She is not of the Hinterlands. We must find out what she wants, and offer it to her in return for her cooperation." Again heads bobbed in agreement along the table.

Kon spoke up, agitation barely concealed beneath a cool facade. "Then the traitor Maegi stays, at least until we speak with our Mage." Again the heads nodded, and this time when Cirillia sipped her steaming Kercha she closed her eyes in enjoyment, allowing the spicy taste to soak its soothing warmth into her bones.

Lessoran

"Les? Les, look at me!" Sylvia's nearly frantic voice grew muffled as he drew his filthy tunic over his head, then it pierced through again, "Please tell me what's going on! What's wrong with you? What's a trial?"

It was surprisingly easy to turn away from her imploring face in his current state of mind. Usually her distress ate away at him until his every thought was of how to make her feel better, but right now he was cushioned from it, held at a distance somehow. *Shock,* he told himself, *I'm in shock.* He shucked off his trousers and turned to the steaming pool taking up the majority of the large room. Candles rested in recesses throughout the space, casting golden light over the gently rippling surface of the hot springs and throwing glittering spangles of reflection over the rocky ceiling. He eased one hoof down onto the first submerged step, distantly hearing Sylvia muttering angrily to herself over the soft noises of her own disrobing.

He stepped down twice more, watching in fascinated disgust as the slight current dislodged weeks of grime from his body to muddy the clear liquid. Murky water trailed off to the far edge of the cave where the rock had been cleverly chiseled away so the spring fed pool always remained at the same height. The dust and dirt of their travels joined the flowing water to cascade over that edge and into the carved trough behind, which then dissipated through a dark crevasse in the wall. He submerged fully, turning onto his back to float in the scalding water with closed eyes. Liquid covered his ears, blocking out all sound, leaving him isolated in the warmth and movement.

Is this what awaits me afterwards? The sensory deprivation of a womb? It would be fitting for life after death to resemble the life that lay before true life. Maybe it's a cycle, and in entering that womb-like space I am simply waiting to be born again. His mind then turned to what he had always been taught, that the Afterlife was reserved for those who died gloriously, in battle or after years and years of living. Only the kiss of fire may release a Hinterlander to live with the Gods in the next life, he knew, and fire would have no part in his demise if a trial took place. With a start he felt fingers trail through his hair, jarring him from that other-world space. He dunked his head under, wetting his face before he rose to his feet, facing Sylvia, seeing her pale face clearly for the first time since the new Morgal of his tribe had spoken to them.

She was up to her collarbones in the water, a surprisingly cautious look on her face when he would have expected ire. The water lapped at his navel, the steam rising fended off the slight chill in the room and beaded Sylvia's still dry hair in droplets of water. The thin wisps of fine hair at her temples curled into the moisture and framed her face in a halo of dark curls. She was achingly beautiful. He took her shoulders in hand when the silence stretched, turning her around and latching his arm under hers to tow her back into the shallows so when she stood her back and the swell of her bottom was bared. He grabbed a coarse woven cloth from one of the shelves by the edge of the pool and began methodically washing her, until her pale skin was pink from the scrubbing.

Little was said aside from his occasional commands to 'dunk' or 'turn'. He was grateful for her unspoken compliance. He needed some time, needed to process before explaining to her what was going to happen. She would need him to comfort her when she found out, and he didn't know if he was capable of that yet.

Now that the muck was scrubbed clean, she glowed. He had thought her skin had browned from all their time outside in the elements, but it had just been that overlying layer of dirt. Now she shone, so pale and white that a fine tracery of blue veins beneath her skin was clearly visible. Pink tinged her cheeks and her incredible eyes were half closed in enjoyment as he massaged his hands through her hair to clean the dark strands. She was squeaky clean, reclining in the water as he crouched by her side, but he didn't want to stop touching her yet, so he simply continued. Finally, her eyes opened all the way and fixed on him, and he knew the brief respite she had granted him was over.

"What is this trial?" she asked calmly, finding a bar of lavender scented soap situated conveniently near, and taking the washing cloth from his lax hands to run it over his chest as they kneeled in the water.

"A way for the tribe to agree to pass sentence on a tribe member," he said evasively as her hands pushed him back into the water so she could lather his hair. A stray soap bubble caught his eye and he hurriedly dunked his whole head, escaping her clutches and pushing into deeper water.

"Why does your tribe want to pass sentence on you?" The question came in fits and starts as he surged from the water to rub at his eyes. He smoothed his clean hair back from his face, leaning back into the water to wash the last few suds away.

"For stealing another man's property. For leaving the tribe unprotected without their head Maegi." He finally looked at her, "For conspiring against the new Morgal."

"Weren't you just doing what the last Morgal told you to?" Sylvia asked.

"When we left, the old Morgal had been defeated. He was not the Morgal anymore, even if he had lived."

Her head cocked to the side as she digested that information, then she walked out towards him until her feet no longer reached the bottom and pushed off, gliding through the water to reach him. She wrapped her legs around his waist so she wouldn't have to tread water, and then asked the question looming between them. "What's the sentence for your crimes, Lessoran?"

He cupped her bottom, pulling her as close as he could and buried his face in her neck, smelling lavender and clean skin and Sylvia. "The punishment for stealing another man's property is that you relinquish that property back to him, along with your most prized weapon. I have a beautiful iron dagger, made from ore mined in these Caves. I will have to give it, and you, to Pralick." She nodded against his hair as if that was expected and squeezed her thighs around him to prompt the next punishment.

"For leaving my people in a compromised position, the tribe will likely want penance. Most commonly they choose the lash, the number of strikes will be voted upon." She shivered against him and her hands tightened convulsively on his back.

"Disloyalty to the Morgal is a crime the Morgal decides how to punish. The tribe will get their say, and a smart leader would follow the wishes of his people. But I don't count Pralick as smart, nor a good leader." He decided to not mention that the Morgal could, and likely would, call for his death due to their long-standing antagonism.

"How do you think he'll punish you? What's the worst he could do?" she pushed.

Les leaned back from their twined bodies so he could see her face in the soft light. With a heavy sigh he gave in to her prodding, laying down the heavy burden of knowledge that had been sitting in him like an anvil since the Ancients had confirmed their support of a trial. "You heard the Ancient didn't you? She said to say goodbye. Pralick will kill me, Sylvia, a traitor's death by stoning."

"No," her head shook side to side helplessly, "no, no, no! That's not going to happen, we can leave. We'll just leave and go somewhere else." Her eyes pleaded with him to alleviate the sudden terror that had taken hold.

"It's not that simple. They were waiting for *you*. The Ancients, seven tribes and their best warriors, all waiting for you. I don't know why, but they're not just going to let you walk out of here, and Pralick will not let me go either, not without his revenge."

"I don't care if it's not simple!" she raged, hitting his chest and splashing water into both of their faces. "We'll escape! We'll trick them! I don't care how we do it but we will get out of here! And you will be alive and then we can go find Ryland and Torman, they will keep us safe." She was out of breath and wiping water from her face by the time her words wound down.

Vaguely disturbed by the thought of her rushing to other men for protection Les smoothed her hair, drawing her close again to run a hand down her back soothingly. He was strangely elated that she so easily forgot her own quest to find home when his life was threatened. "What about asking the Ancients how to get you home?" he asked.

"Oh screw that! If they want to let that beast of a man kill you, then I don't want their advice anyway. And I sure as hell don't want to owe them any favors!" She scowled fiercely, making him smile.

"Then we need to escape." She nodded vehemently, easing the tightness in his chest slightly. "I haven't the faintest idea how we are going to do that," he admitted.

"Well, if the Ancients were waiting for us then maybe they need something? If they need something we have, then we could trade it for safe passage."

Les considered, impressed that her mind moved so quickly. "That's possible, but it depends on what they want. They called you Mage, so I'm guessing they want to use your magic in some way."

"I don't have any magic!" she said in exasperation.

"They don't know that," he reminded her, "And them thinking you are more powerful than any of them might just be our only way out of here."

She nodded in agreement. "Okay, so we talk with the Ancients and then try to bargain? What happens if what they want isn't something we can bargain with? Do you know the Caves very well? Is there another exit we could make a run for? They are pretty old, I bet we could outrun them as long as we don't have to go back through all the tribes out front."

He almost laughed out loud at her casual dismissal of the Ancients as "pretty old'. "They may be old Sylvia but they are far from helpless. Only the most powerful Maegi become Ancients and their magic when working together is formidable."

"Right, magic." She sighed dejectedly, fiddling with the Morgal's medallion Les still wore around his neck, he was supposed to give it to the Ancients, he reminded himself. "I always forget about the damn magic."

"We just need to go talk with them. It seems they are giving us at least tonight before they allow the trial to proceed. So we talk with them, and if nothing comes up to barter for our release, then tonight we run," he said, feeling like he was finally on solid ground again.

"Alright then. Plan made," she affirmed, "I just have to act like some powerhouse Mage and intimidate them into compliance!" She drew herself up, nose in the air and an overly disdainful sneer twisting her lips.

Les laughed, and then, grabbing on to that fleeting levity, he moved in quickly, sealing his mouth over hers. His hands slid over her, and he found himself striding to the wall of the pool as they kissed so he could brace her against it, loving the instinctual spread of her thighs as he pushed against her softer body. She broke the desperate kiss with a gasp to whisper in his ear, even as her legs pulled him closer, "I'm still mad at you."

He slowed his advance, giving her every opportunity to stop him, even as his body screamed at the delay. "How mad?" he asked.

Her heels dug into the backs of his legs forcefully, urging him forwards, uniting their bodies, and eliciting a gasp from both of their mouths before she spoke again, her voice higher than before and pleasingly breathy, "Not *that* mad."

Sylvia

The clothes she found laid out for her in the bathing chamber were too big, but wonderfully clean. A light and exquisitely soft shift in pale blue was paired with a much heavier knitted robe in charcoal gray. They had even provided a woven leather belt to hold the loose folds tight to her body. She was glad for the luxurious warmth of the outer robe when she cracked open the door of the bathing room, letting in a gust of chilly air along with the kindly looking Ancient that had first escorted them into the Caves. She had scrounged around to find a replacement set of clothes for Lessoran, and she and Sylvia went out into the hall to wait while Les dressed.

Outside the largest of the old Seers stood like a sentinel, his dark horns capping his head a good two feet above her own before they curved down in onyx ridges. His lined face was scarred and leathery, and when his lips parted in a smile she saw the tips of his teeth were pointed like a carnivore's. He gave her the heeby-jeebys, but when he slanted a wink her way after she shied away from his slight bow of acknowledgment, she felt strangely comforted.

"This is Wertal," the female Ancient said, smiling at her in a friendly way.

"Hello. I'm Sylvia," she offered to the giant who nodded in return. Turning to the woman she asked, "I'm sorry but I forgot your name in all the commotion."

"Cirillia." That friendly smile came back and Sylvia had to reel in her immediate liking for the grandmotherly figure, reminding herself she could very well be her enemy.

Les walked through the door in a billow of steam, leaving it open behind him to circulate the moist air. His borrowed garments fit much better than hers did. A thrill raced through her just looking at him, all hard muscles and clean skin wrapped up in deep green cloth and an open necked robe. He went to Cirillia immediately, taking her hand with a bow and brushing his lips over the back of her liver spotted hand. "Cirillia, it's good to see you again," he said, shocking Syl into realizing that he knew the withered old woman.

"And you Lessoran. Last I saw you, you were tormenting your young friends with their own personal rain clouds," she teased familiarly.

Les's cheeks blushed faintly, much to Syl's amazement. "That was a long time ago," he said with a faint laugh.

"Yes," Cirillia said, looking him up and down, "Yes it was. Now come, we have hot Kercha and food for you, along with a few questions about your adventures."

Cirillia and the silent Wertal led them through the carved corridors. A pervading smell of wet iron permeated the Caves, emanating from the streaks of rust weeping down the walls. It made her feel like she was walking through the site of an ages old massacre. The remaining Ancients awaited them at a long table in a cozy kitchen room, along with heaping plates of steamed vegetables, roasted meat, various cheeses and freshly baked bread that set her mouth to watering in record time.

The old woman who had first spoken to them outside the caves gestured for them to join the informal gathering. "Come, eat. I know we all have questions, but fill your bellies first, then we can talk." Syl and Les took a seat on the long bench at the outer edge of the table, tucking into the feast without a word. She kept her leg pressed close to his under the table, needing his warmth to settle the nerves that had come to flutter in her stomach as soon as they stepped from the sanctuary of their bath.

Soon enough her wooden fork was scraping the last remnants of creamy mashed cheerum from her empty plate, and she let her eyes rise from her hands to scan the intent faces surrounding them. Les's hand found her leg under the table and gave it a squeeze, reminding her they had decided it would be best if it looked like she was the leader in their tiny band of two. It would make it more believable that she was an insanely powerful Mage, if he deferred to her.

"What are your names?" she queried, and then listened with half her mind as they went around the table to introduce themselves, already knowing she wouldn't remember all the foreign sounding titles. She counted their number absently, and then tallied it once more in confusion. "Where is the seventh?" she asked suddenly.

They exchanged glances, and the smallest of the men, with a brilliantly white shock of hair bushing out from his head, spoke up. "We lost one of our number just a few days ago" he said with a sad shake of his head, "Freyton welcomed him home as he slept and we await a new brother or sister from the Diarmas tribe, but Freyton hasn't yet told us when they will arrive."

"You said you came to the Caves of Orr to ask us a question?" Cirillia prompted when the silence after the man's statement became overlong as Sylvia searched for a way to proceed.

"I did. I want to know why I'm here," she said, feeling immediately uncomfortable at the pleased looks that flashed across the six elderly faces.

"Freyton knows why you are here, and he has shown us your destiny," the man with the white, white hair said.

"And why is that?" she asked cautiously, trying to read meaning into the sudden tightening of Lessoran's hand on her thigh.

"He's shown us visions of the Battle Mage's coming," chimed in another of the Seers.

"Of how she unites the Hinterland tribes behind her," came the deep voice of Wertal.

"And leads our people to glory against the Jorgens"

"Leads us to reclaim Fallon, to usher in the Age of the Hinterlanders"

"Freyton told us of you, Battle Mage, and promised us your help in defeating his oldest enemies," a tiny woman with long, braided hair finished for the group.

Their smiles seemed suddenly sinister to her, and the way that they finished one another's thoughts creeped her the hell out. She wanted out of here, away from their ridiculous insistence that she was something she was obviously not. But in order to begin their escape, since magic was the one thing she could *not* use to bargain with, seeing as she didn't have any, she had to get them to leave her and Les alone together.

"You think I'm this Battle Mage?" she asked incredulously, hiding a wince as Les's hand clamped down on her leg in a clear warning.

"We saw your face, and that of your companion," Cirillia explained, smiling at them both. "Behind you rode the combined tribes, and in your hands was the torn standard of the Jorgens."

"Why do you want to defeat the Jorgens?" she asked in confusion, completely blindsided by this turn of events. She knew the tribes raided the Holm, she had seen that first hand, but an all-out war?

"To recover Fallon, the seat of Freyton in our mortal world." Wertal answered for the other Seer, his voice suggesting it was a fact she should know.

Not wanting to reveal her ignorance of this world, she moved on, "Why would I fight for your cause?" she asked, feeling Les caress her with his thumb as she moved back into less dangerous territory.

"Yes, why would you?" the white haired one said, making it obvious that he was asking what it would take to gain her cooperation.

"Well that depends..." she hedged, unsure where to go from here. The Ancients were essentially playing right into their bargaining plan, but she did not actually possess what it was they wanted, the power of a Mage. How far could she take this ruse? Far enough for them to escape? Or would lying about her abilities get them into a worse situation?

"We are being such rude hosts tonight!" Cirillia barreled in, rescuing Sylvia from her indecision, "Kon, we do not use the kitchen table as a bartering platform, and we should not pressure our guests so incessantly on their very first night safe from their travels!" She clapped her hands together, rising to bustle about, urging the others to their feet with stunned looks still on their faces.

"We have chambers prepared for you both, a real bed, and some sound sleep should restore everyone. We can get down to this more serious business in the morning. Sylvia dear, I assume you can light the fire in your room by yourself," the woman shot her a challenging look, "so pop on down, third doorway on the right once you turn left outside this room. I will come make sure everything is to your satisfaction in a few moments. Lessoran, you have the first room on the left." She chided everyone into action, propelling Sylvia and Les out the door and whisking the platters from the table and into the waiting hands of her fellows.

The tiny woman, Aerin, wandered out into the hall with them, shrugging as they looked at her leaving the cleaning work up to the others. "I'm too short to reach the dishes in the bottom of the wash sink, and far too small for putting anything away," she explained with a rueful air. She escorted them down the long hall, shutting the door behind Lessoran firmly when he entered his room. Syl began to panic as they walked the long yards away from his door to where hers lay, remembering the challenge in Cirillia's eyes as she told her to light the fires in her room. She had a sneaking suspicion that it was a test, and that no handy matches or lighter would be waiting for her. They wanted to know if she could perform magic.

Thinking fast she rushed into the room to collapse on the bed with an exaggerated yawn. Aerin looked on with a smile. "This room will do wonderfully, thank you. I'm so exhausted from the last few weeks I think I'll just go straight to bed," she told the woman, aiming to dissuade Cirillia coming to check on her.

"Sleep well then Sylvia, until tomorrow," Aerin replied easily, shutting the door and plunging her into total darkness.

Syl sat up immediately and pulled back the heap of fur covers that graced the bed, clambering in with her clothes still in place. She nearly tipped over when she tried to get back on the bed, disoriented by the blackness around her. Then she lay still, eyes closed, feigning sleep as she waited for Cirillia to come. Minutes passed and she strained her ears for any sound, impatient for the rest of the Caves to take to their beds also, hopefully allowing her and Les free reign of the halls to attempt their escape. Sometime later a soft knock sounded and the door cracked open to the bright glow of a globelight. Syl focused on breathing slowly and evenly until, endless moments later, the door snicked shut once more.

Over an hour later she crept down the dark hall by touch, listening intently for any sign that the Ancients had posted a guard of some sort between her and Lessoran, but she heard nothing beyond her own quiet breathing. Then the slight squeal of hinges resounded through the hall, freezing her in her tracks. With relief she saw a light emanate from the door Les had disappeared into earlier, and his lithe figure appeared as a shadow on the opposite wall. He stooped to touch the hinges of the door and then shut it, quietly this time.

He met her in just a few steps, pressing a finger to her lips in warning and glancing up and down the hallway warily. "Les," she whispered as quietly as she could, "We need to get out of here, I want no part of this." He nodded in consent and then took her hand to lead them back up the hallway towards where the kitchen was. The door was shut, but enough light leaked out from the edges that Les extinguished his globelight. Murmurs could be heard from within, a female voice rising above to argue that 'they still had no proof she could use her powers'. Syl and Les exchanged a glance, confirming that they needed to leave as soon as possible. This place was becoming too dangerous for both of them.

She felt like they wandered the dank halls for hours. She became hopelessly turned around when they had to dash down a small side corridor to hide in what looked to be a laundry room, when the voices of the Ancients seemed to be chasing them down. But the voices passed, and they crept out again, Sylvia having to trust in Les's sense of direction as her own was dismally confused. Eventually they found themselves peering out of the thin cracks that edged the giant stone door at the entrance to the Caves. Fires still burned on the plateau, and men's voices could be heard occasionally despite the late hour. The camp sprawled to the very edges of the clearing where the trees began. Looking at the spectacle, Syl began to doubt they could possibly win their freedom this way. There were simply too many people who might detect them.

Les took her hand and towed her close so he could speak right in her ear. "I thought long and hard about this Syl, it's our only option; we can't just wander around in hopes of finding a different way out. I'm going to call a storm, as powerful and loud as I can," he said, "Hopefully it will be enough to cover us and wash away any tracks we leave." She nodded her assent, glad that he had a plan, because she was officially out of her depth.

Les's eyes closed and that familiar tingle rushed over her skin from where they touched. She stepped back, rubbing a hand up and down her arm to settle the goose pimples that rose. Long moments passed and she watched the dark corridor behind them apprehensively, until a low roll of thunder sounded from outside and the first smattering of raindrops cascaded down, wafting the familiar scent of wet dirt into the Caves. Les's eyes opened tiredly and she winced at how haggard that fifteen minutes of magic had made him. "You okay?" she asked.

He nodded. "This is a big one, it'll take a while to build fully." He went to the wall by the door and slid down until he was sitting with his back fit snugly between two carved pillars heavily knobbed with stone roses. "The storm is going to feed off my power until it peaks. I can't stop it at this point," he paused as another peal of thunder sounded, "I'm not going to have much left in a bit, so we can't rely on my magic after about twenty more minutes here."

Frowning, she looked at him, worried by how exhausted he seemed already, especially if the storm would take more of his strength in the next half hour. "Shouldn't we go now, then?"

He grimaced, "Probably."

He grabbed her proffered hand to help him to his feet. Approaching the door, they could feel the wind pushing at the cracks, rising in power. Les swept her into a hug when she reached for the door handle, kissing her almost painfully. "We can do this, Les," she said, worried that the amorous moment felt a little like a goodbye. "Just turn left, go for the trees. You said we should make our way northeast right? Head for the other side of the Skypeaks and the coast?" He nodded against her neck, still holding her tightly.

She tugged at an antler to get him to look at her and then kissed him, smiling as she repeated, "We can do this, Les". He smiled back shakily, and abruptly loosed her to unlatch the silver necklace that had been around his neck everyday of their travels. He draped it over her head, and the circular charm nestled warmly between her breasts. Then she was reaching for the handle and once the latch opened, the wind tore it from her hands; it crashed resoundingly against the inside wall, and she thought she saw a light flare up from down the corridor as they fled out into the gale. Rain came pelting in sideways, making it hard to see straight ahead. Shielding one side of her face with her hand she headed left, her other hand engulfed in Les's warm grip. Their clasped hands slowed her down, and she found herself tugging him behind her as he staggered along in her wake. The globelight he had conjured when they left the Caves guttered out mere seconds after he brought it to life, and Sylvia began to fear he was too weak to even find their way out of the crowded camp.

The tents around them had been buttoned down against the storm and few men remained outside in the weather. Campfires guttered, lending the air an unpleasant ashy odor. She saw the tree line ahead as she wound around another tent, but then she reversed her forward momentum, crashing into Les and sending them toppling down behind a tent in the nick of time, as two sentries exchanged posts just ahead. Beneath her Les groaned in time to another crash of thunder and she felt the muddy ground soak through her new clothes. Behind them, another noise was rising. At first she thought it was just another facet of the storm, but then she saw lights shooting up into the angry sky, illuminating the plateau dimly. Heads poked grudgingly from tents and voices rose in question, adding to the cacophony that raged around them.

Sylvia lay still atop Lessoran, ignoring his feeble attempts to push her off as she kept them low to the ground and below eyesight between two tents. She leaned out and around one tent, looking back towards the Caves. Seeing the growing crowd of warriors, she quickly pulled back and wiggled off Les to peer out in the other direction. "Les!" she yelled over the pounding rain, "They know we're gone! We have sentries between us and the forest, looking our way, but it's our only chance!"

Far above, the globelights spread out, covering the plateau equally with their brilliance, urging Sylvia to move. She stumbled to her feet and tried to heave Les up after her, tucking her hands into his armpits and pulling with all her might until he got his hooves back under him. Shouts neared, and the tents they sheltered between showed signs of movement within. Tossing Les's arm over her shoulders she ran towards the beckoning trees, seeing the pale blotches of two soldier's faces turn towards them from where they stood at the edge of the encampment.

"Stop them!" The furious cry barely topped the noise of the storm, but it was then taken up by more voices, until the mountains rang with the call. An arrow skittered over the muddy ground to their left. Sylvia tried to shoulder more of Les's bulky weight to gain speed, but his tired legs couldn't move any faster and her urging almost sent them to the ground once more.

"Go! Syl, just go!" Lessoran panted in her ear. "I'll get away on my own!" He tried to push her onward but she clung to him furiously.

"Shut up and run!" she screamed at him, her breath coming in heaves and her legs starting to tremble from the added weight. The two soldiers in front of them had arrows notched to their bows and were advancing cautiously.

A sheet of fire lanced through the air to her right when she attempted to swerve them away from the men, prompting a scream of terror from her that the storm snatched away almost before it had left her mouth. Spears of fire fell around them in earnest now and with dismay she saw one bury itself into the meat of Les's shoulder, even as she tried to pull him from its path. He threw his head back in agony, dislodging her from beneath his arm as he instinctively reached for the wound. And then the roar of a horribly familiar voice from behind nearly stopped her heart.

"No fire! Don't touch the traitor with fire! He is mine!"
Pralick's command was almost immediately followed by another
voice, this one trembling with age.

"Bring me the girl! Do not hurt the Mage!"

The fire began to fall in a wider swath, hemming them in on
the sides as the mob at their back advanced, and the men to the front
stood their ground. Behind the two lone sentries she saw the trees
twisting unnaturally as a hedge of vines sprang into sudden life
between them, completely blocking off their escape. "No!" she
screamed in fury, scrabbling for Les's arm again and trying to drag
him to his feet from where he had collapsed to his knees. "Get up,
Les," she sobbed, tears and rain mixing on her cheeks, "Get up,
please!"

A hard hand grabbed her and tossed her like a doll back
towards the milling crowd, where she careened into the arms of a
large soldier whose face was obscured by a leather helm. He held her
arms fast to her sides as she struggled to get back to Les. The man
that threw her pushed his hoof into Lessoran's back, shoving him
face first into the mud. A brilliant strike of lightning sizzled through
the air, illuminating Pralick's grinning face as he dashed his wet hair
out of his eyes. Sylvia felt hands on her face, and vaguely noticed the
grandmotherly visage of Cirillia in her periphery. Questions
peppered her, but she couldn't take her eyes off the man standing
over Les.

"Sylvia, are you okay? Are you hurt anywhere? Let's get you
back inside where we can dry you off and figure this out..."

She only had eyes for Les. He was stubbornly trying to gain
his feet despite the sharp hoof centered in his back. His efforts did
little but allow him to turn under the pressure until his face was
visible to her, streaked with mud. He caught sight of her, held
captive but still struggling to free herself, and stilled, the connection
of their eyes almost a physical thing. Then his efforts redoubled and
Pralick howled with laughter.

"You deny me a trial?" he crowed at the Ancients in the
crowd, brandishing the ax that had sliced easily into the old Morgal's

belly. "I make my own trial!" Tendons stood out in his thick neck as he yelled, hatred twisting his face. "Maegi! I find you guilty!"

Pralick lifted his leg upwards, easing the pressure keeping Les pinned, and then, when the tired Maegi surged upwards, he kicked out, sending him tumbling head over heels to lay winded on the ground. Pralick advanced, bringing his ax arcing up, and then flashing down.

Time seemed to stop. The fall of the ax an endless thing that allowed Syl's eyes to take in every inch of the scene in exact, terrible detail. The position of Lessoran's exhausted body sprawled in the mud, heaving to bring air back into his lungs. The utterly animalistic snarl that turned Pralick's homely face into the visage of a monster. The inevitably falling ax that abruptly terminated into Lessoran's neck.

She screamed, disbelief and horror coupling inside to freeze her, holding her immobile as the scream went on and on. Pralick tugged the ax out, and it came grudgingly, as loathe to leave Les as she was. An impossibly bright spray of blood spurted after it, and Sylvia's scream died to unintelligible ranting as her lover's face slowly paled, his green eyes becoming dull and lifeless above his ruined neck. The pulsing blood stopped and so did her voice. Only sobs escaped her now as she shoved uselessly at the arms holding her captive.

"Sylvia, oh Sylvia, look at me child. Don't watch." Knobby hands forced her gaze away from Les's body and angled her head towards Cirillia's sad eyes. Sudden, helpless rage spilled out of her, from every pore in her body the anger spewed outwards. How dare this woman look sad! Sad at an action she could have stopped, sad for a girl she knew nothing about and simply wanted for her power.

"NO!" she screamed and the soldier holding her was inexplicably flung to the side. Cirillia, too, rebounded to go sprawling in the mud, a look of utter disbelief on her aged face. After one stunned moment where everyone stood in shock, more soldiers rushed in to grab at her.

"LES!" she howled as arms reached for her, "LES!" She fought towards him through a thicket of grasping hands, each of her outbursts somehow sending the mob around her tumbling back until incredulously, she realized she was slowly rising above the soldier who had previously held her captive. He was now scrambling away from her on all fours, her waist reaching head height of the crowd hastily backing away, and now her knees. Her ascent stopped when she hovered with her feet even to the tallest antlers of the hesitant crowd. And she saw in distant fascination that the blue glow suffusing the plateau now came from her, like she had sucked all the brilliance from the Hinterlander's globelights, and was now throwing that light back out into the world.

From her vantage she could see a little patch of bare earth, the small hole in the mass of Trewal below her that held Lessoran. The Hinterlanders gave that blood spattered tract of mud a wide berth. Her eyes found his face. He was barely recognizable to her, death stealing the color and humor from his handsome features and leaving only white skin and red blood. Emotion surged and she felt like she was coming apart at the seams, as a wave of grief and horror came boiling up from inside until all she could do was throw her head back in a scream to try to relieve the terrible pressure.

Cirillia

Agony flared from the wrist she had braced against the ground when she fell. But Cirillia pushed it to the back of her mind, focusing instead on the sight of the Mage rising up into the air despite the hands trying to drag her back to earth. The winds, already raging because of the storm, rose to a frenzy, whipping her robe this way and that and sending dusty grit from the mountain sailing through the air to sting her flesh. She saw the moment Sylvia's eyes connected with the body of her companion, saw the grief twist her young features into a semblance of old age, her beauty stripped away by pain. And then all of Freyton's fury burst loose into the world.

First there was a concussion of air, a detonation that centered from the Mage's lips as she screamed her loss. The world twisted sideways as Cirillia was tossed into the heavens and pushed away. The cliff at her back arrested her flight jarringly, but from her slumped position at the base of the cliff she saw some unfortunate souls sail over the edge of the plateau and off into open air. Their feeble cries paled in comparison to the inhuman wail being emitted from the eerily glowing girl; but she barely had time to note its high whine, before the spattering rain thickened to a deluge dense enough to make drawing her next breath nearly impossible.

As she fought for breath, she saw the towering form of the Trianti Morgal fighting his way towards the hovering Mage. His cloak was pulled up to shield his nose and mouth, creating a small pocket of oxygen for him as the air was too thick with pounding water to provide breath. She copied his posture, gasping in moist air as the rain sheeted down the cloth of her robe. The unnatural blue light flickered in time to a crashing noise, bringing her attention back to the Mage, barely visible through the downpour. Pralick flung himself at her, a huge leap that should have carried him well within striking distance, but he was flung aside at the last second with a sound like a gong, and the light flickered again.

Sylvia was screaming at him, words lost in the fury of the storm. Then Cirillia saw her point at the fallen Morgal, her pale face frozen in a rictus of hate. Lightning flashed downwards, so bright it forced her eyes away from the point of impact, but she knew the Morgal was no more. Moments later she was struggling upright as the people around her began to run, crawl and limp away. She saw swarming masses of giant Windthorn roses crawling over fallen bodies towards her. The tangle grew up under Sylvia like some grotesque stem upholding the blooming Mage and raced outwards, impaling still struggling Hinterlanders upon wicked thorns and silencing their cries with strangle holds. She saw the fit young bodies racing past her and knew she could not outrun the flood of thorns. Cirillia grasped inside herself for the coppery well of Earth magic, pulling it into her body and pushing it outwards to fill every space in her skin.

How long she held onto her magic she didn't know. It could have been seconds, or minutes that passed as she pushed every ounce of her will power outwards to ward off the titanic flood of Earth, Air, Water and Fire that drenched the base of the Crooked Peak. When she opened her eyes the air was strangely still. Sunlight beat down on her sopping head from above, the clear blue of the sky tempting her to believe what had transpired when her eyes were open last was nothing but a dream. But then her gaze drifted to the destruction that surrounded her.

Blooming Windthorn roses covered the plateau, disguising the stains of blood with their brilliant red petals. The men who were killed by the first concussion, or drowned in the rain, were nothing but lumps under the tangled mat of vegetation. Creeping vines snaked up and between the Listenbarks at the edge of the forest, traveling outwards farther than her old eyes could track. Her eyes snagged on the cliff that sheltered the doorway to the Caves, now rendered into an arbor for the roses trailing up its side, clinging to cracks and crevices that had not been there before. Far above, the scooped tip of the Crooked Mountain had been flattened, its distinctive shape reduced to rubble that trickled down the mountainside to end a few hundred feet from her position at the base of the cliff.

She stumbled forward, her legs catching and her clothing tearing on the sharp thorns. She could not see where the Battle Mage had gone, but the platform of vegetation underneath where she had last seen her teemed with flowers. Looking to the right she saw the plants had left the charred body of Pralick alone; he was nearly unrecognizable but for the distinctive ax still clutched in his hand. His skin was blackened and cracked, clothing and hair burned to ash by the power of the fire from above.

The Mage's companion too, had been spared the fury of the magical growth. Instead the vines had crept close to him, cradling his body so he appeared to be lying in a lush bed of waxy green leaves studded with blooms. A thick branch banded across his torn throat, as if to anchor his nearly severed head back to his body.

Cries and groans began to fill the air as the stunned remnants of the tribes and their Morgals ventured forth. Few of their numbers still remained. As she approached the cairn that rose where the Mage had been, she saw the bloodied forms of Wertal and Pernal picking their way forward also. Together they inspected the tightly clustered rose vines. Wertal even boosted her up to his shoulder so she could peer at the top of the formation, but they found no sign of the Mage until the burly Ancient began to tear his way through the tough green stalks.

They were slowly joined by other survivors. Cirillia saw a mangled Aerin join their number with relief, but saw no sign of either Kon or Folt among the living. Soon, younger hands took over the task of clearing the vines encasing the Mage, leaving she, Pernal and Wertal to lick their numerous wounds and Heal their people, while the unconscious Mage was slowly revealed. She tumbled from the embrace of the plants to lie unmoving on the ground, scored countless times by the thorns that had grasped her, and soaked to the skin. As she kneeled to check her pulse Cirillia saw with horror that a number of the Windthorn roses stemmed from the girl's skin itself, growing right out of ragged ruptures in her body even though her pulse beat steady and strong under her shaking hand. Wertal wordlessly took out a knife and cut the vines that originated in her, shearing off the blood stained stalks close to her skin.

When the last stalk was sawed through, Sylvia's eyes fluttered, revealing their crystalline glory and sending a wave of Hinterlanders stumbling back in fear. Cirillia remained kneeling by her side, ignoring the countless points on her body that screamed for Healing. She met those blue orbs with her own, trying to gauge the danger the girl may still present.

"Les?" she said brokenly, a thorn prick on her lip weeping red down her chin. Her eyes scanned the chaos around them but did not truly see the destruction that spread out from her position.

Her pain was so evident that Cirillia felt it like a physical blow. A tearing in her chest, a fierce ache of her heart. She grasped for Sylvia's hand impulsively. Tears fell from her eyes as she saw the young woman's face turn unerringly to the body of her lover, and when the Mage's breath caught audibly in her throat, Cirillia pressed their joined hands to her tired, old, breast.

"No Sylvia, I'm sorry. He's gone."

Chapter 14

Ryland

Who dreamed up this tortuous mode of transportation?
Ryland wondered through the pervading sensation of nausea.
*Because he would quite happily, and with a free conscious, hold
them under water until they drowned.* The ship gave another
sickening lurch, sending his stomach heaving up into his throat like it
was trying to crawl out of his body and escape. He shielded his face
from the spray that came careening through the rail off the crest of a
nearby wave, and spat a mouthful of salty brine back out into the sea.
Ryland had hoped the fall of complete darkness would help alleviate
the some of his sea sickness, as his eyes would no longer be able to
track the plunge and rise of their boat upon the water. But when the
ambiance of the sun had fallen, the Demandron had come out of their
cabins and taken the reins, driving the fleet to even greater speeds
with their magic and unsettling his stomach further.

They raced over the water. The horizontal speed itself was
fine, it was the ceaseless vertical movement necessitated by the huge
swells that had sent him staggering, over and over, for the rail. And
now he huddled up against the aft rail, his exhausted body wedged
between a crate of water casks and the wooden railing, soaked to the
bone and with nothing left in his stomach to purge. He had
envisioned this trip much differently. *Romanticized it*, he amended
bitterly. He had pictured clear skies and crisp wind. Crystal blue
waters and an escort of Spinner Fish frolicking in the wakes of the
fleet. *Where had this notion of him standing at the bow of the boat,
hair blown back from his face, not a care in the world, come from,* he
wondered? He had known the facts, that their Maegi would be
calling near constant storms to shield them from farscrying, and that
they would travel mostly by night, flying over the water to the
insistent push of Demandron magic. *Romkin*, he berated himself.
And that wasn't even the worst of his self-deception. There would be

nothing glorious or adventures about war. Especially not this war, waged in secret against innocents who considered them allies.

He had let the magic of the Sareth Isles draw him in, he knew. The last few days before the wedding his father had allowed him to visit the Academy Library, with an escort of course, to aid him in his research. Unable to safely research about humans and magical travel, he had spent the time learning all there is to know about the Isles, their many ties to the Age Beyond Memory, their governing system, their exports, their culture and their God. If events had played out differently in Prium, he could have seen himself happily petitioning to spend a year at Saerin's University. A center of learning much like the King's Academy, but one rumored to have access to a trove of texts and artifacts from the Age Beyond Memory. The Saerin Royalty had no Demandron to secret such information away, and hide it from those who wished to study the bygone times of their ancestors.

The scholar in him yearned for those fabled halls of the University. For the chance to study the nearly intact ruins the Sareth people had taken over as their capitol, and learn the secrets of the ancient architecture no one seemed able to replicate. He would journey south across one of the impossible Skyroad bridges connecting the Isles to spend time on the Isle of the Dead. But only in the light of day, as legend said that once night falls on that tiny burial island, all it's ghosts come forth to feast and drink together; and that any mortal to witness the opulent celebration of the dead would so yearn to join them, that by morning the poor soul would have left their body willingly to walk with the ghosts. And then there was Jeale's Sanctuary, an incredible feat of masonry that could be seen from miles out to sea. The statue of the Sareth God, Jeale, rose hundreds of feet into the air, her features at once young, and ancient, a mammoth stone sword held before her, and the honeycombed Sanctuary living within the folds of her robes at the base of the statue. He had also read about the mines that riddle the stony heart of Mount Qee on the northernmost Isle. But the refining of the many gems and deposits of precious metals at that site held little interest to him other than the finished products, which were the finest Augments found in their world.

The boat dropped out from under him as they nosed into the trough of a giant wave, then shot up to meet his body, clacking his teeth together painfully and knocking his knees into the rail. In astonishment he realized he had been so wrapped up in his thoughts about the Isles that he hadn't been sick for long minutes. He grinned into the night, cautiously wiping salt streaked hair back off his face, testing his new found health with small movements. Eventually he got to his feet, feeling almost like a real person again, rather than a shivering ball of misery. The deck still heaved unpleasantly under him, he was still wet and the night was no less cold, but the paralyzing sense of helplessness seemed to have fled his body and stomach.

He swayed along the deck, nodding at the few crewmen standing watch over the boat as they gave the Demandron at the stern a wide berth, and trying to ignore their knowing smirks as he stumbled past. He found his way below decks and to the tiny cabin that was his for the journey. The mate had given up the space for him, and it still smelled of the portly man's tobacco and sweat. The stench nearly sent him right back out the door, but he managed to breathe through his mouth while he rinsed his face of its salty coating and changed into drier clothes. He then made his way to the galley to escape the close confines of his room, and in hopes of some Kercha to restore his strength. He found the Kercha, blacker and spicier than any he had ever tasted, already hot on the stove, and his father and the captain of the ship heavy into battle plans.

"Our greatest advantage is tha' they have no idea we're coming," Captain Jeralt said, pushing a large contingent of tiny ships into Saerin's main harbor on the map spread between the two men. "While not a great move if they were prepared, it's the quickest way to capturing the city and the royalty," he leveled a challenging stare at the Jorgen before dropping his eyes back to the detailed map before him.

Ryland took a seat on the bench a few feet down from the Captain, studying the layout of their fleet as Captain Jeralt thought it should be. The map showed the three large harbors of the Isles, each housing portions of their troops and fighting vessels. The Harbor at Mount Qee in the North, Saerin's main port fronting the capital city, home of the Royal Palace, Saerin University, and the majority of the Isle's populace. Farther south was Sanctuary Harbor, housing the largest squadron of fighting ships, the majority of Saerin's disciplined navy. Jeralt had positioned their 'fleet' of wooden ships in a three-pronged attack, one for each port. The two groups of ships he wanted to send to Sanctuary Harbor and the capital were roughly the same size, while the grouping at Mount Qee was significantly smaller.

The Jorgen, never looking at the map, kept his gaze steadily on the grizzled sailor. "You hinge out entire success on the Saerins behaving normally. You take no account for the happenstance events that the Gods are so fond of throwing at us mortals. What if the ships of Sanctuary Harbor are out, performing drills when you sail our men into their berth? Then when they get word of the attack they are free to attack any of our fronts from behind. We are deploying with stale intelligence, attacking without knowing the positions of our enemies. We need to be more cautious than this." He gestured dismissively at the model, a sneer on his lips as Jeralt nodded in contemplation.

"Ryland," his father barked, making him jump in his seat and sending a splash of scalding liquid over the rim of his mug to sting his hand. "How would you attack?" Wiping his hand gingerly on his pants, Ryland scooted in close to the Captain.

"Pardon me Captain, may I look at the map please?" he said even as the older man slid down the bench to make room for him.

"Look yer fill son," he replied, "Let's see what that brain o' yers can dream up."

His mind ran through possible scenarios rapidly. The harbors were the only real means of accosting the string of islands, as the majority of the coastlines of the rest of the Isles were impossible to make landfall due to sheer cliffs and shallow reefs. So he agreed with Jeralt that a three-pronged attack upon the Isles weakest points was wisest. That would also tie up the three enemy forces so they would not have reinforcements show up on any front to swing the tide of battle in the Saerin's favor. But he also saw the wisdom in his father's words. Without true, real-time knowledge of the positions of the enemy, sailing into the harbors in full force could leave any one of their fronts in a weak position.

"The three harbors must be attacked," he said slowly, taking a number of boats from the two southern fleets so each contingent had the same number of vessels. "But it would be best to have a pool of reinforcements available should an unknown variable tip any one battle in the Saerins' favor," he finished, placing the wooden models in a group some distance outside the Main harbor in the center, at easy sailing distance to assist any of the initial attacks.

Captain Jeralt nodded happily, a grin splitting his homely face. "I knew this 'un had a mind in his head," he said before launching into a detailed account of how many ships and of what kind should stay in reserve.

Ryland looked up from the map to see a strange expression on his father's face, but it was quickly wiped away once the Jorgen saw his eyes on him. "A much better approach," he said with a pointed look at the Captain, who feigned unawareness. "Ryland, how would you divide our galleys with a bridge for archers between the attacks? How would you distribute the ships carrying catapults and Pitch Fire?" The Jorgen's voice took on the all too familiar tone of the many lectures Ryland had endured upon his return to the Holm.

"A greater number of the catapult bearing galleys should go south to Sanctuary Harbor so they can set fire to the fighting ships there, and the majority of the ships carrying archer's bridges should head to the main port to deal with the larger number of soldiers they will face. Two each of those vessels should stay with the reinforcements," he said promptly, knowing that taking his time would cause worse repercussions from his volatile sire than answering incorrectly in a timely manner.

"You made no mention of the northern front. What of the harbor at Mount Qee? Are you forgetting what is manufactured there? How will you combat it?" The Jorgen's questions fired off rapidly, and Ryland blinked as if each query was a physical rap on the head. He tried to kick his seasick weary brain into higher gear, but could not seem to recall from all his hours of research what, other than ore and gems, was exported out of Mount Qee.

"I don't know," he finally said despairingly, watching as deep lines bracketed his father's lips, his face falling into a frown.

"Pitch Fire. They make Pitch Fire there, out of the Gum trees. Not as easily spread as our own, but much more explosive." The tone of his voice pinpointed his son's idiocy so harshly that even Captain Jeralt winced.

"Oh yeah," Ryland said weakly, wishing he had stayed in his bunk, even if the rancid smell brought about more retching. He stayed silent under the scrutiny of his father's eyes, knowing he was waiting for him to answer the original question again. Ryland stubbornly looked at the map, as if considering, until his father impatiently broke the silence himself.

"An equal number of ships carrying catapults and Pitch Fire should go north and south. The northern ships will target the buildings on the shore that store the Saerin's Pitch Fire, igniting them so they cannot be used against us and causing damaging explosions to the barracks there." The Jorgen's voice was flat and factual, utterly at odds with the emotions the picture he painted evoked in his son. Those buildings would explode, ruining most of the harbor and docks, killing anyone in the vicinity, man, woman, or child. Ryland sunk his fingernails into the meat of his palms, attempting to hide the shudder of abhorrence, that tried to race through him, from showing.

"Right, of course," he said weakly, "I'd forgotten about that."

Jeralt

Jeralt looked between father and son in the galley, feeling the cozy room was far too small for the first time in his memory. Ryland had entered the room looking drawn and tired, but his back had been straight and his mind eager to tackle the problems his father posed to him. Now the young man slouched on the bench they shared, his shoulders curled inward protectively and a look like that of a wounded puppy in his eyes. Jeralt physically bit his tongue to keep from breaking into their conversation and coming to the rescue of the boy. He had been chastised enough times this night by the Jorgen for speaking his mind to know his input would not be welcome.

Silence stretched uncomfortably. The clink of the mugs on

their hooks jostling their neighbors the only sound aside from wind and water in the close space. Jeralt focused inward to keep from bursting into speech. He reveled in the sting of his teeth sinking into his tongue, daring himself to bite down just a little bit harder, making a game of holding the same pressure while attempting to wiggle his tongue free. Finally, finally, the Jorgen seemed to accept Ryland's admission of forgetfulness with a tight, smug smile. He rearranged the boats in front of them according to his own plans. The layout was strikingly similar to the plan proposed by his son, trading only the type of vessels included in each squadron, but leaving the overall numbers intact.

Jeralt swung one leg over the bench and took the other men's mugs in hand, filling them to the brim before measuring more Kercha into the pot to heat. The Jorgen considered the map in silence, occasionally moving a piece here or there as he ran through possible scenarios in his mind. "Thank you, Captain," Ryland said in a quiet voice when he handed him his refill. There was a genuine smile in the young man's eyes as he accepted the mug. *The likes of which have never graced the sire's face*, Jeralt thought. He tried to focus back on the coming battle, run through all the variables and 'what if's' like the Jorgen was doing. But his eyes were drawn back to the quietly attentive young man at his side again and again.

There was an entire world visible behind those brown eyes. An innate softness that seemed to spark the Jorgen's ire every time he saw it. What the Jorgen didn't realize was that a kindness such as that in his son could be a boon if wielded by a strong enough man. Coupled with Ryland's obvious intelligence, the lean muscles and broad shoulders under his tunic, it all spoke of the blossoming of a more than ordinary man. What he wouldn't give to have a son like him. Steeped in potential, pliable enough to learn and young enough still to be molded into something a father could be proud of.

Jeralt's mind drifted to his own son, the only one to live out of the three tow-headed boys his wife had borne him. He had spoken true to the Jorgen earlier; he had made his peace with the weasel Garrin had seen fit to bestow upon him as a son. He had taken the time to visit the brothel Kess ran, and as he stood amid the squalor and too-young whores, he told him exactly what he thought of him and his nefarious ways. Now, if Garrin chose to take him back into his arms in this war, he would leave no unfinished business behind. He swung his head between father and son again, fingering the long braid hanging from his chin. There was nothing but unfinished business and unsaid words between these two, and he feared for young Ryland's sake, that that is all there ever would be.

Jorgen pointed abruptly to the ships held in reserve, "Ryland and I will vacate your ship before the attack begins. We'll need an archer's bridge to see from if our magic is to be of any use. We will keep three such galleys in reserve, choose the best captained for us Jeralt."

Ryland started at his father's words, surprise painting his face. "Father, I'd thought we would split up and each go with one force. I'm not sure our magic will even reach the shore from that far out. What good can we do hanging back?"

"I am commanding this fleet, and the commander has to make the call of who needs the reinforcements. We cannot remain on board here with my Second, because if the ship falls there will be no one to take command. And as for magic, we have ten mostly trained Demandron scattered through the fleet, two Maegi will not tip the tide of this battle. But you will have your chance to fight, with your sword and your magic, when we sail to whichever front needs aid."

Ryland's voice got very quiet, "Will you be taking my power or are we to fight separately?" He kept his eyes on the table top and the map there as he asked, and did not look up to receive the answer; but Jeralt did, and the cold consideration in the Jorgen's eyes chilled him.

"With the Demandron so close I will have power readily available. I should not need you," he said dismissively, and then added as an afterthought, "But I require you to remain close in case that changes."

Clearing his throat loudly, Jeralt broke in, "I got jus the ship for ya sir. Thyrem and his *Windstorm* have an archer's bridge, a good tall one. He's as good a seaman as you'll ever find, and that tub has weathered many a squall I thought would drag 'er down."

"Fine, fine, I leave that decision to you, Captain Jeralt. Yours also is the decision of who will go where, as long as the numbers remain true to this model," he said, gesturing between them and absently straightening a toppled ship. "Keep in mind your best catapults should go north to Mount Qee. It is imperative we are able to hit the buildings housing the Pitch Fire to disable that port." With one last look at the map and a nod of satisfaction, the Jorgen strode from the galley, his cloak whipping wildly in the wind that screamed in as soon as the door was opened.

"Ten laughs a minute yer father is," Jeralt said conversationally, once the door snapped shut, prodding Ryland from his deep contemplation of the tabletop.

He laughed darkly, "That he is. That's why my brother and I secretly named him Chuckles," he deadpanned, before cracking a smile at the absurdity of such a nickname.

Jeralt's laughter filled the small space and he clapped Ryland on the shoulder, before digging out a sheet of crumpled paper to jot down the details of the plan for his own keeping. He would have to draft up the list detailing which ship was to sail where tomorrow. They would reach the Sareth Isles by sundown, and would be splitting up to attack in the dark of the night.

"Shouldn't a leader be at the head of the battle? To, you know, *lead*?" Ryland asked.

Jeralt almost laughed again, but then truly considered the question. It was deceptively simple wording, but he found himself thinking at great length before he spoke. "Taken literally, the title does mean that the Commander should be at the forefront o' one of the prongs of attack. But it's also true that the first into battle often fall. A leader has to weigh the options. Is it a greater risk to the overall fight for him to stay back and let his men fight? Or is charging headfirst into battle, with great magic and skill as a warrior 'nough to win the battle regardless, if he happens to fall?"

Ryland's head cocked to the side. "Then the Jorgen is right, the safest play is to stay with the reinforcements to direct the battle. If I ever spent time thinking about it I guess I would have come to the same conclusion," he admitted, "but I didn't get much farther than imagining charging off the boat and into Saerin's harbor, sword in hand," he finished ruefully.

"Have you seen battle?

The boy nodded, a slightly haunted look on his face more than enough to tell Jeralt the truth of the statement. "Jorgenholm weathers raids from the Hinterland tribes nearly constantly from the autumn through to the spring. The snows force the tribes farther south out of the Skypeaks. But I always fought those skirmishes from inside the Wall, with my bow." Ryland's brown eyes gazed into the past and Jeralt kept quiet, knowing there was another tale to come.

"On our way to Seaprium the Hinterlanders attacked our camp, days south of the Holm. It was completely unexpected, and likely very successful for them because of that. We lost a lot of soldiers, and others. It was the first time my magic was used to kill." A shudder went through him. "I barely remember most of what happened, but I can recall in great detail each man who died as my power touched him."

"War's not a comely maiden," Jeralt said in commiseration, "though young men often think her to be, and their blood is stirred at the prospect to meet 'er. But in truth she's a bloody ole hag, spiteful an humorless, an just as likely to leave you maimed as to bring you to completion." Ryland grimaced at the crude analogy, but nodded in agreement all the same.

"What happens if we win, Captain? What do we do with the Saerin royalty? I heard the King say he still plans on marrying his son to Princess Veraline, but I can't imagine she would want to marry the son of the man who defeated her people." The young man's voice rang with sincere concern for the princess he had never met, and Jeralt silently cursed the Jorgen for not seeing what a treasure of a son he had. What an incredible leader he could be shaped into.

"Have you asked yer father these questions boy?" he stalled.

Ryland's open features dropped to the table once more at the mention of his sire, his face closing off at the mention of his sire.

"No sir, but mayhap I should go do that now. Sorry to bother you Captain." He rose gracefully to his feet, and long ingrained habit made Jeralt rise also, keeping their eyes on a level as he backpedaled, searching for that comfortable ease they had shared just seconds before.

"Yer questions are no bother son. I merely thought yer father might have known the answers better than me. But I can take a gander at 'em if you like. Let's see, iffin we win tomorrow night, the King and Queen of Saerin are like to be executed, then the Princess will wed our Prince Fragon, she will not be given a choice in the matter. It's wed him and retain some stewardship of her land and people, or die. Then the newlyweds will rule 'ere in Saerin together, likely with a council o' advisers to aid them. We will sail on home to a happy King, an I bet yer father will have you all back on the road to Jorgenholm quicker than a wink." Jeralt winked comically at him, but Ryland was already speaking.

"Then all we are accomplishing is what we would have gained anyway? Fragon and Veraline would have wed, and once the King and Queen died they would have ruled the Isles. I just don't understand why we are doing this, the price for speeding up that time-line seems too steep. So many lives and resources spent, not to mention the danger of terminating a solid alliance if anything goes wrong! This is a stupid crusade! Pointless and wasteful and I can't believe everyone is just going along with it!" Jeralt stepped back as Ryland's anger grew, leaving him out of breath at the end of his tirade.

"Those be heavy words young man, and treasonous to boot. Even if I happen to agree with you." He checked the galley door before speaking again. "Someday you might be in a place to speak such wisdom in the right ears, on account o' yer birth. But today, all the likes o' you an me can do is obey orders, and try our best to stay alive. That's yer job tomorrow night Ryland, stay alive, no matter what. Kill the men who would kill you, swim if ya end up in the water, run if you lose yer weapon, surrender if all hope is lost. If you are alive, then maybe one day you can be the one to keep bad decisions like this from takin place." He flicked the tip of one of Ryland's antlers, watching as all the temper fled the young man's body, leaving him looking deflated and defeated. "Now shoo, back to yer cabin boy, get some sleep."

"Aye, Captain," Ryland said tiredly, turning to the galley door. He paused with his hand on the rough wood planking, looking back at Jeralt. "Thank you sir, for answering my questions," he said quietly.

Jeralt nodded, "I'm here any ole time you have more questions for me son." Ryland smiled and moved to exit the galley, wind tossing his hair into disarray. "Ryland?" Jeralt called, a smile tugging at his lips, "Iffin my deck isn't clean when I wake up in the mornin I will set you to bailing out the bilge," he said mildly, keeping his face straight until Ryland's startled "Aye, sir," was cut off by the closing door. He chuckled to himself as he poured more Kercha into his chipped mug and settled back at the table to finish his notes.

The Jorgen

It was an ideal night for their ambush. His Maegi had not even been forced to drain their powers by calling a storm as cover. Fog lay thick upon the isles, and the night was nearly windless, leaving the misty blanket intact to hide their approach. His only concern was that in the stillness, some noise would alert their enemies to their approach. He had cautioned Captain Jeralt of this danger, and told him to make sure the Demandron and Maegi passed that message on to the captain of each and every ship. Oars were muffled by rags, men wrapped their hooves for the time being, and all orders were voiced in whispers.

He and Ryland transferred to the *Windstorm* at dusk, and had been waiting on the bridge with Captain Thyrem since. Watching from the heights the ominous bulge of fog that covered the Sareth Isles grow ever closer. Now they were in the thick of it, and the air was soupy and moist, heavy with water. The *Windstorm* lay at anchor a few hundred yards from the mouth of Saerin's main port, and the three squadrons who would attack first were slowly making their way north, south, and east to their respective destinations. The stir of water from the pull of hundreds of oars seemed too loud, and the gurgle of water sliding under the hulls echoed eerily in the ghostly fog.

"Ship the oars," he ordered the stout Water Maegi at his side. He was determined to limit the noise of his men's approach. The Maegi bent dutifully to a brimming bowl of water, his focus on the small granule of roughly cut ruby that swam blearily at its center. Farscrying was impossible this close to the Isles, a trick no one outside of the Royal family of Saerin knew how to accomplish. Gartlan had cited this knowledge as one more reason they were waging this battle in the dark of night, against men who believed them to be allies. Such a large scale dampening spell would be hugely beneficial as a defensive tactic for Seaprium. As it was here, where it forced his fleet to communicate by a much simpler method, limiting their contact to flares of light from the fragmented pieces of a single ruby. Each ship had a Maegi, some with barely more than a scrap of magic, aboard to monitor their own ruby, and a scroll detailing how to communicate with it.

The ruby flared to life for a long second, and then ignited again two times in quick succession, passing along the order to ship the oars and proceed by the magic of the Demandron alone. The cold essence of their power licked at him from under his shirt. The stone there lay heavy and cold, making it hard to draw a full breath for the icy intrusion. He pushed the small bundle of screaming fear and the tinge of hot blood that came along with the cold far to the back of his mind, trying to hide it in the recesses and memories there, so he could focus on the utter stillness around him.

Ryland stood close by his side, his face paler than the chill of the misty air could account for, and his teeth worrying at his bottom lip. Jorgen found the hot sting of his anger towards the boy to be a helpful distraction from the swirl of darkly arousing emotion inside his own head, and latched onto it in desperation. "You look as terrified as a child," he hissed at his offspring, "Stand up straight, boy!"

Ryland merely looked over at him, his eyes nothing but darker patches of black in the night, highlighted by the bloodless skin surrounding them. Then he turned from him, settling his arms on the rail in front of them and staring off into the fog, his shoulders still hunched. Jorgen tried to quell the unease the uncharacteristically challenging response stirred in him, shrugging off his son's seeming indifference as battle nerves. But the queasy unease of that small moment ate at him, co-mingling with the violence being committed somewhere back in Seaprium, even as it echoed in his mind. His heart sped up and breath escaped him for a moment. He had never felt so unsettled before a battle. From the corner of his eye he caught the red glow of the ruby coming to life within its wide lipped bowl. The ships sailing towards the capital had reached the mouth of the harbor with no incident. Soon after the stone had fallen dark, it lit again in rapid sequences; the forces at Mount Qee and Sanctuary were entering the harbors also.

Long minutes of stillness passed, no light from the ruby, no sound from the shore. And then Ryland spoke in tandem with the flaring of the gem, "Did you hear that?" He turned from his perusal of the unseen shore to look at the ruby with wide eyes, "Are they landed? I heard a noise." Jorgen waved off his questions, focusing instead on the hurried code flashing from the bowl and the translations spilling from the Maegi's lips.

"No signs of movement from Sanctuary. Archers firing on the ships in Saerin Harbor, but they are staying out of range in the center of the water. Catapults are being readied at Mount Qee," the man read out quickly. A flare of diffused light flashed to the north and Jorgen grinned in grim pleasure, turning to face the direction of the light so he could witness the spectacular light show which would result from his fleet's Pitch Fire hitting the Saerin stores of the same volatile material. That small light arced through the air three more times and he growled in frustration.

"Damn you Captain Jeralt, I said to send your most accurate catapult teams to the north!"

"Father," Ryland piped up with some urgency, "did you hear that? Something is wrong at Sanctuary." Ryland went so far as to grip the Jorgen's arm, turning him from the north back to the Maegi muttering under his breath, eyes flying over the scroll in his hands as he decoded the flashing gem. In horror Jorgen focused in on his words.

"Fifteen vessels leading the Sanctuary front have sunk, some unseen object punctured their hulls. The remaining boats are rescuing as many soldiers as they can, but cannot sail forward through the wreckage."

"Trollit!" the Jorgen breathed, sucking in a breath at the viciously potent flush of arousal that careened through his mind as the Demandron drew on the stone hanging from his neck, likely in response to the sinking ships at Sanctuary. He frantically clawed his way back to the present, shoving the brief glimpse of a young boy's violent defilement from his mind.

"Orders, sir?" the Maegi prompted, before diving back into translation as the ruby flickered into life once more. "Ships in the Harbor at Mount Qee are foundering on shallow rocks at the center of the harbor," he said in panicked confusion, "Their Pitch Fire has set the entire town on fire but no explosions from enemy stores have happened." He looked to Jorgen solemnly. "No enemy has been seen at either harbor."

"They're not being attacked?" Ryland asked in confusion. "Then how are the ships sinking?"

Jorgen brushed his son and his useless question aside, asking the Maegi, "No enemy forces? Are you sure?"

"Only the archers at Saerin, sir," he replied, and then amended, with his eyes to his bowl, "And now catapults with Pitch Fire there also, Commander."

"By Garrin's antlers, they knew we were coming," Ryland breathed, voicing the knowledge that had all but paralyzed the Jorgen. Fighting through the stupefying pull of the increase of the Demandron's magic, he rummaged under his tunic for the ebony stone and tore it from his breast. Blessed freedom sunk into his body like an elixir, and in the clarity it provided he flung his troops into movement.

"Recall the fleets from Qee and Sanctuary!" he roared, no longer concerned with keeping quiet. "All able ships sail to the main port, the Saerins have pulled all of their forces back into the ancient stronghold there. We land, take the harbor and surround the Palace until both northern and southern units join us, then we take the damn Saerins in their beds!" The ships around them stirred to audible life, voices calling orders, oars clacking into their oarlocks, anchors being pulled onto decks still dripping seawater.

"Those clever bastards saw this coming," he said to stout Captain Thyrem, who had appeared at his side as the boat lurched into motion on the smooth water. "They must have an informant loyal to them in the Palace by the Sea." He shook his head in amazement. He may not agree with his King, and he may hate him for waging this war, but he would never betray his land and people to such a degree.

"Ryland," he barked, "I've severed my connection to the Demandron, you will stay at my side at all times, I will have need of your magic once mine is tapped out," he said, hating how the command was a subtle admission that his son's power far outstretched his own abilities.

"Severed your connection? Why?"

Jorgen snapped, the adrenaline of the coming battle and the lingering quickening of his blood from the Demandron magic a potent cocktail. His rigid control broke and he felt his facial muscles pull into unfamiliar lines, as he rounded on this youngest son, fist rising. "Do not question me, boy!" he snarled, watching Ryland reel back from the heavy blow of his gloved fist. "Fetch our weapons, keep quiet, and keep close," he said when his son regained his feet, a trickle of blood leaking from his split lip.

"Enemy incoming!" The call came from far above, where a sailor was stationed in the crow's nest, and was echoed by every hand on deck, the message traveling from their ship to the next, and the next, by those calls alone. Out in the swirling mist a ship's prow pierced the gray tatters of fog, the lithe lines of Saerin's fighting vessels becoming visible as they barreled towards them, a rising wind at their back.

The ruby shone its tired red light again and the Maegi started speaking, forcing Jorgen's attention away from the incoming ships as he absorbed yet more unwelcome news. "More than twenty ships in the main port have hit something and are taking on water. Just like the other harbors sir. The boats are now in range of enemy fire and we are taking heavy casualties. They are calling for reinforcements. They say the fog is lifting inland, and a storm is rolling in, making their approach tough. The Saerins have also launched ships from the harbor to board them."

"Tell them they are penned in, the Saerins had boats lying in wait. The harbor is a trap. Their only chance is to fight their way ashore and take the harbor," Jorgen told the Maegi hastily, and then rapidly turned back to the arresting sight of nearly a hundred Saerin vessels bearing down on his small reserve fleet. Ryland rushed to his side and pressed the pommel of Warbringer into his hand. Then father and son stood in stillness for a breath, each drawing on the well of magic they contained. Jorgen grasped for Control, feeling instantly more alive as his magic suffused him, bringing greater light to the dark night, strengthening his hearing and making his blood hum with energy. He poured that energy into his sword, feeling the familiar words of his ancestors fall from his lips, igniting the ancient blade with Garrin's own fury.

Ahead of them grappling hooks from the Saerin ships clattered onto numerous decks, pulling vessels inevitably closer until soldiers could drop gangplanks and board the ships. The Jorgen's force was too tightly compacted to perform evasive maneuvers and the Saerin fleet had arrived with the fore-running wind at their backs, off of what must be a magically called storm. The wayward gage was theirs, effectively trapping his boats so all they could do was wait to be boarded. Retreat was not an option. The sounds of fighting reigned, even above the prevalent sounds of wind and water. Ryland had a bow in hand and was shooting steadily down off the bridge with the ship's archers, igniting the tips of his arrows with magic before losing them to sink effortlessly into the hulls of the Saerin vessels. They would do the most good on the main deck with their swords and magic once they had been boarded, the Jorgen knew. Down below, grappling hooks were already skittering across the deck, catching and being pulled loose again until they lodged solidly into the ship's rails.

He pulled Ryland back from the edge of the archers' bridge,

forcing them both into a crouch as a stray arrow sailed by. "We need to get to the main deck," he told him quickly, and at his son's immediate nod of assent, that niggling feeling of pride flashed through him once more. He clapped his hand down on Ryland's neck and pulled him even closer, so he could be heard over the cacophony of fighting that battled with the rising winds for precedence. "Stay close and watch yourself." Captain Jeralt's face crossed his mind briefly, his open features spouting honesty Jorgen hadn't wanted to hear. "Be careful, son," he finished reluctantly, spinning away and starting for the ladder that would lead him down to the deck, not wanting to see the reaction Ryland had to his telling words.

He dropped the last few feet, knowing that continuing to climb down the ladder would leave his back vulnerable to attack. He landed hard, stumbling to the side as the deck rolled gently at just the wrong moment. The Jorgen brought Warbringer up to parry the down-swinging blade of a swarthy Saerin man just in time, but his balance was still off from his landing and he was forced to follow up the parry with a forward lunge because his momentum was too great to stop. It launched him into the thick of the fighting on deck, rather than letting him stay near the ladder to wait for Ryland's descent. He tried to fight his way back towards the bridge as Ryland's booted feet appeared on the rungs, but the tide of battle was against him as he crossed swords with a tanned Trewal boasting an astonishing rack of antlers atop his thick body.

The man slashed at his right side with an already bloodied ax, and Jorgen brought his own sword up and around to deflect the clumsy blow, then he grasped his Control and launched a spear of Air at the man's torso, battering the breath from his lungs and forcing him to double over from the impact. Jorgen casually lopped off the man's head, his huge antlers clattering to the deck and nearly tripping him, as he searched the throng of fighters for Ryland. He found him, his lean body taut and straining, his sword motionless at his side as he threw bolt after bolt of pure energy into the men that pressed in on him where he was trapped against the ladder and the broad beams supporting the bridge above. He was out of his element here, with no Earth readily accessible to feed his magic. But magic in its basic form was still a force to be reckoned with. The coppery bolts of light sank into Ryland's foes, leaving burned flesh and cracking skin in their wake. A wide swath of dead soldiers ringed the young man, and Jorgen turned his attention back to his own surroundings, confident his son was fending for himself.

He whipped the air around him into a mini windstorm, sending two arrows that had been heading his way flying out harmlessly to sink into the sea. He then bounded up to the forecastle, dispatching two men quickly, one with magic and one with his blade. From his new vantage he surveyed the *Windstorm's* deck in an attempt to read the battle. Of the seventy or so men who had sailed on this ship, many lay dying on her decks, their blood shed in dark spreading stains, devoid of color in the night. Three of the smaller Saerin ships hemmed his vessel in, tied to her with grappling hooks and thick ropes thrown over by the crews as soon as the boarding warriors had cleared themselves enough space to tie the lines off.

Jorgen hammered the pommel of his sword down on the head of a soldier trying to make his way up to the forecastle, and then loosed a huge blast of magic, nearly depleting himself, but managing to topple all of the still boarding warriors into the water where their heavy armor and weapons dragged them down. In the suddenly clear tangle of ships he could make out an enemy Maegi bringing down small spouts of water to drown the men in his way. He was heading towards the destruction Ryland had left around him, with obvious intent to eliminate one of the powers still holding the Saerin forces at bay, when the majority of the rest of the battle had already been lost.

"Ryland!" he yelled, hoping to alert the boy to the incoming danger. Ryland's head twitched in his direction, but stopped halfway, caught on the skinny Maegi as he drowned Captain Thyrem with his Water magic. Sending the burly captain to his knees, and finally to the deck, twitching the last of his life away. Jorgen sent a bolt of Air careening across the deck in hopes of throwing the Maegi off balance, but the paltry amount of magic that answered his summons was only wind by the time it reached the man. He was tapped out.

He cast another look around him, taking note of the swarmed decks of the nearby boats, and the cries of surrender already coming from the ships beyond his eyesight in the dark. They were outnumbered three to one. There was no chance they could turn this fight around, not unless the southern and northern forces somehow knew to come find them here, floating out to sea from the harbor where the rest of his fleet had been slaughtered. He eyed the broken scrying bowl that lay beneath the archers' bridge, his eyes scanning for that drop of ruby red in the mangled bodies that lay beside it, knowing that even if he found the ruby, there was not a drop of magic left in him to call to the rest of his men.

Jorgen drew a deep breath, dropping his sword, and on his exhale he raised his voice to its loudest, "Surrender! The Royal fleet surrenders!" The call was taken up by other voices, and the sound of knees hitting the deck and weapons being lowered resounded across the waves.

Ryland

He sat next to his father on the long ride into Saerin's harbor, his body aching and his mind floating in a strangely calm space. Their hands and legs were tied tightly together and then linked to the man sitting next to them, he to his father, and his father to some unknown soldier on the other side. The poor man had suffered a head wound that had torn one dark spiraling horn completely from his skull, and was reeling drunkenly on the crate they had been tethered to, incoherent and unable to answer any question put to him. Saerin men hemmed them in on all sides, bodies taunt with anger and suppressed violence, eyes full of distrust, many of them fixed pointedly on the Jorgen and himself.

Their skin was tanned darkly from the tropical sun, a deep brown complimented by the spiraling ivory whiteness of the typical Sareth short horns, and Ryland found himself mesmerized by the rich textures and tones. Their eyes, to a man, were as brown as his own, not even the odd green or hazel to lighten the monotony. They seemed tilted to Ryland, as if the Gods had nudged the corners of their eyes upwards, lending the Saerin people an exotic beauty. The boat rang with the fluid tongue of the Isles, the syllables dripping from their lips like rich drops of wine. Their mouths were overly pursed and sometimes comically wide as if they were indeed savoring the taste of each word as they spoke it.

Even through his shocked state, Ryland reveled in the

glimpses the slowly lightening sky afforded him of the towering palace of rosy stone that rambled back into the steep hillside of Saerin. Flags flew gaily from many towers of impossible height. Graceful arches dominated the stone walls in the forms of windows and doors, leaving the heavy stone structures feeling airy and lite, despite their solidness. He immersed himself in contemplation of the foreign architecture, in categorizing the differences in the people and wares in the crowded markets bordering the docks where the boats tied up.

It helped him to ignore the offal that was thrown at them, the slight pain emanating from his chest as he breathed, and from translating the beautiful language that flitted around him into the hateful words he knew were being said. The boat neighboring theirs was unloading, blocking their chain of prisoners from moving up the dock and onto shore towards the milling mob of commoners awaiting them. In muted horror he saw a darkly tanned Saerin soldier with white horns set wide on his heavy brow glance at his fellows, and seeing their inattention to his actions he agilely slid one hoof between the shaky legs of the Priush soldier currently disembarking, sending the poor man stumbling off the gangplank and into the murky water between boat and dock. His legs bobbed sharply back to the surface as the bindings tying him to the next prisoners dragged the two men surrounding him partially down.

His cloven feet kicked desperately as the whole line of chained men tried to shuffle back and tighten the line so the fallen would be pulled free of the water. The Saerin man who had tripped the drowning soldier solidly pressed the line forwards again, sinking the man even farther into the water much to the horror and helplessness of his comrades. The partially submerged legs stopped kicking long before his peer's forward movement and efforts pulled his body clear of the water. His waterlogged corpse dragged along the dock, leaving a wet smear as they were prodded into the noisy marketplace. Ryland's eyes found the big Saerin soldier as he was marched past, and found his furious scowl had been replaced with a smugly curled lip.

His father was stiff and silent throughout the ordeal, his tension only lessening somewhat when they walked through the heavy metal doors that led them to the property reserved by the Palace in the crowded city. Once the jeering calls of the crowds stopped, and the various projectiles ceased, Jorgen strode with more ease, making Ryland wonder if he had feared true danger from the angry populace of the city. Here, inside the Palace walls, the streets were quiet and clean; heavily manicured gum trees and flowering azalea bushes lined the elegant statehouses. He saw not one person traveling by foot. Instead carriages passed, pulled by straining horses whose hooves rang on the cobbled roads, or palanquins were carted about, gauzy window drapes fluttering above their bare-chested bearers.

"We are not here to sight-see, Ryland," his father commented quietly, earning him a glare from the guard who plodded uphill closest to them.

"Why are we here?" Ryland asked in an even lower tone. "Why didn't they kill us?"

Jorgen shrugged, "They might want to ransom us back to Seaprium. They might want to use captives to leverage good behavior out of Gartlan. Or they might just want to execute us where they can watch," he finished, each horrid situation outlined in the same bland tone.

Ryland examined his father's stoic face thoughtfully, and a little fearfully. Tradition held that when the King of Prium was crowned, he took the title, leaving all other names and ties of his former life behind him. It was only through his extensive studies of the Jorgen's ancestry that he knew their current King's former name had been Gartlan, and that he was a distant cousin to his own family. His father had slipped up, calling the King by his former name, showing his unease to his son in a way that his emotionless face did not.

"What happened back there? How did they know we were coming?" he asked, ignoring the smirk that crossed the nosy guard's face at his query.

"Someone warned them. It's the only answer which makes sense. Seaprium is harboring a traitor." His father's voice was still strangely devoid of emotion when Ryland would have thought he would be bristling with temper at the betrayal, and their subsequent defeat.

Before he could ask his father if he had sustained some injury that was causing his peculiar behavior, they were forced into a single file line in order to squeeze through a narrow door that tunneled through a thick wall of the ever present red hued stone. It was a feat made awkward by their linked state and he ended up thudding heavily into the wall as the guard behind him shoved impatiently at his back, eliciting a groan of pain as the aches from the beating he had been given when he relinquished his sword on the boat, flared into life. His chest hurt abominably after he rebounded off the hard wall, and the act of breathing that had pinched uncomfortably in his chest before, now spiked a fiery pain, deep in his sternum, at each inhale. They broke out of the darkened tunnel and into full sunlight, bathing a training yard in stark relief. The bright light, as it so often did, triggered a massive sneeze when it hit his eyes, and the world tilted around him as pain flared from his ribs and lungs. His surroundings faded into blackness.

When he came to he found himself draped across his father's shoulders, a firm hand from behind anchoring him in place as the Jorgen stumbled along with the added weight. Each jarring step was agony, and he scrabbled with his bound hands for purchase on the Jorgen's back in an attempt to alleviate the pain of his weight being pressed into the other man's hard shoulders. His struggles nearly sent them both to the ground, but that harsh grip from behind steadied them before they could topple.

"Stop moving," came his father's breathless voice, but he could only whimper in response. He could feel the Jorgen's heavy sigh through their connected bodies. "Just breath Ryland, focus on the next breath. One after the other," his tone turned cajoling and Ryland found himself pulling in air in time to his words, his focus on keeping the rhythm allowing him to relax his stiff body slightly, making his father's work easier.

They were being prodded along a torch-lit hall. Every few steps the metal grate of a cell would appear at the top of Ryland's line of sight, and then fade back into the rose colored stone that the ancient Trewal who had inhabited this island had made all of their dwellings from. They moved in fits and starts as Priush soldiers were shut into the cages one by one. The bottoms of the metal grates were now populated by upside-down hooves to Ryland's fuzzy eyes. Hanging slumped as he was, all the blood congregated in his head, and he could feel the beat of his heart in his eyes as pressure built. Finally, that pressure eased as his father walked him into a cell and lowered him with a labored grunt to the hard floor. His stern face swam into view, and he felt the brush of a cool hand on his overheated face.

"Just keep breathing Ryland, in and out," his father whispered fiercely, and then the cell door swung shut with a clang; Ryland was left slumped on the floor, with nothing but a few wisps of straw and a bucket to keep him company. The noises of the remaining prisoners moving down the hall grew faint as he tried to settle his body more comfortably on the hard floor. But breath was almost impossible to draw when he was prone. So he ended up sitting propped up against the wall, cushioned as comfortably as he could be with the bits of straw he could reach without moving from his position. Slowly he peeled his sweaty tunic away from his chest and stared down into the darkness forlornly. Unable to see what, if any, damage was visible. Instead he pulled the hanging ends from his britches and bared his stomach to his eyes that way.

Flickering flames through the grate revealed large purple bruises covering his ribs and torso. One bruise still held the shape of the hoof that had created it, a stunning replica of the cloven crescent Ryland could recall in great detail, stomping down on his curled body. He touched the imprint and winced. *What I wouldn't give for one of Torman's rough Healings right now,* he thought ruefully. Any sort of Healing would be a blessing from Garrin at the moment.

He stilled as a number of hoof-falls beat against the stone floor from down the corridor and their guards swept past his door, rapping the knuckles of one prisoner's reaching hand so sharply that the resulting crack must have been bone breaking. Low laughs filled the air at the man's pained gasp. Now free of all of their prisoners, the soldiers extinguished the torches as they went, plunging the entire dungeon into darkness before they shut the final door with a resounding thud. His eyes slowly adjusted to the dark and he found he could see the faintest outline of his legs on the light colored stone, but not much beyond that. Voices began to sound out in the dark around him.

"Jeron? Jeron are you out there? It's yer mate Ryen. I thought I saw you go down with 'a arrow, but Matty said he saw ya on a boat coming here!"

"Matty? Matty Feldman? From the *Rain Racer*? Is that who you 'eard it from? Is Matty alive?"

"Those vermin knew we were coming, twasn't even a fair fight!"

"My son! My son!" one man wept over and over, a litany that beat below all the other voices in continuous grief.

"Commander Jorgen?" a voice close to Ryland's cell asked into the blackness.

"I'm here," came the tired reply, and quiet as it was, all the other voices tapered off after the Jorgen's affirmation.

"Your orders sir?" the first voice asked.

A slight rustling sounded from further down the hall, and then the clink of metal on metal made Ryland think his father had grabbed onto the bars of his cell, the seal ring of the Jorgen family chiming off the hard metal. "Your orders are to survive, and to help your brothers to stay alive. Lick your wounds, and aid any you are able to that cannot. We don't know what fate the Royals of Saerin have in mind for us, but it is best to face it in strength and health in any way this could be resolved. I have heard not but of the fair ruling of this King and Queen of Saerin. I hope that you men will be returned to Seaprium if a bargain can be struck, or at least have your lives spared and be put to work here on the Isles." Murmurs whispered through the space at the optimistic words, but the Jorgen spoke on, "Rest your bodies, ready your minds, if you have magic, recharge your stores. If a weapon falls into your hands, secret it away. If the chance to free ourselves presents itself, then we will be ready to take it," he finished, the iron back in his voice.

Ryland was glad to hear his father acting more like himself. The dead tone of his voice as they traveled to the Palace had scared him more than being taken captive, or being tied and at the mercy of his enemies, ever had.

"Ryland," his father's voice rang out, just as Ryland was allowing his exhausted eyes to close in preparation of getting some rest. He snapped them back open and instinctively struggled to attention, only to freeze in pain and remembrance that his father could not see him, propped up against the wall.

"Aye," he croaked.

"They will come back for us. They know who we are. See that you are fit to stand before a King when they do. I will not have you leaning on me in the presence of royalty."

Yep, Ryland thought, *the old Jorgen is back, hooray for us.* And then he let his lids fall shut, the darkness behind them somehow kinder than the blackness of the dungeon.

———————

Ryland woke slowly. A voice was calling his name, but his eyes didn't seem to be working. No matter how he rubbed at them the darkness of sleep remained. Slowly memory filtered back in and he realized that his eyes were fine, the cell that he had fallen asleep in was just shrouded in darkness.

"Ryland?" the voice called again, and Ryland groggily recognized his father's stern tone.

"Yeah. I'm awake," he said, pulling himself up against the wall with a wince.

"Sorry for the false alarm sir, but I hadn't heard 'im move in a long while," another voice said, this one much closer. Ryland moved to the open front of the cell and saw the vague shadow of a man standing against the bars of his own cell, across the hallway, a mirror image to Ryland's own position.

"I thought you were dead," the man spoke to him, "I could hear your breathing cause it was so raspy, and then I slept a little an when I woke I couldn't 'ear it no more. Sorry to wake ya," he said apologetically.

"That's fine," Ryland replied, even as his battered body cried out for more rest. "Any idea how long we've been down here?"

"Ole Matty got the first cell up there and he can see daylight from under the door. He figures it must be 'bout midafternoon on the outside," the nameless soldier said.

Three quarters of a day. He'd been asleep for nearly ten hours and still exhaustion pulled at him. He took stock of his body; broken ribs and a badly bruised chest were the worst of it. There were also a few tender spots on his arms where he had deflected kicks to his head when the soldiers had subdued him after the surrender. One of his wrists was puffy and wouldn't bend much. When he attempted to use it to sit back down on the floor, it gave way and sent him tumbling into an aching heap.

By the time he had found a mildly comfortable position and was contemplating sleep again, the door at the end of the row of cells was flung open and light flooded into the dank space. He met eyes with the young man in the cell across from his, wincing at the colorful black eye he sported, before giving a nod of commiseration. He made his way to the bars, curious as to what awaited them.

"I hope I look better than you do, Lord Ryland. Those are some mighty pretty colors yer face is sporting," his neighbor said with a grin.

"I'm not sure I am lord of anything right now, and your own face could put a rainbow to shame," he replied. "What's your name?"

"Ryen sir. I'm glad to see you moving about," he lowered his voice with a glance farther down into the dungeon, "I think he was serious about not letting you lean on him when they come for you. Either way its safest for you to be able to move on your own."

Ryland barely had time to nod in response before two guards

in pristine tabards of pale green were at his cell. One poked his metal tipped spear through the bars, warding him off while the other worked his jangling ring of keys at the lock.

"I see one hint of magic from you, boy, and I'll gut you like a fish," the one with the spear warned, his accent lilting and strange as he spoke the words. The man with the keys walked off, farther down the hall to his father's cell and soon reappeared with him. "The same goes for you, Jorgen," he spat, leveling his spear at him.

The second guard had his father's hands tied together, but they didn't bother with the precaution for him. *I must look even worse than I feel,* Ryland mused as he tried to walk at a normal pace towards the blinding golden light that blazed outside of the door. His ribs made breathing difficult, but whenever he paused to catch his breath the spear tip of the guard behind him pricked repeatedly at his back, goading him into motion once more.

This time not even the wonder of the architecture around them could distract him. He had to put too much effort and concentration into walking and breathing. He didn't even have the energy to thank his father when his bound hands reached out to steady him as he stumbled over the threshold of a large room, the transition from flagstone floor to lush carpet catching him by surprise.

"What is the meaning of this?" a quiet but authoritative female voice rose, "Untie him at once! And fetch us a basin of water and some clean cloths." The woman speaking walked towards them like a vision from a dream. Her brown hair was piled high in an intricate knot of some kind at the back of her head, and a long rose colored dress hugged her womanly shape, leaving little to the imagination. Her face was tanned with high cheekbones, and she had the tilted eyes Ryland was beginning to expect from the Saerins, along with the slight, pale short-horns. Her lips shone red in contrast with her smooth skin, and spots of color darkened her cheeks as she glared at the guards who had escorted them into her presence.

"Calm yourself, Madeline. They are prisoners of war, not guests."

Ryland's eyes slid past her to the man who had spoken. He

sat upon a large chair at the center of the room. The back of the seat was heavily inlaid with opalescent shell in the shape of a Fian, the geometric pattern of the shell growing ever larger towards the edge of the backrest. The mammoth throne overshadowed the elderly man sitting upon it so much that Ryland hadn't seen him sitting there until he spoke.

His father bent at the waist in a cordial bow. "Your Majesties," he said in acknowledgment, prompting a similar bow from Ryland as he came to realize that this was the King and Queen of Saerin.

"How like the Priush, to bow to my face, and attack me by night," the King said bitterly. "Shall I expect an attempt on my life now that you have made your pleasantries?"

The Jorgen's face remained impassive. "I am sorry for the insult you sustained from our attack last night, your Majesty. My men were but following orders, as was I. I hope we can come to some sort of agreement that does not take the lives of the innocents who were ordered to fight for their King."

A contrite look flashed across the man's face, replacing the angry scowl. He tugged thoughtfully on a long lock of white hair that frizzled out from under the slim circlet resting on his brow, then glanced to his much younger wife.

Queen Madeline stepped forward. "You speak truly, and with dignity, Jorgen of Jorgenholm, as I remember you doing so before. I wish we were meeting on different terms than this. It seems to me that you and the King would have much to say to one another if you had not just lead an attack on our shores, unprovoked." The Jorgen nodded gravely in response, a hint of shame in his bearing as he directed his nod at the man seated on the throne, but he did not take his eyes off of the proud woman standing next to it.

The Queen placed one slim hand on her husband's shoulder, and gave a brief squeeze before helping him to his feet. Standing, Ryland could see the ghost of the younger man the King had been in his long bones and broad shoulders. But where he would have once towered over all of them, his back was now stooped with age, and he kept a tight grip on his wife's hand as he approached them.

"My wife speaks truly, it is all she ever does," he said, "But for all that it is true, the laws of my country come before what I may wish for, and I find even my wife's temperate demeanor hungering for blood after the night we have passed. And according to those laws, my Lord Jorgen, you have stolen onto my land in the dark of night with the intent of taking my throne. Your punishment has always been written, and they are not words that can be undone." Ryland sifted through the painfully polite exchange, knowing there was some point he was missing, but unable to pull its meaning from the overly cordial words.

"Fortunately, the same sentence is not necessary for your son, not yet. I hope that at least will bring you comfort, Jorgen." Madeline spoke softly, with a sidelong glance at Ryland.

"It is always good to know your bloodline will survive you," the Jorgen said, and then moved on quickly. "May I ask what you plan to do concerning Prium?"

Ryland blocked out the words the royals were speaking as he replayed his father's words. *'It is always good to know your bloodline will survive you'* he said to himself, finally coming to the conclusion that the Jorgen had likely drawn as soon as the word 'surrender' had left his lips. *They are going to execute him. They are going to kill the Jorgen.* A strange blankness followed his realization. But Ryland would be spared. *To what end,* he wondered? Would he remain a captive in Saerin, or be ransomed back to his own people? Poor Elaine. And poor Torman, he thought absently. His brother always had mixed feelings about becoming the Jorgen in the case of their father's death. He had joked tirelessly that he would run away if it ever happened, and leave the job to Ryland. But he would have no choice but to take the title if Ryland never returned to Jorgenholm.

"...Your concern for your men is admirable and fitting with what I know of your leadership, Jorgen. I too, usually move to spare the lives of innocents. But the men groaning in our dungeons are not innocent in any Saerin's eyes, not when they have come to our shores and spilled our blood! Orders or not! We cannot afford to relinquish to our enemies more men to fight for them, even when those men were once allies. I am sorry, Jorgen, but they will not be leaving the Isles," the Queen was saying, her color high. His father nodded curtly, his face as impassive as always.

Ryland was struck by the oddity of the conversation, the strange dichotomy of the people who were sentencing his father to death, treating him with such respect. They spoke on at length about where the captured men of the Royal fleet would end up; the King felt execution would do much to appease the anger of the Sareth people, but the Queen serenely mentioned a need of hard manual labor in the mines and elsewhere on their ever expanding islands. Ryland tuned them out again, as a gangly young man in the green livery of the Saerin royalty rather sullenly provided him with a clean cloth and warm water to wash his hands and face.

After he had cleaned up marginally, Ryland was provided a chair that he sank into gratefully. Not long after he had sat, however, their audience came to an end. His father seemed pleased with the outcome, as far as he could tell, having argued convincingly for the safety of his men, who Queen Madeline would see working on the Isle of the Dead, a much safer occupation than being sent into the mines of Mount Qee, and a far kinder end than the executioner. The Saerins always had a shortage of people willing to work on the infamous isle, as their superstitions painted the lonely rock in a dangerous light to mortal men.

"Jorgen, the headsman will come for you on the morrow, I suggest you make whatever peace with your God you wish to make, tonight. Our people will not stand for a private execution, someone must answer for the sons and husbands killed today, and tomorrow that someone will be you. I know you can understand their call for vengeance," the queen said, laying a hand on his father's arm as if she were not the one ordering his demise. The Jorgen nodded that same curt nod of acceptance, and Ryland wondered if he would ever be that strong, to face his own death with such calm acceptance.

"We shall take your Ryland into our care now, and have the Healers see to him. As I said, I cannot promise you his survival in these coming days, that largely depends on your backstabbing fool of a cousin your people were unlucky enough to have as their King, but he will be treated with respect while he remains in our care, as his station demands. Please take the time to say your farewells." The queen patted the King's hand, clutched in the crook of her arm, and with one final nod, swept regally from the room.

He turned to his father, hating that tears welled in his eyes. *Their relationship may not have been the closest, but he was still facing the loss of his father*, he tried to rationalize.

"Wipe your eyes boy, don't disgrace yourself," his father said harshly, effectively ending Ryland's emotional response. Pushing aside the crushing disappointment, Ryland looked into his father's dark eyes, searching for some connection, some tie other than their shared blood, and found nothing.

"You get word to the Holm as soon as you can. And find your way back there to make sure your brother doesn't run the place into the ground. This war is not over, but I have hopes that we can seclude our people from the bitterness the King has provoked here," he said. "Warbringer will be held for you to return to the Holm for Torman. Queen Madeline knows enough of our ancestry and respects Garrin too much to leave something so tied to our blood, after she sheds mine, alone." The Jorgen slipped the Ice Lion seal ring of the Jorgens from his thumb and pressed it into Ryland's slack grip. "Now go." Jorgen pushed him in the direction of a waiting servant, nodding at him when he hesitated, "Go, Ryland." And then he turned on his heel. The guards set to watch him trailed after his strong strides, looking more like an honor guard than gaolers returning a captive to his cell.

Ryland almost stumbled into the pretty girl flanked by armed guards waiting to take him to a healer, his focus was still so intent on his father, waiting for that last glimpse. But when his father's heel, and then his long shadow had slipped around the corner, he finally looked up. Behind the young woman, peering out from around one of the large pillars that dominated the throne room, a pair of brilliant blue eyes were locked on his face. A slim hand pushed long black tresses of hair back to catch behind one long ear, baring copious freckles that spangled across sun kissed skin. Petite horns rose pale in contrast to that dark fall of hair, their creamy spirals the iconic mark of an Islander. The small rosebud mouth was pursed in surprise, and a familiar blush rose to stain freckled cheeks as the girl realized she had been seen.

"Sylvia?" Ryland gasped in confusion, his mind grappling with the stunning similarities and glaring differences embodied in the partially concealed young woman. Her face colored further, the familiar features wrinkling into a mask of confusion before she slid back behind the pillar, the soft ring of hoof on stone the only evidence proving he had not imagined her.

The servant, still clutching his arm from when he had stumbled to her, looked worried, her tan forehead wrinkled, and her plump lips clamped tightly shut. She said nothing in response to his questioning gaze, only towed him in the opposite direction after casting nervous looks at the two stoic men behind them. Her hands were firm and unyielding when he tried to look back, pulling him forwards at such a rate that his tired body could barely keep up.

Glossary

Age Before Memory- Mysterious past era no one knows much about.

Arrowcatch- Protection spell that warns of incoming arrows.

Asodin- Tribe member who "owns" a _Kurianit_

Augment- Precious stones holding a reservoir of magic to be used by any Maegi or Mage.

Banded Monkey- Breed of monkeys found in the Sareth Isles.

Blitherly Sea- Body of water between Prium and the Sareth Isles.

Bloodhunger- Hinterland Berserker magic, performed with the blood of the warrior to make him stronger, faster, and fiercer. Warriors rape after conquering, kill rather than capture, destroy rather than pillage.

Caves of Orr- Sacred abode of The Ancients, Freyton's Seers.

Cetrian- Hinterland ceremony of cleansing, _Kurianit_ emerge as _Ianit._

Cheerum- A hardy plant with oniony taste common in the Skypeaks.

Corep- Small fruit that grows on a tree, similar to a kumquat.

Crossroads- The convergence of the three roads leading to Jorgenholm, Galmorah, and Seaprium.

Cyn- Healer's robe, always pale green, in any Hinterland tribe.

Draconis Tussis- Dragon's Cough, deadly plague created by magic.

Dreamweed- Drug much like opium.

Fabriel- A large bird good for cooking and use of its down feathers.

Fen- A small throwing or close combat knife.

Fian- Shellfish with iconic spiral shell, similar to a conch.

Flaix- A foxlike creature, red or orange, hunted much like a fox, with hounds.

Foraul nu' Groth- Challenge by battle for leadership in a Hinterland tribe.

Galeshorn Ocean- Ocean East of the Sareth Isles.

Galmorah- Second largest city in Prium, located by the Serpent's Tongue river.

Gum Trees- Jungle tree with flammable sap used to make Pitch Fire.

Ianit- Meaning, "of us". A Hinterlander who joined the tribe after being *Kurianit.*

Ilyria- The name of the Trianti Morgal's broadsword.

Jeale's Sanctuary- Huge statue on the Sareth Isles, from the Age Before Memory and believed to be the goddess Jeale. Inside the all-female priesthood of Jeale lives and worships.

Jorgenholm- Third largest city in Prium, a stronghold located in the Skypeaks mountain range at the northernmost tip of Prium. It is ruled by the Jorgen, the eldest male in the ancestral line of the Jorgens.

Kercha- A coffee-like drink made from a blend of spices.

Kurianit- Meaning, "not yet of us", a Hinterland indentured servant captured during battle.

Lirel- A *Kurianit's* distinctive dress, one shouldered, dyed the color of their tribe.

Listenbark- A silvery evergreen tree with needles and a sappy trunk.

Loria- The largest moon.

Maegi- A Trewal capable of using one type of magic, Earth, Air, Water, or Fire.

Mage- A Trewal with blue eyes capable of using all types of elemental magic.

Merchant Triad- The three wealthiest trading families in Saerin

Mount Qee- The Northernmost Island of the Sareth Isles, comprised of a dormant volcano. Mount Qee is mined heavily for precious stones, Augments, metals, and minerals.

North Gorge- A large canyon and river marking the end of the Skypeaks range. Not a part of Prium.

*Opening-*The five step process taught to young Maegi which is used to access Trewal magic.

Pitch Fire- A highly explosive, viscous liquid derived from Gum Trees. Used primarily in catapults as projectiles.

Poisonleaf- A jungle plant with electric green fronds, very dangerous to touch.

Prium- The Kingdom ruled by the King of Prium, including the cities of Galmorah and Seaprium, along with Jorgenholm.

Reedwood Forest- A woodland area of Prium south of Jorgenholm, bordered by the Sacred Plains and the Galeshorn Ocean.

Renaldis charm- Defensive magic that dries a power-source activated within its range, be it Maegi, Mage or Augment.

Roan- A grassy bladed plant, low growing and prolific.

Romkin- A common Layette expletive similar to 'dumbass'.

Sacred Plains- A large plain at the center of Prium where the majority of the Kingdom's grain and weaving materials are produced.

Sacred Square- The largest city square in Galmorah.

Saerin- The Capital city of the Sareth Isles, home to the Saerin University and the Royal Palace.

Sapbeetle- An insect found in the Reedwood forest and Skypeaks that feeds off Listenbark sap. It sings at night.

Sareth Isles- A string of five islands off the coast of Prium.

Sareth's backbone- A volcanic mountain range running along the largest of the Sareth Isles.

Seaprium- The capital city of Prium, the largest city in the Kingdom and home to the Palace by the Sea.

Serpent's Tongue- A forked river separating the Sacred Plains and the desert surrounding Woletor's Crater.

Skycastles- A mazelike valley full of rock spires high in the Skypeaks.

Skypeaks- Mountain range in the North of Prium, acting as the border for the Kingdom.

Sorret- The smallest moon.

Spineback- A river fish found in the Skypeaks with white meat.

Spinner fish- An aquatic mammal similar to a dolphin.

Stalkwing- A nocturnal bird of prey.

Starsh- A word of binding to keep magic in an item, or performing its set task.

Steelskin trees- Large trees common in Prium.

Streamcress- An edible algae common in the Skypeaks.

Terling- An adornment worn around an antler tine. Matching Terlings worn around the antler base are important in the wedding ceremonies of Prium.

Tern- A fruit that grows on a tree, pitted, and similar to a plum.

Traumek- The journey to the next world for Hinterland warriors slain in battle.

Trollit- A common Layette expletive similar to 'shit'.

Warbringer- The Jorgen's ancestral sword, a Relic from the Age Before Memory.

Weiring- Someone with God Eyes, able to see the influence of a God on mortal Trewal.

Windthorn roses- A hardy briar rose with a sweet smell.

Woletor's Crater- A mysterious crater in the desert south of Galmorah. The Trewal believe it to be cursed by the Dark God and do not venture there.

Characters

Meanwhile back on Earth...

*Arianna-*A friend of Sylvia's
David Granger- Sylvia's high school sweetheart
Dr. Attebury- Surgeon operating on Sylvia's knee
James Eldritch- Sylvia's father
Janet Eldritch- Sylvia's mother
Sammy- Fat cat #1
Sarah- A friend of Sylvia's
Suzie- Nurse at Sylvia's surgery
Sylvia Eldritch- High school senior
Toby- Fat cat #2
Rachel- Co-captain of Sylvia's Rugby team

Jorgenholm

Camus- Royal Maegi at Jorgenholm
Cara- The Jorgen's deceased wife
Chir- Jorgenholm messenger
Councilman Jeston- Noble who visited Jorgenholm
Fria- The Jorgen's middle child, a daughter
Gambria- The head cook for Jorgenholm
The Jorgen- Ruler of Jorgenholm, formerly Dourith
Johan- Holm soldier who had family taken by the Demandron
Kaur- Common child living in Jorgenholm
Lana- Ryland's head chambermaid
Lear- A soldier making maps of Jorgenholm's warrens
Lourn- Common child living in Jorgenholm
Metra- Torman's lover, a commoner and the Holm's agriculturist.
Perlt- Jorgenholm's head steward
Retcha- Common child living in Jorgenholm
Ryland- The Jorgen's youngest son
Saul- Common child living in Jorgenholm

Torman- The Jorgen's eldest son
Willa- Kaur's mother, a commoner, seamstress at the Holm

The Palace by the Sea
Demandron- Mages who control the Priush throne
      The Circle- Ten Mages of full power
      Disciples- Ten Mages in training
Elaine Herrion- The daughter of Councilman Tager Herrion
Fragon- The only son of the King, Prince of Prium
Jeralt- Ship's captain, the Royal Commander's second
Kess- Captain Jeralt's son
King of Prium- Formerly Gartlan, cousin of the Jorgen
Matty- Soldier
Ryen- Soldier
Serena Herrion- Wife of Councilman Tager Herrion
Tager Herrion- Councilman in Seaprium, very powerful
Thyrem- Captain of the ship *Windstorm*

The Hinterlands
Ancients-
      Cirillia- The youngest Ancient, from the Trianti tribe
      Kon- The oldest Ancient, from the Baroun tribe
      Pernal- Ancient from the Diarmas tribe
      Aerin- Ancient from the Verie tribe
      Wertal- Ancient from the Kla'routh tribe
      Folt- Ancient from the Rishal tribe
      Skalin- Ancient from the Proult tribe
Baroun Tribe
Diarmas Tribe
Kla'routh Tribe
Proult Tribe
Rishal Tribe
Trianti Tribe

Breanne- Female Trianti loyal to the Morgal

Chrisyne- Deceased *kurianit* of Pralick, Lessoran's former lover

Courit- Lessoran's good friend, killed in the most recent raid

Horout- Old man known for making alcohol for the Tribe, loyal to the Morgal

Jamae- Male Trianti loyal to the Morgal

Jerra- Trianti child who spotted Syl's "hooves" first

Lessoran- Head Maegi of the Trianti tribe

Morgal- leader of the Trianti tribe

Pralick- Trianti warrior who captured Sylvia

Tamol- Trianti *Ianit* woman, Healer for the Trianti, loyal to the Morgal

Teegar- Trianti warrior loyal to Pralick

Verie Tribe

The Sareth Isles

Madeline- Queen of the Sareth Isles

Veraline- Eldest daughter of Madeline and Willem, betrothed to Fragon, Prince of Prium

Willem- King of the Sareth Isles

Gods

*Freyton-*The patron god of the Hinterland tribes

Garrin- The patron god of Jorgenholm and Seaprium

*Jeale-*The patron goddess of the Sareth Isles

Woletor- The Dark God, has ties to the Demandron

Historical figures

Bejeweled Witch- A villain Vorrion the brave defeated

Cinsul Garson- An explorer whose books are in the King's library

Firetongue- A dragon of legend

Pealer Grunswer- A Sareth Scholar who traveled widely

Vorrion the Brave- A famous warrior of stories

Acknowledgments

This book was a labor of love. The love of my husband, mother, sister, and friends fueled me to finally finish this endeavor and pushed me to release it to the public. Thank you.

I'm not usually a fan of clichés but in this case, it really did take a village. Thank you to my wonderful Beta Readers, Alyssa, Earl, Ema, Jan, and Mitch; your enthusiasm and time is more appreciated than you can ever know. To 'The Mean Cousin', you rock. Thanks for all the pushing, and researching, and support.

I couldn't have accomplished this without all of you. Thanks will never truly be enough, but I figure it is at least a step in the right direction.

Thank you!

*A special preview of
the next book in*

*The Ending Balance
Chronicles*

by M.J. Burr

Steelskin

Coming soon...

Gartlan

"Your Majesty?"

The soft voice broke the silence of his study, making him jump. He tried to turn the convulsive move into a smooth turn, but ended up dumping his goblet of wine onto the finely woven Galmorish carpet. The young serf who had spoken bent hastily to aid him, sopping up the ruby liquid with her thin robe.

"I'm so sorry my King! Please, let me clean it up. It's my fault!"

He stood back up to let her work, feeling bad as he saw her hands shaking with nerves. He decided to do the right thing and alleviate her guilt, but in straightening back to standing an abominable headache began its slow pulse behind his eyes, so he simply waved his hand weakly, "It's fine, all fine." He sank down into a handy chair, pouring more wine into the goblet he still held.

Something had gone horribly wrong. It was the only explanation for the abrupt termination, three night ago, of the pleasure coursing into him from the stone that connected him to his Demandron, and for the overwhelming crash of power that had then snapped into his head. It had to be the backlash of the loss of Control that he had only ever read about, and never thought to experience himself, having no magical abilities. *What had happened? And why hadn't he had word yet from the Isles?*

"Tager Herrion has requested an audience with you, Your Majesty," the serf said timidly, startling Gartlan, who had managed to forget her initial interruption as his thoughts turned inward.

"Again?" he groaned. *Would the fool never leave him alone?* "Does he think asking for the twelfth time will make me want to see him any more than before?" he roared, rising from the chair to pace angrily in front of the hunched form of his serf, who wisely remained silent, letting his temper play itself out.

"I refused him the last eleven times, and he dares to request an audience again? He dares!" His pacing took him in a winding path around the chair he had just been sitting in, and the serf's head followed his progress, her eyes lowered to watch his hooves as he walked. He came to a stop before her, knowing there was more to her interruption of his solitude. "And…" he prompted.

"And the Council has called a meeting tonight to address the unrest in the city." Her mouth opened again to say yet more words he didn't want to hear, but she hedged, her eyes flicking around the room like she was seeking for an escape route before she fixed her eyes on his hooves once more. "…And the lone Demandron who remained in the city has still not been found, and the Council of Merchants has officially petitioned the crown for recompense for revenue lost due to the silence from Saerin." She finished in a rush before bowing so low he thought her breasts would spill from the neck of her robes.

He clenched his fists, feeling that tightening of muscle and sinew throughout his body, relishing in the physical manifestation of his frustration, then he collapsed back into the chair once more, feeling drained of every emotion but anxiety. "Leave me," he commanded, and the girl ran gratefully for the door.

What a gods-forsaken mess. He didn't know what to do now that the Demandron where not here whispering in his ear. His path had seemed so clear before, but now the lay of the land around him was blurry, concealed from him in ways that only highlighted how out of touch with reality he had been these last years. The merchant council was blaming him, their King, for payments and deliveries left unfulfilled when the Sareth Isles abruptly cut off all contact on the night his Imperial forces should have taken the city. He could hardly blame them, but he also could not beggar the crown to fulfill those contracts.

He didn't know what to think, which way to look to lay blame, so many possibilities for treachery filled his head. Had the Jorgen taken Saerin for himself? He had been so against the war in the first place, maybe he was making a bid for a more powerful Name than he already had. And he could have been working with the Saerin royalty! Or he could have taken them out, either possibility stood with what he knew of his cousin. And that dour man's very first move would have been to assassinate or imprison the Demandron, which could account for the terrible sensations he had been subjected to three nights ago.

Then there were the Demandron themselves. Those dark unknowable Mages. He would not put it past them to have taken the Sareth Isles for themselves, even though he had done all he could to appease their appetites here in Prium. But why the loss of Control from them he had felt? Was it a ruse? A tactic to shed blame onto some other party?

Lastly was the possibility that the Jorgen and his army had been defeated, as unbelievable as that seemed with their superior numbers and the Demandron Mages at their side. He dragged his hands down his face and then cradled the heavy weight in his cupped palms. Not knowing who his enemies were was far worse than any political intrigue he had experienced to this date. And he had weathered three assassination attempts soon after being Named King. At least when he knew what he was up against he could prepare a defense!

He had to do *something*. His inactivity was beginning to cause more problems than it was holding off. The Merchants Council could only be delayed for so long before they would simply hike the price of supplies for the Palace to an ungodly sum to make up their losses. But in order to deal with them he needed to know if trade between Seaprium and the Isles would ever resume. He had already dispatched five small sailing vessels to approach the isles to learn of the fate of his troops, but had not heard a whisper from any of them since they left the Seaprium harbor.

Then there was Herrion. That fat, pompous little *romkin* was seriously trying his patience with his arrogant appeals and demands for information. The old man acted as if Gartlan *owed* him an explanation! *The King owes no one anything*, he thought fiercely, *but every Trewal in this realm owes their King allegiance!*

He stood up resolutely, still unsure, for all of his hours of contemplation, how to approach his many problems, but knowing that *something* had to be done, soon. He would attend the Council meeting tonight, something he usually avoided at all costs, and he would schedule an audience with the detestable Tager Herrion sometime in the next fortnight. The Council would aid in the decision of what to do about the Merchant Council's demands, and hopefully by the time his audience came around, he would finally have the information he needed to put all the fires in his realm out. Hopefully by then he would know who his enemies were, and where to expect the next attack.

About the Author

M. J. Burr loves words, and even more so, stories. It's her dream to create a world for readers to get lost in, with characters that become friends, and a plot that enthralls your mind. She hopes that Prium is as good an escape for her readers as it has been for her since she began writing the Ending Balance Chronicles in 2011. She lives in the beautiful wine country of Southern Oregon with her husband and a furry pack of animals who are more children than pets.